Don't miss these other exciting titles by bestselling author

Vickie McKeehan

The Pelican Pointe Series
PROMISE COVE
HIDDEN MOON BAY
DANCING TIDES
LIGHTHOUSE REEF
STARLIGHT DUNES
LAST CHANCE HARBOR
SEA GLASS COTTAGE
LAVENDER BEACH
SANDCASTLES UNDER THE CHRISTMAS MOON
BENEATH WINTER SAND
KEEPING CAPE SUMMER (2018)

The Evil Secrets Trilogy
JUST EVIL Book One
DEEPER EVIL Book Two
ENDING EVIL Book Three
EVIL SECRETS TRILOGY BOXED SET

The Skye Cree Novels
THE BONES OF OTHERS
THE BONES WILL TELL
THE BOX OF BONES
HIS GARDEN OF BONES
TRUTH IN THE BONES
SEA OF BONES (2018)

Promise Cove

A Pelican Pointe Novel

VICKIE McKEEHAN

beachdevils
PRESS

Promise Cove
A Pelican Pointe Novel

beachdevils
PRESS
ISBN-13: 978-0615720456
ISBN-10: 0615720455
Printed in the USA

Cover design by Vanessa Mendozzi
Pelican Pointe map designed by Jess Johnson

Visit the author at:
http://www.vickiemckeehan.com
http://www.facebook.com/VickieMcKeehan

For Gene and Keith,
the real-life men who inspired the Promise Cove story.

And to the outstanding men and women
who serve in our military, the sacrifices they make,
and the promises they keep daily.

He who has gone,
so we but cherish his memory,
abides with us, more potent, nay,
more present than the living man.

Antoine de Saint-Exupery,
French writer and aviator 1900-1944

Promise Cove

A Pelican Pointe Novel

VICKIE McKEEHAN

beachdevils
PRESS

Welcome to Pelican Pointe

Prologue

One year earlier
Twenty miles southeast of Baghdad

The combat post was rural, more like a farming community stuck out in the boonies. The roads were primarily unpaved, dusty twenty-four-seven, and at the moment littered with burned-out equipment. The convoy they were riding in was going a sluggish twenty-five miles an hour in hundred-twenty-degree heat. There was no AC, no hope of grabbing an artery-clogging, delicious-tasting, fast food burger with a pile of over-salty fries, or even indulging in an after-duty dip in a cool, sparkling blue swimming pool.

Because this particular stretch of road had seen its fair share of hostile action the past couple of days, the entire unit had to be extra vigilant.

As they made their way up a rise, a grove of palm trees came into view. The wind picked up causing the fronds of the trees to bend and sway. The hot, arid breeze kicked up the loose grit, causing the tiny grains of sand to become airborne and burrow in and under any exposed pore and crevice of skin it could find. A thick layer of sand stuck to their faces, to their uniforms, and to their weapons. Homemade masks made from scarves and bandanas hid their sweaty faces and did little to protect them from the elements.

Dressed in full combat gear, the stifling heat inside the Hummer caused perspiration to pool down their backs. The prospect of a hot shower, a mere dream in the back of everyone's mind, was as far off at the moment as the idea of ever getting to go home.

But even in a war zone, confined in the cramped space of the Humvee, the soldiers did their best to make light of their predicament by laughing and cracking jokes. Sitting in the back seat, two officers kept up a steady stream of chatter. At least one did. Glancing up briefly when another new barrage of sand hit the windshield, Captain Scott Phillips barely noticed as he yanked the bandana from around his mouth so he could talk. And the Captain loved to talk, especially any bit of conversation that crept into his head that had anything to do with his wife, Jordan, and their baby daughter, Hutton, a daughter he had yet to lay eyes on or hold.

As had become his habit, 1st Lt. Nick Harris listened as patiently as he could. What else was he going to do in such close quarters but listen to the Captain's long-winded stories about home? Nick indulged him, not only because he was a captive audience but because, like most everyone in the unit, he genuinely liked Scott. The men who served under Phillips liked the no-nonsense way he ran his unit, liked the man who could routinely go from all-business to light-hearted in the blink of an eye.

And light-hearted usually meant Scott kept up a non-stop monologue about his family back home. After spending a year of active duty with the guy, Nick felt certain he knew every nuance about the man's personal life. There wasn't much info Scott held back or didn't share. When it came to his wife and newborn daughter, the man simply refused to shut up.

On the surface the two men had little in common. Scott was blissfully married while Nick, unattached, single, and happy about it, had a bevy of women waiting for him back in Los Angeles. But despite their differences, Nick's affection for the guy overrode any annoyance over knowing every detail Scott chose to share. It seemed to Nick, Scott's family life back home in California was an open book, which made him long ago accept the fact that Scott just liked to talk. Period.

Nick watched as Scott tapped his flak jacket and reminded, "I promised Jordan I'd wear this thing 24/7 as long as I'm over here. I didn't have the heart to tell her it won't do a damn thing to stop an IED."

"There's no stopping an IED," Nick agreed amicably.

"When we get out of this mess promise me you'll come to Pelican Pointe for a visit, meet Jordan and the baby."

Here it comes, thought Nick as he shook his head, Scott crowing once again about his hometown and the people in it. Nick responded the way he always did whenever Scott mentioned Pelican Pointe—he made some smart-ass comment—making sure to insult the Captain's small town in a good-natured, guy kind of way. "Now why would I want to spend time in a Podunk town that sounds like a bird sanctuary? I'm a big city kind of guy, Captain. I'd go nuts in a small town. Besides, small towns are cliquish."

"Pelican Pointe's different."

"I doubt that. Everybody knows your business in a small town."

"When we get out of this mess, you come for a visit. I guarantee you'll see for yourself what a great place it is, how great the people are. They'd do anything for you, Nick." Without taking a breath, Scott went on, "God, I sure miss Jordan. And I haven't even laid eyes on Hutton. I wish I'd been there the day she was born. I hate it Jordan had to go through childbirth without me. She's almost five months old, can you believe it?"

"How does it feel to be a dad?" Nick didn't have a clue about being a father, but it seemed the right thing to say at times like this when Scott got that distant look on his face, that wistful gaze in his eye, the look that said he was homesick and wanted nothing more than to get back home to his family.

"Being a father is great, I think. I'd like to be able to hold her though, you know. Pictures aren't the same thing. You ever thought of having kids, Nick?"

A panicked look crossed his face. "Hell no. I can't even see myself married."

"Marriage is exactly what you need. Might settle you down."

Nick couldn't imagine it. "Marriage would be like a rock around my neck. Too many sweet things out there in the proverbial sea I haven't sampled yet." He wiggled his eyebrows up and down.

"Get yourself in trouble is what you're gonna do. You need to think about finding that special someone. If you ever found a woman like Jordan, you'd change your mind in a heartbeat."

Before Nick could argue, he heard the sound of a rocket blast pierce the air.

Someone yelled, "Look out, incoming!"

Nick heard an explosion, saw a blast of fire, and then a wave of smoke surrounded the vehicle so thick, he could barely see or breathe anything but fire and heat. Soldiers started running toward the lead Hummer. He heard more yelling. His lungs burned.

"Go. Go. Go!" someone shouted.

Chaos reigned as Nick watched the Humvee just ahead of theirs disintegrate into pieces. He saw burned metal fly through the air before he realized it wasn't the lead Hummer at all. He turned to where Scott had sat beside him and saw his buddy's face twisted in pain. Nick heard screaming.

"Promise me, Nick…"

Chapter One

Present-day
California coast

Nick came awake, trembling. Sweat beaded on his body. He ran a shaky hand over his face before glancing at the clock by the bed. Three-fifteen a.m. He'd gotten less than four hours sleep.

Insomnia was proving to be a bitch.

Living with the dream was even worse. Every night to be taken back in time to that day, as if watching the same scene play out, burned in his brain, he had to relive it over and over again. One image in particular. Seeing Scott's face for the last time always did him in for the night.

Nick did his best to blank his mind. But it took some time before that day's images completely left him. It always did. He'd known for months what he had to do, but until last week he'd been unable to take that first step.

"Damn you, Scott, why can't you leave me in peace," he muttered as he slowly swung his legs out of bed switching on the bedside light. He glanced around the four walls of the dingy motel room that had been home for the past two days. He was stalling. There was no other word for it. He'd never been afraid of confrontation. But every time he thought of facing Scott's widow, fear made him break out in a cold sweat. Months ago, he'd given up the notion of ever feeling like his old self again. Not at work, not at home, not anywhere. He was afraid to talk about that day, even though he relived it nightly, he was afraid of that promise he'd made in the heat of battle, the one that hadn't counted because he'd only told Scott what he'd needed to hear, what he'd wanted to hear. It hadn't meant anything. Scott had known that. The man had merely needed comforting and Nick had obliged, repeating a bunch of words strung together to make Scott feel better before he...

That's all it had been.

A lump of panic caught in Nick's throat. He closed his eyes until it passed, until he got the shaking under control. He finally got up on unsteady legs, forced his feet to make the walk across the shabby carpet into the bathroom, where he turned on the light, and then the faucet. As the water ran, he stood in the bright spotlight looking into the old chipped, bathroom mirror, staring at his reflection. Streaky red lines rimmed his lake-blue eyes. It looked as though he'd been on a drinking binge for a couple of months. He hadn't. He ran a still shaky hand through his coal-black hair. Locks that hung almost to his shoulders had replaced the military cut he'd worn most of his life. The other hand reflexively ran across the puffy, red scars on his chest and torso. A stranger stared back at him from the mirror. He might be able to conceal his mental scars from the world, might be able to deny he had any, but there was no hiding the jagged, ugly marks on his body.

He splashed cold water on his face, and decided he needed to stop being such a coward. There were only so many times a person could put off something before they had to man up and take that step, get it done.

Taking another long look in the mirror at the man he barely recognized, he knew it was useless to try to get back to sleep.

He reached over to start the water in the shower.

At five-thirty, dressed in jeans and an ancient black T-shirt, Nick started packing up the meager belongings he'd brought with him. Throwing toothpaste, razor, and toiletries into his small travel duffel, the memory of what his life used to be like flickered in his head like a video. That carefree life he'd lived before war belonged to someone else. There was no recapturing what he once had or how he once felt. Hadn't he spent the last year trying?

Satisfied he wasn't leaving anything behind, he swung the bag over his shoulder, crossed to the bureau, and picked up his motorcycle helmet. Taking one last look around the room he sucked in a deep breath. He hesitated only briefly before turning the knob. "Best to get this over and done with," he muttered, as he threw open the door and strode out into the parking lot.

Despite a February marine layer, the sun made enough of an appearance in the eastern sky to brush along the horizon, stringing out dabs of orange streaks here and there. For him daybreak had always been the best time of day. He took a minute to enjoy the crisp air, before stowing his gear. Reluctantly, he straddled the Harley, snapping the strap on his helmet. He turned the key in the ignition and the engine rumbled to life. Slowly he made his way out of the parking lot, made a right turn onto the 101, and headed north along the rugged California coast.

When the wind hit his face, he gunned the engine, picking up speed, trying to outrun the dread of what he had to do. He couldn't call her ahead of time. He didn't dare. If he could have merely picked up the phone it would have made things so much easier. The idea of finally having to face her pissed him off. He increased his speed, angry that what he had to say to Jordan Phillips couldn't be said over the goddamned phone.

Eighty miles to the north, along a rugged section of cliffs and vistas, Jordan Phillips stood on the creaky, wooden front porch of an old Queen Anne Victorian house, trying her best to wake up. She tipped up a steaming cup of coffee to her lips and let a sigh out. She could see her breath in the winter air. This was her favorite time of day, watching the first hint of sun tip the sky a brilliant pastel when it seemed to her the beginning of each day held so much promise. She felt she could do anything. For about half an hour each morning she felt energized, invincible even. Okay, so the feeling didn't last long. But out here alone for two years, Jordan sometimes wondered how she'd managed by herself for so long. First, Scott had been deployed and there had been that expectation he'd come back in one piece.

But he'd been dead now almost a full year, that hope gone like so many others.

It was time she got her act together, stop the lack of focus, finish the house and get ready to open her home as a bona fide bed and breakfast to paying guests. It was what Scott had wanted.

When a rabbit jumped out of the woods and into the clearing, scampered next to the house and scurried across the lush green lawn, she squinted into the morning sun. She watched as the furry little guy sniffed the air, and sensed he wasn't alone before quickly making a beeline back into the thick underbrush. She hoped the vinegar she'd poured around the perimeter of her garden yesterday would keep out the critters from dining on her thriving patch of herbs. She'd hate to lose them after all the time and effort she'd poured into cultivating the seedlings from scratch. But then she spotted another one dash out of the row of hedges and could only hope his breakfast had been from the healthy patch of clover at the side of the house and not her precious plot of lettuce.

When her fifteen-month-old daughter, Hutton, toddled over, she forgot about rabbits and gave the little girl her best smile. She turned her attention to the baby. Eyeing Hutton's runny nose, she set the coffee mug down on the railing and instinctively reached into her pocket for the ever present Kleenex. Like a seasoned mother, Jordan wrapped the sweater tighter around Hutton's little body hoping to keep her warm. Even though spring was still officially six weeks away, the morning breeze right off the ocean had a bite to it, making the salty air damp and chilly.

But it was too beautiful a morning to spend inside. The sun shone bright. A new nest of robins serenaded them from the row of cypress trees lining the driveway. Jordan took a moment to listen to the birds before inhaling the fresh air coming in off the ocean. Times like this, she loved this place almost as much as Scott had. But she knew things were about to change. She steeled her spine, stood up a little straighter. Despite her determination though, nerves made her stomach clinch with dread. March was right around the corner and would soon turn into April which brought her smack dab up against a deadline she'd been avoiding for a year. Thinking about losing this place sent Jordan fighting the panic fluttering in the pit of her stomach. She had to get the house ready to open as a bed and breakfast. She needed to show the bank that The Cove was a real business venture with a real cash flow. If she couldn't pay that first bank note she'd lose everything Scott had loved, everything he'd fought and died for, everything that had been important to him, the reason they'd moved back to Pelican Pointe in the first place.

She contemplated all the work she still had left to do. The dilapidated porch needed sprucing up. She'd put that off long enough. Today was the day. She didn't want potential guests driving up to their anticipated lodging only to get a good look at the porch and decide they'd made a terrible mistake. If the porch looked shabby they might think the whole place did. No way did she want unhappy guests asking for their money back. She didn't want to start out with a hassle right up front. Success depended on keeping revenue coming in and guests happy…and willing to come back.

She could have easily left and headed back to San Francisco to the comfort of her family and let the bank have the house. She knew her family would make room for her and Hutton. But the bed and breakfast had been Scott's vision. She wouldn't abandon his dream, their dream, she corrected, because she was afraid of what the next few months might bring. Scott had probably been scared in Iraq, she reasoned, and with justification. Scott hadn't given up and neither would she.

Her resolve to make this work grew.

"We'll be cutting it close, Hutton. But we can't give up now. Mama has to get this old porch sanded today, and then re-stained so the guests will see a wonderful place to sit outside, a place to enjoy the view. I took four new reservations this week. That makes six in all. Okay, it isn't much, but opening day is still a ways off. We've got time to make this work. It's a start. We have to stay positive."

As she reached down to Hutton and swung the baby up to her hip, she swiped at the baby's runny nose again, telling the toddler, "Your daddy would be so proud of his girls."

Imitating her mother, Hutton reached out and touched her mother's nose, gave a little squeeze. "Mama."

"That's right, baby girl." Jordan bit her lip to keep from crying. Scott might not have come back from Iraq, but she had part of him right here in her arms. She felt his presence in this place, this house he loved so much, every single day.

"We have to be strong for daddy. We can do this Hutton. We have to."

Doing a steady seventy-five, Nick cruised along the Coast Highway and blew right by the city limits sign of Pelican Pointe, an old-fashioned wooden marker touting a meager population of two-thousand-eight-hundred and seven. Just to prove a point, mainly that he did not want to be here in this particular town he gunned the engine. The noise turned a few heads as he flew past the strip of fishing village to his left that snuggled up against the bay. He followed the sign directing him to the town's business district, and headed down a tree-lined Main Street. He breezed past another sign in front of the Community Church on the corner, proclaiming they'd had seventy-five people in attendance the previous Sunday. He didn't slow his speed until he reached the heart of downtown. He eased past a bank, a pharmacy, a hardware store, a beauty shop, along with a spattering of neatly trimmed little houses lining both sides of the road. By the time the diner caught his eye, his stomach rumbled. He remembered he needed to eat. He spotted the market and decided it would have to do. He wasn't ready to sit down yet and mingle with the good people of Pelican Pointe. Even though he needed caffeine like an addict needed a fix, he'd forgo the diner and make do at the convenience store. At that moment he would have given fifty bucks for a couple of shots of espresso. Eyeing the convenience store, he grimaced at the idea of having to settle for a cup of crappy coffee. But he reasoned, he could avoid people in the store. The diner might be more difficult.

As he pulled to a stop in what looked like the newly paved parking lot of Murphy's Market, he reluctantly cut the engine and sat there looking around at the sad little excuse for a town. So this, he thought, was the infamous Pelican Pointe Scott had bragged so much about. To Nick it pretty much looked like any number of small towns along the coast he'd passed on the trip here. But this town seemed in worse shape, as if it didn't see enough tourists to make stopping here worthwhile unless you had to. And there was no denying it was a helluva long way from the interstate. So why would anyone bother?

It sure as hell wasn't L.A.

When his stomach growled again, he grudgingly crawled off the bike and headed inside to see what he could rustle up for breakfast.

The place was larger than it looked from the outside, no convenience store at all, but rather a tidy compact market. Even though the store was whistle clean, the narrow, cramped aisles seemed as if the owner had packed so much into the undersized space, a sudden panic of claustrophobia descended. Nick fought for control three feet inside the glass doors, pretending to orient himself to his surroundings. He started forcing in deep, calming breaths, putting his mind to relaxing his need for air. When the breathing exercises began to quash the anxiety, he nervously picked up a brown, plastic basket to gather his breakfast. Calmer now, he circled the aisles, picking up an array of mostly junk food, a couple packages of donuts, a bear claw, a bag of Doritos, before spotting the self-serve coffee pot on the side wall hiding near the deli counter. He grabbed the largest to-go cup he could find and filled it to the brim. Letting the black liquid cool, he sipped the strong brew before finding a lid to fit the top. He'd tasted worse, he decided as he headed to the checkout.

For the first time he noticed the small, gray-haired clerk standing behind one of two checkouts stands. The fifty-something man stood a mere five feet in height. He wore a starched dark green apron tied around his neck and middle. He reminded Nick of an aging leprechaun minus the suit. And wouldn't you know it, his name tag read Murphy. According to Scott, this was the mayor and owner of the only grocery store in town.

"Wouldn't you rather have a hot biscuit with bacon and egg instead of that junk food?" Murphy asked jovially. "Two sausage biscuits with egg for three bucks. Can't beat the price. Best deal in town."

Nick's eyebrows went up. "Competing with the Hilltop Diner?"

"Baked fresh from the Diner this morning, Margie sees to that, delivers them hot seven days a week even on Sunday."

"Sold," Nick said, absently letting go of the basket filled with junk food and leaving it on the vacant check-out stand nearby. He watched as Murphy went over to a microwave on the front wall under a bank of windows, threw in two wrapped biscuits, and hit a couple of buttons on the panel.

"Just passing through?" Murphy asked to make conversation, as he waited for the biscuits to warm.

"Actually, I was wondering if you might know where I could find Jordan Phillips." Nick had no sooner gotten the words past his tongue when he noticed the man's friendly demeanor vanished. To Nick it looked as if he was sizing him up. He supposed he couldn't blame him. After all, he was a stranger who had driven up on a loud, big-ass Harley.

Even though Nick towered over him, Murphy put on his sternest face and gruffly asked, "Who wants to know?"

Nick shifted his feet, uneasy, hesitant to say too much. But he did need directions. "I...know she runs a bed and breakfast around here called The Cove. Thought maybe you could tell me how to get there."

"So, you're looking for a place to stay? Ah, well, she hasn't opened up yet. Since her husband died in Iraq, Jordan's struggled to get it going. They sunk all their money into that place before his reserve unit got called up. The bank's extended her out as far as they can, if she can't get a cash flow going, they'll have no choice but to put the place up for auction. She'll lose everything. Shame too, after Scott didn't come back."

Murphy scrubbed a hand over the stubble on his chin. "You know Jordan?"

"Not really. I knew Scott." Now why had he volunteered that? But it was too late. He saw Murphy's ears pick up, watched his curiosity pique before the microwave timer dinged.

"That a fact?" Murphy asked as he rang up the biscuits and the coffee. To Nick the man seemed to be pondering which tack to take. So it was no surprise when Murphy asked, "How'd you know Scott? Same reserve unit maybe?"

Nick nodded.

"You down here from the Bay?"

The man was too nosy, Nick thought, so much for slinking through town without announcing his presence. What would prevent this guy from picking up the phone and giving Jordan a heads-up that a stranger was asking about her? She'd be expecting him then. He'd be committed. Something about that pissed him off. So much for unobtrusively stopping and getting directions, thought Nick. He pulled a ten from his wallet. "No," he finally answered, as he tossed the bill down on the counter. He had no intention of answering anymore meddlesome questions. He'd already said too much. But instead of giving up, the man surprised Nick and went into a detailed account of Jordan's predicament.

"It's been a rough year for her and the baby, out there alone, trying to fix that big old house up herself. Doing what she can anyway, can't afford to hire any help. If you ask me, she's in a helluva hard place right now with the balloon payment coming due. She could use a friend."

As Nick waited for Murphy to count out his change, he listened intently as the guy started telling him the best way to get to Jordan's.

As soon as he got outside, Nick removed the wrapper from his biscuits. Leaning on the bike he scarfed down breakfast all the while brooding over Murphy's words. If the man knew Jordan needed help, why wasn't he rallying the good people of Pelican Pointe to step up to the plate and help Scott's widow? After all, Scott had painted the townspeople as a bunch of home-grown good Samaritans. Didn't sound like that to Nick.

As he headed out of town, the question nagged at him. He did his best to shrug off the why. Jordan Phillips wasn't his problem. He was here for one reason. And it wasn't to get drawn into the woman's problems or do a good deed for anyone but himself. He didn't give a rat's ass about anything in Pelican Pointe, least of all Jordan Phillips. He didn't need anyone else's problems right now. He had enough of his own. He certainly didn't want to hear that Scott's wife had fallen on hard times. What he had to say to the woman would take no more than an hour, two at the most. He was sure of it. Once he explained what happened, his conscience would be clear. A couple of hours, a long talk, maybe a shoulder to cry on and he would be done with Jordan Phillips. He could head back to L.A., and get on with his own life.

Maybe then Scott's ghost, or whatever it was, would leave him the hell alone.

Following Murphy's directions, he took the Coast Highway until he spotted a narrow turnoff heading farther west toward the ocean. In the distance, down the winding road, at the end of a long paved driveway he spotted a freshly painted apple-green and white sign that read, "The Cove Bed and Breakfast, Scott and Jordan Phillips, Proprietors."

As he drove past the sign, seeing Scott's name there gave him a jolt. Despite the fact that Scott had described the place more times than he could count, Nick hadn't expected that. Slowing the bike, he took the time to glance around at the surrounding woods. Some thirty yards ahead, he noticed the grove of trees that guarded an old house and then suddenly the rundown-looking Victorian came into view. Just like the town, the house looked like it had seen better days. It needed a fresh coat of paint, new shutters, maybe a new roof. The wooden porch sagged, the rotted wood of the railing needed replacing. From the end of the drive, he spotted some kind of activity on the porch he couldn't quite make out.

As he got closer, it wasn't the condition of the house that caught his attention and held, but rather the striking woman about five foot six with caramel-colored, honey-blonde hair pulled back in a ponytail, standing on the wraparound porch struggling mightily with a large commercial sander. Trying to keep a steady hold on the constant motion, she was fighting the machine or maybe the machine was fighting her. Either way, the battle raged on and it looked like the sander was winning.

Pulling up beside the porch, he quickly shut off the engine to the cycle. Before he could slide off the bike, however, the woman lost control of the machine. The sander became airborne, flew through the wooden railing, sailed another five feet in the air and landed with a grinding thud in the middle of a bunch of flowers. Pink and purple blossoms shot out from every angle, along with green vines going every which way. The sander sat there among the flowers, whirling, spewing forth enough dirt and noise to deafen the neighbors or scare a baby.

From somewhere on the porch, Nick heard the wail of a small child. The harried woman rushed over to a mesh, crib-like box where she bent down to scoop up the unhappy little bundle dressed in pink overalls. Clutching the baby to her chest, she began bouncing her up and down trying to soothe the little girl. Over the din, Nick heard her say, "Oh, sweetie, I'm so sorry. Don't cry now. Hush now. It's okay. Shhhh. It'll be okay. Mama's right here, she didn't mean to scare you."

Nick bent down over the sander, located the switch, and flipped it to the off position, silencing the deafening noise. Hauling the machine out of the bushes, he set it upright. Out of the corner of his eye, he watched as Jordan simply dropped down on the porch steps with Hutton on her lap as if exhausted, defeated.

During their time together in Iraq, Scott had forced countless photographs from home on Nick, whether he wanted to look at them or not. Now, snapshots of this woman, this child flickered through his head in rapid-fire succession. He realized, the photos hadn't done either of them justice. The baby, no longer an infant, had grown. The woman had features he didn't recall from pictures, which told him how little attention he had paid to them at the time. He certainly had not remembered Jordan's warm expressive, big brown eyes. Or her long narrow face with the high cheekbones. Or that sweetheart-shaped mouth. Or those long legs in a pair of jean shorts.

And she'd lost weight.

Nick stood back long enough to let her go through the rituals of calming the baby. But once he felt it was okay to proceed, he approached both with caution. "Are you okay?"

Sniffling, cuddling the child, Jordan stared at the stranger as if he'd lost his mind. "Do I look okay? They shouldn't rent that thing without detailed instructions on how to keep it under control."

In spite of her meltdown, Nick couldn't help but chuckle at her words. Wisely though, he hid his smirk by leaning down to check the damage to the wood-splintered porch railing.

"That's just one more thing I'll have to fix," she sobbed. "I'll never get this place ready to open." Turning to Nick, her shoulders slumped. She sighed. "If you're looking for a place to stay, we aren't open yet." Her earlier morning optimism and pep talk forgotten, she groaned, "Looks like we may never be."

How to proceed, he wondered before taking a long look around at the picturesque surroundings, those huge cypress trees guarding the house, their peeling branches swaying in the soft breeze from the ocean. You could smell the water from here. He breathed in the fresh air heavy with some indistinguishable sweet mixture from the blooming buds lining the rest of the walkway. Without thinking, without preamble, he heard himself slide out the words, "Murphy at the store said you might need help out here."

"He did?"

Nick noticed she seemed bewildered at that. Her big brown eyes grew even wider. She actually stammered before her voice evened out. "I...I...well of course I need help, but I can't afford to hire anyone right now. Murphy knows that. He shouldn't have told you there was work. I can't pay you, not until I open up anyway." Staring at the man, her heart suddenly raced with undefined hope. She so needed things to go her way for a change. "Are you looking—for work, I mean?"

He squinted into the distance at a flock of seagulls circling overhead, refused to meet her eyes. He hadn't come this far to lie to her. That's the last thing he wanted to do. But at the moment, he couldn't stop the words from spilling out of his mouth. "Seems I am. If you know a place for me to stay, I could ride it out, until you get open." He didn't have a clue what had happened to the man who had all but chanted the entire way here, "I refuse to get involved."

In the blink of an eye, her anticipation turned cautious. "Why would you do that? I don't know you from Adam— you come riding up here on a motorcycle—out of the blue. You aren't in trouble with the law, are you?"

Nick shook his head. He contemplated how not to lie because he'd never seen a woman more in need of help than this one. Murphy had been right about that. And damn it, how could he turn his back on her now? Even he wasn't that cold. He heard himself say, "Nope. I'm a fair carpenter. I can handle a hammer, a saw...and I can handle that sander." Eyeing the condition of the place, he added, "But at this point, I don't think you can afford to be too picky. Murphy says you've got a deadline approaching."

"Murphy's got a big mouth." Her shoulders slumped again—visibly. She sighed again. "It's a small town. You'll find that out soon enough. Nothing but busybodies who know everything about your business. I'm Jordan by the way. Jordan Phillips." Bouncing her daughter, she added, "And this is Hutton."

"Nick Harris." He watched her face for any sign of recognition at the name. Surely, Scott had mentioned him in his letters home. But when she appeared more distressed and deeper in thought, he realized the name meant nothing to her. What now? he wondered. The woman didn't seem to have any idea who he was. He wasn't sure what to do. He had counted on her recognizing his name. Should he mention how he knew Scott, blurt out here and now, admit why he'd come to Pelican Pointe in the first place? He sucked in a quiet breath. She looked so vulnerable sitting there with the baby on her lap. Her eyes still glistened with tears. He'd witnessed the woman's breakdown over a sander. What would she do if he dredged up painful memories about her dead husband now? She'd start crying again, that's what. He didn't see any reason to take the chance. His courage plummeted.

As he watched her face, Nick knew she was weighing her options. He could tell how intently she studied him over the top of the baby's head. He didn't blame her. He was a stranger riding a Harley. For all she knew he could be a serial killer. He racked his brain for inspiration. What could he say that might reassure her that she could trust him? But then why should she trust a total stranger? Suddenly, he blurted out, "I'd stay in town, work here during the day, go back to my room at night if that'll make you more comfortable." It was the only thing he could offer.

"You aren't from around here." It wasn't a question.

"L.A."

"There isn't another place to stay in town. The Cove is it."

He knew the minute she made up her mind about him. She stood up with purpose, sat the baby on her hip. "Well, Mr. Harris, I'm in kind of a fix right now, desperate even. I'll pay you the going rate for a carpenter." She'd have to find out exactly what the going rate was.

"You don't..."

She held up a stubborn hand. "As soon as I open, we'll settle up. Keep track of your work, your hours. In the meantime, there's a studio apartment in the back over the garage. It isn't much. In fact, it's a dump." With a nervous laugh she added, "Frankly, it's a mess. But I could give it a thorough cleaning and see what I could do to get it livable while Hutton's taking her afternoon nap."

"That'd be fine. While you clean the place, I'll finish sanding the porch, repair that railing. How would that be?"

She stood up, glared in the direction of the sander. "Be my guest. This porch will rot before I go near that thing again."

Chapter Two

Holding a tray laden with sandwiches and a pitcher of iced lemonade, Jordan assessed her work force from just inside the front doorway as Nick, saw in hand, cut another piece of two by four replacement wood to put the railing back together. After she'd directed him to Scott's plethora of tools kept out back in the overstuffed garage, Nick had been out here hard at work for hours as the miter saw buzzed and the busted balustrade, once again, took shape. She watched as he picked up a hammer and began to nail the wood in place, the muscles bunching in his arms with each whack of the mallet.

She sucked in a breath. It had been a long time since she'd felt attraction to a man. Not only was Pelican Pointe a small town without an overabundance of single guys, most of whom were thirty-plus years her senior, she lived pretty much out in the boonies. The closest thing to a hunk she'd seen recently was the UPS man. He gave her a three-minute-thrill once in a while when he delivered whatever she managed to order online.

But even though she hadn't had sex in forever, Jordan appreciated watching a fit, in-shape male swing a hammer and work a saw. He'd shed his black jacket, which had hidden a set of ripped abs. Now, the thin fabric of his T-shirt clung to his sweaty body in clumps. Since the day had grown quite warm, she found herself wishing he'd simply take off the shirt. She watched, though as he seemed to delight in the work at hand as though he enjoyed being outdoors. Every so often he stopped to bask in the sunshine holding his face up to the cloudless sky while his longish black hair hung around his face in damp curls.

While he seemed to take pleasure in the ocean breeze cooling off the heat from his body, Jordan took delight in the way he packed himself into a pair of jeans.

She needed to get a grip. And fast.

The minute she stepped out onto the sagging porch, their eyes met. She didn't imagine the pull in her lower belly because it all but yanked her out of a lust-packed daydream. "You've been out here for hours. How about a sandwich?"

"I could eat. Thanks." He set down the hammer, took the tray from her, put it down between them on the steps. As soon as his butt hit the wood, he picked up a ham and cheese sandwich and dug in. "Mmmm, this isn't the cold sandwich I expected." The ham was warm and covered with melted mozzarella, the bread crusty and smeared with a tangy dollop of some kind of tasty spice.

A little insecure when it came to her culinary skills, Jordan couldn't help but ask, "How's it taste?" Tentative, she sat down on the other side of the tray on the top step, watching him eat. He must have been ravenous, she thought, as she picked up one of her own concoctions and dug in.

"Delicious. What's that spice in the mayo?"

"Pesto. It gives it a little extra kick."

"I'll say."

"I got the studio clean, well, clean-er."

After two tours in Iraq, he could sleep in a barn. "I'm sure it'll be fine."

An awkward silence descended. She'd spent such a long time here alone, it felt strange to be in a position of having conversation with someone other than

Hutton. "You finally got all that peeling paint sanded off, makes it look better already."

"After a couple of coats of stain it'll look even better."

"You did a good job putting the railing back together."

"Getting there. It'll need a couple coats of paint though."

Nick polished off his sandwich, downed a glass of lemonade and poured another. "I'll finish the railing after we eat." He dusted the crumbs from his shirt and hands, zeroed in on the chunky, chocolate chip coconut macadamia nut cookies on the tray. He broke one in half, stuffed it in his mouth. "You make these?"

"I did." Pleased he liked the food, she added, "Desserts are my specialty."

"Best cookie I ever ate. What all needs doing around here?"

That made her laugh. "How much time do you have? And where do I start? Up to now, I've been concentrating on the inside, getting the guest rooms ready upstairs." When she saw the willing look on his face, she reluctantly added the bad news, "But the bathrooms, they need a lot of work. Old plumbing. I've put that off too long. I know that was a mistake. Do you know anything about plumbing?"

"Some." Another white lie. What he knew about plumbing would fill a thimble.

"If you think it would help, I have a how-to book on plumbing. And every other book on do-it-yourself projects known to man," she said with a nervous laugh.

Nick drained his second glass of lemonade, suddenly craving a cold beer. The lies, he thought, could make a man thirsty. Knowing he should keep his mouth shut, he asked anyway, "Did you have a plan when you started all this?"

Jordan looked away, drew in a breath then calmly blew it out. "The plan was...for Scott, my husband, the plan was for us to turn this place into a B & B. But that only lasted until his unit got called up to Iraq. From that point, from the time I found out...he wasn't coming back...things got..." She took another deep breath. "Since Scott died, I haven't had a plan. But, if I don't get this place up and running by May first, get paying guests in here, get a cash flow coming in to show the bank this is a real business, I'll lose everything that meant anything to Scott. The bank has given me several extensions already. You might say I've hit the proverbial brick wall."

"May one, huh? There's still time. How about this? I'll read your plumbing book, see what I can do to get the house ready and we'll take it from there." He stood up. "Why don't you show me around, show me where to start—after the porch that is."

She started with a walk around the grounds. To her, it was better if she showed him the hidden cove below the cliff, the beach, the grounds, hoping he'd see the potential of the place right off rather than hitting him over the head with all the work that needed doing inside the house. For some reason it became all important to get him on board with seeing the house as a legitimate B & B and all it had to offer.

Since he'd already dug around in the black-hole-filled garage firsthand and since she'd pointed out the garage apartment earlier, they bypassed that and crossed a grassy courtyard. The quad included an outdoor eating area set up with several teak tables all sporting a variety of colorful umbrellas. Flower beds filled with an assortment of moonbeam coreopsis, day lilies, lanky bromeliads, and purple peonies lined the walkways, bursting with color and fragrance. The place looked like a snapshot out of a garden magazine.

"How many acres?" Nick asked trying to take in the picturesque setting.

"Fifteen," she advised, as she continued down a well-worn path, past blossom-laden dogwoods and magnolias, shrub vines filled with plump wild blackberries and strawberries just beginning to ripen. Jordan led the way following another trail through the grove of cypress trees before reaching the cliff where they began their descent down to the cove and the beach.

The hike down the side of the cliff was steep and intimidating but the steps built into the side of the slope made the climb down much easier.

As they started down, a little pang hit Jordan's heart when she remembered how long it had taken Scott to build the wooden steps into the side of the rough terrain. He'd spent months on the project before adding the iron-pipe railing just weeks before his unit had been called up to leave for Iraq. Over her shoulder, she reminded Nick, "Be sure to hold onto the railing. The footing here is tougher than it looks and even the most seasoned hiker can sometimes get a little winded." She hoped he wasn't insulted by the reminder.

But she had no sooner gotten the words out than she glanced back and noticed he looked as if he might be having some sort of panic attack. His face had turned a clammy gray as beads of perspiration formed on his forehead. "You okay?"

"I'm fine," he whooshed out.

When she reached the last step, Jordan jumped onto the loose, sandy soil and looked back at Nick, who stood on the last step a little breathless.

Like a bubbly tour guide, Jordan hit the high points, anxious to show off what the place offered. She spread her arms out and said, "Nick Harris meet The Cove, forty yards of pristine private beach hidden away from public access that no other house in the area offers. This place is ideal for surfing, whale watching, picnicking. What with six guest rooms, which is more than most B & Bs offer, and with beach access, something even some of the larger hotels in Santa Cruz don't offer, I shouldn't have a problem keeping this place full during the summer. At least that's what I'm hoping."

She stood watching him walk up and down the stretch of sand near the water. A little nervous, she went on, "That's rosemary and sage you smell along with Monterey pine. The trail is lined with the stuff. It grows wild here along with plenty of ginger, beach grass and alfalfa. There's a tide pool, all kinds of cool rock formations in the area." But as Jordan went on with her pitch it appeared as though Nick wasn't listening but trying to recover from the climb down. Relieved that he didn't seem to be as pale as before, she went on determined to give him the full treatment. "Scott planned to offer the guests surfing lessons. He'd be the instructor, of course." She chuckled almost to herself before adding, "I used to tell him I thought it was a sneaky way to get to go surfing. When we got things up and going, he wanted to offer scuba diving, too. There's a shipwreck just off the coast not far from here. He thought it would be an interesting selling point to lure guests."

"Shipwreck?"

"Yeah, you know, stay at the B & B, dive while you're here and explore a shipwreck during your stay." She pointed offshore toward the horizon. Jordan saw Nick take his time, scope out more of the cove. It was after all a spectacular spot to just sit and enjoy nature. But the guy seemed to be distracted, a little preoccupied and a whole lot winded. With that body, she wondered why. As she watched him walk to the water's edge and back, checking out the rocks and shells along the way, she finally shut up long enough to give him time to get his breath back.

The climb down told Nick what he'd known for months, after several surgeries, he still wasn't yet back to full strength. But even so, he had to tamp down the urge to shed his clothes and take a dive right then and there into the blue water.

Standing there at water's edge he wondered how many times Scott had walked this same beach. His heart clutched at the thought.

To get his balance back, he took several gulps of ocean air, filling his lungs with the salty smells of the sea and reluctantly admitted to himself the place was as beautiful and peaceful as Scott had described. He'd talked about this place so much it made Nick feel like an imposter, which he was. He knew he'd have to pay for posing as a carpenter slash handyman. Maybe he needed to come clean. That idea crashed and burned when he looked over at Jordan. She was obviously off in her own world. It wasn't until the wind whipped her hair from her face that he realized she was politely waiting for him to recover enough for the trek back up. He shook off his melancholy mood, gave her a brief nod to let her know he was ready, and turned to head back up the cliff.

Once they got back to the top, he followed her along another path that took them past a vegetable garden, where she instinctively checked on her neatly planted rows of fragrant onion, thyme and basil. "I've got rabbits. Trying to keep them out is like trying to keep a vampire away from blood."

"Why would a rabbit stay away from a readymade smorgasbord like this?"

She laughed. "Exactly. But there has to be a way. I've tried all the natural remedies, mothballs, marigolds. I'm down to trying vinegar." She stood up to continue the tour.

"That explains the pickle smell."

He continued to tag behind as she led him past still more well-tended flower beds filled with pink blossomed hydrangeas, purple delphinium, and native blooming yellow and white ice plants. They passed budding magnolias, ancient pines, and another row of cypress where a couple of rope swings swayed in the breeze. To Nick the entire fifteen acres looked like something out of a travel guide, an idyllic snapshot of coastal living. It sure wasn't smog-infested L.A.

No wonder Scott hadn't been able to shut up about the place.

When they got to the house, they entered through a sunny mud room with banked high windows on one side, and a roomy, well-organized laundry space on the other. They made their way into a bright, airy open kitchen. A commercial six-burner stovetop and double oven took up one side of the room, while a spotless marble-topped island planted in the middle held an array of ancient, well-scrubbed pots and pans overhead. A desk took up one corner, a stone fireplace the other.

Brand-new chrome appliances complemented chestnut cabinets. The newness of everything, including a spotless Italian tile floor, told him this room had already been remodeled. "You must have started in here."

"It needed the most work. It made sense to get the kitchen up and going before we did anything else." She didn't add that the remodeling had pretty much ended here in this room when Scott left for Iraq.

They moved on to the back staircase and up to the guest bedrooms. He listened as she pointed out the rooms she'd already painted, light fixtures she'd already replaced, a bathroom floor she was ripping up before putting down new tile. "The larger bedrooms are on the back side of the house with the view of the ocean." She walked into one, stood at the double French doors looking out. "You can see the trail we walked through earlier leading down to the cove just beyond that grove of trees. And then of course there's the ocean."

For some reason, Nick got the impression she wanted him to see the possibilities of the place. He wasn't sure why his opinion mattered. He wanted to tell her he understood the plan, and that what she was trying to do out here without Scott wasn't crazy or impossible for a woman here alone.

But as she stood nervously twirling the simple gold chain dangling from around her neck, all he could do was think about Scott's hopes and dreams for this place. After all, he knew Scott's plans almost as well as Jordan. But he couldn't mention that.

Instead, he wanted to know, "Jordan, where do you and the baby sleep?"

"Downstairs. There are two bedrooms off the front of the house. I'll show you the rest of the downstairs as soon as Hutton wakes up."

She opened one of the French doors. They both stepped out onto a long, wooden deck running the length of the back of the house. The ocean breeze instantly made an impact. The cooling, aromatic wind rustled through the colorful pots of flowers lined up along the wall where patio chairs waited for guests to sit outside and either enjoy a sunset or maybe stargaze through the telescope already pointed skyward.

"That's some view," Nick remarked, as once again, he filled his lungs with the smells from the ocean. It was obvious why Scott had talked so much about home. He'd had so much to come back to, any man who'd had all of this waiting would have talked about it nonstop.

Nick had nothing like this back in L.A., not even close. Not this woman, certainly not a child. Nothing in his life remotely resembled Scott's. For whatever reason, Nick's life had been spared that day in Iraq while Scott's had not. It made no sense. For years, Nick had distanced himself from commitment, from serious relationships while Scott had settled down, made a life here with Jordan. And for what?

Jordan's voice brought him back from questions with no answers.

"The smaller bedrooms across the hall don't have this view, of course, but they're nice size. Hopefully these larger rooms will be my bread and butter."

Nick kept his thoughts to himself as they went back inside, down a long hallway where he noticed three of the rooms stood empty. He wondered how she intended to have guests without furniture. "Aren't you missing something in here?"

She laughed nervously. "I wanted to paint each of the bedrooms a different color so they'd have their own special theme." She smiled tentatively. "Now all I have to do is come up with one and finish painting before I bring up the furniture. My aunt's been generous enough to donate some antique pieces that will go well in here. My sister and her husband are bringing the last of the stuff down first chance they get. As you saw, the rest of the furniture is stored in the garage. It's out there gathering dust." But looking at the bare rooms now, she should have already furnished these rooms. There was so much she should have already taken care of, seen to. How could she explain to anyone how difficult the past year had been, the grief, the depression?

He was staring at her.

She sighed. She might as well level with him and get the bad news out in the open. "The building inspector was here yesterday. He said I'll have to bring the wiring up to code."

"Whew! I'm no electrician. You'll have to hire a professional for that."

Terrific. The do-it-yourself vibe he gave off didn't include wiring hundred-year-old houses. "Murphy gave me the name of several in Santa Cruz. I'll start making some calls this afternoon."

But suddenly, Nick thought of another way to help. "I could handle that part for you. I might know someone who could do the job." He was certain, Ben Latham, and a former Guard buddy would have no qualms about helping out. And he could also arrange to pay him without Jordan ever knowing about it.

Her eyebrows rose. "Really? That'd be great. Umm, any idea how much he'd charge?"

He shook his head. "No idea."

When they got to the first bathroom off the front landing, Nick looked in, came to a decision of his own. The room needed a new toilet, a new sink, a new faucet, and new flooring. Had to be four for four, he thought, anything less would come off as unfinished and tacky. "You weren't kidding. What made you think you could fix this place up?"

"Scott grew up here. The house belonged to his grandparents. But they lost the house in the early '90s and had to move out after his grandfather made some bad investments. When his grandpa died, Scott promised his grandmother he'd get the house back for her. Of course she died before he could. But when we got married, we bought the place and moved back here to raise our own family. Six months after we moved back, his unit got called up."

"You've been living out here alone," he declared aloud, not really expecting her to comment.

"Until Hutton came along, yes."

A pregnant woman, alone, living all the way out of town like this? No wonder Scott had worried himself sick. What if she'd gone into labor out here? When he saw the shadow of worry flutter in her eyes, he did his best to make her feel better. "There's still time to get it done, Jordan. It can still happen." And by God he'd make it happen for Scott, for her.

"I don't know, there's an awful lot left to do. I should have had the place ready to open by now, been further along with everything."

For some reason, he desperately wanted to reassure her. "You shouldn't be that hard on yourself. This is a huge undertaking for one person to handle. Together, we'll pick up the pace."

Around five-thirty, Nick stepped into the apartment over the garage Jordan had described as a dump. Hot and sweaty after the all-day sanding and staining job on the front porch, badly in need of a shower, he looked around and decided she'd exaggerated its poor condition. The place was actually spacious, almost loft-like, and smelled like lemon wax from the old oak, hardwood floors she'd polished to a gleam. She'd left the windows open. The ocean breeze on his sweaty body felt good to the skin.

The place was sparsely furnished. And what was here looked like leftovers from the '70s. An ancient sagging green sofa divided the living space, creating two rooms out of one. Beyond the sofa sat the double bed, an old urn top maple that looked in better shape than the rest. Glancing around the room, he decided, despite the lack of furnishings, he could be comfortable here. When he spotted the tiny kitchenette, which consisted of a small refrigerator and a two-burner stovetop tucked into the corner on one wall, he went with impulse. He walked over and threw open the door to the refrigerator. Sure enough, there inside, his hostess had stashed six cold beers. Grateful, he twisted the top off, guzzling the cold brew down like a man plucked off a deserted island. He crossed over to the back window and scanned the view of the ocean. As he drank his beer, he thought of Scott. Nick could envision him walking on the beach, surfing, living here with his wife and child. Hell, even in broad daylight, Scott's ghost refused to let go.

Sweaty, he started shedding clothes, wanting nothing more than a hot shower. He plopped down on the bed to pull off his boots, tested the mattress. He'd been in worse, he decided, as he began to pull off his jeans.

And it would have to do. Even if he had to pitch a tent to stay somewhere on the property, he was committed now. As he pulled out his shaving gear and walked into the bathroom, he couldn't help but wonder what he'd gotten himself into. He was here for Scott even if his wife had no idea who he was or how he'd known her husband.

Lathering his face with shaving cream, he knew it wasn't fair to keep his secret. How did he intend to remedy that? For a man who hadn't wanted to get involved, he felt chained to a block of cement. "Thanks Scott," he grumbled sourly, as he pondered his descent into what felt like quicksand.

Or like a drowning man going down for the third time. Not only had he never lived with a woman for any length of time, he certainly had never been around a kid, much less a baby. Then there was the work itself. He could drive a nail, but he was no carpenter. Could he fake that? He was pretty much all thumbs when it came to plumbing, too. So how was he going to install bathroom fixtures? As he reached over and turned on the shower, he considered the entire ruse. Getting through the next two months would definitely take some creativity on his part.

Plus, at some point, he'd have to find the right time to confess who he was.

But he had to admit, he didn't miss the office, or the daily grind of work, which for the past several months, had been going badly. Working outside with his hands had been almost therapeutic. He'd built up a good sweat, which had made him forget to think about the war, and how chaotic his life had become over the past year. Okay, so maybe the respite had been brief but who knew, maybe physical labor might be the answer to his problem.

Stepping into the shower, he turned the knob as far too hot as it would go, felt the water bead over his body, and fought the weary feeling that always seem to hit him this time of day.

Sleep deprivation could be a bitch.

As he began to relax, his mind drifted to the possibilities of the place. Scott had been right about The Cove's potential. But could they get everything done that needed doing in just over two short months? He stepped out of the shower, grabbed one of the thick towels Jordan had stacked on the shelf and began to dry off. Striding back into the bedroom he stopped. For the first time, his gaze landed on the bedside table where a vase full of red blossoms sat, a homey touch to be sure, just like the beer. Instinctively, he walked over, breathed in the scent of the buds. Inexplicably touched that she'd taken the time to leave fresh flowers for the room—for him, he smiled. An image of Jordan's slim body standing on the porch struggling to keep that sander under control had him smiling as he pulled on a clean pair of jeans.

He'd been invited to supper by a beautiful woman, a woman who was so completely not his type he had to admit she made him nervous. And Nick Harris had never been nervous with women. When he thought about Jordan he shouldn't be picturing her as any type but rather as a mother. Could he help it though if her long, sexy legs and her cute little butt in those shorts kept popping into his mind all afternoon as he worked?

As he walked over to the main house he decided he'd have to work on reining in those thoughts. It wouldn't do to have more guilt layered over what he already had to deal with.

Over dinner, an upbeat Jordan passed Nick the scalloped potatoes and decided it was good to have a man around the table again. She missed Scott. That was a given, but living on the outskirts of town without Scott, she had missed having company, missed being around people in general. With no one but Hutton to talk to had been difficult. But having Nick at her table was both a pleasure and a weight. Glancing over at Hutton, squirming in her high chair, Jordan soon realized she was rusty at making simple dinner conversation and mentally kicked herself. No pity party tonight. It wasn't everyday she had a guest. After all, before she opened up for business, she could use all the practice she could get at preparing meals and entertaining guests in her home around the dinner table.

Out of the corner of his eye, Nick watched Hutton play with her food. The baby's task seemed simple enough. From the tray of her high chair, she picked up her bright green peas, one pea at a time, and dropped them onto the floor. She would then lean over the side to check out all the little green specks dotting the tile.

When Jordan noticed what she was doing, she said, "Hutton, stop that." Jordan tore apart a crusty roll and handed it off. "Here, try some of this bread." Desperately, wanting dinner conversation, Jordan tilted her head and studied Nick's expressionless face. She decided it was up to her. "Pelican Pointe is kinda off the beaten path. There isn't much in the way of jobs here. Were you just passing through looking for work and Murphy pointed you out here?"

Wincing slightly at the question, not wanting to lie to her any more than he had to, he wondered how he might answer. For several long seconds, he sat there contemplating his response. Finally, he picked up his iced tea and settled on a partial version of the truth. "You might say I've had a rough couple of months. I needed to get away from L.A. for a while. About a week ago, I got on my bike and did just that. I ended up in Pelican Pointe." He might have taken his time making the journey here, coming to see this woman, but now that they were sharing a meal, he couldn't remember why he'd been so apprehensive.

"I guess these days there are a lot of people going through rough times."

Thoughts of the last year whirled through his head. "You could say that."

But all at once she caught what he'd said and wanted to know, "You've only been gone from L.A. a week? You were looking for work, right?"

Like a man hoarding a secret, he guiltily changed the subject. "Where do you get your cuisine? This beef dish is excellent. I didn't see any place in town that offers this kind of food."

A smile transformed her face. "Beef bourguignon. You think it's restaurant quality? I'm flattered. I was worried my culinary skills were a tad on the weak side for a B & B. For the past few months I've been experimenting with recipes, trying to broaden my menu, shore up my skills so to speak." Eyeing him with a steady gaze, she added, "You might make a good test subject. Up to now, it's just been Hutton, and she's going through her picky-eater stage."

The picky eater dropped another pea on the floor.

Nick had never known a woman who liked to cook or for that matter liked to go near a kitchen or was content to stay home. The usual women on his radar lived a high-octane kind of existence, much like him, hell-bent on the fast track up the corporate ladder to financial security as fast as they could get there. They didn't cook anything that couldn't be slid into a microwave, and lived primarily on delivery or take-out. And like him, having kids wasn't even on the agenda. As he stuck another bite of tender meat in his mouth, he decided this odyssey might have a few added benefits after all, like home cooked meals. "If every meal tastes as good as this, I'm happy to be your test subject."

The man had a voracious appetite. He took seconds of everything except the peas. And then she realized he'd worked like a dog since getting there that morning. That in turn had her wondering if he was comfortable in the studio apartment. Before she could ask though, she saw Nick lean over in Hutton's direction, push his plate toward the baby, and whisper something in her ear. "I don't like peas either. If you want to drop mine on the floor, be my guest."

Hutton shot a grin his way. Her smile was so like Scott's. The baby had his mouth. And he saw her father in those blue eyes. His heart sank. What was he doing here anyway creating more problems for himself? He felt the urge to run.

Oblivious to Nick's mindset, Jordan watched the byplay as Hutton, sensing a kindred spirit, clapped her hands in glee before scooping up a handful of peas from his plate. At the sight of her daughter interacting in such an easy way with Nick, Jordan almost dropped the pitcher of tea she'd picked up to refill their glasses. Keeping her thoughts to herself, she eyed Nick's plate and then the peas in her daughter's hand. "So we aren't fond of our green veggies, are we?"

Snapping out of his gloom, Nick pasted a smile on his face for Jordan's benefit. "Meat and potatoes, that's my kind of meal."

"Hutton seems to agree. I made cherry pie for dessert. I guess you wouldn't…"

He never let her finish. "Love cherry pie. I don't have to eat those peas or clean my plate, do I?"

"Since you're a guest, I think I'll let it slide for now. Want ice cream with that?"

"You read my mind."

When dinner was over, Nick offered to clean up the kitchen while she gave Hutton a bath and got her ready for bed. A generous offer Jordan had no intention of turning down. Relishing the prospect of having adult conversation, Jordan hurried through Hutton's bath. After getting the baby down for the night, she practically floated into the kitchen with the idea of maybe offering him a glass of wine, only to find the kitchen spotless but Nick already gone. Disappointed, she stared out the back window of the kitchen across the courtyard at the light on in the apartment over the garage. That would take some getting used to, she thought, as she put the kettle on for tea, the glass of wine forgotten. At dinner, she'd studied his hands. They didn't appear rough or calloused, not the hands of someone used to manual labor. She couldn't help wondering what secrets Nick Harris held.

Whatever they were he didn't seem the type to disclose his private thoughts.

After preparing the tea, she picked up the novel she'd been reading from the counter and headed to her bedroom. But getting ready for bed, she fought back tears that finally started to spill. Disappointment filled her. "Honestly, why would a man like that want to stay and talk to a boring housewife like me? Keeping me company would be the last thing on his mind. And besides, you're talking to yourself."

Crawling into bed, she opened the book and forced herself to concentrate on the storyline. But an hour later, a restless Jordan finally got out of bed and strode over to the bureau, retrieved a box from the drawer. On nights like tonight when she was missing Scott and unable to sleep, it helped to read his last letters from Iraq. Reading his words, knowing his thoughts, hearing his voice inside her head, talking about his dreams for the bed and breakfast somehow inspired her enough to keep going. When she'd settled back in bed, she opened the box and started reading the letters, as if they brought her comfort, she soon fell asleep.

Chapter Three

In spite of the constant wind whipping sand across the bumpy road, the heat was brutal inside the Humvee. The faces of the soldiers and any other exposed areas were covered with a mixture of grit and sweat. They bitched good-naturedly about their circumstances. Riding side by side, Nick and Scott had gotten past the complaining and were deep in conversation as they talked about their lives back home.

"I miss Jordan. And I wish I could hold Hutton, you know. I couldn't be there when she was born. I can't wait to see her for the first time. I didn't exactly plan on Jordan having to go through childbirth without me."

"How does it feel to be a dad?"

"Great, I think. It's hard to feel like a father when I'm so far away and can't rock her to sleep or put her on my shoulder like I've seen other dads do. I was hoping to get to do that before she gets too old. Jordan e-mails me plenty of pics, but pictures aren't the same thing. You ever thought of having kids of your own, Nick?"

"No. Nor do I want to get married. I don't like the idea of being tied down. I'm glad you're happy, Scott, but marriage isn't for everyone."

"If you ever found a woman like Jordan, you'd think differently."

Nick heard artillery fire right before a rocket exploded. Someone yelled, "Look out, incoming."

Nick heard another explosion and saw a flash of fire.

"Promise me, Nick..."

Nick came out of the dream as if he'd been back on that littered road near Baghdad talking to Scott. Dripping wet with sweat, he threw back the sheet. He rubbed a hand over the scars on his chest and glanced at his watch. One-thirty. He needed fresh air. Crawling out of bed, he made his way to one of the windows and slid the glass higher to let in more of the cool night air. Gulping the moist marine breeze had him fighting the urge to give in and take one of the sleeping pills the doctors had prescribed. He had a bagful. But he'd taken enough pills, seen enough doctors and hospital rooms to last a lifetime.

He backtracked to the nightstand and turned on the lamp. He found his jeans, slipped them on without buttoning them, before heading outside to the landing. He stared up at the night sky. Stars glittered down at him.

Suddenly squinting across the shadowy courtyard he spotted Scott, or at least his image, this time lifelike, heading his way. He could tell it was Scott by the way he walked. And he'd know the guy's walk anywhere. When Scott's image finally looked up at Nick, he smiled and lifted a hand in a wave as lifelike and real as if he'd just walked out of the main house. The gesture so familiar, just like Nick had seen him do six dozen times in Iraq. As if real, Scott spread his arms out wide and yelled up, "Took you long enough, you finally got here. Welcome to The Cove, Nick. How do you like it so far?"

Nick considered the fact he might possibly be going insane, slowly, deliberately, off-his-rocker-crazy. What was he supposed to do, answer a ghost, talk to one? How could he have thought coming here to see Scott's wife would make anything better? He scrubbed a hand over his face. "How's that working out for you, Harris?"

And now he was talking to himself. In the midst of it all, by coming here, he had a nagging feeling he'd just made the situation a helluva lot worse. What would Scott say if he told him he was attracted to his wife? Ridiculous, he thought. Scott was dead. And had been for ten months.

Nick glanced up at the stars again and tried to make out the brilliant twinkling light of the brightest star. Venus, he decided. The night sky shimmered back at him. He couldn't remember the last time he'd taken the time to just gaze up and enjoy that view. Insomnia aside, there was nothing like watching the night sky for falling stars. He'd forgotten how to do that in L.A.

As a boy, he'd spent hours looking through his telescope trying to locate everything from the Milky Way to the Little Dipper to Cassiopeia. Funny, he hadn't thought of that in ages. But for the past three years his life hadn't exactly been his own. Leaning on the railing, he looked across the courtyard at the main house.

Scott was nowhere in sight.

Shrouded in darkness even he could tell the rambling old Victorian looked as if it needed a complete overhaul. A sudden idea hit him. What kind of fool would be thinking about getting to work right about now? And what would Jordan say?

A couple of hours later, roller in hand, Nick glanced at his watch and yawned. Four-twenty. Standing on the ladder he'd found in the garage, he spread another round of Banana Cream paint on the living room wall. He looked around the room. Once he'd thrown down drop cloths to cover the upright piano, the sofa and loveseat, he had pretty much been good to go. And it didn't take much thought to slapping on paint.

But the mindless task soon gave way to exhaustion from lack of sleep. When he decided to take a break he simply climbed down off the ladder and sat down on the floor. Stretching out his long legs, he leaned his head up against an unpainted portion of the wall and closed his eyes. It didn't take long for him to drop off into a deep slumber.

As was often her habit, Jordan walked past the living room on her way outside to enjoy her morning cup of coffee on the front porch. Glancing into the room, she came to an abrupt halt. Startled to see the ladder guarding the front window, along with the butter color now splashed across the white part of the walls, she drew in a breath at the sight of Nick slumped on the floor.

Oh, my God, was the man breathing? Had he fallen off the ladder and broken his neck?

As she got closer, she saw his chest move up and down. The man was sound asleep. Instinctively, she moved toward him. The guy had flecks of pale yellow dotting his black hair. In his right hand he still clutched the paint roller. She leaned down to study his face. The involuntary pull of attraction hit her first before mortification. She hadn't had feelings like this since Scott. And the UPS man didn't count.

As if he could feel her intense stare, his eyes flew open. He jerked to attention.

Jordan stood up so fast she sloshed hot coffee all over her hand. Trying to back away, embarrassed at her wayward thoughts, she tripped over the drop cloth, caught her balance just in time to keep from falling.

Self-conscious at the idea of her finding him asleep, Nick immediately started to get to his feet which caused Jordan to stumble again on the drop cloth, putting more space between them. "Sorry, didn't mean to wake you." That was a ridiculous statement. The man was sleeping on the floor of her living room. Balancing the mug of coffee in one hand, she nervously pushed back her hair with the hand that held the baby monitor she always took outside with her.

"What are you doing in here?"

He rubbed his face. "Couldn't sleep. I decided to get a little work done. I didn't think you'd mind if I started painting in here." He came more awake—or tried to. The bright sunlight drifting in through the windows hurt his eyes. His mind refused to work. But he did his best to come up with a reasonable explanation as to why he was sleeping on her living room floor. "You said you hadn't gotten to this room yet, so—I thought—what the heck? But I sat down to take a break for a minute, must have dropped off."

"I'll say." Clutching the cup tighter in her fist, she asked, "Let me get this straight, you couldn't sleep and got up to paint my living room—in the middle of the night?"

"That about covers it. Back door wasn't locked. You really need to remedy that. I tried not to wake you. What time is it?"

"Six-fifteen." When Hutton's baby babble crackled through the monitor, she immediately turned to leave and then stopped suddenly. She backtracked, held out her cup of coffee to him. "You look like you could use this a lot more than me. Breakfast will be ready in about twenty minutes. Eggs and bacon okay?"

Taking the cup from her in one hand, he scrubbed at his face with the palm of his hand, rubbed his eyes. "Fine. That's...fine."

Nick watched Jordan walk out of the room. It might have been through bleary eyes, but all he could think was what a punch he'd just taken. This early in the morning, wearing no make-up, she looked—nothing short of amazing. That thought kicked him into gear.

He took a much-needed pull on the caffeine, mentally trying to shake the cobwebs out of his brain.

Jordan was Scott's wife. Had been, he corrected, as he looked around the room at the mess he'd made.

Thank God the woman wasn't his type. His type had always been women who liked to party, women who didn't have a domestic bone in their body. He'd cleverly managed to avoid women like Jordan. After all, the girl next door type could destroy a guy's player status. Of course, lately he hadn't exactly been at the top of his game.

He shook his head and stood up. How long had it been since he'd been with a woman anyway? Obviously, it had been too long. He needed to remedy that. Maybe he'd slip into Santa Cruz the first chance he got, find a willing, available female.

Okay, that made him feel better.

Standing there trying to wake up, his mind went back to what Scott had always said about his wife every time he had taken out her picture. And now after being around the woman for less than twenty-four hours, he had to agree...Jordan was a natural beauty, an all-American kind of girl with a sweet-nature.

Definitely the kind of woman he made a point to avoid, the kind you kept at arm's length.

He worked the kinks out of his neck. Avoided that kind of woman for a reason, he decided, as he got to work cleaning up the caked and dried paint mess he'd created hours earlier when he'd fallen asleep on the job.

As Jordan headed in to get Hutton, she decided as awkward as it was to have Nick working in the house, it also felt like the right thing to do. She couldn't exactly explain that, except for the fact that for the past two years she had been lonely living out here with only Hutton for company.

While she put a clean diaper on Hutton, she made a mental checklist of things she needed to discuss with him about the work. After all, they had a common deadline to meet. There was a work schedule to organize. When would she have gotten around to painting the living room? She took a deep breath, blew it out. Her lack of organization and direction needed to change. Over the next few weeks, she needed to focus better and stop this habit of not finishing anything. She'd have to make sure she kept a tally of all the work he did. She couldn't deny the prospect of having someone to discuss her plans with felt good though. As she set Hutton down on the floor to walk, as she watched her daughter toddle out the door, she decided she'd made the right decision to let Nick Harris stay.

It took a couple of days for them to settle into a work routine. Jordan would finish painting the guest rooms while

Nick tackled the myriad plumbing problems that always seemed to occur in an old house with five full bathrooms, all of which had ancient fixtures.

For a novice plumber Nick had problems from the beginning. It didn't take a genius to figure out for the next two months his time would be spent replacing and fixing dripping faucets, wobbly toilets, and broken tile. Sprawled on the bathroom floor, his arms wrapped around an unsteady brand-new porcelain bowl, he did his best to hold it in place while attempting to bolt it to the floor with a wrench. One of Jordan's many how-to plumbing books lay open next to him. But it wasn't exactly going textbook perfect. "Son of a bitch."

Jordan suddenly appeared in the doorway with an amused look on her face. "Problem?"

"The damn bolt is stripped. And it's the only one left." He'd gone through three already. "Is there a hardware store in town? I'll need another bolt, probably several." More like several boxes.

"Ferguson's on Main. You drove past it to get here. Can't miss it. If you're making a trip to town, would you mind picking up the flooring while you're there. It's been on back order for four weeks, should be there now for sure. I haven't had a chance to pick it up. Would you mind bringing it back?"

Nick stood up, his large frame filling the rather small space. Instinctively, Jordan backed up into the hallway. "Sure, but I can't bring flooring back on the bike."

"Why do you ride it, the bike I mean?"

"It's open." Eyeing the puzzled look on her face, he added, "I don't like closed-up spaces, being confined inside a vehicle for too long."

"That might rule out the SUV then. No problem. I can pick up the flooring when Hutton wakes up from her nap."

As he dried his hands on a rag, he calmly told her, "Jordan, I think I can handle a ride into town and back." At least he hoped he could.

"Then take the SUV. The keys are on the peg by the back door."

Fifteen minutes later on the ride into town, he rolled all the windows down on the Explorer and fought off a panic attack by gulping in deep breath after deep breath. When the trapped feeling began to abate, he started to worry over Jordan's situation. He remembered in detail his talks with Scott who had given him the impression that the house was pretty much good to go, even ready for guests. Ever the eternal optimist, that assessment was so like Scott. Nick shook his head. He could almost hear Scott's voice.

"Yeah, now that I think about it, I might have been a little too optimistic in that regard."

Nick almost drove off the road when he glanced over to look at the passenger seat. There sat Scott with a big goofy grin on his face. "Sorry buddy, but you weren't ready for the truth."

"Shit." Nick forced himself to focus on the two-lane roadway. "You aren't here."

"Of course, I'm here. Why wouldn't I be here, the place where I was the happiest? I'm all around here, everywhere here actually, especially The Cove, to help you adjust, Nick. Jordan needs help. And whether you want to accept it or not, you're it."

"I'm not a contractor or a carpenter. She needs both. The house is nowhere near ready for paying guests. Even if both of us worked twelve hours a day for the next ten weeks, it's gonna be cutting it close."

"Just do your best. That's all I ask, Nick. You promised me."

As Nick hit the city limits, he pointed out, "You've sure gotten a lot of miles out of that, too. Look, installing plumbing fixtures isn't my forte. I could offer to hire help, bring in a professional, but how would I explain that to Jordan."

"You'll figure it out, Nick."

Nick spotted Ferguson's on the same side of the street and pulled into a slotted space. He cut the engine and looked over at the passenger seat. Scott was gone. Nick puffed out a shaky breath. Maybe sleep deprivation caused hallucinations. Maybe he needed to look that up on the Internet. He continued to sit there and rack his brain for inspiration. Maybe he should simply head back to L.A. It was, after all, the easy way out and would make more sense than this crazy idea ever had. But if he did that, he knew he probably wouldn't be able to sleep again in this lifetime. And if he walked away now knowing what Jordan was going through alone, he was sure Scott might never stop harassing him.

No doubt about it, he felt trapped between a promise that hadn't meant anything and his guilty conscience. He crawled from behind the wheel of the SUV, muttering something that sounded like, "Thanks Scott.

I'm stuck here and something tells me you're loving every minute of it."

Feeling pissed off at the whole situation, he walked through the double doors of Ferguson's with an attitude. Looking around the store he spotted the hardware section and dug through the shelves until he found several boxes of nuts and bolts he thought he could use.

He then followed the signs for customer pickup to the back counter, only to find he had to wait his turn behind five other people. There was one lone man behind the counter trying to take care of everyone—and at a snail's pace no less. But he got in line behind a little old lady with blue hair, who as it turned out, wasn't picking up anything at all, but rather wanted spring planting tips on what kinds of perennials thrived best in this zone. After standing behind her for ten minutes, Nick suspected she wanted nothing more than to have someone listen while she berated her lazy, good-for-nothing excuse for a son-in-law.

By the time a balding, overweight man in his late forties finally greeted him from behind the register, Nick was looking for a fight.

"I need to pick up flooring for Jordan Phillips."

The man shook his head and didn't even bother to stutter when he said, "Sorry, mister, but that flooring's not going anywhere until I get some money on the account. It's way past due. I've been patient up to now, but I've got to have payment on her account before I let her have the flooring. I'm not in business to give away my inventory."

"How about if I speak to the owner, Mr. Ferguson?" Through Scott's descriptions of the town, Nick felt as if he knew the townspeople well enough to ask for him by name.

"You're looking at him."

Nick raised an eyebrow in disbelief. So much for Scott's misguided assessment of the citizens of Pelican Pointe. "She needs that tile."

But Ferguson was steadfast. "Sorry."

Just as obstinate, Nick pointed out, "You know her husband died in Iraq, right?"

Ferguson shook his head defiantly. "For his country and all that. Look, I've carried the account for well over six months. That's more than most would do. I can only be charitable for so long, I've got a business to run, bills of my own to pay."

"How much will it take to bring her account current?"

"I'll need at least twenty percent of the balance."

Nick reached for his wallet, pulled out his credit card. So much for being a returning war vet and getting help from the good people of Pelican Pointe. He had to fight the urge to tell off the balding gasbag. As he handed off the credit card something occurred to him though. He lowered his voice when he demanded, "I don't want you hassling Jordan about paying on her account every time she walks into the store. From now on, you talk to me about it. Got that?"

When the man looked even more sheepish, it only made Nick more determined. "If I find out you've bugged her, I'll come back in here and ream your miserable ass. Are we clear?" While the man stood there with his mouth open, Nick leaned over the counter and made another point. "And I want help loading the damn flooring."

Later Nick stood on the loading dock and watched as two Ferguson employees carried heavy square boxes of tile flooring and pushed them into the back of the SUV. With a satisfied smirk on his face, Nick didn't see Murphy amble over.

Noting the men were loading Jordan's Ford Explorer, Murphy asked, "How's it going? I see you found Jordan's place."

"Seems like I'm working for her."

Murphy sent him a dubious look. "Now how did that happen?" But suddenly Murphy understood. "You didn't tell her who you were, did you? Something tells me Scott's name didn't even come up. Am I right?"

Nick let out an audible sigh, ran his hands nervously through his hair. "When I got there, she was having a crisis of sorts, a meltdown. It wasn't a good time to start throwing Scott's name around in the mix."

"You have to tell her. Jordan's had a rough time."

"I know that. She's under the impression you sent me out there to find work." He let that register for a couple of minutes before adding, "Look, I know you don't know me, but when I told her my name, it didn't register, didn't mean a thing to her. She was upset, the baby started crying, and I didn't want to add to that. I haven't found the right time to tell her yet."

"Trust me. There is no right time. You wait and it'll get tougher to find the right words, not easier. I don't want to see Jordan hurt."

"You think I do? That's the last thing I want. So, could we ride with this for a while, Murphy, just until I find the right time?" Knowing small towns, a thought occurred to Nick. "And just so you know, she fixed up that studio apartment over the garage. I'm sleeping there. "

Murphy shrugged. "What do I care?"

"Yeah. Right. Gossip is the small town way of life. I don't want people getting the wrong idea about Jordan and giving her a hard time."

Murphy shook his head. "I'll make sure people know. But Nick, tell her about Scott soon, okay? The longer you wait, the tougher it'll be."

Once back at The Cove those words came back to Nick as he finished unloading the boxes of tile flooring and stacking them into the packed garage Jordan obviously used for storage. There was barely enough room for the flooring. As he took advantage of the only available floor space, he stopped long enough to look around at all the stuff. There was an assortment of antique dressers, chests, and beds. He spotted boxes of new plumbing fixtures. There were two new pedestal sinks, another new toilet still in the box, new faucets, and a cherrywood vanity. Behind all the clutter, he spotted an old television set, and wondered briefly if it might pull in enough of a reception in the apartment to get a Lakers game.

Looking closer, behind the clutter, Nick sucked in a breath. His gaze fell on half a dozen surfboards leaning up against the far wall. Scott's surfboards, he realized, as he worked his way past the dusty junk to get a better look. But Scott was gone. Nick was here with Jordan and Hutton doing all the things Scott should have been doing.

Even though he'd promised Murphy to tell Jordan who he was, he doubted there would ever be a right time. She wouldn't understand, she couldn't. Why had he ever thought coming here was the answer? He wondered for the hundredth time in two days what he'd gotten himself into and how he was going to get out. He came out of his reverie long enough to crawl further into the abyss to discover four brand-new bicycles hiding in the corner and wondered why there were so many. Then he realized the bikes had to be for guests to use for sightseeing in the area. For some reason, they caused him to wonder if Jordan had been out of the house much in the last year. When was the last time she'd had any kind of fun? In fact, he wondered what exactly a woman with a baby did for fun. Before turning back to finish unloading, he decided to find out.

Standing on a ladder, drill in hand, she almost had the cornice mounted over one of the bedroom windows when she heard footsteps out in the hallway. Listening to his steps grow closer, it dawned on her how glad she was that he was back from town. How silly, she thought, days ago she didn't even know the man existed and now... She reeled in her emotions. She couldn't have missed him. He'd only been gone a couple of hours. Frustrated with her own thoughts, she got down off the ladder and met him going into the bathroom to start work on the toilet again. Knowing Pelican Pointe wasn't the friendliest of towns, she wanted to know, "How'd it go? Any problems?"

"Nope. Flooring's unloaded and stacked in the garage. Hope that's okay."

"That's fine. You don't have to put the flooring in by yourself, Nick. I can lay flooring. If you weren't here I'd have to do it anyway." She grinned. "Besides, it seems I have this how-to book that says it's easy as 1-2-3, a piece of cake. Why do you suppose the books make it sound like do-it-yourself projects are so easy?"

Nick grinned back. "They want you to buy the book, their book, the easier they say it is, the more books they sell." She looked around at the mess. "With the new fixtures and new flooring this bathroom should be good to go, don't you think?"

"Should be. Does the shower work?"

"I haven't tried it in...well, a long time."

Absently, Nick reached over and turned on the shower head. All at once, water spewed out from every direction, drenching him from head to waist. "Figures," he muttered as he turned off the water.

"Sorry about that." But she giggled in spite of the look on his face. "Uh-oh. Guess it could use a new shower head, huh?"

Soaked, he took a playful step in her direction. "So you think my being all wet is funny?"

This time Jordan stifled the chuckle. "Of course not." She took a step backward to keep from getting wet.

But Nick took another step, squeezing out the excess water from the tail end of his shirt and flinging the drops in her direction. "Next time, you get to play the drowned rat."

"Who me?" Eyeing his approach, she skipped playfully out of reach just in time to avoid another splatter of water. "Get me wet and you die," she warned teasingly as she threw him a towel from the rack. Their eyes locked. She stepped back again not wanting to appear obvious about seeing him take off his shirt. But when he just stood there staring at her with those intense blue eyes of his that made her feel sixteen again, she forced herself to back out of the room.

What was wrong with him? he wondered. Why did the woman make him feel like a green kid again? He needed to get to Santa Cruz...and soon. He had to remind himself he'd had plenty of success with women ever since he'd first persuaded Mary Kate Frasier into the backseat of his Chevy Cavalier. He didn't need to moon over a woman with a baby. Frustrated, he started mopping up the water on the floor. The annoying scene at the hardware store completely forgotten.

That evening after supper Nick walked into the kitchen to get a beer out of the fridge, and take a break from the plaster job that had consumed him for the better part of two hours. The sounds of U2's With or Without You drifted from the CD player on the kitchen counter. Jordan had her head down at the kitchen table looking through various flower catalogs.

Remembering the damage the sander had done to her flowers, he asked casually, "What are those red flowers? The ones you left in the studio by the bed."

"Red flowers? Oh, you mean the crimson stargazers." She smiled when she saw the baffled look cross his face. "Lilies."

"They smell great."

"They're my favorite. But I thought I'd plant red tulips out front. Maybe put in some white and yellow daffodils for contrast, lining the walkway up to the porch which, by the way, looks one hundred percent better painted and sanded. And I was wondering, since the porch looks so much better, maybe you could help me hang a porch swing I bought online last summer. If we hang the swing it might make the place look—I don't know, homier, more inviting."

"Sure, I'll take care of it. But the place is plenty homey, Jordan. This house makes a nice B & B."

Some of the worry left her face. "You think so? Really? The past year I've had so many doubts. Sometimes I feel like it's just an old house that's way past its prime."

"It has a solid foundation. Whoever built the place didn't cut corners on quality, quality lasts. It just needs some sprucing up, a little TLC. We'll get the place ready for opening day."

"You have no idea how much I needed to hear that, Nick. Thanks. It's good to hear something positive for a change. It's like validation."

"Do you have money budgeted to hire roofers? That roof will only last until the next big Pacific storm."

Her good mood went south. She didn't want to hear that right now. She couldn't handle another major expense of any kind. The wiring was a setback, but a new roof, she couldn't think about that now. "The roof has been patched a couple of times already. It's the best I can do for now. Do you think it will last till next spring? I might be in better shape to take out a loan for the roof by then."

He drew in a deep sigh knowing she was doing her best. What would she say if he offered her the money? But looking at her face he knew she wouldn't take it. And it would invariably lead to her asking all kinds of probing questions, wanting answers he was in no frame of mind to deal with yet. Instead of going there, he said,

"I spent some time down in the basement today, looking at the wiring. The inspector wasn't lying to you. The wiring must be at least fifty years old. It definitely needs replacing. I found an electrician, but he can't come out until next week." He didn't mention the buddy doing him a huge favor.

"Just remember, Nick, you don't have to do everything by yourself. I need help hanging the swing on the porch, I wasn't asking you to do it for me. I've been here two years by myself. I've gotten rather handy with tools."

"Just not a sander," he teased, sending her a grin. Her shy smile made her eyes twinkle, her cheeks flush.

"No, not the sander. That wasn't exactly my finest moment."

He couldn't remember the last time he'd said something silly enough to cause a woman to blush. And that raised all kinds of red flags as to how completely out of his element he was with this particular woman. Just one more reason to keep his distance, he thought, as he drained his beer and headed back upstairs to finish the lousy plaster job before the damned stuff dried hard as concrete and he had to start all over again.

Chapter Four

Scott's easy laugh all but filled the inside of the Humvee. They rode sitting side by side on the same bench seat.

Smiling, Scott held several photos out to Nick. "Jordan's got the prettiest brown eyes. But look, Hutton got my eyes. And she has my mouth, too. What do you think?"

Taking the pictures, Nick replied diplomatically, "I'd say, thank God, she looks like her mother."

"I'm sure Hutton has my chin. She's a cutie that's for sure, don't you think? How'd you escape getting married all this time?" "Never wanted that kind of commitment. There are too many women in the world to be tied down to just one. Don't tell me you haven't ever felt like you're weighed down by one woman. Doesn't marriage choke the life out of you?"

"Nope, not with Jordan."

Nick heard the sound of artillery fire. A rocket exploded around them shattering metal into a thousand pieces. He heard the pang of shrapnel.

Someone shouted, "Look out, incoming."

He heard another explosion. Flames shot into the sky, while billowing smoke poured from several vehicles. The air smelled like burning fuel and then he breathed in the unmistakable smell of burning flesh.

"Promise me, Nick..."

Nick's eyes flitted open. His body shook uncontrollably with spasms. He could almost smell the burning oil and fiery smoke. He felt like he was burning up. With the sheet, he mopped at the sweat on his body and rubbed a hand over his face, then through his hair. Weary of the dream, he glanced at the alarm clock on the nightstand. Two-thirty. How long would he be able to function without a good night's sleep? And would the dream ever leave him in peace? Would Scott? Drained, he rolled over in bed and turned on the light. He grabbed the book from the bedside table about plumbing. As he began to read, he asked out loud, "What's the big deal about plumbing? Shift gears Harris. It's all in the book." Then with a sigh, he added, "In another life I hired people to do this."

After thirty minutes of plumbing how-to, he closed the book, bored out of his mind. Looking around the sparse accommodations, he decided what the place needed was that old TV from the garage.

Getting dressed, he yearned for that other life, the one he'd had before Iraq. But he knew there wasn't a chance in hell of recapturing his former happy-go-lucky world. Hadn't he been trying to do just that for months since he'd been back stateside?

The night air felt good. He glanced across the courtyard for any signs of ghosts. The place was deserted. He raised the garage door and felt around for the light switch. Eyeing the mess inside, a sigh escaped his lips. He began sorting through the clutter, convinced Scott hadn't thrown anything away since he'd moved here. Standing there, he felt like a different person altogether. And wasn't that just a bitch, he thought, as his eyes landed on the reason for his quest.

He ran a hand across the old television set, swore at the dusty top. How had his life come down to this? Without spending too much time in thought, he shouldered the old model and carried it out of the garage, up the stairs, and into his charming new digs. "Ahh, nothing like home," he muttered, as he plugged in the TV and immediately began fussing with the snowy reception.

A sleepy Jordan walked into the kitchen at just after six o'clock, carrying a wide-eyed Hutton. She wasn't prepared to see Nick standing at the stove fixing breakfast at this hour. A little tug of delight lapped at her stomach at the prospect of someone making her breakfast. Her happiness quickly faded though as she looked around her tidy kitchen and saw the mess he'd made. The counters were a wreck, full of a half dozen messy bowls. Her spotless stove was under a layer of flour residue. In an instant though, the glee came back twofold when Nick turned around from the stove. The relaxed look on his face told her all she needed to know. The tension that had been there since his arrival was gone from his face.

"I hope you don't mind, but the stove in the apartment refused to work. And I was hungry."

Jordan settled Hutton in her high chair. "No problem. That old thing probably hasn't worked in twenty years. Do I smell coffee?"

When he put a steaming mug in her hands, she groaned in appreciation. "You're a saint. You cook? Are those pancakes?"

"Yeah. Breakfast I can do. My specialty is pancakes. I thought we could take turns fixing breakfast. No point in you doing it every morning. Does the munchkin eat pancakes?"

"The munchkin loves pancakes. And so does the munchkin's mother."

Jordan filled a sippy cup with milk and handed it to her daughter. But Hutton ignored the milk and clapped

her hands as Nick set a plate in front of her with a stack
of pancakes so high the baby couldn't see around it.
There were enough flapjacks to feed three starving
people. Jordan grinned as she went over and forked up
some of the pancakes onto her own plate. After pouring
syrup on Hutton's pancakes, Jordan started cutting
them into pieces. Suddenly, she caught the intent stare
on Nick's face as he watched in wonder as Hutton
began to use her fingers to stuff her mouth full of food.

"She hasn't mastered spoon or fork yet. You have
kids, Nick? Are you married?"

He had just taken a sip of coffee and almost choked
at the question. "No, on both counts. I'm about as
single as you can get. Never even had a dog."

"Never? Really? Why not?"

"Moved a lot. My father was a colonel in the Air
Force. But after my mother died when I was ten, my
father took a position at a military academy back East."
God, he remembered how that had pissed off the old
man to give up his career in the military to take care of
a kid he didn't seem to like very much. "You can't
have a dog in that kind of environment." And not much
of a father-son relationship either, he thought with
regret, as he remembered his father's detached, aloof
demeanor. Growing up with the man he'd felt at odds
with on just about every level, he realized now that
maybe that's why he'd joined the Guard, hoping he
could finally make his father proud. As he sat there
watching Hutton he had to wonder if maybe he'd
inherited some kind of a gene that prevented him from
forming emotional attachments. His father certainly
hadn't formed one with his own son, nor had he
provided a warm, fuzzy environment after his mother
had died.

"Is your father still alive?"

"You bet," Nick said a little too cheerily.
"Remarried, retired, and lives in Florida." And the only
time he talked to him was twice a year, on his birthday

and Christmas. Unable to keep his eyes off the baby, he asked, "She feeds herself at this age?"

Jordan smiled. The man knew nothing about children. Everything Hutton did seem to fascinate him. "She does. The whole thing's a bit of a mess and cleanup usually takes several wet towels but she manages to get the food in there. Don't you, baby girl?"

Hutton ignored her mother and continued to eat.

Determined to make conversation, Jordan wanted to learn more about the man. "What brought you to...L.A. is it?"

"Yeah. Work." He didn't give her an opening to pursue that line of questioning and neatly changed the subject. "What about your family?"

"I'm from San Francisco. I grew up there. Mom ran a catering business. Dad taught bio-chemistry at San Francisco State until he retired last year."

Noticing the wistful look on her face, he realized she was homesick. "You miss it."

"I do. I met Scott there."

At the mention of Scott, the conversation ground to an abrupt halt. Nick cleared his throat, got up to clean up the dishes. She watched the man's engaging mood morph into cool detachment. It was impossible to miss the tension tightening his face again. Feeling somewhat responsible, Jordan tried her best to get back on better ground. "You cooked, it's only fair that I clean up. That's the way it works."

"I made the mess, I don't mind."

As soon as Hutton began to toss pieces of her pancakes on the floor, signaling she'd had enough, Jordan wiped down Hutton's face before setting her down on the floor to play. Resolved to make Nick feel better, wanting very much to pick up the conversation, Jordan tried to make amends. "We were just getting to be friends, getting to know each other a little bit."

"There isn't much to know."

"You get up early, I know that. If you're having trouble sleeping, it might be that old bed. We could change out…"

As he loaded the dishwasher, obviously annoyed at the conversation, he told her bluntly, "Trust me, it isn't the bed."

Patrick Murphy had found Pelican Pointe quite by accident some twenty years earlier when he'd gotten lost on a sales call during one of his trips down from the Bay. From that point he'd wandered down to the little coastal town on numerous fishing trips whenever time permitted. But it had taken the breakup of his marriage and the loss of his job before he'd finally gotten tired of the big city and packed up lock, stock, and barrel, and headed to Pelican Pointe for good. At the time, a little more than fifteen hundred people called the town home. As soon as he'd settled in he'd set his sights on the ancient mercantile, a rundown shell of a building left over from the '40s that had gone to seed. He decided a town this size needed its own store, one where the residents could shop without having to make the trip into Santa Cruz every time they needed aspirin or toilet paper. He'd opened a renovated Murphy's Market that first year, and ran for mayor the next.

As the only grocer in town Murphy prided himself on knowing what inventory he needed to stock to keep his customers happy. For the vegans in town, he kept a line of organic and healthy foods. For the bottled water drinkers, all they needed to do was make their favorite brand known and he'd see to it they got it. He had fresh produce delivered four times a week making sure his store rivaled any of the markets in San Fran several hours to the north. He knew down to the customer which non-essential items they bought on a frequent basis and made sure not to run short. He ran two checkout stands, and with five regular part-timers, Murphy's Market was the third-largest employer in town behind the bank and Ferguson's Hardware.

With his store such an integral part of the town and the fact that he was mayor, it was a safe bet that nothing much happened in Pelican Pointe without Murphy knowing about it—in detail. This morning he watched a young woman in her early twenties named Lilly Seybold, at least he thought that was her name, do her grocery shopping, or try to. Lilly had only been in town since Christmas and rented a rundown, old trailer on Derek Stovall's land on the outskirts of town with her two young kids, a boy about eighteen months and the girl, barely three years old.

Living on assistance from the county, Lilly didn't have much money. On a tight budget she usually shopped clutching a fistful of coupons along with a well-worn, hand calculator, which allowed her to know to the penny how much the bill would be before the cashier totaled it up. Carla Vargas, the county social worker, was in the process of helping Lilly get a divorce from her husband, who was serving time in state prison for a laundry list of charges, the least of which were several drunk and disorderly incidents, a polite way of saying he had beaten the living crap out of Lilly on more than one occasion. It seems Lilly had finally found the courage to file charges and the police had seen fit to lock him up. But according to Carla's reports, there weren't a lot of employment opportunities in Pelican Pointe for Lilly. She and her two young children, Kyra and Joey, were having a tough time making ends meet, hence the assistance from the county.

This morning the store was busy. Murphy watched Lilly make her way to the other open checkout and then nervously eye the scanner as it rang up her meager groceries, a generic carton of diapers, a gallon of milk, peanut butter, and a day-old loaf of bread. When the clerk gave her the amount, Lilly pulled a ton of loose change from her ragged purse, barely coming up with the twelve dollars and fifty-six cents to cover the bill.

After paying, she led the kids out the front door to a beat-up old Ford.

Watching them go, Murphy made a mental note to ask Carla if Lilly had enough money coming in each month to cover her bills. It was barely the middle of February. But with rent due on the first, the young mother might not have enough left over to buy food.

As he turned to ring up another customer, he spotted Jordan standing in the produce section. His thoughts turned to her situation, a different kind of hardship entirely, but still a hardship, he decided. That had him wondering how things were going between her and Nick Harris. He couldn't help but think whoever said life was dull in a small town obviously had never lived in one. Turning his attention back to running register number one, he began scanning Myrtle Pettibone's twenty cans of cat food.

As Jordan walked up and down the narrow aisles she had to keep a sharp eye on Hutton, who every now and again tried to latch on to anything within her short reach. The fruit wasn't safe as she tried to lean over and capture a bright red tomato. When she came up empty, Hutton tried again, this time scarcely missing her opportunity to grab an orange. Jordan barely caught her daughter's arm in time to prevent the neatly stacked apple pyramid from completely collapsing into a mess on the floor. Avoiding the mishap, Jordan didn't see Sissy Carr barrel straight for her. If she had, she would have tried to duck behind the greeting card display.

But since she hadn't yet made the turn into frozen foods, it was too late to try and hide from the tall, bleached-blonde in her mid-thirties who was Scott's ex-girlfriend from high school and the spoiled daughter of the president of the First Bank of Pelican Pointe. Although she'd already been through two messy divorces, Sissy considered herself the pillar of the community, serving as the only woman on the city council. Since Scott had brought Jordan back to Pelican Pointe, Sissy hadn't hidden the fact that she didn't like Scott's wife. It was a fact that Sissy, like many residents here, considered Jordan, an outsider. And Scott was no longer around to defend her or set them straight. So much for the friendship of a small town.

At first glance, Sissy looked harmless, but Jordan knew better. They'd encountered each other several times in the past, each meeting more awkward and unpleasant than the last. Niceties were nonexistent. This morning was no exception.

"Daddy says you're still trying to turn that rundown old house into a motel, of all the silly notions I've ever heard."

Mindful of Hutton's presence, Jordan tried to keep her cool and watch her language. Through gritted teeth, she managed to spit out, "Bed and Breakfast, Sissy, not a motel. There's a difference."

"Whatever. I can't believe you really think anyone's gonna pay good money to stay in a dump like that. I'd be insulted if a man even tried to take me to a place like that for the weekend."

More like a quickie, thought Jordan. Temper flaring she bit her lip to keep her nasty thoughts to herself. "You're talking about our home, the place where we live, Sissy. It's supposed to be quaint."

"Quaint's just a fancy name for dump. Daddy says you won't make it anyway. And you owe money to practically everybody in town. It must be so embarrassing for you. Scott deserved better."

Jordan moved to get by the woman to continue her shopping, but Sissy's obstinate stance had her blocking the narrow aisle.

"You're wasting the bank's money, Jordan, and too stubborn to realize you're throwing good money down a rabbit hole. That house should've been demolished years ago. It was rundown when Scott lived there and it hasn't improved one bit. No one wants you here. Why don't you pack up and go back to San Francisco where you belong?"

Jordan finally managed to push the cart past Sissy and sent the woman a sweet smile in spite of the way she felt. "It was nice seeing you again, Sissy. Be sure to set aside some time to stop by for the grand opening."

After that Jordan wrapped up her shopping in a matter of hurried minutes. Murphy was waiting at the checkout. "How are you, Jordan?"

She breathed out an angry sigh and for the time being let her frustration with Sissy go. "I should probably thank you for sending Nick out my way. He's really making progress. The guy already fixed the porch, has one of the bathrooms almost done and he's been here less than a week. I'm grateful Murphy."

Sheepish, Murphy wasn't about to give away Nick's secret. But he didn't want Jordan finding out his part in the subterfuge and that fact blowing up in his face later. He cleared his throat in an attempt to hide his deceit. "I'm glad he's working out then."

When other customers started lining up behind Jordan, he let the conversation die a quick death. The townspeople didn't need any more fodder for the grapevine. Nick's arrival out at The Cove had spread like wildfire through town. Jordan didn't need spiteful gossip making things any worse for her.

Once outside, Jordan pushed her cart toward her Ford Explorer and noticed a woman squatting next to it holding a tire iron in her hand. She was trying desperately to get the lug nuts off a flat-as-a-pancake rear tire on a faded-out red Escort parked in the space next to the SUV. The trunk stood open. Two small children with runny noses were hunkered down next to their mother watching as she struggled to loosen one of the bolts holding the tire like glue onto the wheel. The lug nuts refused to budge.

"I hate that," Jordan commented, pulling the cart to a stop at the rear of the Explorer. "Got your milk and eggs in the car, your perishables, and the car leaves you stranded." It had happened to her last spring when Hutton had been just three months old. Fortunately, she'd been able to use the phone in the store, get Wally Pierce from the gas station to come over and change the tire for her. But this woman dressed in her worn-thin jeans and a ratty old T-shirt didn't look like she could afford to do that. And trying her hardest to pull on that tire iron, she couldn't have weighed more than a hundred and five pounds.

"I thought I could just...you know, get the old tire to come off, but these things won't budge," she squeaked in a quivering voice as if she'd reached the end of her rope. "I've been trying."

"Those things are hard to get off." Not to mention they looked like they'd been welded onto the car's wheels since the eighties. Jordan knew nothing about cars or tires or lug nuts. But she did recognize thread-bare tires when she saw them. All four tires looked in bad shape. "I'm Jordan by the way. Jordan Phillips. And this is Hutton. Do you have a spare?"

"There's a tire in the trunk." The woman blew out a breath. She had no idea what shape it was in. "I'm Lilly. Lilly Seybold."

Jordan smiled at the two kids. "And who do we have here?"

"That's Joey, the baby," she pointed out as she gently reached down to pat the little boy's head leaving a trail of grime on his forehead before pulling the little girl into an embrace. "And this is Kyra."

Jordan looked at both little brown-eyed tots and said what any mother never got tired of hearing, "What pretty children you have, Lilly? Well, let's see what we've got." She peered into the trunk. Again, Jordan was no expert, but to her the tire in the trunk looked in worse shape than the flat one. "This happened to me just last year. Right here in this very parking lot. I had all my groceries in the car, Hutton was fussy. Then I noticed the tire was flat." But she'd had a brand-new spare tire to replace the flat one while this woman didn't. Tentatively, Jordan offered, "Can I make a suggestion, Lilly?"

"I guess," Lilly answered shyly.

"I don't have a cell phone, but how about if I run you over to the gas station and…"

Before she could finish Murphy walked up to the women. Looking over the situation he remarked, "Flat tire, huh?"

Relieved, Jordan said earnestly, "Murphy, just the man we need. Lilly here's been trying without success to change a flat tire."

"But the lug nuts won't budge," Lilly confirmed.

"Can't have my customers stranded in the parking lot," Murphy declared with a smile. When Lilly started to protest, Murphy held up a hand and added, "All part of the service." Murphy bent to get to work. He might have been just over five feet, but he had more muscles than Lilly had or Jordan for that matter.

Watching him work, Jordan reluctantly felt the need to tell him, "I'm not sure her spare is in such good shape, Murphy. Better take a look."

Glancing in the direction of the trunk, he groaned, "This old thing won't cut it. You'd be better off patching the one that's flat." He reached in his back pocket and pulled out a cell phone, dialed a number by heart. "Wally, I've got a customer with a flat tire. And we need a patch job as soon as you can get to it."

As Murphy talked, Jordan loaded her groceries into the back. As the cart emptied, a thought occurred to her. On impulse, she dug into one of the sacks, pulled out a box of Lorna Doone's and a couple of juice boxes.

When Murphy hung up, he turned to Lilly and held up a hand when she started to protest at what she'd overheard. "Wally can put a patch on the tire. It costs almost nothing." He wasn't absolutely certain of that fact, but in the event he couldn't patch the tire they'd fix her up with a retread. He had no intentions of leaving Lilly stranded.

Jordan picked up his intent. With a cheerful tone, she piped up, "That's great. A patch is almost as good as a new tire. And I know for a fact Wally needs to get rid of that stack of old tires he's got over there." She knew no such thing. But Murphy and Jordan exchanged a knowing glance before she motioned to the grassy common area next door and said brightly, "Murphy, we're going to walk over to that park bench there and take the kids, get them out of the parking lot and the traffic." The only moving cars anywhere near the parking lot were the ones doing a slow twenty-five down Main. As she snatched Hutton out of the shopping cart, she said casually over her shoulder, hoping Lilly would follow, "Come on, Lilly. Grab the kids. Hutton's ready for her snack and there's plenty here for Kyra and Joey."

Lilly looked worried about leaving her only means of transportation. No one in this town had been nice to her except for Carla Vargas and she had to be because she was the county social worker. But she followed Jordan holding Kyra by the hand and carrying Joey on her slim hip across the parking lot to the grassy park where one ancient, wooden bench had been bolted to a poured cement square block. She settled Kyra and Joey on the bench and stood nervously over them as if she already regretted the decision to leave her car.

Before she ever sat down, Jordan tugged open the box of cookies and looked into the children's wide eyes at the prospect of getting a treat. She wondered how long it had been since these kids had had any kind of extra in their lives at all. She plopped down on the grass with Hutton on her lap and started doling out juice boxes and cookies. All the while wondering how to broach what she wanted to say. Jordan felt like she understood Lilly's reluctance. After all, she didn't have any friends in town either and certainly not any with children. She was certain Lilly didn't either. If she was wrong about that then she'd leave it to Lilly to set her straight. Hutton had no children her own age to play with and Lilly's kids looked like good prospects. "I'm fairly new in town, Lilly. I've only been here a couple of years." She didn't mention how rough those years had been. "I live out near The Cove."

Lilly's eyes bugged. "I've seen that big old house before from the road. You live there?"

Jordan nodded. "Do you live nearby?"

"Trailer about a mile out of town the other way. I lived there once with my mother a long time ago before she died. When my husband…left, my stepfather said I could come back here and stay in a trailer he has on his property until we got up on our feet. I mean it's not free. I have to pay rent and all, but it's a roof over our heads." For some reason Lilly felt like she needed to tell this woman the rest. "It's kind of a dump. But we came back here after…my husband, my soon to be ex-husband is in prison." She spoke the words as if Jordan might want to rethink her choice of friends.

And just as needy, Jordan told her flatly, "My husband died."

"Oh." That threw Lilly. "I'm so sorry."

"Me too. Anyway, I was thinking that maybe you and I could get the kids together, like a playdate. I've been busy with the house, and Hutton has no one but me to play with. It couldn't hurt if the kids got together at least once a week to keep each other company." She didn't add that the get-together might mean she'd have someone to talk to as well.

"You want to do that even though my husband's—
my ex is in jail." Lilly couldn't believe anyone wanted
to be her friend, not in this town. Most of Pelican
Pointe did their darnedest to avoid the three of them
whenever they saw them on the street. Her kids sure
weren't responsible for anything their daddy had done,
but the townsfolk here had acted as if they were
contagious or something.

"What's he in for—your ex?"

"Assault."

"Did you hurt anyone, Lilly?"

Lilly looked appalled. "No. I never hit him even
when he hit me."

Jordan winced. "Well then, why don't you plan to
come out to the house next Wednesday afternoon? I
could really use a friend, someone to talk to, couldn't
you, Lilly?"

Lilly nodded almost in wonder. "You want me to
bring anything?"

"Nope, just yourself and the kids."

Lilly's face looked as if someone had handed her a
gift.

Forty-five minutes later after Murphy had discreetly
talked to Wally and Wally had assured Lilly no less
than four times that the retread he'd just put on her car
had been sitting around taking up space at the station,
Jordan and Murphy stood by the SUV talking.

"That was a nice thing you did for her, Murphy."

"It's a retread." As if that explained everything, he
cocked his head and looked at Jordan. "What was that
about her seeing you next Wednesday?"

Jordan chuckled. "Okay, I guess we're both saints. I
could use a friend here, Murphy, and I think she could,
too."

He nodded. But unfortunately he knew that most
people in town didn't share that sentiment.

"Before sending Nick out my way did he tell you
anything about himself, Murphy?"

Murphy looked a little desperate at the question. Damn, he thought that had certainly come out of the blue. To stall, he took out a handkerchief from his back pocket and wiped the grease off his hands. "Uh, I talked to him at length. I know he'll do a good job for you. Look Jordan, if you're worried about him living out there with you...I could..."

"That isn't it..." But when she picked up on the disturbing undertone, she turned to face him. "Oh, for God's sakes. Are the townspeople beginning to talk, Murphy? Is the rumor mill kicking into overdrive? Are they thinking the stranger in town might just be living in my house, too? For your information..."

Murphy held up both hands. "Not my business, Jordan. Or anyone else's."

"Don't try to smooth it over, Murphy. This town never accepted me, not since Scott brought me back here. He loved this town, couldn't wait to get back to it. After living here the last two years, I'm not sure why. They didn't exactly welcome us with open arms, certainly not me. And now..."

Murphy finished for her. "You're stuck here."

"Well, if I don't open up on schedule, it won't be for long."

Nick paced back and forth on the new and improved front porch, as he talked into his cell phone. "Dave, the place is called The Cove." He rattled off the phone number. "The sooner you call the better room you'll get. Go first class and ask for the ocean view. Yeah, they still have rooms available, but the place is filling up fast. It'd be a wonderful place for you and the wife to spend your anniversary, don't you think? You can fly into San Francisco, spend some time there if you want before heading down the coast to spend a few days in a peaceful, quiet bed and breakfast by the ocean. Thanks Dave, no trust me, you'll love it. Beach access, the surf's great. Wonderful food."

With his spiel done, he hung up and searched his iPhone for another number. Pressing buttons, he waited until he got an answer before going through the same routine with that person before going on to the next and the next and the next until he spotted Jordan pulling into the driveway. He quickly tucked the phone into the back pocket of his jeans. Hopping down from the porch, he went out to help her unload.

She'd been gone a long time, he thought as he opened the rear door of the SUV to get to the groceries. He wouldn't admit to worrying about her. He'd never worried about anyone but himself. And he didn't intend to start now. But as he watched Jordan unbuckle Hutton he stopped to enjoy the distant sound of the surf coming from the cove. He inhaled the country air. Here he was happy doing mundane, very ordinary things, and was far more at peace than he'd been in two years. This was the life, living in the country, he thought. No pressure here, he told himself, as he picked up a carton of diapers. He realized he had worried about her and Hutton on their trip into town. It was only because he was looking out for them, he told himself. It was perfectly understandable under the circumstances. "What took you so long?" He heard himself ask.

Jordan told him about Lilly, about how she'd invited her and the kids over to the house. When she'd finished she added mischievously, "And giving the townspeople a new reason to dislike me."

When she reached to pick up a sack of groceries while still holding Hutton, he stilled her hand in the process. "I've got this."

Her eyes met his. Their hands touched as they reached for the same sack. For several long seconds they stood at the back of the car with his hand over hers. There was heat here, she realized and she wanted…what? What did she want? When he leaned in ever so slightly to get a better grip on the bag, her hand instinctively dropped away.

Acting as if nothing had happened, Nick picked up another bag and turned to head into the house. "By the way, you're going to need a fence around your vegetable garden. Your garden under mass attack."

"Oh, no. What did they eat?"

"It's more like what they didn't."

"Shoot. I've tried everything I've read on the Internet, even black pepper, chili powder, hot sauce, but so far…"

He shook his head. "A fence is the only way. I found material to build one in that black hole of a garage. I think I can go down about six inches in the ground, build one that will get the job done. How about the fireplaces in this place? I counted four. Do they all work?"

Jordan followed him into the kitchen. "Sure. Except the one in the living room might need a good cleaning. It's been used more than the others. I've been meaning to take care of that. Why?"

"I found the woodpile behind the garage. Thought I'd split some wood for a fire."

Did he plan to cut firewood or build a fence around her garden the same way he'd painted her living room in the middle of the night? she wondered. "What? In your spare time you're going to cut wood and put in a fence? Nick, you don't have to do so much. The truth is I ran out of wood last month, haven't had a fire since. Tried to cut some myself and almost chopped off a toe. Who would have thought cutting wood could be so hard?"

"Splitting wood," he corrected as he sat the diapers on the floor and the sacks on the counter.

"Huh?" She plopped Hutton down on the floor and started putting away the groceries.

"Never mind." He sent her a wide grin. "I think I can handle an ax."

With a body like his she had no doubt he could handle just about anything physical. But why was he trying so hard? "I'll just start lunch while you go play Paul Bunyan then."

"Hey, it got cold last night. This close to the coast it gets chilly. The firewood will come in handy."

With that, he disappeared through the doorway, leaving her standing there wondering where he got his energy. In fact, it crossed her mind that he acted like a man possessed or with something to prove. She just wasn't sure what it was.

Shortly after lunch he was sitting at Jordan's desk sketching out his plan for a garden fence when he heard a car door slam. Jordan must have heard it too because she rounded the corner quickly hoping to reach the front door before the visitor rang the doorbell. "I just put Hutton down for her afternoon nap. I don't want anyone ringing the bell and waking her up."

"How's that going to work when guests start showing up?"

"Good question. I guess I'll have to work something out once guests become a reality," she told Nick as she raced for the door just in time to see Frank Martin striding up the front steps. The banker was Scott's age but was already losing his hair and had a nice comb-over going on.

Jordan opened the door and stepped outside, a bit breathless, more from nerves than anything else. This man wasn't exactly a welcome sight. "Frank. How's it going?"

"Afternoon Jordan." Looking around, Frank sighed audibly. "I was afraid of this. Not making much progress, are you?"

Just as she'd done at the store earlier with Sissy, Jordan's temper flared in a rare show of irritation. Couldn't the man see how much better the porch looked? Nick had not only stained and sanded, but he'd also shored up the sagging boards, replaced the rotten wood from the railing, and repainted. Jordan had no intentions of letting his comment slide. "On the contrary, I'm moving right along on schedule."

The door behind her opened and Nick joined them on the porch, stuffing his hands in the back pockets of his jeans. "Everything okay out here?"

Jordan felt like reinforcements had arrived. No longer facing Frank alone, bolstered by Nick's emergence, she gave Nick a subtle smile. "Everything's fine. Nick, this is Frank Martin, vice-president in charge of loans at the First Bank of Pelican Pointe. Frank, this is Nick Harris. He's my…contractor slash carpenter."

Nick stuck out his hand and didn't miss Frank's hesitation. The man's entire body grew rigid before he half-heartedly shook Nick's hand. His reluctance didn't get past Nick.

"Nice to meet you, Mr. Harris, is it?" The man looked as if he wanted to wipe his hands on something after touching Nick's.

"Frank stopped by to get a progress report for the loan committee. See how things were shaping up. I believe he thinks we're going to miss our deadline." She looked Frank in the eye before adding, "But we aren't. We're going to open on time."

"I admire your optimism, Jordan, I really do, but as you know, I've come to check on your progress. The bank wants its payment on time, no excuses. I'm getting reminders from Mr. Carr on a weekly basis now. You can expect a weekly visit from me until you open."

"Message delivered, Frank."

"I wish you luck, Jordan, I really do. You know, this isn't personal, don't you? I went to school with Scott from first grade to high school. We played on the basketball team together. I knew Scott's grandparents."

He wrung his hands as if he'd have to remember to wash them at the first opportunity.

When Jordan said nothing, Frank added, "I just wanted to stop by and see how you and Hutton were getting along. I didn't know you'd found the money to hire a contractor."

"Thanks, Frank. I appreciate all you've done. If he were here, Scott would say the same."

Frank turned to Nick, before retreating to his car, he thought for a moment before saying, "Next time you're in town, Mr. Harris, stop by, and open an account. We'd love to have the new business." With that, the banker turned and walked staidly back to his car.

Not in a million years, Nick thought. He had to wonder if in his former life he'd ever been that much of a cold-hearted prick. He hoped not. But why on earth Scott would have such a high opinion of the people in this town was a mystery to him. Except for Murphy, everyone had been a huge disappointment. What was wrong with the townspeople here anyway?

"Would you mind, Jordan, if I took a look at those loan papers? See if there might be any other options in case we run into an obstacle."

"Sure. But it's pretty straightforward. I went over the loan papers in detail when Scott...after..." Her sigh caused a slump in her shoulders. "It won't change anything, Nick."

He stifled the urge to reach out and put his arms around those shoulders. "Maybe not, but it won't hurt to take a look." He paused, looked around the porch, and felt a wealth of pride at how much better the place looked. "We'll give the second coat of paint another day to dry. Then we'll hang that swing you wanted."

Later that afternoon Jordan was spreading chocolate frosting over the top of the cake she'd baked while Hutton sat on the floor, digging in the cabinets, pulling out every pot and pan she owned, when the phone rang. Jordan wiped her hands off and moved to pick it up. "The Cove Bed and Breakfast, Jordan speaking. Memorial weekend? Could you hold just a moment while I look? Yes, thank you." Carrying the cordless phone she moved to the desk in the corner of the kitchen, quickly pulled open the reservations book and leafed through the pages. "The twenty-sixth and twenty-seventh will be fine. And what's the name? Williams, Dave, Mr. and Mrs. Dave Williams. Ocean View. Okay. Ocean View is $275 a night. Yes, there's beach access, meals are included, that's right." She went on to take credit card information, glancing up when the back door opened and Nick stepped inside. "Yes, thank you. Thank you very much, Mr. Williams." As he closed the door behind him, Nick immediately saw Jordan doing a happy-dance in the middle of the kitchen. Spotting him, she ran over, grabbed both of his hands in hers and continued to dance this time with him. "I have another reservation for Memorial weekend. Can you believe it? May is starting to fill up. That's the third call today."

After an exhausting afternoon installing a sink in one of the bathrooms upstairs, he'd dragged himself over for dinner. Tired and hungry, he'd been in a bitch of a black mood. But at the sight of Jordan dancing and obviously happy, the blackness somehow lifted. He stood there without saying a word and just watched the contented look on her face. Her smile lit up the room. Suddenly, he wanted nothing more than to keep her that way—smiling, glowing—and dancing. As to his question of how women with babies had fun, he pretty much had his answer. Jordan seemed to get such a kick out of the simple things. Despite her dire situation she seemed to have an eternal optimism that came from within, a never-give-up-attitude that seemed inexhaustible.

When she noticed he hadn't said a word since coming in, but stood instead staring at her, she stopped dancing and instinctively reached up to slide her hand along his jaw. "What's wrong? Are you okay?"

"I'm fine. I just saw you dancing and..." He couldn't finish. Instead, he stilled the hand touching his face. On impulse, he whirled her around as if they were on the dance floor. "You're happy."

"I am." When he danced her over to the refrigerator to dig out a beer and let her go, she announced, "Dinner's almost ready."

Making himself at home, he twisted off the cap and turned the bottle up for a long drink. "I'm starving whatever we're having smells great."

All at once, from her position on the floor, Hutton piped up, repeating his words, or tried to. "'mells gate."

Having never been around a baby before, Nick slowly turned from the fridge to stare at the child on the floor. Startled to hear Hutton talking, repeating the very thing he'd just uttered, or at least her version, he moved closer. "Did you hear that?" Fascinated, he finished the walk around the counter to get a better look.

Although Jordan had turned her attention to throwing a salad together, his rapt manner had her studying him, amused at the astonished look on his face. "She's at that stage where she tries to repeat everything she hears. And what you smell is plain old meatloaf."

To test out the theory that she'd repeat what she heard, Nick set his beer down on the counter and picked up an apple from the bowl. Sitting on his heels in front of Hutton, he held out the apple as an enticement. "Say apple, Hutton? Here's an apple for Hutton."

Hutton, finger to her mouth, had a look on her face that clearly said she didn't perform on demand. But after a lot more urging and much prompting, she finally leaned her little face closer to his and with a shy grin said, "Abble."

Jordan wanted to laugh out loud at the look of wonder on Nick's face. He was clearly impressed with her daughter. The next words out of his mouth proved it. "Did you hear that? She said it. Hutton said apple. Isn't she awfully young to be talking like that, repeating words like that? She seems exceptionally bright for her age. Maybe you should have her evaluated."

Jordan laughed out loud. The man obviously knew nothing about toddlers. "Of course she's brilliant, but I suppose I could be biased." Noting he was serious, she added, "According to the books I've read, she's right on schedule with her vocabulary skills."

"You have books on the subject?"

"I do, and I've also been reading to her since she was born. Every night before bed is story time." Intrigued at his interest, she offered, "Maybe you'd like to take a turn after dinner?"

His eyes went wide. "Read to her? A kid this size? Okay. Sure. You mean like, The Three Bears or something?" It was the only children's story he could bring to mind.

"Oh, I think we can do a little better than that, can't we Hutton?"

By this time, Hutton had lost all interest in the fruit and turned her attention to banging a pot with a wooden spoon. In an impromptu move, Nick picked up another spoon. In sync with the toddler, he started tapping it on a pot in time with hers. Hutton found his drumming particularly funny and started giggling before she went into a full-blown belly laugh.

Watching her daughter play with Nick, watching them interact, Jordan suddenly got tears in her eyes. To hide her wet face, she went over to the stove and pretended to check on the meatloaf. After a few minutes she got herself more under control, and turned around just in time to hear Hutton let out another belly laugh. She looked at Nick who was now down on all fours playing peek-a-boo with her daughter. For some reason, the playful scene caused her heart to flutter in her chest. She opened her mouth to say something, but closed it when no words came out.

After that, it was all Jordan could do to get through supper.

In a routine now, Jordan and Nick split the chores. She gave Hutton her bath while Nick cleaned up the supper dishes. But while putting on Hutton's pajamas, as story time approached, a gnawing sadness engulfed her. This would be the first time a man had read to her daughter and it wouldn't be her father. It would never be Scott.

By the time Jordan was done getting Hutton ready for bed, Nick had brought in an armload of firewood and built up a cozy fire in the living room. When all three of them were settled on the sofa, Jordan handed Nick one of Hutton's favorite books. She watched and listened as Nick read to her daughter about a panda bear living at the zoo. As soon as that was finished, Hutton handed him another. This time the story was about the adventures of a fun-loving red fish swimming in the ocean. The minute he read the last word, Hutton handed him another one, this time he read about a clever monkey swinging from tree to tree in the rain forest. During each story, Nick remained patient as Hutton kept interrupting him with comments in baby babble that were unintelligible to Jordan let alone to Nick. But he didn't complain about the interruptions any more than he did about Hutton's wanting one story after another.

"She likes books, doesn't she?"

Getting up from the sofa, Jordan explained affectionately, "She likes to stall. Don't you, baby girl." Scooping Hutton up in a bear hug, she told the child,

"But it's time to go to bed now. We need to go find Mr. Bear and get him to bed. He's sleepy. Say thank you Nick for the stories." Now, suddenly shy, Hutton ducked her head down on her mother's shoulder. "Tell Nick, night-night, Hutton."

As Jordan carried Hutton out of the room to bed, over her shoulder she heard Nick say, "Night, Hutton."

And before they got out of the room, Hutton lifted her head, waved a little hand in Nick's direction, and softly cooed, "bye-bye."

The gesture got to Nick. He suddenly got a glimpse of his own mother. And it had been more than twenty-five years since he'd experienced such memories. After his mom had died, he remembered how his father had retreated into a shell, leaving his ten-year-old son to wonder what he'd done to make him so withdrawn, so moody, and so harsh. He had missed his mother, and when he'd tried to turn to his father for comfort, his father had shut him out. He'd lost the one person in his life who had shown him unconditional love. For the first time, he realized that emotional void might be why his life up to now had been one empty relationship after another. He hadn't wanted to get attached to anyone for fear of losing them.

Maybe that realization had him appreciating Jordan. She had a way with Hutton. It didn't take a genius to see she was a good mother, gentle and loving, much like his own had been. He realized now as he sat there staring into the glowing firelight, thinking about all the times his mother had been there for him, he hadn't allowed himself those kinds of thoughts in years. Memories from boyhood flickered through his mind as he saw her sitting next to him on the bed reading him stories just as he'd done with Hutton. Or the times his mother had helped him with his math and spelling while they sat at the kitchen table. He could see her sitting on hard bleachers in the scorching heat rooting for him at summer little league games and how she'd always managed to make it to every school event he participated in. Leaning his head back, he closed his eyes. He allowed the images from childhood, the good times, the ones of his mother, to crowd out the more recent pictures of his life, all the ugly parts and all the painful memories that had come after. Soon, his breathing slowed and he fell asleep.

Jordan found him like that.

Without waking him, she pulled an afghan from the blanket box and covered him up. She took a seat by the fire. Tucking her legs under her, she got comfortable and stared into the firelight, letting her thoughts drift to another night when Scott had fallen asleep like this after they'd first moved into the house. Their dreams then had been fresh, new, and filled with so much promise and hope for the future. Their future together. Her eyes grew moist. She fought back tears, knowing crying wouldn't help. Besides, she'd cried her eyes out and knew for a fact it didn't help and wouldn't bring Scott back.

Scott was gone.

She glanced over at Nick. The man had read to her daughter. Abruptly, she saw him start to shake, right before he jumped and came awake. He sat up so fast his leg hit the coffee table. For a few moments he acted as though he were someplace else and unable to get his bearings. Spotting Jordan, he immediately acted embarrassed. "Sorry. I guess I fell asleep."

"And you look like you could use another twelve hours," she pointed out, as she continued to stare at the bewildered look on his face. This wasn't embarrassment but something else. The man looked downright disoriented. Her heart went out to him. "When's the last time you got a solid eight hours, Nick?"

He got to his feet, not bothering to answer. "I should be going." He grimaced when he saw she was still staring at him. Clearly uncomfortable, he looked away, not meeting her eyes. "See you in the morning," he mumbled, as he turned to leave.

He was halfway out of the room before Jordan calmly spoke up, "Are you sure there isn't anything you'd like to talk about, Nick? It might help you sleep to get whatever's bothering you off your chest."

Nick stopped. For a few seconds Jordan thought he might open up. But instead, he simply stuck his hands in his pockets. Then, as if coming out of a daze, he shook his head and backed out into the hallway. "Thanks for dinner," he muttered as he turned to go, almost knocking over a vase full of flowers on the table in the hall.

"Thanks for reading to Hutton," Jordan said quickly as he retreated into the kitchen and then out the back door as if the house were in flames.

"Oh, Nick," she whispered. "You seem so troubled, why won't you talk to me?"

Chapter Five

Hours after she went to bed, Jordan was still playing over the scene between Nick and Hutton in the kitchen before dinner, as well as his reading to her. Restless, in the king-sized bed too roomy for one person, she'd spent the last several hours tossing and turning, unsettled, trying to drop off.

"You'd think after almost two years, I'd be used to sleeping alone by now," she confessed aloud. Before Scott had gone to Iraq, she had never talked to herself, either. Not once. And now it seemed living out here alone had her acting more like her elderly grandmother, whom she'd witnessed as a child, talking to herself while baking or knitting or doing a hundred other mundane chores. Was she turning into her grandmother before the ripe old age of thirty? Well, that was unacceptable.

"When you're used to having someone to sleep with at night, it isn't fair to have to go back to sleeping alone." She crossed her arms over her chest. "Damn it." A few minutes later, she blurted out, "Just stop feeling sorry for yourself. Geez, you are so pathetic."

Upset with herself, she didn't think her restlessness tonight was all about missing Scott. No, the interaction between Nick and Hutton drove home one clear point she couldn't shake. Scott had died without ever getting to see his daughter in person. Hutton had been five months old when a government car had pulled up in the driveway. Some army major had told her Scott wasn't coming home. He never even got to hold her. And the realization that Scott would never get the chance to play with his little girl like Nick had done earlier simply broke her heart and had her feeling sorry for herself and that made her miserable. She crawled out of bed. Once again, she dragged the box from its hiding place in the dresser drawer.

She got out Scott's letters, one after another. She reread each one. Tears streamed down her cheeks. But after the fourth letter, she couldn't take it anymore. Deciding she needed fresh air, she quickly threw on a pair of jeans and pulled on an old sweater over her pajama top. Grabbing the baby monitor which she routinely left beside the bed at night, she headed for the door.

Under the half light of the moon, Jordan followed the trail down to the cove. Tonight she needed to hear the sounds of the surf. It might make her feel better. It had certainly worked in the past.

Once she reached the beach, she plopped down on a rock nearby and listened as the angry waves smashed up against the rocks. The wind blew straight in off the water. She shivered inside her sweater and realized she should have grabbed a jacket.

She'd been there no more than ten minutes when she spotted a shadowy figure in the distance, slowly making his way toward her in the moonlight along the water's edge. Alarmed at the sight, she'd almost decided to climb down off the rock and make a run for it when she recognized Nick. At about the same time she saw him, he glanced up and spotted her sitting on the rock. He headed her way. Cautious in his approach, he kept his hands jammed in his pockets. "Couldn't sleep?"

"No. I see you couldn't either. That's getting to be quite a habit. Why don't you tell me what's troubling you, Nick? It helps to talk. Or so I've heard."

He didn't even look at her. Instead, he focused his eyes on the water, listening to the waves as they crashed over the jutting rocks. "It's beautiful here. Quiet. Peaceful."

"Scott loved this place. He moved back here because he thought it was the perfect place to raise his family, the place where he'd been raised. From the time I met him all

Vickie McKeehan

he talked about was moving back to Pelican Pointe, living here, buying this place, turning it into a B & B. He had this idea we could run it together and make a living at something where he'd be around every day to help raise his family. It was actually a brilliant idea. If only..."

Nick knew. Hadn't Scott told him a hundred times about his plans? He was tempted right now, this minute to tell her, to simply get it off his chest once and for all how he'd known Scott, tell her how Scott had died. But when he turned to look at her to open up, to unburden his secret, he noticed tears shimmering in her eyes. His heart turned over in his chest. "It'll be okay, Jordan."

"I don't know. Even if I get the business up and running on time, I'll still need a full house for a couple of months to get enough to make ends meet after I make the first note payment. I've calculated the numbers to the penny. It'd be nice to get another extension for a couple of months, to have some breathing room. But I don't think the loan committee will go for that. You met Frank."

"Is that what brought you out here tonight, Jordan, worrying about the bank note?" He didn't think that was it.

She rested her chin on her knees never meeting his eyes. "Sometimes it's overwhelming. It'll never be the same, my life."

"People tend to forget that life is all about change, a constant state of flux." He knew it was weak, but the only thing he could think to say. He didn't even recognize his own life. He had no right to try to give her any kind of a pep talk about making adjustments, turning to alternate plans.

She lifted her head. "That's easy enough to think, to say. It sounds good until it happens to you. Try living every day with life-altering changes."

If she only knew. "I can only imagine how hard it is. Come on, I'll walk you back. It's getting colder. And it's too late to start another fire." He took her hand momentarily to help her off the rock. But once she slid off, he continued to keep the link between them holding her hand in his as he led her back up the trail and the steep steps. Keeping his touch light, he guided her up the path as it twisted and turned in the dark.

Once they began walking through the grove of trees close to the house, Jordan asked, "Will you be able to sleep?"

"Probably not. How about you?"

"I should try. Hutton will be up soon."

"If I start painting the entryway, will I keep you up?"

"Nick, that's crazy. It's three o'clock in the morning. Maybe you should see the doctor, get some pills or something. There's a clinic in town…"

"No thanks, I don't need pills." He already had a year's worth of pills and still half a dozen prescriptions. They didn't work—none of them did—so why bother?

As soon as they reached the back door, he reluctantly let go of her hand, missing the contact almost at once. He watched her go and couldn't help wonder what was happening to him. When she'd disappeared inside, for some reason his thoughts turned to his mother, the only other woman he'd loved enough to miss. He looked up into the night sky, located the brightest star.

When he looked back down, there he was.

Scott stood ten feet away intently watching Nick. "I told you, she's something, huh buddy?"

"I'm going crazy."

Scott laughed a belly-gut laugh that reminded Nick of his daughter. "Hutton laughs just like that."

"I know. It's music to my ears."

"You can see Hutton?"

Scott smiled. "She's everything I wanted."

"This is nuts. I'm having a conversation with a ghost."

"You always did have a tough time thinking outside the box."

Nick shook his head and made his way up the steps to his apartment, wondering with every step if pills would keep the delusions at bay.

Over the next couple of days it was easy for Nick and Jordan to stay busy and out of each other's way. Jordan spent her days painting the guest rooms, baking bread, perfecting her recipes and taking care of Hutton while Nick struggled with plumbing installations and bathroom flooring. In his spare time, he built the fence to keep out the slew of pesky rabbits, split another cord of wood, rearranged the packed garage into an organized system where he could at least find a drill bit without tearing the place apart. Hard physical labor seemed to keep his mind from wandering into places he had no business going, like his growing attraction to Scott's wife.

Today though, he had decided to tackle laying the tile, to put the finishing touches on one of the upstairs bathrooms and be done with it. He was taking the last of his measurements, making sure he had enough flooring when he stopped long enough to watch Hutton play a few feet away out in the hallway. She'd discovered one of the empty cardboard boxes containing some of the supplies he'd brought up from the garage and was now happily pounding away on the cardboard with a plastic hammer he had picked up at the hardware store. Wrapped up in her antics, fascinated, he watched in horror as she suddenly lost interest in the box and toddled over to the top of the stairs. At that moment, he noticed the safety gate had been left open and Hutton was headed straight for the stairwell. It happened in an instant. In the blink of an eye, he moved like a shot, his movement so fast he crashed into the wall, catching up to Hutton just before she reached the stairs. Scooping her up from behind, he clutched her to his chest. Nick closed his eyes, and dropped to the floor breathing hard. Shaking, trying to recover from the narrow escape, he told her, "God that was close. You scared ten years out of me, Blondie"

When his nerves settled enough, still holding on to Hutton, he reached over and swung the gate closed, latching it securely in place. "For someone with such short legs you move like a running back. What do you say we keep this little close call just between the two of us. Your mom has enough on her mind without knowing this."

As soon as Jordan walked out of the bedroom though she saw the look of panic on Nick's face, saw him clutching Hutton as if he were scared to death, her mother-radar went on red alert. Something was wrong. Dropping down on one knee in front of Nick, she asked, "What happened?"

He blew out a breath. "The gate was left open. She almost made it to the stairwell."

"Oh, my God." She leaned in to Hutton, rubbed a hand through her blond baby-fine hair, placed a kiss on the top of her head. "It's my fault. I had my hands full when I carried up the mirror from the garage for the dresser. I forgot to go back and close it."

"Scared ten years off me," Nick muttered as he relinquished Hutton to Jordan.

She grabbed his hand. "Thanks Nick. I'm grateful you caught her before she got to the stairs."

So was he. God, if she'd fallen... He didn't even want to think like that.

Chapter Six

The Hilltop Diner was old, something out of a 1950s malt shop. It had a black and white checkered floor, a faux black marble counter with eight padded red stools, all of which had seen their fair share of fannies over the years. A Wurlitzer jukebox stood at the end of the counter where, at the moment, Patsy Cline belted out *Walkin' After Midnight* for the smattering of patrons who sat at one of the eight mismatched square tables, or one of the four red-vinyl booths lining the front wall with window views of Main Street.

Without an official city hall, the Diner acted as a substitute meeting place for the town council, especially when, like today, Reverend Whitcomb refused them space alongside the ladies bible study group. Normally, the town council could be found at the Community Church at ten o'clock in the a.m. every third Thursday of the month. But this morning Mayor Patrick Murphy had to settle for the corner booth, the largest booth, presiding over an impromptu meeting to discuss the finishing touches for the annual spring Pelican Pointe Street Fair.

The fair was a three-day event cooked up twenty years earlier to add another source of revenue to the town coffers.

Sandwiched between the Christmas off-season and Memorial weekend, the street fair brought in money without waiting for the start of the summer tourist season which didn't kick in officially until Memorial weekend. This year, the fair started the third week of

March. That gave the town less than three weeks to get everything finalized.

Tapping her ballpoint pen absently on top of her clipboard, Sissy batted her eyes at the men sitting around the table, even if the youngest one was at least fifteen years older and said, "Ricky Oden's band is the last to sign up so that takes care of the music." As the only female member of the town council, Sissy used manipulation and a flirtatious nature to try to get her way even if she had to twist the facts to do it, a routine she'd perfected since junior high. While the tactic worked like sugar on some, including her own father, it didn't always work with this crowd.

She listened impatiently as Kent Springer, the married real estate developer she'd been sleeping with off and on for the better part of three years, went over the list of carnival rides they could expect. "They've agreed to set up on Tuesday, the night of the twenty-fourth, and gear most of their rides to the younger kids."

"But we asked you to check and see when the rides had last been inspected." Wade Hawkins, a long-time council member and a retired history professor, reminded Kent.

"You can be a real pain in the ass, you know that Wade," Kent responded.

But Wade wanted an answer from Mr. Slick, as he was known around town, and refused to let it go. "When's the last time the rides were inspected? That was the question."

When Kent looked away, Wade persisted, "Are they safe or not?"

"Of course they are," Kent answered absently. He didn't really give a shit. He was getting a kickback from the owner of the carnival for every time this particular vendor came to town, which happened seven times a year because he was in charge of the bookings.

What did he care when the last time anyone had inspected the damn Ferris wheel?

Eyeing Kent with equal skepticism, Murphy added, "We don't want the town put in a position over lawsuits about unsafe rides, Kent. It's just that simple." Having made his point, Murphy turned to Sissy. "So with Ricky on board that makes five bands providing the music for all three days, correct?"

Sixty-five-year-old Bran Sullivan, the town vet didn't wait for Sissy's confirmation. Instead, he proudly pointed out, "Ricky plays a mean bluegrass. Donna says the band's going professional and cutting a record." Ricky was married to his daughter, Donna, and as a son-in-law, Bran couldn't ask for better.

Sissy rolled her eyes. "CD," she corrected, mildly annoyed at the elderly, outdated mentality of her cohorts on the town council. Every one of them except Kent was well over fifty and he was knocking on the door. If she had anything to say about it, she intended to change that come next election and bring in some younger blood. Sissy had been trying to get rid of these old codgers for years to no avail. But for now, she checked her notes. "We'll have a total of thirty booths set up. That's five less than last year. Ten booths for food, the rest will be arts and crafts. The bad news is it looks like we're down to twenty-five floats this year. And thank the Lord, they are all cars or trucks, with the exception of crazy old Marabelle Crawford and her sister who insist on riding those damn golf carts."

Once again, Wade took issue. It wasn't so much about the floats, but rather the fact that Sissy and Kent kept trying to selectively enforce who got to participate in the parade and who didn't. It irked Wade to know that the two couldn't be trusted with details or to simply do the right thing where the folks in town were concerned. When it came right down to it, Sissy and Kent always seemed to be trying to pull a fast one. And pretty much everyone in town knew about their long-standing affair, probably even Kent's wife. It wasn't so much about the cheating but rather the fact they were both notorious for looking out for themselves. And Wade felt duly bound to keep these two honest if at all possible. "We need to use more horse-drawn floats like we did two years ago, and let the kids decorate their bicycles. Both cut down on the gas fumes polluting the air. We're a coastal town and as such we should do more to protect the environment."

Sissy snorted. "Wade, twenty-five cars rolling down Main Street for less than an hour won't hurt the air one day out of the year for chrissakes. Get real."

"Sissy, we have seven parades in this town a year, this one celebrating spring, plus the others on Memorial Day, Fourth of July, Labor Day, Homecoming, our own version of the Thanksgiving parade, and Christmas. We need to set a better example. And the kids love to decorate their own wagons and bikes. It makes even the youngest kid feel like they're a part of the festivities. It isn't right you keep trying to limit who participates. That's what Pelican Pointe is all about, community, making sure everyone gets a chance to feel involved."

Doing his best to put an end to their sniping at each other, Murphy tried for calm. "We've been over this." But as usual it didn't take long before they chose up sides even further, three against two. Wade had Murphy and Bran, his weekly fishing buddies, in his corner, while Sissy and Kent always teamed up against anything that had Pelican Pointe looking outdated. Kent and Sissy didn't hide their desire to bring the town kicking and screaming into the twenty-first century, all the while trying to figure the best angle whereby they could make a fast buck for themselves in the process. Fortunately the rest of the town council knew the drill.

"Using the horses would make the parade more rustic," Bran offered, just to get a rise out of Sissy, which wasn't difficult whenever she was in a snit, which was practically all the time.

But as usual, Sissy was ready for a fight. "Then you clean up the streets, Bran. Horses leave shit in their wake. And nobody cares about rustic or quaint. I'm sick of hearing that. Pelican Pointe still languishes in the backwoods. God, will you people ever be able to leave the '80s behind for good?"

"The kids like the horses, Sissy," Murphy pointed out.

"The horses are tradition," Wade reminded. "Not to mention the parade's more fun when the kids who don't own horses get to decorate their bicycles and show 'em off."

As the argument heated up, so did Kent's libido. Watching Sissy get all fired up had Kent reaching his hand under the table and rubbing at Sissy's soft flesh. His fingers inched up Sissy's bare thighs as far as they could without going all the way in. The forty-eight-year-old balding, wheeler dealer owned the only real estate office in town and thought of himself as the town's mogul. Since the early nineties, he'd made a small fortune off the misfortunes of others, buying up foreclosed California property in the area at a low price then selling it at a tidy profit. The man was ruthless and not just in real estate. Years earlier Kent had set his sights on the Phillips property long before old man Phillips had to let it go because of his bad investments. It had been Kent's bad luck that when the property had eventually been put on the auction block, he'd been out of town.

And to make matters worse, three years ago, he'd missed another chance at it when the Phillips' grandson, Scott, had beaten him to the punch once again, offering the owners an outlandish price for the place. He might have missed his window of opportunity twice, but he didn't intend to make it thrice. From everything he'd heard around town the widow would be out on her ass approximately sixty days after she couldn't make that bank note on May first. As he saw it, he had four months before that piece of prime real estate rightfully belonged to him. And when that happened, he planned to bulldoze every building on the place to the ground so that he could build a five-star resort and spa in its place. Screw the quaint bed and breakfast angle, he thought now. Scott Phillips might have messed up his plans three years earlier, but by God, he had no intentions of letting it escape his grasp this time. Kent had heard through the town grapevine about the newcomer helping out the poor widow. He had no intentions of letting that happen either. If Nick Harris thought he could save the place from the big bad bank, he had a surprise coming. It wasn't the bank he needed to worry about. Kent planned on getting that piece of land no matter what or who he had to go through to get it.

At that moment, he glanced out the window and watched as the newcomer climbed out of an SUV and sauntered into Ferguson's. Good, he thought. Let him do all the back-breaking work in vain. He planned on keeping a close eye on the situation. He really hoped Harris wasn't putting in too much of an effort to fix up that dump. It was a waste of time and money. If Kent Springer had his way that ramshackle old house had a short lifespan.

Completely oblivious to what was going on across the street at the diner Nick went about his business, picking up the supplies he needed and ordering the materials to patch the roof. Thirty minutes later, in a good mood, he walked through the double doors of Ferguson's stepping outside into the warm afternoon sunshine, almost giddy at the prospect of a job well done. He couldn't believe the progress they had made in such a short amount of time. Every day the house looked a little bit better. He had almost started to believe they'd make the deadline.

He came to an abrupt halt when his gaze landed on a boy of about ten, who sat on the sidewalk a few feet away guarding a cardboard box. Curious, Nick went over to where the boy sat and squatted down in front of him, checking out the contents inside the box.

"What have you got there?"

The boy fixed him a good pout. "Puppies. They can leave their mother now. My mom says I got to find them a new place to live."

Nick peered into the box. Six lively, wiggly balls of fur, their breed unrecognizable, looked back at him with big black soulful eyes they hadn't yet grown into. He set down the sack he held and focused on the puppies. "What kind are they?"

The boy shrugged. "Don't know exactly. Little bit of everything I guess. Got one that's brown and white, one's solid brown, one has all kinds of colors."

"Which one do you recommend?"

Turning sharp eyes on the man, the boy thought he recognized a novice. "You know anything about dogs, mister?"

"Not really. Maybe you can give me a few pointers."

As the boy began his best pitch, Nick rubbed his jaw, wondering what Jordan's reaction would be. Without putting much more thought into it though, he decided on the multicolored one and headed to the SUV.

Arms full of puppy, Nick set the little guy down on the pavement long enough to get the front passenger door open. He set the sack on the passenger seat and was in the process of settling the puppy onto the floorboard, when a passing delivery truck suddenly backfired. The noise sent him into panic mode. At the first tremble, he knew what was about to happen. Loud noises had a tendency to set him off. He leaned on the

SUV for support but the shakes took control. For a few moments, he stood there planted where he was, not moving, and did his best to get his breathing under control without success. Self-consciously, he looked around. Finally he managed to shove the passenger door closed before making his way around the other side and crawling behind the wheel. He rested his head on the back of the seat. All the while trembling so badly, he hoped no one had witnessed the episode. He sat there unable to drive until he got his bearings back. It didn't seem to matter that he'd spent a year in therapy. They'd called it hypervigilance. Fight or flight among returning vets could be difficult to overcome after experiencing the daily stress of war, being on high alert in a combat situation. Some days could be like living in a fog. Other times, the loud noises set off the shaking. Whatever it was on whatever day, the attack left him embarrassed and humiliated. He never knew when or where it might happen.

"You're gonna be fine, Nick, just breathe."

Nick hesitated to check out the passenger seat. But there sat Scott holding the new puppy on his lap. "Damn it, will you stop doing that."

"Cute dog. Jordan's gonna have a fit, though. But if you play it right, she'll cave. A little advice here, bro. Play the Hutton angle." And with that, Scott dissolved into thin air.

Nick scrubbed a hand over his face and once again looked around self-consciously to see if anyone had seen him sitting in a car talking to himself.

From his seat in the booth by the window, Murphy saw Nick's struggle. He glanced around the table to see if anyone else had noticed. Fortunately, they were deep in discussion. No one but him had watched as the scene unfolded across the street. Murphy had heard the truck backfire, and looked up to check out the noise. The last thing he had expected to see was Nick Harris shaking. Murphy felt for the man he was beginning to think of as a friend. He quickly turned his attention back to the round table argument, grateful no one else had witnessed the incident.

Nick had just set the puppy down on the grass in the backyard, watched as the little guy sniffed the ground before hunkering down to pee, when he saw Jordan fly out of the house with Hutton in her arms, as if she'd been watching from the window.

Halfway there, she came to a stop. "Nick Harris, you pick that fuzzball up right this minute, take it back wherever you found it. And don't give me a sad story about how you never had a dog."

Spotting the dog, Hutton began to squirm in her mother's arms. "Down. Ma-ma. Down."

Jordan set Hutton down to walk. As soon as her feet hit the ground the little girl ran over to the multicolored puppy, her legs pumping as fast as they could. When she got close, Hutton let out a long squeal of delight and started clapping her hands. The dog responded and began circling the baby.

Jordan needed to be firm. "Please tell me this is a joke. That dog is not staying here."

Nick thought Scott might be right. His best chance was with Hutton. "Look at her reaction. She loves him." For good measure, he added, "And I can't take him back. He has no place to stay. He's homeless." But he was grinning from ear to ear as he said it.

"And if he stays here, he might not have a home for very long. Did you think of that?" Pleading her case, Jordan pointed out, "Nick, with everything that's going on, I can't get the house ready for business, take care of Hutton, and look after a dog. He isn't even housebroken."

"We'll work on that."

Sensing defeat, Jordan circled both the dog and the baby, who by now had thrown both arms around the puppy.

Jordan eyed Hutton's face. The entire time Nick never took his eyes off Jordan. And in that instant what he saw told him the dog wasn't going anywhere because Hutton, and now possibly Jordan, had already taken to the furry little thing. Nick plopped down on the grass. Instinctively, the puppy wandered over, followed by Hutton. Nick picked up the little guy to hold him in his lap, and before he knew what was happening, Hutton had followed suit, dropping down across Nick's lap. For a man who'd never spent much time around a kid, he was beginning to get used to the funny little expressions Hutton made. With a lap full of little girl and dog, he swung his head down to the child's level. "We have to think of a name for your dog, Hutton. What do you think we should call him?"

The little girl stuck her finger in her mouth, clearly thinking it over. Before long she uttered, "Dog."

Giving up, Jordan joined them on the grass. Sitting cross-legged, she began to stroke the dog's fur. "He is kinda cute. Hutton's dog."

Touching a little hand to the dog's head like she'd seen her mother do, Hutton gleefully repeated, "Dog."

"He might be stuck with that name for awhile," Jordan reasoned.

"Dog, simple and to the point, I like it."

"Okay, he can stay, but you brought him, that means you have to clean up after him."

"Deal." He leaned back on the grass. As had become a habit around Jordan and Hutton, some of the tension drained out of him. The earlier episode forgotten.

Later that afternoon, Jordan was busy in the laundry room folding clothes. Hutton was doing her best to help. Dog was underfoot. When Jordan turned to put another load of clothes into the washer, Hutton pulled some of the clean clothes out of the basket. The clothing landed on the floor. Quick as a fox, Dog snagged something pink in his mouth and took off into the kitchen. Giggling, Hutton toddled after him.

Taking a new load out of the dryer, Jordan turned to see Nick standing in the doorway, carrying Hutton in one arm and holding a pair of pink panties in his other. "I think you've been the victim of a panty raid." He held out her underwear, a snicker on the verge of his lips. It didn't escape Jordan's notice that the man looked completely at ease standing there holding women's panties.

She laughed good-naturedly, but grabbed for her underwear. "Sneak attack. And he was lightning fast." Taking the panties back, she realized the pair wasn't her best. When Nick walked away, she glared at Dog. "Couldn't you have at least taken something black and sexy, instead of a pair of granny panties?"

Dog didn't even have the decency to hang his head. He simply blinked those big eyes of his, and hung out his tongue while his tail flopped back and forth on the floor.

When supper was done and Hutton was tucked into bed, Jordan sliced two generous pieces of chocolate cake and arranged them on a tray with a pot of coffee. She carried it to the kitchen table where Nick sat studying the loan documents she kept in a tattered accordion folder.

"I've been through the papers. I don't think you'll find a loophole anywhere."

"Hmm, no, no loophole. Are you aware the bank here in Pelican Pointe is only managing the loan? They resold the note to a larger bank out of L.A. more than a year ago before they gave you the first extension."

Jordan sat up straighter. "I didn't know that. Is it significant?"

"Might be." He held out a letter. "The bank here in Pelican Pointe sent you notification when they resold the loan."

She took the paper, barely giving it a glance. "But what difference does it make who holds the note? It's been extended out as far as it can be. Right?"

"I was thinking. If we contact the L.A. bank directly we might be able to get a refi, or maybe get the loan extended to the first of September. That way you'd have the summer months to take full advantage of the entire tourist season, time to get a healthy cash flow going. I think they'd go for that."

Jordan blinked in realization. "You've done this before."

"In my former life I was an investment banker." And worked for the largest investment bank in Los Angeles that just happens to hold your note. But he wasn't going to mention that. She might start asking questions. How could he tell her that the very serious-minded, hardworking financier he'd once been, seemed to have no interest in that life now. In fact, he seemed to find anything to do with the banking business these past few months sucking the life right out of him. While he was trying to come to grips with this revelation, he realized she was saying something to him.

"Why would this L.A. bank give me an extension when the bank here in Pelican Pointe is pressuring me for the first payment?"

"Simple. We bypass the bank here and go directly to the source of the loan. I'll make a few calls. Have you advertised, Jordan?"

"I've been online since January. My sister Ellen got a friend of hers to design a website. And I put the listing in the B & B trade magazines. I started running an ad in the San Francisco paper. The ad will continue through the end of May. It's costing a fortune, but I have to get the word out somehow."

"Sounds like you've covered your bases then. If we could show the bank in L.A. that you're booked up at least ninety percent through the summer, they might go for an extension to let's say, Labor Day."

She couldn't help it, hope soared. "Really? The reservations are picking up. I'm getting one almost every day now. And people who have seen the ad are beginning to call, ask questions. They may not be making a reservation yet, but they're interested enough to call. I don't mean to pry, Nick, but why are you a former investment banker?"

"Lately, I've had some personal issues to deal with, so I took a leave of absence to try and sort things out." Sensing the perfect opportunity for full disclosure, and before he lost his nerve, he sucked in a breath. "Speaking of that, I think there's...there's something I've been meaning to talk to you... to tell you."

At that moment, Hutton began to fuss through the baby monitor. Before he could say any more, the baby began to cry in earnest. Without another word, Jordan rushed from the room, telling him, "Hold that thought." She never noticed the look of anguish on Nick's face or the fact that his hands were shaking or the fact that he'd broken out into a cold, hard sweat.

Or the tears blurring his eyes.

Chapter Seven

At breakfast the next morning there was no mention that their conversation the previous evening had ended abruptly. Truth was Jordan had been up most of the night with a fussy Hutton cutting a new tooth. The last thing on her mind as she stood at the stove scrambling eggs was Nick on the verge of some dynamic disclosure. Instead, her mind focused on the part of the conversation that had been the most encouraging news she'd had in months—the fact that maybe this bank in L.A. might consider refinancing her loan—or at the very least give her an extension. Either one would take a huge amount of financial pressure off her. The last year without Scott's income had made her a pro at stretching a dollar. But in trying to get a new business up and running there had been plenty of expenses. Not to mention all the materials they had purchased before Scott had ever set foot in Iraq. They were in debt then but hoping to open up the B & B only months shy of his getting his deployment notice. With so much work still left to do, the opening hadn't happened and now Jordan was almost out of money, even after budgeting to the penny. The idea of having to go back to San Francisco broke had her petrified.

Across the kitchen Nick sat at the table watching the intense expression on her face. He didn't think she was that into scrambling eggs. She hadn't asked about what it was he'd started to tell her last night. Instead, she looked a million miles away. He took a sip of coffee and absently spread jam on his toast. That is, until he noticed Hutton's bobbing up and down in her high chair trying to reach the bread he held in his hand. Relinquishing it, he got up to put more in the toaster.

"How'd you sleep last night? I didn't see you down at the old haunt."

She recognized the teasing tone, but looked at him in disbelief as she dumped the eggs onto a platter. "You were down at the cove again last night? Nick, you can't keep this up. At some point you have to get eight hours. You can't work like a dog around here all day and go without sleep. And Hutton was fussy. New tooth," she explained absent-mindedly.

Ahh, that explained her distracted mood, he thought, before he pointed out, "Then you didn't sleep either."

When the phone rang, she strolled over to the corner desk to answer it, rolling her eyes at his comment. But as she picked up the cordless phone there was a twinkle in her eyes. She continued to look at him while going through the standard routine greeting before getting down to thumbing through the reservations book.

The call was obviously another potential guest. When she was done, she hung up and turned around with a brilliant smile on her face. "That's amazing. That was a woman from Cincinnati." She leaned closer. "Ohio. She saw the ad in the paper when she was on a business trip to San Francisco last week. She wants me to send her some information about holding a retreat here the third week of June for eight people. Four couples, Nick. Can you believe it? She also made a reservation for her and her husband to spend their wedding anniversary here May seventeenth as a kind of trial run in preparation for the retreat." She sighed with pleasure. "This whole thing may actually take off. Can you imagine that?"

He sipped his coffee, smiling at her enthusiasm, and said, "Actually Jordan, I can."

Later, as she rolled melon-colored paint on the wall in the hallway upstairs, Jordan heard the whir of a drill coming from the second bathroom where Nick was busy replacing the vanity. Glancing over at Hutton playing with a set of soft blocks in her Pack 'N Play while Dog snoozed like a baby, Jordan thought she could get used to this feeling. She felt more hopeful about things than she had in almost a year. She knew the man down the hall was responsible. An investment banker who hopefully had a little pull with a bank in L.A. Imagine that. And he'd found Hutton a dog. When the doorbell interrupted her optimism, she climbed down off the ladder, went over and picked up Hutton before heading downstairs to answer the door.

Her good mood lasted only long enough for her to peer through the screen door to find her closest neighbor in distance, seventy-year-old Edmund Taggert standing on the porch ready for a fight.

When he saw Jordan, he didn't waste any time getting to the point. "Missy, you are making way too much damn noise again. This was a peaceful place 'til Scott brought you back here and you started this...this dang remodeling."

She pushed the screen door back and stepped outside onto the porch. Instead of arguing with the old coot or asking him how in the world he managed to hear every sound they made from a half a mile away, she said simply, "I'm sorry Mr. Taggert, but you know I'm in the middle of getting this place ready to open."

"Silliest damned notion if you ask me, turning this place into a motel. Don't know why the city council ever gave you the permit to do such a thing. But you've got to keep the noise down. My Bessie isn't used to all this noise. She's already tried to run off on me."

"Sorry, Mr. Taggert, we'll try to keep it down. Would you like to come in for some coffee?"

"Come in? Missy, you are crazy if you think I'm spending my time listening to that blasted racket while trying to drink a cup of coffee. Drilling and hammering indeed."

Over a half a century of smoking had the old man stopping in mid-sentence long enough to wheeze in her direction before he added, "And keep that mutt you got away from my Bessie, he's a growler." Having stated his business, Taggert turned to leave.

After listening from behind to the old man's bitch-fest, by the time Nick came down the steps to give Taggert what for and put in his own two cents man to man, it was too late. He watched as the old man shuffled down the driveway. Nick shook his head, remembering Scott's claim about the good citizens of Pelican Pointe. Nick had seen friendlier people in L.A. When he looked over and saw the disillusionment on Jordan's face, he tried for levity. "Who is Bessie?"

Jordan threw him a sly smile. "His ancient cat."

"I didn't mean to make more trouble with the dog, Jordan."

"Trust me, you didn't. Mr. Taggert owns the organic farm that borders our property. He's been over here at least fifty times the past two years complaining about something or other. If he isn't nagging me about the noise, he's bitching about the condition of the place. Taggert isn't a happy man. Don't worry about it, Nick."

"Nice guy."

She sighed and said softy, "Taggert and the rest of Pelican Pointe." Nothing ever seemed to be enough for this town, she thought as she carried Hutton past Nick and back upstairs to resume her painting. But Nick saw the look of disappointment in her eyes. Every time she turned around she had to deal with another problem, some stupid infraction she'd committed against the residents of Pelican Pointe.

It was getting old.

Later that morning, a few minutes after eleven, as Nick stood at the work table he'd set up in the garage measuring laminate flooring, he heard a vehicle pull into the driveway. On the off chance it was another Mr. Taggert-like neighbor come to complain, he intended to head them off before they upset Jordan. Stepping out of the garage, he saw a man get out of a black pickup. When the man looked up, met his eyes, he started grinning at Nick.

"Son of a bitch," the man said good-naturedly as he shook hands with Nick, and then slapped him on the back in the way of man hugs. "My lieutenant's really out here in the boonies. When I got your call, I told Sheryl you were probably pulling a joke on me and that I'd drive all this way only to have you call and say, 'gotcha.'"

"No gotcha," Nick said, as he pulled Ben Latham into a bear hug. "It's good to see you. But drop the officer shit, though. Okay? Thanks for coming, Ben. I owe you one for this."

"Nah, we both know that's not true."

"How are Sheryl and the kids?"

"Great. Sheryl's pregnant again. Just found out yesterday. Number three." Ben wiggled his eyebrows up and down.

"Congratulations. Three, huh?" Thinking of what a handful Hutton could be sometimes, Nick wanted to know, "How do you handle three?"

"Three's not that much different than having two." At least Ben hoped that was true. In spite of his doubt about it, Ben gave him a confident laugh remembering something his wife had told him. "You just recycle all the baby stuff, like strollers and clothes and don't get too hung up on gender-related things and pretty much takes it from there." Eyeing the look on Nick's face, all of a sudden Ben got curious. "What's really going on here, Nick? What are you doing out here in the middle of nowhere?"

"As I told you on the phone, I've walked into a mess. Come on, Ben, let's take a walk. I need to explain a few things." As the two men took off through Jordan's flower garden then further out into the backyard away from the house, Nick proceeded to bring Ben up to speed about Jordan's predicament and the lies he'd told her.

Sgt. Ben Latham had served under Captain Scott Phillips and Lieutenant Nick Harris in Iraq. If anyone could understand the situation Nick found himself in, it was rock-solid Ben Latham. When Nick had finished laying all his cards on the table, he looked straight into Ben's eyes. "She can't know that you and I knew Scott. No mention of Iraq. That's bottom line, Ben. I haven't gotten around to explaining who I am, how things were in Iraq, how things went down that day."

"Sounds like a covert op. Imagine here with Captain Phillips's wife. I hope you know what you're doing, man. Wouldn't it be a helluva lot easier if you just told her what happened?"

"You want to talk about that day, Ben? Walk her through what happened to her husband step by step? How about while you're here you sit her down and have a heart to heart with her about all of it. How's that? I'll head into town, grab a beer, and let you take care of it."

Ben shook his head and held up both hands. "Okay. Okay. It was just a suggestion. I get it. I just hope you know what you're doing."

"I'm just trying to help her out. She could use all the help she can get right now, don't you think?" Nick said nothing about seeing Scott's ghost, or nightmares at two in the morning, or how he woke up drenched in night sweats. He didn't say anything about making promises in the heat of battle when a man lay dying in your arms. Besides after months of going to therapy, where he mostly sat and stared at the counselor, he wasn't sure himself why he couldn't just talk about that day. All he knew was that he couldn't do it—to anyone, least of all Jordan.

"Why can't you just come clean about knowing him? When she finds out the truth don't you think she'll be a little upset? Women are like that."

"I might if I thought it would end there. But it won't. She'd ask questions, want answers. I guess it's complicated." Ben nodded, but clearly didn't understand the situation. He looked around the yard. "Nice place. It's a shame about the captain. You know I'll do whatever needs doing here, Nick, that's why I made the trip. Let's take a look at what we're up against."

As they stood in the basement, Ben unrolled the blueprints of the house and wrote down more figures on his clip- board, handed the whole thing over to Nick. "It's bad. Some schmuck used rubber-coated cable. The rubber wiring's got to go as well as these corroded terminal connectors. And there's not enough amps for a house this size. I'm surprised she hasn't had fuses blow before now. With eight bedrooms and five baths if she gets a full house here with people running blow dryers and other small appliances, the wiring's toast. I can bring the wiring up to code, spread the amps out over two systems, put in a new breaker box, and add a few more outlets in more convenient places throughout the house. It helps to have the blueprints."

"When can you start?"

"I'm here now." He grinned. "And Sheryl knows where I am. Might as well get started." He made a thumbing gesture upstairs and asked, "Is she as good a cook as the captain said?"

"You can't say shit like that." But Nick smiled in spite of the warning. "You're in for a treat. She's a helluva good cook." He slapped Ben on the back again. "You lucked out. Meals are included with the job."

When the two men emerged from the basement, Jordan was standing at the island counter kneading bread dough. At that moment a timer dinged and she turned to open the oven door. She looked up to see Nick, standing just inside the doorway talking to a tall, good-looking, sandy-haired man with huge brown eyes.

The two stepped farther into her kitchen.

"Jordan, I'd like you to meet a friend of mine, Ben Latham. Ben this is Jordan Phillips owner and proprietor of The Cove Bed & Breakfast. Ben is your electrician."

Jordan pulled the quiche out of the oven, set the hot dish down on the counter and wiped her hands on her apron, all in one competent motion. Holding her hand out, she smiled, and said, "Nice to meet you, Ben. How is it you know Nick?"

Ah, Nick thought, right to the sham. Let the lies begin. He didn't wait for Ben to answer instead, he said, "I handled some investments for Ben a while back."

As buddies go, it didn't take Ben long to get into his role. He slapped Nick on the back. "And he did a wonderful job for the wife and me, got a nice little nest egg and college fund going for the kids." Which wasn't a lie at all, Ben thought as he sniffed the air, pointing to the steaming dish. "That smells great, by the way."

Hutton who'd been crawling around on the floor stood up and toddled over to her mother. "And who's this little doll," Ben asked, as he squatted down on his heels to get a better look at the baby.

Jordan swung Hutton to her hip. "This is Hutton. You'll stay for lunch."

"I thought you'd never ask."

Over salad and a bacon and cheese quiche, Jordan found out the two men had known each other for ten years, that Ben lived in San Jose with his wife and two kids, a boy five and a little girl three, and that his wife Sheryl was expecting their third child. And the way the men polished off the entire quiche put an end to the myth that men didn't eat such things.

After making small talk, Jordan steeled herself to ask the question she'd been avoiding. "Have you had a chance to come up with an estimate?"

Ben exchanged a knowing look with Nick.

When neither man said anything, Jordan sighed, "That bad, huh? Will three thousand do it? I've got that much set aside for emergencies." It would drain her savings account, but the building inspector had insisted she had to bring the wiring up to code in order to open. She didn't have many options.

"I can do it for two." Ben already knew Nick planned to foot the bill.

"Really?" Relief filled her. Then she realized he must be giving her a discount because of Nick. "Are you sure?"

"Absolutely."

"That's wonderful, Ben. Thank you."

To change the subject Ben patted his full stomach and leaned back in his chair. "That was the best quiche I've ever had. Maybe you could share the recipe with Sheryl before I leave. You're every bit as good a cook as I'd heard you were."

Nick choked on his iced tea.

"I am?" She stared at Ben then over at Nick knowing he must have been the one to sing her praises.

Ben caught his blunder. "Uh, yeah, Nick mentioned it."

Nick cleared his throat. "Jordan, the wiring job is going to take Ben a couple of days to complete. I was thinking if it's okay with you he can bunk on the sofa in the studio."

"Don't be ridiculous. That couch doesn't have a decent spring left. In fact it's barely viable for sitting let alone a good night's sleep. Ben can take one of the guest rooms upstairs. He'll be much more comfortable."

"No ma'am, I couldn't do that."

Baffled, Jordan asked, "Why on earth not? You're giving me a discount on the wiring. I can offer you a room for the duration of the job plus meals."

Ben looked uncomfortably at Nick for help. "I just couldn't, ma'am. I'm a stranger. You don't know me."

"That's absurd. You're a friend of Nick's and that's good enough for me. And I have to get used to having guests in the house anyway." She stared at Nick in frustration. "Look guys, this is a bed and breakfast. After May one, I'll have strangers in the house all of the time."

"The couch is good enough for me, Jordan. But thanks for your hospitality. It isn't the first time Nick and I have bunked together." And after two hitches in Iraq he could pretty much sleep standing up.

Jordan shook her head and plucked Hutton out of her high chair. "I've got to put Hutton down for her nap. We'll discuss this later."

As she left the room, or rather stormed out of the room, Nick started clearing the dishes from the table and Ben got up to help. The purely domestic scene didn't escape Ben's watchful eye. He'd never seen his buddy in this kind of role before. Ever. This wasn't the Nick Harris he had known in L.A. Something was going on and he needed to find out what it was. He chose his words carefully. "It breaks my heart knowing she's up against so much out here alone. I can see why you came. She's really something."

"She is that." Nick said as a strange sense of pride spread through his chest.

"Little girl looks just like Scott. Has his eyes."

"She's the sweetest little thing too, just like her mother. Did you know she's talking?"

Okay, that told Ben...a lot. Nick was a nice enough guy. They'd been through a lot together even before Iraq. They'd met back in college and remained friends. Ben knew all about Nick's childhood, at least what he'd been able to pry out of the guy. He'd always felt Nick's lack of a family life contributed to the fact that he'd never been able to form attachments. But Nick, even on his best day, had never been kid-friendly. For Nick to take an interest in a kid, even Scott's kid, was a big deal. It seemed to Ben that the committed bachelor looked a lot less committed than he'd ever seen him look. Because they'd acted as each other's wingman on numerous occasions long before he'd ever met Sheryl of course, Ben used his astute fatherly voice to tell Nick, "Of course the baby can talk, you doofus. That's what toddlers do."

"Yeah, well I don't have two of them. This is my first." Ben shook his head and slapped Nick on the back.

"You've got a lot to learn, my friend. I'm just the man to help teach you." He headed for the door. "School is in session tonight after supper. But for now, I've got a job to do."

By the time Jordan came back in, Nick had finished cleaning up the kitchen. "I like your friend," she admitted.

"He's a good guy."

"You're telling me. That price is incredible. Discounted no doubt. I just can't believe you talked him into coming all the way here from San Jose to do the job."

The guys in his unit would pretty much do anything for each other. How could he explain that to her? And then he realized that he probably didn't have to. She was after all the wife of a guardsman, one who had

given his life in service. She would already know that
their unit consisted of men from all walks of life, and
the men had spent years training together for not only
war, but for any and all civil emergencies like floods
and fires. Jordan probably knew that after all those
monthly maneuvers were behind them each month the
relationship between the men was often more about
camaraderie than one of rank and file—and after
serving in Iraq together—that friendship had grown
tighter.

Without giving anything away, he said quietly, "He
knows I'd do the same for him in a heartbeat." Scott's
image flashed into his head.

Jordan took a long look at the man standing in her
kitchen. He wasn't that different from the man she'd
married. Scott had been a successful software engineer,
a graduate of Cal Poly who'd gotten in on the ground
floor of a video game company that took off. But
before all that, he'd joined the Guard during his college
days along with a couple of his buddies. And for a guy
who pretty much had been considered a nerd most of
his life, the Guard allowed him to pursue his love of the
outdoors while earning extra money he'd used for
college.

A California native who loved hiking the hills
around San Francisco, where he worked, Scott had
been especially fond of the water. A surfer at heart,
Scott had spent most of his days after college
graduation in pursuit of a good time, any good time.
That is, until a particular warm, sunny day at Ocean
Beach where he'd gone to surf. He'd happened upon a
beautiful college senior with big brown eyes and
honey-blonde hair, trying to tackle some serious waves.
She'd gotten in trouble with the undertow, and he'd
pulled a struggling Jordan out of the surf. By the time
she'd dried off, he'd cajoled a dinner date out of her.
From that point on, he'd been a goner. They'd hit it off
and moved in together after she graduated college. Six

months later there was a wedding. With marriage came the talk of kids and settling down in Pelican Pointe for real to raise those kids.

But Iraq had come along and put a serious dent in those plans.

Jordan remembered how close Scott had been to the men in his unit. So looking at Nick now, told her everything she needed to know about the two men she considered her first real guests. Nick had made one phone call and gotten an electrician, a friend to show up for him. It sounded exactly like something Scott would have done for someone.

Jordan gave Nick a shy smile. "You really like my cooking?"

"We just scarfed down a whole quiche in one sitting, you have to ask?"

"A girl likes a little validation every now and then."

As he turned to head out the door to catch up with Ben, he looked back at her and said solemnly, "Anytime, Jordan. I'm right here."

Before she could reply, he closed the door leaving her standing there with her mouth open.

At supper that night, Nick bit into the lasagna. "Oh. This. Is. Fantastic. Woman, you could easily open a restaurant serving food like this. Taste this, Ben." He forked up another bite and closed his eyes.

Ben dug in earnestly to his own plate. "Mmmm. I like Italian but this is the best lasagna I've ever eaten. Uh, you might not want to mention that little tidbit to Sheryl though." He laughed but his pleasure was obvious. He continued eating before finally telling her, "You're a culinary genius, Jordan."

She looked around the dining room table. Once again, her daughter hadn't bothered with a spoon. She had red sauce all over her face and in her hair. The two men were obviously enjoying their meal. Her spirits lifted. At times like this, she thought everything might be okay after all.

After getting Hutton down for the night, she went into the kitchen to make herself a cup of tea. As she ran the water to fill the kettle, she heard the thud of a basketball hitting the concrete, before hitting the rim and bouncing off, and then male voices. Sure enough, when she glanced out the kitchen window she saw them. With only the outside garage light to illuminate the area in the middle of the driveway she saw two grown, sweaty men going at it in a fierce game of one-on-one. She listened to the grunts and good-natured ribbing that accompanied the battle, and then watched as Ben elbowed Nick for position. Nick, the taller one, blocked Ben's shot, caught the rebound, spun and put it up for two. Jordan watched in fascination as these muscular men resembled two power forwards shoving and pushing each other and yet played the game with as much enthusiasm as two twelve-year-old boys might before their mothers called them inside to get ready for bed.

When the kettle whistled, snapping her back to the moment, she suddenly lost her taste for the tea. Neither was she ready to settle into that big empty king-sized bed to read more of Scott's letters. Or worse still, another novel, where someone else's life turned out just fine in the process.

On impulse, she went to the fridge and pulled out three beers, twisted off the lids. With her hands full, she stopped long enough to pick up the baby monitor from the kitchen counter and headed outside.

Just as Nick went up to block a shot, she announced from the driveway, "You two look like you could use a cold beer." Her words had Nick stopping and turning. But not Ben. He continued to the basket, took the lapse in judgment on Nick's part to send a hard shot to

Nick's ribs knocking him off balance and to the concrete. Nick landed hard on his butt. Ben scored the goal and gave himself a little hand pump in the process.

"Oww," Jordan said automatically. "That had to hurt."

"Don't be such a girl," Nick responded with a grin as he got to his feet.

"I'll take that beer," Ben said winded.

"You would," Nick challenged. "You're behind. And out of shape."

"Fuck you—oops. Sorry Jordan."

Jordan couldn't help it, she giggled at these two. "No problem." She handed off the beers and the two men sat down at the picnic table, trying to get their breath back. Both of them chugged down the beer as if it were water.

Ben stopped long enough to look around the courtyard. "You got a nice place here, Jordan."

Nick wished, not for the first time today, that Ben would keep his mouth shut. It seemed every time he opened his mouth, he feared the man might give away his sneaky, lowdown little secret. But Nick had learned a long time ago that Ben, much like Scott, loved to talk. And Jordan was easy to talk to. So he sucked it up and tried to cut the guy some slack as he listened to Jordan tell Ben about The Cove.

"Have you taken the trail down to the beach yet?"

Ben shot a quick look toward his buddy. "Yeah, Nick and I took a walk down there after supper. The place is gorgeous, Jordan. Being this close to the ocean, I thought maybe I could go surfing if I get an early enough start in the morning."

"By all means, take all the time you need. There are plenty of short and long boards to choose from in the garage. Nick can show you. You should bring your wife here for a visit. I can guarantee you'll get my best room at a terrific discount."

Ben laughed, but suddenly got to his feet, looking around for his watch which he'd taken off before the game. "What time is it?"

"A little after eight."

"Great, if I hurry, I can call Sheryl, give her an update on Nick here and say good night to the kids before she puts them to bed."

He took off toward the apartment at a jog. "Thanks for the beer Jordan. I gotta talk to my kids before they go to sleep."

Nick hollered after him, "Be sure to remind Sheryl how much better off she would've been if she'd married me."

"Yeah right. Like she doesn't know how lucky she is to have yours truly. You gotta watch this guy, Jordan. He's a major player," Ben yelled over his shoulder. "He has a long track record of conquests."

"Shut up, Ben." He didn't need a reminder of his past. But unfortunately, he couldn't argue with the assessment. He looked head-on at Jordan who was simply smiling at their banter. "Don't pay him any mind. Ben's always been high maintenance."

She didn't doubt Ben's comment. She might be a widow who hadn't dated in years, living on the outskirts of a tiny town, but she'd grown up in San Francisco and was hardly naive. With Nick's good looks, combined with his own admission he'd avoided any emotional attachments like the plague, she didn't doubt the major player label. But instead of following that tack, she asked about Ben. "He seems like a good father, calling to talk to his kids before they go to bed and all. How long's he been married?"

"Hmm, let's see, a little more than six years I guess. He was the first one of us to take the plunge." Had it been that long? It seemed like another lifetime ago, a time when things had been a whole lot simpler and life had been easier.

"The plunge? You mean that dreaded trip down the aisle of wedded bliss?"

He laughed. "Something like that. Marriage might be great for most guys but…"

"It's not for you."

"No, not me," he said emphatically, draining his beer.

Watching two good-looking men perform physical labor had its benefits. Over the next couple of days no one enjoyed Nick and Ben's playful nature and wicked sense of humor more than Jordan. The two worked together like a well-oiled machine. They installed conduit, ran wiring, put in a new breaker box, and replaced old, outdated connectors. When the electricity had to be turned off for the work to be completed, Jordan coordinated the cooking and baking with Ben, who promised they'd all get to take hot showers right on schedule.

Despite Jordan's pleading, Ben had opted to sleep on Nick's old green couch, not in the soft bed in one of the guest rooms. Why, she couldn't say for certain, only that she thought it had something to do with keeping her reputation sterling as a young widow with a baby who lived alone and away from town. Little did both men know there wasn't a thing they could really do to prevent the town from talking about her anyway, nor from the ugly rumors she was certain Sissy delighted in spreading.

Jordan had tried to reason with both men. There was no one around to know what exactly she did out here miles away from anyone. And as proprietor of a bed and breakfast there was every chance a single man would happen along one day in the very near future and want a room in her coastal B & B. The fact that she would eagerly take money from a male guest, a stranger, had neither man changing his mind. Nor did they give an inch. Even though she thought their stance rather silly, it was also very sweet. Both men seemed to genuinely care about her well-being.

The first night on the sofa, Ben had gone to bed around ten-thirty. He'd been fast asleep when around two o'clock, he'd heard a noise. Sitting straight up, it had taken him several minutes to realize where he was. He heard groaning. It took him a few more minutes to realize the noise was coming from somewhere behind him. The only thing behind him was Nick's bed, so he swung his legs to the side and caught movement to his left. Standing up in nothing but his briefs, he caught a glimpse of Nick just in time to see him run into the bathroom. The door slammed shut and Ben heard retching. He stood where he was until the door opened again. "You okay, Nick?"

"Sorry, didn't mean to wake you. Go back to sleep."

"You wanna talk about it."

"No."

And that had been the end of that. Nick had refused to talk to him. And like any buddy, Ben let it go.

When the alarm sounded at six the next morning Nick hadn't said another word and neither had Ben, even though he knew Nick had been unable to get back to sleep. The way Ben saw it, they didn't really need to talk. Ben had been there the day Scott died, and knew exactly what had happened. He'd been riding in the Humvee just ahead of theirs and knew it could have easily been him. It didn't take a genius to figure out Nick felt guilty about surviving. But for the life of him, Ben had no idea why. He didn't understand it. But then, PTSD didn't have to make sense. That's why Nick was here in Pelican Pointe helping Scott's wife. Ben had no doubt, if he'd been the one who hadn't made it back, Nick would have been there for Sheryl and his kids. And that thought tumbled into something else. Was

Nick falling for Scott's widow? Was it possible Nick Harris could change his ways and settle down here in the boonies with a woman like Jordan? Ben shook his head. The idea was ludicrous. The Nick Harris he knew would never in a million years be able to give up his fast track life in L.A. for this backwater existence no matter the woman.

Feeling more settled about that, Ben got up and got dressed, intending to take full advantage of the surf while he was here.

The two-day job actually took three but went by in record time. Before Jordan knew what was happening, Ben had packed up his tools and his truck and was heading back home to his family. Jordan had given him at least a dozen recipes she'd written down for Sheryl. He'd also made reservations for a couple of days in June to bring his wife back to spend several days at The Cove surfing and fishing.

What Jordan didn't know was that long before he'd ever reached the interstate to head back to San Jose, Ben had torn up the check she'd written him for two thousand dollars. Hell, he'd even torn up Nick's.

It was the least he could do for Scott's widow.

A couple of hours after Ben left, Nick disappeared in the SUV telling Jordan he had a couple of errands to run. He'd been gone about fifteen minutes when Jordan looked out the window and saw Lilly's Ford Escort lumbering up the driveway. She picked up Hutton and went out to greet her guests.

Lilly emerged from the front seat and immediately started unbuckling car seats. She plopped Kyra down first and then Joey before turning around to look shyly at Jordan.

Jordan noted Lilly had washed her hair. In the sunshine it had a nice sheen to it. She'd put on clean jeans and worn a crisp white cotton blouse. The difference in appearance made the woman look years younger. And the kids were just as clean. Jordan brushed a hand over Kyra's head and said, "I wasn't sure you were coming."

"I got a late start. Joey took a longer nap than usual. I would've called, but I don't have a phone in the trailer. Sorry about having to cancel last week, but the kids had colds, didn't want Hutton getting sick."

Jordan paused at the knowledge. The woman had no phone living out in the country away from town with two little kids. She wondered what would happen if Lilly had an emergency. Jordan sent up a silent prayer that Lilly would never have to find out.

"How about we go inside for some chocolate cake and milk?" That offer got everyone drifting toward the porch and then inside.

The minute she stepped into the foyer, Lilly smelled the paint and looked around. "Wow, you are fixing this old place up. It looks great by the way. And to think you live in this big old house by yourself." Compared to the small trailer the place was a mansion. She couldn't imagine living here.

"It's a work in progress. And very shortly, I'll be having a houseful of paying guests," Jordan reminded her as she led them into the kitchen.

"It'll make a nice bed and breakfast. Will you need any help out here when you open up? Maybe like a maid or some other kind of helper? I'm pretty good at making beds and doing laundry. Or, I could wash dishes, help out that way."

"Thanks Lilly, that's an idea. You know, I actually have no idea what I'll need once the place opens. I'm doing this by the seat of my pants. Some days I feel totally out of my element."

"You?" It was hard to believe this woman couldn't handle anything, or any problem. "You look so put together so—cool."

"Thanks, but that isn't the case." Jordan put Hutton down on the floor while she pulled out plates and glasses from the cabinet. She cut slices of cake, found an extra sippy cup for Joey, and poured milk for the kids. "In fact, I'm anything but cool. Would you like coffee instead of milk?"

"That sounds good." Distracted, Lilly chewed on the inside of her jaw until she said, "Jordan can I ask you something?"

"Sure."

"Aren't you lonely living out here by yourself?"

She turned and stared at the younger woman for a long time. Tears brimmed her eyes. "Oh, Lilly, you have no idea." Over cake, Jordan unburdened the facts about her life for the past two years right up until Nick had appeared out of the blue. And from there the two women settled in like old friends and chatted in spite of the boisterous play of the kids. Jordan discovered Lilly was originally from Monterey where she'd graduated high school with the dream of becoming a design artist. Lilly recalled how she'd met her husband at seventeen and how she'd been so incredibly young and stupid to think he was the answer to her dreams. He'd been a charmer right up to the night of the wedding when he'd gotten drunk and beat her senseless. The sad thing was it hadn't been for the first time.

Jordan shivered at her own good fortune. And then remembered her good fortune had died in Iraq. Good fortune it seemed could take a major turn downward very quickly.

The staggering news was that while Lilly had two children and in less than a month would be a divorcée, she was only twenty-three years old.

"Looks like we've both had some rough times," Lilly offered quietly, as she tucked a strand of brown hair behind her ear.

As bad as things were for her, Jordan realized Lilly had it worse. After all, she had a family back in San Francisco who'd been her support system. After Hutton's birth they had been there for her as she waited for Scott's return. They'd begged her to stay in San Francisco and wait with them. But hoping to make Scott's dream come true, she'd stubbornly packed up the baby and come home to Pelican Pointe. After getting word of Scott's death, her family had once again tried to talk her into packing up everything and moving back in with them. But again, she'd tried to hold steadfast to Scott's dream—and single-handedly make it a reality. She smiled at Lilly. "You know, I don't know what it is, maybe it's because I've just poured out my whole life story, but I feel better."

Lilly laughed. "Well, that makes two of us. I haven't had anyone to talk to since I came back here. I don't confide too much in my stepdad. He's an ornery cuss. And I'm afraid to confide too much in the social worker for fear she might tell everyone in town my personal problems. She knows too much as it is. It seems the town has decided not to like me."

"Are you kidding? No one in Pelican Pointe wants anything to do with me. That's something else we have in common."

"Really? Wow, we make a great pair."

After chatting away two hours, they walked out into the front yard just as Nick drove up and squeezed the SUV in beside the little Escort. He got out, smiling at the ladies, but when he spotted the three kids, his smile grew wider. "I see Hutton's got her some new friends."

Jordan introduced Lilly and the kids to Nick.

Nick asked Lilly, "You sample Jordan's chocolate cake yet? I hope you guys left me a piece since she wouldn't let me go near it before you got here."

Lilly giggled. This man was a hunk. "I think there's some left. Jordan's a good cook."

Nick locked eyes with Jordan. "She is that."

"Thanks for having us." Lilly could see these two looking at each other as if she wasn't even standing there. She cleared her throat nervously and started loading the kids into their car seats. "I was telling Jordan I could hire on after she opens, maybe maid duties, do laundry, or whatever to help her out around here."

"Sounds like a good idea. What did she say?"

"She's thinking about it."

Jordan smiled. "What I said was I don't have a clue what I'm doing. I can only imagine what I'll need after I open. But you know what, in about two weeks I could use some help with the cleaning. You know keeping the furniture dusted, getting the place spiffed up before opening day."

"You just tell me when and I'll be here."

"In the meantime though, why don't you plan on bringing the kids back out? Hutton had a blast."

Lilly looked relieved to know this hadn't been a onetime event. And the idea of a permanent job had her feeling downright giddy.

After saying their goodbyes, Jordan watched Lilly back the car out of the drive while Nick busied himself at the back of the SUV. He began unloading tray after tray of brilliant blooming red tulips, sunny yellow daffodils, and an assortment of colorful lilies, lining them up along the walkway.

Looking over the collection of flowers, Jordan was overwhelmed at the gesture. "Nick, they're lovely." Inhaling the fragrant blossoms, all of a sudden her excitement faded as she thought of the cost. She'd have to take the money from her grocery budget. Or maybe take them back. "Nick...did you get these at The Plant Habitat, the nursery at Beach and Main? I...my account there is past due...I...can't afford these."

"They were on sale. And you need some color in that flower bed there. That sander took out a whole row of your best flowers."

She should have been embarrassed at discussing her sorry financial state with him but somehow after spending an afternoon with Lilly her troubles paled in comparison. Instead, she said quietly, "You shouldn't have spent the money, Nick. I'll go write you a check."

"You will not. Maybe if I hadn't come riding up on the motorcycle when I did you wouldn't have lost control of the sander."

She knew what he was doing. "It wasn't the motorcycle and we both know it. But thank you for the flowers, Nick. They'll look wonderful lining the front walkway, don't you think?"

He continued unloading the SUV, picking up a tray of lilies. "I do. Just tell me where you want these and I'll get started."

She eyed the determined look on his face and hefted a tray of tulips herself, carrying it to the front flower bed. She set it down on the concrete. "Right here. I want these to line the walkway up to the porch. We'll both get started. Hutton can help." Turning to Hutton, she asked, "Want to play in the dirt, sweetie? Plant some of these beautiful flowers Nick brought us?"

"I may not know much about kids, but if memory serves, even I know dirt and kids and dogs just automatically go together. I was a kid once myself." He set another tray down on the ground at her feet, grinning.

Getting into the rhythm, she teased back, "But that had to be light years ago when kids had nothing to play with but sticks."

"Keep it up and I'll reconsider helping plant these babies."

An hour into the project, on bended knees, Jordan had just finished working her way down one side of the walkway, setting a nice balance of daffodils combined with red tulips in the bed when Nick pointed out, "I think we're losing ground. For every flower we plant, we're losing two."

Jordan glanced up in time to see what he meant. Hutton and Dog were alternately pulling up every flower she'd so painstakingly just put into the ground. "Oh, no, my tulips." She jumped up and started chasing Dog trying to retrieve her precious buds before they were too far gone to replant. "Come back here you mangy mutt. That Dog's a bad influence. Hutton stop that, put those daffodils down this minute." But Hutton and Dog were having way too much fun to listen. Thinking what a great game they were playing, Hutton began giggling and yelling, "Dog. Dog."

Taking pity on Jordan, Nick tried to grab for the dog to keep him from stealing anymore of the flowers. "Dog. Sit. Sit. Heel." But the harder Nick tried the friskier Dog got, destroying more of the stems in the process.

"I see obedience school in Dog's future. He's a menace to my flower beds."

When Jordan finally retrieved the flowers, the stems were so broken, the roots destroyed there was no chance of replanting them. She sat down on the grass with slumped shoulders as Hutton toddled over. "Mama." She reached around Hutton and pulled her in for a hug. "It's okay, sweetie, they were just flowers. I'm sorry, Nick."

Nick laughed. "Like you said, Jordan, they were just flowers. Have you ever considered one of those lighted walkways instead?"

Kent Springer was so red in the face he looked like he was about to pop a blood vessel. "Damn it Gonzalez, you promised me. I drove all this way."

Despite Springer's money, Ron Gonzalez, the county building inspector, wanted no part of his plan. "I said I'd think about it. I thought about it and the answer is no."

"The least you could do is hear me out. You can't just change your mind like this."

"I can and I'm not doing it, Springer. I know what your angle is. I won't do it to her. I found out her husband died in Iraq, I'm not doing it."

Kent removed a wad of bills from his pocket. "Okay, another five hundred but that's it."

Ron shook his head. "Put your money away. It's too late. The electrician called me out yesterday morning to inspect his work. I already signed off on the rewiring job."

Kent stepped further into Ron's face. "Goddamn it. You promised me. You can't do this to me."

Ron took a step backward and headed for his truck leaving Kent standing in the middle of the church parking lot spitting venom.

"You'll pay for this you son of a bitch." But Ron just kept walking.

Kent crawled back into his Seville. He hit the steering wheel with a fist. A setback, he thought, this was a setback nothing more. There were other ways to thwart the opening of that ridiculous B & B than bribing the building inspector. He wanted that property and no one was standing in his way this time.

Kent decided to move on to plan B.

Chapter Eight

As Nick showered, the thought kept rolling over in his head and no matter how hard he tried to ignore it, he couldn't. He'd seen it in Jordan's eyes when he'd brought the flowers. The beginnings of dependence, need, something. Whatever it was, it scared the crap out of him. He didn't want her feeling reliant on him in spite of her situation.

When he was finished here, when he'd fulfilled whatever promise he needed to fill, his life was back in L.A. After he came clean, if he decided to head someplace else other than L.A., it certainly wouldn't be Pelican Pointe. He wasn't staying in this crappy little town any longer than he absolutely had to. It was time to make that clear to her the only way he knew how.

Jordan climbed the stairs up to the garage apartment carrying a stack of clean towels and Nick's laundered shirts. When she reached the landing, the door to the studio stood open and without a second thought, she stepped inside and came to a halt the minute she saw Nick. He stood with his back to the door, wearing nothing but his jeans. The man had obviously just taken a shower. His black hair glistened. Shirtless, she got a good look at his muscled back as the skin shone still slick in places. The rest of him was just as lean and well-built. The way she gawked, anyone would have thought she'd never seen a man without his shirt before.

She must have made a noise because he turned. His movement sharp and quick, he reached to get his shirt.

But not before Jordan saw the ugly, red scars that streaked across his chest and down his stomach. Staring at the damage, she sucked in a breath. Nick's head whipped in her direction. Their eyes met. As he slipped into the shirt, he continued to stare and so did she. Finally, Jordan found her voice. "I...I brought your laundry. I didn't mean to...the door was open." "You startled me. I left the door open because it gets hot in here. The AC doesn't work."

She didn't miss the brusque tone in his voice. "Oh. Well. I'm sorry." If he stayed she'd have to fix the AC come summer. Then she realized a man like this would never stay here in such a rundown studio apartment. He was out of place here and they both knew it. Trying to think of something to say, she blurted out, "You get the ocean breeze at night."

It was then her eyes landed on the plumbing book on the nightstand. She picked it up. "You know, I have other books, novels, mysteries, thrillers at the house, a sight more interesting to read than this. You're welcome to them when you can't sleep."

He continued buttoning his shirt. "Thanks. I may take you up on that."

It felt intimate to watch the man dress. And awkward. But when she saw him start to tuck the button-down shirt into his jeans, she realized he was getting dressed to go out for the evening. "Are you…going someplace?"

"I thought I might go into town."

It was ridiculous for her to feel let down but she did. "But you haven't had dinner." She sounded needy and hated the fact that he recognized it, too.

It was the perfect opportunity to make his point. "You don't have to fix me dinner every night, Jordan. In fact, I've been taking advantage of that. It's time I went out and got my own supper."

Disappointed for some inexplicable reason that he wasn't staying to have dinner with her and Hutton, she started to babble. "Of course. I wasn't thinking. I forgot you might be interested in Pelican Pointe's night life such as it is. For a single guy like yourself, you'd want to know that. I should have mentioned it before now." Clearing her throat, she went on like any good hostess might and explained the local attractions to her guest. "There are a couple of bars in town. One's located inside The Pointe which sits right on Main. It's more upscale, mostly geared to tourists, used to be an old fish hatchery though before Perry Altman, a chef visiting the area from L.A. decided he could turn the place into a five-star restaurant. You can't miss it. Then there's McCready's. It's mostly for the locals. It's located west of Main, in the area known as Smuggler's Bay near the waterfront. Then there's The Hilltop, the diner serves a terrific steak or chili burger, and you can order a beer there with your meal but they don't serve mixed drinks."

"Thanks." He pointed to the stack of clothes she'd set on the bed. "And thanks for doing my laundry. It feels like I should be paying you rent or something."

Awkward. The room reeked with it. But the suggestion brought her back from her embarrassment enough to speak. Appalled at the notion he pay rent when he was doing so much of the work, she all but seethed, "No. No, you're working here. And I can't pay you yet... Laundry is the least..."

Feeling the uneasiness, he made the mistake of looking into her brilliant chocolate-brown eyes. His mind suddenly went blank. He couldn't remember why he'd wanted to go into town in the first place, or why he'd wanted to act so cold toward her. Feeling more and more like a jerk, he admitted, "Jordan, it's okay, I didn't mean anything by it. Thanks for the clean clothes that's all I meant."

But the damage was done. She turned and all but ran from the apartment leaving him feeling like the slithering snake he was.

McCready's turned out to be a cross between a pub and a dimly lit pool hall owned by an ex-Irish boxer from Dublin named Flynn. The place sat between a bait and T-shirt shop amidst a series of vacant storefronts along the wharf overlooking Smuggler's Bay.

Nick sat at the long, scarred mahogany bar, nursing a beer, listening to Dwight Yoakum on the jukebox trying to sort out his feelings about guitars, Cadillacs and hillbilly music. He brooded over the earlier scene with Jordan. He'd put her off all right, enough that she hadn't even asked about his scars. Most women did. They wanted to know what had happened. Usually all he had to do was mention the word "Iraq" and he was flooded with sympathy. He didn't want sympathy from anyone, least of all from Jordan. And she hadn't given him any. She'd run from the room away from him so fast, and it had had nothing to do with his scars. His coldness had not only surprised the heck out of her, coming out of the blue like it had, but it had hurt her feelings. Remembering the shattered look on her face, if he could manage the logistics of it, he'd like to kick his own ass. When he tried to direct his attention to the basketball game on the big-screen TV, all he saw instead was the wounded look he'd put on Jordan's face. He simply couldn't get that picture out of his head.

The bar started to fill up and get noisy. He watched men and women pair off and head over to play pool. As he sat there nursing his beer, he eyed the people around him, listening to their banter. He couldn't explain why but suddenly the entire crowded atmosphere started to annoy him, started to make him edgy.

He thought about going home and realized for the first time in weeks he wasn't thinking about L.A., but going back to the Cove. Damn, he didn't want this. He didn't want a woman like her, not that girl next door thing she had going on. She had a baby for God's sake, Scott's baby. Hell, a blind man could see she was still pining for her husband. And why wouldn't she be? Scott had been good, solid, husband material. While he was... What was he anyway, a man with secrets and problems? Christ. He ran a hand over his face. Thinking about Jordan had him wanting to be there when she put Hutton to bed, wanting to read Hutton a story, wanting to share more than he had a right to.

What was happening to him? The bar was getting to him. Annoyed with himself and the fact that he no longer found solace in a crowded, stuffy barroom, he decided he might as well get the hell out of there.

At that moment, however, a bleached-blonde woman with bright red lips sidled up next to him and slid onto the bar stool, making sure her ample breasts rubbed up against his arm. Any other time Nick would have been all over her, but for some reason all he could muster was disgust at her being so damn close and so different from Jordan. What was wrong with him? Isn't this why he'd left Jordan tonight for this very thing? He sized up the woman from head to toe. Wearing a tube top that showed off enough cleavage to showcase her mindset and a short skirt that bared skin up to her ass, he watched her lean farther into his space.

And felt nothing. Okay, so he couldn't very well blame his non-interest on Iraq.

The woman, however, had no idea what he was thinking and leaned seductively into him. Twirling her hair with a finger and licking her red lips, she managed, "You're Nick the new guy in town, the one that rides that big-assed Harley, aren't you?"

Nick leaned out of her range and drained his beer. "That's me."

"I'm Sissy. The banker's my daddy. And just so you know, that job you've got isn't going to last much longer. The little widow will never be able to turn that rundown house into anything but spare lumber."

If he wasn't interested before, her high-pitched voice ended any and all hope, especially the nasty bite in her tone. "Is that right? And do you get that firsthand information from your daddy?"

"Among others." She stuck out her chest in his direction again and all but purred out every word, "I've just been dying to go for a long ride—on a Harley."

"Maybe some other time, I was just about to head out."

Recognizing a rebuff, Sissy didn't take kindly to being put off. "Don't tell me you're more interested in that prissy Jordan. I went to high school with Scott, grade school too. And if he were here, Scott would tell you firsthand you don't know what you're missing." Seductively, she licked those thick ruby lips again. "You can bet I'm so much more inventive than that boring little housewife ever could be. And I don't have any bratty kids to get in the way. Jordan's life is pretty much a screwed up mess, too."

Now that just pissed him off. And Nick was pretty sure what Scott would say if he were here. In fact, Nick could almost hear Scott's voice telling him to run the other way, like maybe back to The Cove and back to Jordan. "Lady, you don't even know me. Why would you say such a thing about Jordan?"

By that time, the pool players had taken an interest in their conversation and ambled over. "He isn't interested, Sissy. Can't you tell he's getting it from the hot widow out at the Cove?"

Another pool player threw in, "Jordan's a hot little number all right. And Scott's been gone a long, long time. It was just a matter of time before she hooked up with the first guy to come along."

Nick stood up, a little lightheaded, but not from the single beer. "Look guys, I don't know what your problem is, or what the lady's problem here is, but I don't want trouble. In fact I'm out of here."

All of a sudden, Nick caught movement out of the corner of his eye just in time to dodge the pool cue aimed at his head. Without thinking, he swung around and sent a hard right to the jaw of a third pool player who'd snuck up behind him. The man crumpled to the floor, out cold. Nick stood over the man, fists clenched. Looking around the room, he told everyone within the bar's four walls, "I don't know what your problem is, but there's nothing going on between me and Jordan. I'm here to help her finish the house, nothing more. Why are all of you so determined to give her such a hard time anyway?"

And with that, he stormed out of McCready's.

Once outside in the night air, he started to shake. Afraid someone would see him he walked around the corner of the brick building and leaned against the wall until his nerves settled down. When the trembling had stopped, he started walking to his bike, and then as he got closer, began to run. All he could think about was getting back to The Cove, and back to Jordan.

Nick woke in a hospital bed. A gray-haired, fifty-something doctor stood beside the bed holding a chart, looking down at him with a sad look in his eyes. The room appeared foggy, the image not quite clear as the doctor told him, "You're lucky you made it out alive, son."

He looked around the room, but except for the doctor they were the only ones there.

"Where's Scott?"

"Scott? Scott didn't make it. The Humvee blew up. You didn't get him out, Nick. If you'd been faster, reacted quicker, moved sooner, Scott would be alive."

"No. No. He can't be gone. He has to go back home to Jordan and his daughter. No. He can't be dead. All he wants is to get back to his wife and baby. That's all he talks about."

"He's dead, Nick. Scott isn't going home. He didn't make it. You didn't pull him out in time."

Nick's eyes flew open. He slid out of bed and hit the floor running to the bathroom just in time to throw up. Afterwards, he went to the fridge, took out a bottle of water and leaned on the counter for support. He downed the water in one long, continuous gulp. He made his way back to the bed. But he took one look at the crumpled sheets, and couldn't make himself crawl back under the covers. He decided to get dressed.

Outside the night breeze felt cool on his skin. He looked up at the star-filled sky and let the fresh air clear his head. By now he didn't need a flashlight to find the trail down to the cove in the dark, but rather relied on moonlight to guide his way. He headed out past the side of the garage and followed the rocky slope gently angling downward. He made his way past the fragrant rosemary in bloom and savored the smell of the wild ginger ground cover. The smell of pine mixed with the salty sea invigorated him so that by the time he reached the beach, his stomach had stopped churning. He wasn't surprised to see Jordan sitting on the same rock as before and dropped down next to her.

"Come here often."

Despite her melancholy mood, she laughed. "Now there's a line I haven't heard in some time. I'd think with your background, you'd be more original."

"I'm a little rusty on my pickup lines."

"That's too bad. How'd it go in town? Have fun?"

"I think the bar scene has finally passed me by." At least in this town, he thought.

"We all get there eventually."

"It might have run its course."

"Things change, remember?"

She was throwing his words back at him. "You're right. Can I ask you something? I don't mean to make you sad or anything, but...there's something I'd like to know."

Even in the moonlight he saw her eyes flicker with caution. But he had to ask. "Why do you suppose...your husband, Scott, felt so warm and fuzzy about Pelican Pointe?"

Surprised, at the question, she thought for a moment. "Scott's parents died in a car accident when he was five. He came here just a little boy to live with his father's parents. Scott used to say it was like having two sets of parents, two sets of memories, those when he was very young, very small, then those that came with this place. When we first met, he'd tell me such warmhearted stories about this town. Every story made it seem like he was homesick, and couldn't wait to get back here. He made the place sound like paradise. His stories convinced me it must be the greatest little town in the state of California." She laughed and shook her head. "He certainly sold me."

Nick could relate. Scott had done the same thing with him. That's why he had to ask. "Do you think he might have built it up in his mind like something he wanted it to be, but wasn't, an idyllic place that never actually existed?"

Jordan didn't have to think long. "Could be. Scott was overly optimistic...about everything. He might have romanticized the town a bit, exaggerated even. He had such high hopes for us here. But as you've seen, the people haven't exactly lived up to the picture Scott painted."

Nick couldn't have agreed more, wanted to say a big amen to that. Was now the time to tell her he'd known Scott? The thought nagged at him as he ran a tentative hand over his queasy belly. His nerves spiked. After the kind of night he'd had up to this point, the last thing he wanted to talk about was that day.

"Why do you ask?"

"This town could use a swift kick in the ass."

"Uh-oh. I take it your night on the town wasn't the night you thought it would be."

He had no intentions of letting her find out the ugly things they'd voiced about both of them in the bar. It galled him all over again just thinking about it. "You've made several comments about how Scott felt about this place. It doesn't jive with the way these people act, look at Taggert." He remembered how Ferguson had acted at the hardware store. And Sissy. And every one of those pool players.

"It doesn't, no. But Scott had a history here. Maybe it was different for him back then growing up here."

Nick didn't believe that for a minute, but let it go. "Maybe." Then smoothly he changed the subject. Noticing what she was holding in her hand, he asked, "Does that baby monitor really work all the way out here?"

"You bet. It's long range. You want to test it out?" She laughed at the look on his face.

"Could we?"

"Sure." She handed him the monitor. "I'll head back to the house, when you hear me on the two-way, push this button." She showed him what she was talking about and then got up off the rock.

It occurred to him that she was merely humoring him. "You think I'm nuts."

She laughed again. "I think you're curious. You've never been around a baby before and the old saying kicks in, seeing is believing. I was that way right after she was born, I couldn't believe she was mine, couldn't leave her alone for five minutes without making sure she was breathing. But trust me the monitor works just fine from this distance."

"I found bicycles in the garage."

What that had to do with the baby monitor, Jordan could only wonder. "Okay. You want to use one, go ahead. That's why they're out there."

He suddenly realized he might sound ridiculous. But he'd already opened the door. "Maybe we could all go for a bike ride." As if thinking out loud, he suddenly thought of something. "Don't they have some kind of a baby seat that attaches to a bike? I've seen bikes with a baby on board in the park before." And he never in a million years would have thought he'd be interested in carting around a baby on a bicycle.

Unbelievably moved that he would think of such a thing, Jordan saw the seriousness on his face and wondered why he was trying so hard. "Yeah, they do."

Pleased with the knowledge, as he walked her back up the trail, he said, "I'll see if Ferguson's has one next time I go into town."

Chapter Nine

The next day, Nick was standing in the bathtub installing a new shower head when Jordan walked in, all smiles, carrying Hutton. "I ran out of Delicious Melon."

He slowly turned to stare at her as if she'd grown horns since breakfast. "Excuse me."

"Delicious Melon, the paint color for the corner room with the bay window. I need another gallon. I just wanted to let you know I'll be gone for half an hour."

An alarm went off. After last night's altercation at McCready's, it was bound to be all over town what had happened. And then there was Ferguson himself. How could he be sure he wouldn't hassle Jordan about her account. The urge to protect her from anymore of Pelican Pointe's stings had him offering, "The paints at Ferguson's, right? How about if I go? Check on the baby carrier thing for the bike we were talking about."

"No, that's okay. You're in the middle of something. I'll look for the baby seat while I'm there. Anything else?"

Resigned to his fate, he suggested, "You might check the amount of paint colors we have on hand for the other rooms." He couldn't think of any other reason to stop her from heading into the miserable excuse for a town. So he did his best to act as if nothing were amiss when he lamely added, "Make sure we have enough of each color to finish the job."

"Good idea. You know, I was thinking about that theme idea for each room. We should name them, the rooms I mean. Some B & Bs do that. Think about it, if each room had a name, it'd be easier to keep them straight when the reservations are booked, each room could be booked by its designated name."

"Good idea, but naming the rooms after fruit might not work."

Jordan looked puzzled. "Fruit? Delicious Melon?"

She laughed. "Oh. The Melon Room, The Peach Room. That's kind of cute, I like that. It could work."

"Jordan, I was joking. How about an ocean theme instead? The B & B by the ocean offers rooms like The Shell Room, or The Sea Horse Room."

"Oh. I like that even better. The Sand Dollar Room. That's an idea." She sent him a wide smile and turned to leave for town in a good mood.

But the moment Jordan stepped inside Ferguson's with Hutton on her hip, her good mood vanished. Several customers took the time to turn their way and stare at her and the baby—noticeably, even more so than usual. By the time she reached the paint counter, she felt like the butt of some inside joke. A few more heads turned, a few more customers leaned over and whispered to each other. Feeling more than a little put off, she tried to convince herself she was simply overreacting, but to what she wasn't sure. The minute the clerk behind the counter finished what he'd been doing and turned to wait on another customer, which was Jordan, he too gave her a leering look. It was that look that said it all. Something was definitely off kilter.

"I need another gallon of Delicious Melon and a gallon of Butternut."

"Right away, Mrs. Phillips. It'll take me about fifteen minutes to mix up the color. You go ahead and shop. Come back in fifteen and I'll have it ready."

Etta Mae Searcy, a white-haired woman in her seventies, had been looking at wallpaper minding her own business, but moved closer when she overheard the brief exchange. "You don't want to make her wait and get her mad, Gerald. That Nick fellow might come in and punch your lights out."

Appalled, Jordan turned to face Etta Mae. "Why would you say such a thing? Nick would never do that."

Etta Mae snorted, ignoring her loyalty. "Your Nick sure packs a wallop, just ask Sal Turley." She leaned over closer to Jordan. "Your Nick knocked him out cold last night at McCready's. Sal had to go over to Doc's and get his head checked out. Flynn didn't even get a chance to call Ethan out before it was done and over with."

So this was what Nick had meant last night about the town needing an ass-kicking. And he'd already thrown the first punch. Good lord, if Flynn had called Ethan Cody she might have had to bail Nick out of jail last night. The whole town had to be talking it to death. That fact alone humiliated her. Before she did a little ass-kicking of her own, she needed to get more facts. "Let me understand this, Nick…got into a fight…last night…and hit Sal Turley."

Etta Mae snickered. "Wasn't much of a fight from what I heard. Your Nick laid him out stone cold with one punch is what he did. Then made some kind of a speech, told everyone at the bar the two of you wasn't doin' nothin' out there at The Cove."

"What?" Jordan saw stars. She settled Hutton on the counter to get her balance, rubbed a hand to her temple, and wondered if this could get any worse. But then, scooping up Hutton, she hurried out, telling the clerk over her shoulder, "I'll be back for that paint. You just have it ready."

At a fast clip, Jordan walked into the grocery store looking for Murphy, but it was Velma Spears who manned the only open checkout. She walked past Velma and several customers, down every aisle looking for Murphy. With every turn, there was another customer who stopped in the middle of their shopping long enough to stare at her. She finally found Murphy stocking canned goods on the back aisle and tapped him on the shoulder. "I need to talk to you. Could we go into your office?"

She was pissed, Murphy noticed. He nodded and tagged along behind her.

Once inside the tiny office, Jordan dropped into a chair, settling Hutton on her lap and wasted no time getting to the point. "I want the truth about what happened last night at McCready's? Did Nick get into a fight?"

"It wasn't really a fight, more like stopping a rumor before it got started. If you ask me, Turley got what he deserved. He threw the first punch, Nick just defended himself."

"What was said? What started it?"

"Nick did the gentlemanly thing and defended your honor."

Fresh humiliation crept up her throat and stayed there. "Oh, for God's sakes."

With Jordan in town, it was the perfect time to make the call. Sitting on the sofa, cell phone in hand, papers spread out in front of him on the coffee table, Nick leaned back, got comfortable. "You could say I'm calling in a favor, Charlie. We go back a long way. You guys hold the note on the Phillips' property, fifteen acres in Santa Cruz County that includes The Cove B & B. I need at least ninety days more, the end of August would be ideal. More if you can override the loan committee. That would give her time to get all the summer tourists in here. Time to get a healthy cash flow going. Time for her to get on her feet."

"Damn it, Nick, the loan committee is tightening credit on everyone. You know that. A lot of it is out of my hands these days. But if you were to show up and make your case in person that might carry more weight than mine, even if you have been acting funny since you got back stateside. When you coming back to work anyway?"

"I'm not sure." He didn't want to think about going back to those four claustrophobic walls. "Listen, Charlie, just do your best. Try to keep this inside the loan committee, okay, the less people who know, the better. Your recommendation as well as mine should be enough. I'll put mine in an e-mail. I just don't want this becoming common knowledge. Keep it low profile."

And then he decided to use the same spiel on Charlie he'd given everyone else. "While you're at it, why don't you surprise the wife with a romantic getaway to The Cove?" He rattled off the phone number. "Be sure to call soon, the place is starting to fill up."

As if knowing what her mood would be like after getting back from town, Nick got busy putting up the porch swing. He'd just finished drilling the holes, when Jordan pulled the SUV into the driveway and climbed out. It didn't take a genius to read body language. From the porch he could make out the tight set of her jaw and the fact she looked plenty pissed. Even as she pulled Hutton out of her car seat, he noticed she didn't look particularly inclined to open that jaw and talk to him. He was pretty sure he should be grateful for the silence because when she did start talking he figured he'd still be in hot water.

Without a glance in his direction she walked up to the porch and sailed right past him, without so much as a hello. He gave Dog a knowing look. "She's steamed all right. I just hope I can talk myself out of this one." Picking up the puppy, he patted the dog's head. "We need to go find us a doghouse and lie low for a while."

She was still fuming as she ladled soup into bowls to go with the hot ham and cheese sandwiches she'd fixed for lunch. Sitting in her high chair, oblivious to the imminent clash of wills, Hutton stuffed macaroni and cheese into her mouth one handful at a time. When Nick strolled in, Jordan huffed out a breath. She wasn't nearly ready to speak to the man. They'd been avoiding each other since she'd gotten back from town, but with lunch looming, avoidance was no longer an option.

Sensing the frosty atmosphere, Nick did what any intelligent man would do under the circumstances and went for a diversion, keeping up a steady conversation with the baby. Washing his hands in the kitchen sink, he directed his question to Hutton, "How's that macaroni and cheese, Blondie?"

Hutton returned the favor, answering him with a string of baby-speak. Grateful for Hutton's exchange, he fixed himself a glass of iced tea. When the phone rang it broke some of the tension. During the call, Jordan went from pissed off to jovial hostess in a matter of seconds. Since the caller was another reservation, it took some of the bite out of her temper, brightening her mood.

After she hung up, they sat down at the table together. Although in a better frame of mind, Jordan ate her soup in stony silence until Nick decided to meet the battle head-on. He purposefully asked, "How was the trip into town?"

Jordan glared at him. With one quick look at Hutton, between clenched teeth, she said stiffly, "You know perfectly well how it went. And we'll talk about this later, after I get Hutton down for her nap."

As if on cue Hutton held out a spoon full of pasta and promptly dropped it on the floor. When Dog ran over to lick up the unwanted food, Hutton found that extremely funny. She began to clap her hands and drop more on the floor.

When she noticed Nick laughing, she giggled even more and started chanting, "Dog. Dog. Dog." Not one to lose the opportunity of the moment, Nick turned to Jordan and pointed out, "Hutton's talking to me."

"Oh, I'm talking to you. I just don't think you're gonna like what I have to say." With that, she turned her attention to cleaning up Hutton.

Later after Jordan got her down for a nap, she walked into one of the guest rooms to see Nick standing on a ladder, installing a ceiling fan with a lighting fixture. Her heart softened a little just seeing him work so hard and knowing what he'd done for the place, for her. But despite that they had to clear the air.

Out of the corner of his eye, he saw her walk into the room holding the baby monitor in her hand that she carried everywhere she went, night or day, whenever Hutton slept. When he saw her set it down on the dresser, he climbed down off the ladder, prepared to do battle. He watched her cross her arms in a defiant stance. "That's why you offered to go into town, wasn't it? So, I wouldn't find out what you'd done."

"What I did? Me? I don't know what version you got from those nut jobs in town but I was minding my own business, having a beer, and some guy I don't even know throws a punch at me, and then insults you."

Trying to keep her voice level, she tossed back, "And why did that happen? I don't need you to defend me, Nick." She was pacing now, building up a new head of steam. "You've made things ten times worse. Usually, they just ignore me. Now, the whole town is laughing at me and talking behind my back."

"Please." He rolled his eyes. "Like they weren't doing that before?"

"Okay. They talked behind my back. But now they're openly snickering and laughing at me. You should have seen them at Ferguson's and at Murphy's. It's… humiliating."

"So you'd rather have me just stand there and let them say things about you that aren't true. That would have been better?"

"They probably thought that two days after you got here. It's a small town with small-minded people. I can't control what they think about me, or you for that matter."

"What's wrong with the people in this town? Why do they treat you like a leper?"

Jordan blew out a breath, and sat down on the bed they'd just brought in from the garage two days earlier. She hung her head as if she'd just lost all momentum. "Honestly I don't know, but Scott loved this place, loved the idea of moving back here. I'm not sure why. Because once we got here, they treated us like outsiders, both of us, even though Scott grew up here and knows practically everyone in town. Scott kept telling me they'd warm up to us, to me, eventually." Her shoulders slumped and she ran a hand through her hair. "But then he left for Iraq, left me out here alone, pregnant, without a friend in town." It sounded so pathetic, she thought, as she met Nick's stormy eyes.

"You had Hutton here alone?"

She shook her head and looked down, nervously, playing with the string on her hoodie. "I went to San Francisco for her birth to be with my family. Even though it was Christmastime, I think that upset the doctor in town. I guess he thought I'd snubbed him in some way by going out of town to deliver. Another mark against me. But I couldn't help it. I wanted to be with my family. I felt so alone here, Nick. I stayed with my parents until Hutton was three weeks old. But then we had to come back here. And God, once I got back, I've never felt so… miserable. Every time I went into Pelican Pointe, they were standoffish. The longer it went on the worse it got. Then after I got word that— Scott had died, they were downright hostile."

"You have no friends here, not one?"

"No. Lilly's the closest thing I have to a friend. And Murphy, but he's the mayor, a politician. Sometimes I think the only reason he's nice to me is because he wants my vote." He took a step toward her, tucked a hand into hers.

"They just don't see what a terrific person you are."

"They haven't made an effort to get to know me, Nick. And if it hasn't happened by this time, I doubt it ever will."

"You're right. The people in this town are incredibly petty."

"Not just that but at this point, I'm considered the crazy widow on the fringes of town trying to take a rundown, old house, and make it into a business. For some reason, the town resents me for that. I don't get it, either. They welcomed Perry Altman to town, gave him loads of support for turning the old fishery into The Pointe but when it comes to opening this place, it's beneath them. I can't win with these people."

"I'm sorry I upset you."

Jordan smiled, all forgiven. "Etta Mae said you knocked Sal out with one punch."

He grinned. "Had a weak jaw, went down like a falling rock. But I wish it could've been Sissy, she's the one with the big mouth."

"You're telling me. I wouldn't mind clocking Sissy myself. I'd like to see someone wipe that smirk off her face." She sighed, feeling better about everything. "I'm sorry I overreacted. In the future, if I need my honor defended, I know where to find my knight in shining armor."

It was such a nice afternoon after Hutton woke up from her nap, Jordan decided it was time to test ride the new porch swing. That's where Nick found them enjoying the simple pleasure of a lazy afternoon. They hadn't yet spotted him. So he leaned on the doorjamb and stood back and watched the show. Hutton prattled on in gibberish only she could understand while Jordan pretended to hang on her every word. In her hand, Hutton clutched one of the yellow flowers they'd managed to salvage, a daffodil maybe, and Jordan made up a story about the flower. It was an easy scene to watch. Relaxed, he felt better than he had in a year. Even with all the physical labor, it seemed like every day he felt less stress, and in better shape than even physical therapy ever provided.

Jordan finally spotted him and motioned for him to take a seat on the other side of Hutton in the swing. "It's such a pretty day. Almost spring." After he'd settled in, Jordan eyed Nick carefully. He'd been working like a slave for weeks and without much sleep. The brutal timetable they were under had to be catching up with him. "Do you surf, Nick?"

"Not in years."

"Take some time for yourself, go surfing this afternoon. You and Ben should have spent more time in the water while he was here."

"Okay, but only if you and Hutton join me. How does a walk on the beach sound?"

A walk on the beach sounded great. "Fine. Go grab a board. I'll get Hutton's sunscreen and a couple of towels and meet you at the top of the trail."

As he stood on the cliffs watching Jordan's approach, Nick's mouth went dry. The woman wore a red two-piece swimsuit, with some kind of wraparound thing at her hips. It didn't look possible that she'd ever had a baby. She had a body models might envy but with curves in all the right places and not the stick-figure-thin-as-a-rail variety.

Carrying a surfboard, he led the way down the trail while behind him Jordan carried Hutton and Dog plodded down each step at his own pace. But the only thing Nick had on his mind were Jordan's long legs. Until today, she'd mostly been sort of covered up, wearing jeans, except for that first day when he'd seen her legs in shorts. But now, Jordan uncovered was a sweet thing to behold.

He reached the bottom first and got rid of the surfboard so he could help Jordan maneuver the last step carrying Hutton. He spread out the blanket. But Jordan and Dog had other ideas. Jordan kicked off her sandals and moved along the shallow surf. Barefoot now, carrying the baby on her hip, he watched her move along the water's edge until she stopped to dip Hutton's toes into the cold, ocean water a little at a time. The baby giggled while Dog played tag with the waves. But Nick had trouble taking his eyes off Jordan. He knew he had no right to this woman, but his body's reaction was another matter entirely. He forced himself to take a step back—mentally.

Before she caught him staring, he turned his attention to the water. For several long minutes, he stood back reading the currents, finding the best point break. When he spotted his chance, he picked up Scott's favorite board, threw it on top of the water, and paddled out into the surf.

Jordan watched as the man propelled himself through the water on his belly like a pro. It didn't take long for him to find the perfect tube, and popped up on the board, weaving his way through the water. He glided over the waves with some skill, keeping his balance for the longest time before dropping into the wave. When the ride ended, she turned her attention back to Hutton. To entertain Dog the two began to roll a ball back and forth over the sand. When that grew tiresome, Jordan showed Hutton how to use a small scoop to push the sand around. This seemed to hold her interest. By the time Nick plopped down on the blanket next to them, they'd finished building their fourth sandcastle, a fragile fortress waiting for the next wave to come along and obliterate it into mush. The first time the water charged up and ruined her afternoon's work, Hutton had cried, but by the third effort, she pretty much took the damage in stride.

"What are you making there, Blondie?" Nick asked, as he tugged on the cute little pink beach hat she wore covering her head. Her big blue eyes, so like Scott's, locked on his with such trust the look humbled him. In baby-speak, Hutton proceeded to describe her work. Covered in sand from head to toe, she looked like a grubby cherub. But she also looked as though she was having the time of her life. As Hutton turned back to her sand project, something caught his eye out over the glistening water. It looked like a dot of land in the distance, north of where he'd surfed. "What is that?"

Jordan squinted, putting her hand over her eyes to shade out the sun. "Oh. That's Treasure Island." When she caught his baffled look, she laughed. "No kidding. That's what Scott nicknamed it when he was a kid. He used to explore that little dot of land out there. He kept a dinghy inside the sea cave over there so he could make trips back and forth." She pointed to a dark cavern-like entrance at the base of the trail that he'd missed until now. "The dinghy's still there." When she saw Nick's eyes widen, she added, "Well, not the one he had when he was a boy, of course, but rather a newer version, one with a nice double hull, and a seven-horsepower motor."

"A real island?" Now that he hadn't known. Scott had never mentioned Treasure Island to him before. But it sounded like every twelve-year-old boy's fantasy to be able to explore an island of his very own. "What's it doing there?"

"One of a chain, I guess. The tip is all that's left. It's more rock than anything, but there's some vegetation on this side. I haven't been out there since…" Her mind drifted to another day just after they'd bought the place.

Scott had shown her around and then made a point of taking her out in the dinghy to explore the island. They'd made love there. It might have been where they'd conceived Hutton. At that moment Hutton squealed at something Dog did and Jordan snapped back to the present. "You should motor out there one day. Take some time to look around. It's worth the trip. Just north of that little dot of land is where the shipwreck's located."

He might just do that, he thought, as he glanced at Jordan. She'd mentioned Scott's name without looking like she wanted to cry. It was a first. But she'd been lost there for a moment in her own thoughts.

"You looked like you were having fun out there today. Surfing. You're pretty good."

"The surf's great here. You should take a turn."

"I haven't surfed in more than two years. Not since we first moved in. I'd probably kill myself now."

"It's like riding a bike, you never forget how. Go ahead, have some fun, I'll watch Hutton."

"Thanks, maybe another time."

He frowned. "You need to have some fun, Jordan. When's the last time you got out?"

"I get out every day."

"I mean for fun. Once you open this place up for business, you'll be swamped through the summer. You need to have some fun now before you're so busy with guests you can't see straight."

That night, as she got Hutton ready for bed, Jordan pondered Nick's words. How long had it been since she'd gone anywhere just for fun? Three months earlier, she'd gone home to San Francisco for Christmas and to celebrate Hutton's first birthday. But she didn't think that's what Nick had been talking about. The last time she'd gone out was the night before Scott had deployed for Iraq. They'd gone to the boardwalk in Santa Cruz for dinner. They hadn't had much money to splurge, but they'd played games in the arcade, walked along the boardwalk, and then eaten dinner on the wharf. They'd made love that night for the last time. Funny, when they'd been in bed together, she had never once thought it would be for the very last time. How was a person supposed to know something like that would be the last time? She'd been pregnant with Hutton then, just barely. Scott had been ecstatic at the prospect of becoming a father. He'd told her at least a dozen times before his deployment not to worry, that he'd be back in six months. So much for optimism.

When she realized Hutton's bath water had turned stone cold, she picked her up out of the water, wrapping her in a towel. And saw Nick standing in the doorway. "Anything I can do?"

Unlike last night, he hadn't felt the need to run into town. And he hadn't felt like staying cooped up in that studio apartment watching a snowy Lakers game. So he'd wandered over here to the main house to see if they might need him for story duty. A guy could hope. What was it about these two that drew him in?

Glad for the interruption to her thoughts, Jordan gave him a shy smile and said, "She'll be ready for a story after I get her PJs on, how about that?"

He grinned. "Sure. We were just getting to the good part the other night when you whisked her off to bed." He watched how expertly Jordan diapered Hutton and had her dressed in lightning-fast precision. The minute the last snap caught, however, Hutton popped up like a jack-in-the-box as if she'd found her second wind.

"She doesn't look tired," Nick commented, as he watched the child in whirlwind fashion toddle over to the bookshelf to pick out her favorite story books.

Knowing the bedtime drill, Hutton gathered up as many as she could carry at one time and followed her mother into the living room. Nick trailed after both as did Dog. Taking a seat on the sofa, he got comfortable. It took Hutton all of two seconds to crawl onto his lap the minute he sat down as if she'd already gotten into the routine. She opened up the first book about a lost kitty cat. With Hutton on his lap and Dog curled at his feet, for the next thirty minutes, Nick read half a dozen story books.

After the last one, Jordan announced, "Okay that's it, time for bed. Let's go get Mr. Bear. Say night-night, Hutton." "Night-night," Hutton repeated as her mother scooped her up and quickly headed into the bedroom.

After they'd left the room, through the baby monitor, Nick sat mesmerized by the tender scene unfolding across the hall. He heard Hutton making little baby noises. He listened as Jordan spoke in a soft tone, putting her daughter down for the night, telling her another story about how Mr. Bear was tired and sleepy.

It hit him then like a punch to the gut. He'd given up his whirlwind, carefree life in L.A. to go to war. In two short years his life had changed dramatically. Even when he'd returned to his job months after being wounded, he'd failed to recapture that single carefree existence. Even though he'd tried. He'd gone to the same parties as before with the same people, tried dating some of the same kinds of women who'd before given him such pleasure. He'd tried to pick up his life from before. But nothing he'd done since getting back had brought him any kind of peace or joy.

Until now.

When Jordan got back to the living room, she realized she didn't want him to leave. A bit nervous, she tried to think of something to say. "I've got a bottle of wine from the Alexander Valley. Would you like a glass? It might help you sleep."

"Sounds good." He trailed after her into the kitchen. "Let me help."

"Then pop the cork." She handed him a corkscrew and pulled the wine out of the cooler. He worked the bottle open, pouring two glasses of chardonnay.

They took their wine back into the living room. As Jordan got comfortable on the sofa, Nick laid a fire. As soon as the logs caught, Nick turned to her and said, "I've been thinking, I guess I could have handled things better at McCready's."

"Knowing the town like I do, it wasn't your fault. I admit I made a big deal out of nothing. And just the other day I ran into Sissy at the store. She made me so mad I wanted to spit. She made me feel so...like a failure."

"Why, because daddy's handed her everything she ever wanted all her life? You shouldn't let her get to you or make you feel bad. She's probably never had to overcome anything in her life."

Jordan smiled. "Scott said almost exactly the same thing when I complained about her to him. At one time during high school I think she'd convinced herself Scott would marry her."

Nick's eyes grew wide. "I couldn't imagine going through married life listening to that voice of hers." He mimicked her line from the bar. "'I've just been dying to go for a ride on a Harley.'"

Jordan laughed, thinking of Sissy's squeaky voice. "I thought it was just me. We are so mean."

"Hardly. Something tells me that woman wrote the book."

"Murphy said she once got so drunk at the bank Christmas party she started counting on her fingers who was sleeping with whom and naming names."

"That sounds like good old Sissy. How'd it all end up?"

"A fight broke out between Sally Peterson and Adele Simpson over Drake Simpson who'd also been fooling around with Ginger Hampton, a stylist and tattoo artist at the Snip 'N Curl."

"Come on, you're making that up."

She crossed her fingers over her heart and held up her right hand. "Nope. Someone knocked over the punch bowl and a food fight ensued. It happened at the community room at the church. You can ask around if you don't believe me."

He grinned. "I'll take your word for it."

"I've been thinking about Lilly and the kids. There's so much to do out here, I think it's time to make her an offer, maybe part-time at first and then add more hours when we open. I think she'd be a real asset. And she can bring the kids with her while she works."

"Then do it."

"There's a problem. I'm pretty sure she'd have to give up her subsidy from the county. What if she gives that up and The Cove turns out to be a bust."

He gave her a sad look. "Come on Jordan, you don't really believe that. Turning this house into a B & B is a terrific idea. We just have to make it happen. And we're doing that every day." He ticked off several fingers. "First, you have beach access. Second, you offer comfortable, spacious rooms. Throw in meals that many hotel restaurants only dream about serving. Third, you offer the only place to stay within a seventy-five-mile radius. You'll make it work, we'll make it work."

"How is it you always know the right thing to say to me? Thanks." She took a sip of wine, licked her lips. "I think that baby carrier for the bike is a good idea. The guests can always use it if they bring their toddlers with them. How about we see if we can pick one up in town tomorrow?"

"If Ferguson's doesn't have one, we'll go into Santa Cruz."

"Or order one online. It feels wonderful to have someone to talk to. I'm so glad you're here, Nick."

For the first time in a long time he felt as if he belonged somewhere. Here in this house, with Jordan and Hutton. He looked at Jordan over his wine glass, their eyes locked. He said softly, "I am too."

She thought she might drown in those lake-blue eyes of his. She forced herself to look away. Glancing at Dog curled up by the fire asleep, Jordan announced, "I suppose we need to take Dog for his shots. I'll call the vet in the morning, see if he can work us in."

"I'd forgotten about that. I'll take him. Do we need to get him..." He winced, "Uh, neutered?"

Jordan smiled. "Probably." She lifted her glass. "Here's to being a responsible dog owner, which I know you are or you wouldn't have brought it up. Right?"

Nick glanced sympathetically over at Dog whose head popped up as if he knew the subject concerned his immediate future. "Maybe he's too young for that." Nick suggested, hopefully.

"Maybe. But we won't know until Doc Sullivan tells us. Either way, it's the right thing to do."

"I'm sincerely sorry, Dog," Nick said, wincing.

Sitting in front of the cozy fire, drinking a glass of wine, talking as though they'd known each other for years, Nick thought the atmosphere needed something. Glancing at the piano, he asked, "How about some music?"

"The stereo's located under the television, plenty of CDs to choose from. Or we could listen to the radio. The station out of Santa Cruz comes in pretty clear most nights."

And she would know that, thought Nick, as he tried to picture all the lonely nights she must have spent here alone with only the baby for company and before that...total solitude. "I was thinking of something else. Can you play that thing?" he asked good-naturedly, as he pointed to the piano in the corner.

"Six years of lessons three days a week after school," she responded, amused. She got up and went over to the old upright piano, sat down. Making an exaggerated production out of every movement, she wiggled her fingers before flexing them again and then cracked her knuckles. She stretched out her arms, and then paused over the keys for dramatic flair. She started laughing at her own theatrics, which brought laughter from Nick.

"Are you going to play that thing or weave a spell?"

"I'm nervous."

"You're kidding."

She touched the keys, began playing chopsticks before moving lightning fast into the rhythm of Beethoven's Moonlight Sonata. She played on through the stormy finish and then just as quickly shifted gears into a lively rendition of Elton John's I'm Still Standing. When she stopped, she blew out a breath.

Nick noticed tears in her eyes. Damn, that had come out of the blue. "Jordan."

She shook her head. "I haven't played since before Hutton was born. It was…I played a lot when I was pregnant and alone and sitting here feeling sorry for myself and…waiting, and…"

"I get it." He swallowed. He couldn't help it; he opened his arms, and said, "Come here, baby."

She didn't even think, but moved to the sofa and into his arms. She began apologizing, "I'm sorry. Playing just brought back so many memories. When I was alone it used to be therapeutic, but…now… I know that sounds silly."

"You have every right to feel that way." He turned her to face him. Her head fell back on his shoulder. He inhaled the fragrance of her hair and smelled vanilla. When he looked down her big brown eyes locked on his. "I'm sorry. I didn't know."

"Of course, you didn't."

The urge to kiss her overwhelmed him. But the minute he leaned in, she suddenly got up and walked over to the entertainment center, and began flipping through a stack of CDs in the drawer until she found the one she wanted. "I have a CD I bought a couple of months ago." She slid the disk into the stereo. Teddy Thompson's lilting voice filled the room. His haunting, moving melody, *Change of Heart*, drifted from the speakers. She held out her hand. "Dance with me, Nick."

Nick sucked in a breath, got up, and closed the distance to where she stood. He slipped his arms around her and they began to move slowly. Instinctively, he brought her arms up to drape around his neck, while his gathered her in closer.

Feeling his hands on her had her heart racing as it hadn't in two years. Nick holding her like this, touching her like this seemed...so right. She followed his lead around the room as they circled the floor in each other's arms. The beat changed slightly and he let go long enough to dip her to the side and then back again before drawing her even closer than before. He brought one of her clasped hands to his mouth, and gently placed a kiss there. The song shifted to Touching Home. They began moving again, one trip around the room, then another, body to body.

Jordan danced, eyes closed, in a dreamy fog. Being held in his arms felt like heaven. She imagined them stretched out together, her snuggling up to him in bed as they lay side by side. If she moved just so, leaned into him a little more... She nuzzled her head into his neck.

Just as she'd hoped, he brought his mouth down to fit with hers. Their tongues met for that first taste of each other. The playful tag went in and out until he sank deeper into the kiss. Jordan dove down with him, melting against his body while his tongue invaded, tasted, and savored.

Caught up, lost in the scorching heat and arousal, Jordan felt Nick's hands drop lower to her rear, dragging her up against his erection. Wanting to feel all of him, she lost herself in the stormy heat, matching him burn for burn. His fingers roamed to her breast and began to rub and knead until the nipple pebbled to a hard knob.

It had been so long since anyone had made her feel wanted, needed. Jordan let out a low moan.

The sound brought Nick to his senses. And she was trembling. All at once, he let her go.

Her bubble burst. Where warm, wet lips had been, there was empty air. Through lingering lust she saw him take a step backward, away from her, then a few more steps in retreat, leaving them standing a good two feet apart. While they stared at each other, an upbeat song began to play in the background.

"Nick..."

"It's getting late, I... I need to go. Uh, you know we still need to order the drywall and insulation from Ferguson's, right?"

Through clenched teeth she managed to spit out, "Fine. We can take care of that after the vet appointment."

"Good. Then I'll see you in the morning. We'll get an early start."

She watched him disappear down the hallway and listened as the back door slammed shut behind him. With a sigh, she walked over to the stereo and shut off the music. For a while she stared into the dying fire then turned out the lights and reluctantly headed to bed feeling incredibly stupid and let down.

How could she have allowed herself to think a man like that would be interested in her? And she'd been all over him. And...wait a minute. Her brain started backtracking over the scene. He'd been so hard he'd all but busted out of his jeans.

She sighed and closed her eyes. For a few minutes she imagined that hardness moving inside her, filling her.

Disappointed in him, in herself, she went into her bedroom without turning on the light. Instead, she sat down on the bed trying to get thoughts of Nick out of her head. When she looked up she caught her reflection in the dresser mirror. Despite the darkness and the shadows, she could see her lips were swollen, tender from his smoldering mouth on hers. And the way he'd touched her breast. Closing her eyes, she knew one thing.

She wanted Nick.

Getting up from the bed she went to the drawer that held the box with Scott's letters, the last link she had to him. Hugging the box to her chest, she walked to the closet, kissed the box, and pushed it to the back of the shelf. Rubbing the tears from her cheeks she said out loud, "I loved you Scott with all my heart. I can't believe you're gone so soon. But, it's hard being alone all the time. It's time... I let you go."

She shed her clothes, and crawled into bed with tears still streaming down her face and cried herself to sleep.

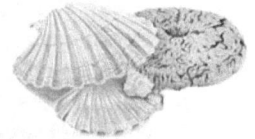

Chapter Ten

When Jordan walked into the kitchen carrying Hutton on her hip at six-thirty, she saw Nick standing at the counter whipping up batter in a bowl. The shadows under his eyes told her he hadn't slept any better than she had. Good, she thought, sourly. Serves him right for being such an ass.

"Morning, ladies," he said as if he were perfectly okay with not having had sex with her the night before. "There's coffee. Waffles okay?"

So, they weren't going to mention their dancing glued to each other, or having their tongues down each other's throats, or him getting her taut nipples to pebble, or his rock-hard erection.

She slipped Hutton into her high chair and went to the refrigerator to pour milk for her sippy cup. She decided she was savvy enough to play it just as cool as he. "Waffles sound delicious." Were they going to discuss drywall and insulation now? she wondered. She poured a cup of coffee and watched as he filled the waffle iron with batter, closed the lid.

They stood there in strained silence until Nick blurted out, "You're a good kisser."

That sent coffee flying out of her mouth. "Gosh, you could've fooled me. The way you ran out of the room, I was pretty sure I hadn't measured up to your player standards."

Okay, she was still pissed he thought as he tore off a paper towel and handed it to her to wipe up the coffee she'd spewed. And who could blame her? He hadn't been that inept since junior high. But everything inside him kept reminding him this was too important, that Jordan was too important to screw this up. "Get real. You think this is easy for me?"

"Easy? I've got news for you, Nick, nothing about you is easy."

He ran his hands through his hair in frustration before turning back to the waffle iron, where he scooped out a steaming crisp cake which he handed off to Jordan to cool for Hutton's breakfast. "Look, I'm not stupid, Jordan. I can see plain as day you aren't ready. You think I don't see how the light goes out of your eyes every time you mention his name."

She stopped cutting up Hutton's waffle and stared at him. "Is that the truth, Nick? You left last night because you don't think I'm ready to move on, is that it?" When Hutton became impatient for her breakfast, she turned back to pour a light dabble of syrup over the baby's waffle and slice an apple to go with it.

"I know you aren't." After serving up two more cakes he sat down at the table and looked up at her. "It's okay. That kiss was rushing you." And should he mention that he had no business being attracted to Scott's widow in the first place.

She sighed and placed her hand over his. "That's for me to decide, don't you think?"

"Yeah, it is. But you don't quite pull off the act."

She bit her lip, reluctant to admit how he must have read her body language in order to pick up on something like that. But was he right? Was she that far from moving on? Scott had been dead almost a year. But he'd been gone for almost two. And she was so tired of being alone. "And how much time are you willing to give me, Nick?"

He reached to tuck a strand of hair behind her ear. "I'm no saint here, Jordan. But I'd be lying if I denied being attracted to you."

That really didn't answer her question. Sometimes you just had to go with your instincts. So she sucked in a breath and moved into his space, took his face in her hands then kissed him softly on the mouth. "You aren't real happy about this, are you, Nick? Being attracted to me."

So she saw through that much of his façade. "I'm a bad bet, Jordan."

"Why is that?"

How could he begin to list all his problems for her? She had a kid. Problems of her own to deal with. She didn't need him screwing up her life any more than it already was. "Let's just say I never should've kissed you and leave it at that."

"Wow, Nick! That's so flattering. How many times have you ignored your attraction to someone? How many times were you able to do that?" She held up a hand. "No, don't answer that. I don't want to know. You're flat out wrong about one thing, though." She didn't wait for his response but moved right on to make her point. "You didn't just kiss me. We danced. We made out..." *Until you got cold feet and ran.* "But why don't you ignore that part, too. And you're forgetting something, Nick, something important to me. I kissed you back. With a vengeance. But you may have picked up on something about me not being ready, which unfortunately makes you a very special man in my book, picking up on it like that."

"No, I'm not. And it's best if you remember that. And I've never been patient with anyone, ever."

"Then maybe I'm not just anyone."

On the drive into town, Jordan sat in the passenger seat playing tour guide, pointing out various sights along the Coast Highway, at one point, showing him where a field full of wild strawberries grew in abundance. "We'll be able to pick strawberries there in a couple of months. And they call that point over there, Smuggler's Point, which used to be the name of the town back in the 1800s because it was originally founded by smugglers who used that area to unload their bounty, rendezvous, and sell their goods."

"You're just full of useful information."

"Useless, you mean. And don't think I don't know you're making fun of me. But Pelican Pointe doesn't exactly offer a wealth of cool places to visit. I'm doing my best to play concierge with what limited points of interest I have at my disposal."

"I find it odd that the town was founded by smugglers. How do the snooty townspeople handle that?"

"They ignore it." She shot him a knowing smile before suggesting, "Once we get there maybe we should split up. You know, you take the dog to the vet and I'll go to Ferguson's, and then swing by Murphy's, pick up some milk and eggs."

He knew what she was doing. "You don't want to be seen in town together. That might jump start the rumor mill."

Her jaw dropped. "Is that what you think? Not at all, I wasn't..." She looked over at him and twisted up her mouth. "Maybe a little" She threw back her shoulders. "I don't care what the town thinks."

"That a girl. I think we should stay together, show them we don't give a hang what they think of either of us. If the vet visit runs long, then we'll talk about getting things done separately. How's that?"

"Sounds like a plan."

Minutes later, Jordan directed him to a renovated two-story Craftsman-style house that served as both a residence and the Pelican Pointe Animal Clinic. Located a block off Main on Crescent Street, where houses more often than not doubled as both residential dwellings and their owners' small businesses. The Sullivan house was no exception. The 1940s style house wore its pastel-blue paint job like a bright happy Easter egg nestled on a bed of plastic green grass. The home reflected the personality of its owners.

Bran Sullivan had been ready to retire for three years since he turned sixty-two. But he was the only vet within a fifty mile radius and he not only loved animals, but he also enjoyed working with his receptionist, Joy, who also happened to be his wife of thirty-six years. It was no hardship for him to continue taking care of the town's animals while working out of his house, and closing the doors to go fishing every now and again when the mood struck him.

Joy, a plump, green-eyed woman with red, graying hair whose disposition reflected her name, sat behind an old beat-up desk, holding a tiny kitten. She eyed the bundle of puppy in Nick's arms and greeted the couple with an overzealous innate style. "New client, right? I can always tell a newcomer. Fill out this form and have a seat. As I told you over the phone Bran's a little busy this morning but we'll work you in."

A little busy? Jordan looked around the room at the various pet owners sitting squeezed into the small ten by twelve waiting area where every chair was taken. There were several cats, a few dogs, a pot-bellied pig and a sick-looking hamster still penned in its cage.

With Jordan holding Hutton, Nick set the puppy on the floor at his feet while he filled out the form. But when he got to the line that asked for the pet's name, he leaned over to Jordan and whispered in her ear, "I think we're going to need to come up with a real name other than Dog. I don't feel right putting that down. Hutton can still call him Dog, but the little guy needs a real name, don't you think?"

The wistful look on his face didn't escape Jordan. She tried to be helpful. "How about Sam or Ollie?"

"Ollie?"

"I once had a cat with that name when I was five."

"That's fine for a cat, but a dog needs a good strong name... How about Quake?"

"Why Quake?" She looked baffled, but could tell he'd given this some thought.

"He sort of quakes whenever he pees and gets in trouble for it."

Jordan looked at the man's face. That look of longing held steady. He'd never had a dog before and this was his opportunity to name one. "Quake it is then."

He finished filling out the form, handed it back to Joy. "Do you think we could go run a few errands and come back later?"

Joy's smile grew wider. "Now, there's a good idea. In fact give him a good two hours and the crowd should be cleared out by then."

Nick nodded. He went back to where Jordan stood with Hutton in her arms and laughed out loud when he saw her trying to corral the dog with her feet and legs much like you would a soccer ball, but without the kicking. When she saw him laugh, she leaned over to explain so no one else would hear. "I didn't want him getting too close to the other animals, especially that sick-looking terrier just in case they've got parvo."

"Good idea," he whispered back. Although he didn't think there was much danger to the dog, Nick picked up Quake just in time to prevent him from wandering too close to the overfriendly, but much larger chocolate lab.

He threw a thumb back over his shoulder at Joy. "She says it's okay if we come back later."

"Great. There's no room to sit down anyway." Once they got outside, Jordan took hold of Nick's arm and pointed him toward the car. "Let's get Hutton's stroller out of the back. We can leave the car here and walk over to Ferguson's."

It didn't escape Nick's notice that she'd grabbed his arm, a gesture that said to hell with what the town thought about them.

From the window of the Snip 'N Curl, Sissy and her hairdresser, Janie Pointer watched as Nick and Jordan took their time walking along Main Street—like a couple. "They make a nice little family," Janie pointed out, as she tried to coax Sissy back into the chair away from the window so she could finish the monthly bleach job on Sissy's hair. But Sissy didn't budge. She stared at the couple, for some reason, envious. As she watched Jordan push the stroller past the beauty shop and Nick walk beside her with the puppy on a leash, she asked Janie, "Why is that good-looking stud of a guy interested in the stuffy house frau?"

"Honey, how long have you known men? Some like hot sauce, some like plain fare. There's no rhyme or reason to their tastes."

"That's bullshit. I can't believe Scott married her. She doesn't belong here, Janie." And now without doing a single thing, Jordan had another good-looking man interested in her. A man who seemed to have fallen under her spell just as Scott had. Jordan's luck with men didn't sit well with Sissy.

Janie, a tattooed woman pushing forty, threw back her black hair and laughed, "From what I've heard she won't be here for long. Even if she does get that place open on time, there's no guarantee she'll be able to keep it going by herself. She still has a long row to hoe if you ask me."

The hope that Jordan might still fail got Sissy back in the chair where Janie once again grabbed foil and began dabbing lightener on Sissy's dark roots.

On their walk down Main Street Jordan spotted a poster in one of the store windows and pointed it out to Nick. "I forgot about the street fair. There'll be carnival rides, a parade and plenty of food booths. We should plan to go." She remembered going last year with her sister when Hutton had been just three months old. They'd had fun looking at the homemade arts and crafts. Then all of a sudden, her shoulders slumped. "I should've been open by now. If I'd planned a little better, the street fair would have brought in guests sooner. If I were already opened, already had guests coming in for the street fair, I wouldn't be cutting things so close now."

"Maybe. Maybe not. Stop beating yourself up. Tourist season doesn't begin for real until June. You're getting a jump by opening in May a full month beforehand. Think of it that way."

She looked up at him as they strolled through the double doors of Ferguson's. He looked as relaxed as she'd ever seen him, well except for when he'd been playing with her nipple. The Cove seemed to be agreeing with him. "Thanks, Nick. You always know what to say, how to make me feel like—I'm not such a failure."

When a new lighting display caught her eye, she turned to touch the glittering crystals of a chandelier. But then, so did Hutton. From her stroller she made a grab for the same display. Luckily, Jordan caught her daughter's hand right before she latched on to a very breakable and expensive, light fixture.

Noticing the sudden save, Nick commented, "Nice reflexes, mom."

"Gotta have a lightning pair of hands."

"Which should we check out first, drywall or the insulation? Drywall, I think it's what we need to put the finishing touches on that hall bathroom. Then we get the estimate for the insulation." And putting down insulation would be a messy, dirty job, one he'd give anything to be able to hire out. Ah, well, he thought as he headed toward the back of the store.

It was true she'd gotten caught up in the shopping expedition but listening to him now, she needed to tell him how things were. After all, pride could only take you so far. She shouldn't be shopping for anything, not even the baby carrier for the bike. And insulation wasn't going to be cheap. She took a deep breath, looking around to see if anyone was close enough to hear and whispered, "Nick, it's like this... I haven't been able to pay anything on my account..."

Nick looked visibly pained. At that moment, he spotted Ferguson heading straight for them. He wondered if he had time to get Jordan and Hutton out of the store. But before he could act, Ferguson was getting closer. And a few seconds later, Jordan spotted the guy, too.

Remembering her overdue account, Jordan wanted to run and suddenly felt like such a loser.

"How are my two favorite customers this morning?" Ferguson asked in what sounded to her like an almost cheerful tone. Was this the same man who'd sent her threatening past due notices for the past four months? Funny, Jordan thought now, she hadn't gotten one of Ferguson's letters lately, which had her chewing at her lip.

"What can I do for you two today? Do you need to order more flooring? I can give you a better price this time around. And good news, there won't be a six-week wait."

Nick was afraid he knew where this conversation was headed. But before he could speak up, Jordan said, "We have enough flooring, thanks. Look Mr. Ferguson, I know I need to make a payment but if you could just be a little more patient with me..."

"No need for that now, this guy already brought your account current weeks ago."

Jordan's knees almost buckled. She turned to gape at Nick. "What is he talking about?"

"Jordan, it's no big deal. It's taken care of." Nick sent a go-to-hell look Ferguson's way just in time for the man to abandon ship.

"Well, I'll leave you two to sort this out. Don't forget we're having a sale on paint and wallpaper this week. Twenty-percent off."

When Ferguson was out of earshot, Jordan turned to Nick. "You shouldn't have done that. I appreciate everything you're doing but... Paying on my account is too much." She looked mortified, like she wanted to run out of the store and hide.

He wasn't about to let this ruin their morning. "Don't do this, okay? We had a heart-to-heart talk about your account the first day I came in here. I gave him a minimum payment and convinced him to extend the line of credit." Okay it wasn't exactly the truth, but he didn't want her to know the exact amount.

Jordan looked skeptical. She didn't want the whole town knowing about this. "Maybe we should head back to the vet's office. The waiting room might be cleared out by now."

Nick realized she was self-conscious. He could offer to pay for the baby seat, but that might just embarrass her even more. If he handled this right... "Tell you what, you take the dog, head back to the vet, I'll check on that insulation and drywall." He grinned, trying to make her feel better. "It shouldn't take long. I'll meet you there in ten minutes."

"Nick, why don't we forgo the insulation and the other stuff? I don't want to run up my tab here."

He took a different tack. "Then let me handle this. You can pay me back first chance you get."

"I can't let you do that."

"Jordan, are we friends?"

"I'd like to think so."

"Okay then. I want to do this."

Vickie McKeehan

"But… What if…?"

"I believe in what you're doing. Think of it as an investment. You'll pay me back. I'm not worried."

Jordan bit her lip again, clearly not at all comfortable with the prospect of owing him money. "But…"

"No buts. I want to do it." The look on her face said he needed to work an angle, so he changed tactics yet again. "Look, you're providing me with employment and a place to stay. I haven't felt this good about myself in a long time. Before I came here I'd tried…a lot to work out my…issues. You have no idea how much it means to me to feel…better about things." More than she'd ever know.

"Really?"

"It's true. Think how much I would've spent on therapy to feel this much better."

"Okay, I'll let you pay but only if you consider it a loan and put it in writing, like a contract. The money we spend today will be added to the total of your investment. Deal?" She held out her hand.

He smiled and took her hand in his. "Deal. Now, let's go see if we can find that baby carrier."

An hour later, they walked out of Ferguson's together heading for the vet's. Nick had enjoyed every minute watching the expression on Ferguson's face when they'd ordered the insulation and drywall and arranged for delivery. If anyone six months ago had told him he'd get such a kick out of spending money on such things he'd have called them crazy. Yet, what he'd told Jordan was absolutely true. He hadn't felt this good in too long to remember. And that was worth something.

At the vet's, Doc Sullivan recognized Quake from the Bronson's litter of puppies eleven weeks earlier, which meant that Quake was still a little too young to get neutered. But he did get his shots and his ID chip. Because the poor dog reminded Jordan of how Hutton looked after getting her shots, they dropped him off at the car for a little nap. They left the window rolled down on the car where he could get plenty of fresh air while Nick treated them to lunch at the Hilltop Diner.

They walked into a busy, noisy lunch crowd. And once again, found there was no place to sit, not an available chair in the entire place. Just when they were ready to turn around and leave, they spotted Murphy in one of the booths waving them over where he was eating with Carla Vargas, the social worker. As soon as Nick and Jordan made their way over to the table, Carla, a stylish, petite woman in her early forties with olive skin and coal-black hair she wore clipped back off her face, got up from her side of the table to slide in beside Murphy, who introduced Carla to Nick.

"Have a seat. We've already ordered but Eileen will be along with our food any minute now and you can tell her what you want," Murphy told them amicably.

Jordan motioned to Nick they needed a high chair for Hutton and he went to retrieve one from the stack next to the cashier. Jordan settled Hutton into a high chair while Nick slid in ahead of her in the booth giving her the outside seat so that she could deal with the baby. About that time Eileen Faraday, wearing a hot-pink waitress uniform, set two steaming plates of food in front of Murphy and Carla. Automatically, she grabbed two menus, and handed them to Nick and Jordan. "What can I get you two to drink?"

"I'll have iced tea."

"Make it two," Nick added as he picked up his menu.

"How's it going, Jordan? Murphy tells me it's just a matter of time before we've got us a bed and breakfast in the area," Carla said, as she dug into the Tuesday special, two cheesy enchiladas with rice and beans.

"Nick's been working like a fiend. He's made so much progress in such a short amount of time I think we might actually pull it off."

Carla glanced up from her plate long enough to notice the look on Jordan's face. The woman radiated with happiness for the first time since she'd known her. Was there something going on between these two? she wondered, as she took a sip of her tea. Carla had heard about Nick's encounter at McCready's as well as the other gossip around town. But a blind woman could pick up on the vibes passing between them. She wondered if Nick even realized how his eyes lit up any time he glanced over at Jordan.

Smiling Murphy added, "That's good news. You two make a terrific team."

Nick noticed Jordan's cheeks redden. He wondered if she might be thinking about last night and how they had gone after each other without much effort. God, how he had wanted her. It had taken everything in him to walk out of that living room without taking her to bed. Looking over at her now, as the sun drifted through the front windows and settled in her hair making it glisten golden, his heart did a funny lurch.

"You fish, Nick?"

"Been a long time," Nick said, trying to get his mind off the way Jordan's body had felt up against his.

"We're taking Wade's boat out this weekend, fishing for surf perch and striper, maybe some cod. You're welcome to join us."

"You should go, Nick," Jordan urged. "It'd be good for you to get out, take some time off from the brutal schedule you've been keeping."

"I really need to finish a couple of the bathrooms before taking time off."

"It's a standing offer. If you don't make it this weekend, we'll go again, but probably not until after we put the street fair behind us. You guys are coming, right?"

Nick looked at Jordan, who was scanning the menu and didn't answer him. Nick gave Murphy a safe answer. "Probably."

Jordan thought about Lilly and the question nagging at the back of her mind. She wanted to offer Lilly a job. But if she had to give up her county assistance and the job didn't work out, what then? She decided to play what-if with Carla and get her answers here and now. Without giving away anything about Lilly, she danced around the issue and presented a what-if scenario to Carla. She listened as Carla verified what Jordan had feared. If Lilly took a job at The Cove, she'd forfeit collecting her subsidy.

Eileen came back to take their order while they kept up a steady chatter about the upcoming street fair. They watched Carla and Murphy finish off their enchiladas and Hutton chew through several packets of saltine crackers before she began to get restless. Even Nick recognized when it was time for the baby's nap. Hutton began to fuss and Jordan turned to Nick telling him, "I'm sorry, but I think she's about ready for a nap."

"Do we need to get the food to-go?"

Considering how long it had been since she'd seen the inside of a restaurant, she so wanted to stay, even if it was just the Hilltop. "If it's okay I'd like to try to get through lunch. Maybe she'll settle down when the food gets here." She dug in the diaper bag for the sippy cup filled with apple juice. Hutton liked the juice and that seemed to buy them some time.

Thankfully, Eileen appeared with their food, the Tuesday special for Nick and a club sandwich with fries for Jordan which she immediately shared with Hutton.

While Murphy stopped to talk to Margie, the owner, and pay the check, Carla hung back, putting her hand on Jordan's shoulder. "It's good to see you looking so well, Jordan." To Nick, she winked and said, "Keep up the good work, Nick. Maybe I can talk Murphy into springing for a romantic weekend once you open up." And with that, she turned to meet up with Murphy at the counter.

From the booth by the window, Nick and Jordan watched the couple walk hand in hand across the street until Nick said flatly, "I didn't see that coming." He looked every bit like a man hooked on a big dose of small town gossip. Chomping at the prospect of a rumor, he added, "That sly, old fox."

"Who'd have thought Murphy and Carla as a couple? I didn't know. The social worker from Santa Cruz. Comes to town every now and then to check up on a couple of families in the area who've had some domestic violence issues. I didn't even know they knew each other. Come to think of it, I wondered where she stayed whenever she'd come to town for a couple of days."

Nick laughed. "Mystery solved."

They ate their meal quickly, trying to anticipate Hutton's changing mood. The meal could have been tense but was anything but. When Hutton grew crankier and louder, in public no less, Jordan simply scooped her daughter up out of the high chair, cuddling her close making a kind of game out of her cross mood until they left the restaurant and got back to the car.

On the ride home, Hutton fell asleep and didn't wake up even when Nick lifted her out of her car seat as if he'd been handling her since birth. Jordan stood back and watched, impressed. As he carried Hutton into the house she followed him into the nursery. When they got to the crib, Nick waited patiently as Jordan removed the baby's shoes as if they'd put her down as a team many times before today. She let Nick do the honors of gently laying her in the crib.

It was the first time in his life, he'd ever put a baby down for a nap. The gesture felt a little awkward, but after watching Jordan, he felt he could handle it. As he stepped back from the bed, he watched as her little puckered mouth made sucking motions in her sleep. He took a deep breath and noticed Jordan's astonished stare. He shrugged. "I've watched you enough." They backed out of the room, Jordan shaking her head, while Nick felt a contentment he'd never known existed.

While Hutton slept, he unloaded the car and busied himself removing the baseboards from the upstairs bathroom where he intended to replace the drywall. As he pried loose the rotted wood, he considered their morning together. Even when Hutton had gotten cranky, her crying hadn't bothered him. In fact, he couldn't remember the last time he'd enjoyed shopping with a woman and doing such ordinary things.

But what would happen when Jordan found out he'd known Scott? That would ruin everything. His lies would surface and she'd look at him different then, for sure.

As he finished gutting the bathroom and cleaning up the mess, bagging the debris to take out to the trash pile, he decided not to think about it. He wouldn't think about Scott not when he couldn't stop thinking about getting Jordan into bed, couldn't stop thinking about how she'd felt against him. Jordan was unlike any woman he'd ever known. She had a sweet disposition, a bubbly, upbeat attitude in spite of the year she'd had. And she was a good mother who seemed to have an instinctive gentle temperament with Hutton.

On his way to the trash pile behind the garage, he spotted the box containing the baby carrier sitting beside the SUV. After dumping the trash, on impulse, he dug out one of the bikes from the garage. Slitting open the box he spread everything out on the driveway and began to assemble the baby seat. After getting the device together, he started attaching the seat to the back of the bike.

As soon as Jordan emerged from the house she noticed right off, he'd attached the baby seat to the man's bicycle. Trailed by Quake, Jordan stood on the back porch and watched him put the final screws into the bike seat.

He looked up and saw her standing on the porch. Their eyes locked. The man who'd bedded more than his share of women wanted to tell her how much he'd enjoyed their day in town together doing nothing particularly adventurous, certainly mundane, but the insecure man who felt like he didn't deserve her wasn't exactly sure how to say what he felt. So, he simply sent her a grin before turning his attention back to the bike, keeping his head down until he'd secured the baby carrier in place. He tested his work.

By this time Jordan had closed the distance between them and stood a few feet away.

"What do you think?"

"I think I'm lucky you were looking for work."

That had him glancing back up, meeting her eyes. Those eyes stayed locked on his. While desire danced in his lower belly, something else nagged around his heart. Lust he more than recognized. But this woman made him feel something else, something no other woman had ever touched. Warmth spread inside like a leisurely drift into sunshine. He forced himself to turn back to his task. He began picking up his tools and saw the baby helmet still in the box. He opened the carton, held it up. "Look at this. I can't believe they make one of these things so small. When she wakes up we're all set to take her for a spin."

Nick had no way of knowing Jordan's thoughts were riding so close to his own. Feelings she thought were dead and buried with Scott whirled in her head, in her heart, in her belly. The man was slowly breaking down every barrier of grief she'd built for Scott. And in just a few short weeks. Where was her loyalty to him? How could she let another man into her heart so quickly? They're just thoughts, she reasoned. *I haven't jumped him in his sleep yet, have I?* She remembered their morning conversation. They were attracted to each other. They were consenting, mature adults. She'd already acknowledged she wanted him. How could she tell him she was closer to making that leap than he knew?

After all, what exactly was she supposed to feel when the man bought a baby carrier and put it on the back of a bicycle so he could take her daughter for a ride, so they could both go for a bike ride? She knew with certainty that he had never done such a thing for anyone else.

Despite riding a Harley, it had been a very long time since Nick Harris had ridden a nine-speed mountain bike. He wasn't even sure he could keep it upright without falling off, so he tried it out a couple of times, stopping and starting, before trusting himself enough to have Hutton on board. But the old adage that once you learn how to ride a bike you never forgot how turned out to be true. After Nick got Hutton strapped into the seat, after he made sure she got comfortable with the sway and give of the movement, he took off down the driveway. With Jordan following on her bike, they rode up and down the long drive from the garage down to the road.

Ten trips back and forth and Nick forgot all about bad dreams and war and forgot about how Scott had died and focused on Hutton's joy at riding on the back of the bike. He listened to Hutton's squeals of delight on the turns, listened to her clapping her little hands in sheer delight from the movement of the ride and the wind in her face.

As he pedaled along the driveway, he couldn't help but think that this was something every man should experience, this feeling akin to complete peace.

Was it possible Nick Harris had found his own piece of heaven right here?

Up on the hill overlooking the Phillips' property, Kent pulled his Seville into the clearing and shifted into PARK.

Before he'd even turned the key in the ignition Sissy crawled over the console and straddled his lap. Pulling up her skirt to reveal her bare butt, she landed a wet kiss on Kent's mouth complete with tongue down his throat. He pushed the seat back, unzipped his trousers, and without preamble plunged into Sissy's moist heat. Their joining lasted all of three minutes and it was over. Breathing hard, they both righted their clothes before Sissy moved back to the passenger seat, flipped down the visor to check her hair and reapply her lipstick. Up to this point, they hadn't said a word to each other. But now as Kent packed himself back into his pants he stared out over the rise, and told her, "Ninety days, just ninety more days and this land will belong to Springer Development."

"Well now Kent honey, that sounds truly optimistic, but what if the bitch makes it. She's got that—new guy helping her out after all."

"Doesn't mean a damn. She isn't going to make it. Trust me on that. I've got a plan." And with that Kent proceeded to outline his agenda.

While Kent planned the demise of The Cove Bed and Breakfast, Jordan struggled with the decision on whether or not to hire Lilly. How could she ask the woman to give up the only income she counted on monthly to come to work at a fledgling bed and breakfast without any guarantees they'd make it? What if Sissy and everyone in town were right and she failed? She waffled back and forth daily with regularity. One day her thoughts soared over all the progress they were making and the next she'd wallow in self-doubt. All she knew for certain was that there were no guarantees and that Lilly needed a regular stable income. Was Jordan ready to be anyone's employer? It was a big step. And one she didn't take lightly.

The next morning Jordan got up and decided the only way to resolve the issue once and for all was to go see Lilly to find out how she felt. Knowing Lilly didn't have a phone she called Carla Vargas for exact directions to Lilly's trailer.

Later that morning she and Hutton headed off bearing gifts. Packed in the backseat she had put together a picnic basket full of fried chicken, mashed potatoes, macaroni and cheese, a bag of apples and pears, and for dessert, dark chocolate brownies. She'd timed her arrival for ten-forty-five, so that it coincided with an early lunch. She knew firsthand with toddlers it was best to get them fed and down for an afternoon nap as soon as possible.

Derek Stovall's land was less than a mile southeast of town. Jordan spotted Lilly's Escort before she saw the broken-down aluminum trailer about fifty yards off the road, well past the main house. As soon as she pulled up, the door of the trailer swung open as if Lilly had heard the car. Jordan watched as Lilly stepped out onto a few rickety boards that acted as a front stoop with Joey on her hip, her mouth wide with shock.

Jordan opened the car door and shot her a smile. "I'd have called to let you know I was dropping by but you don't have a phone." She tugged Hutton out of her car seat and set her down on the dirt path leading to the front door. Jordan reached back inside and pulled out the basket of goodies. Waving the basket, she added, "I hope you guys haven't eaten lunch yet."

"You found us out here?"

"It wasn't hard. I asked for directions," Jordan confided easily. But she noticed Lilly looked uncomfortable, embarrassed.

Without a word, Lilly stepped aside and made room for Jordan to get by. When she saw that Hutton was having trouble maneuvering around the rocks lining the way up to the steps, she set Joey back inside and went back for Hutton, carrying her through the doorframe. She stood there holding Hutton while Jordan looked around for a place to set down the basket. She spotted Kyra in the kitchen area sitting at a table with a coloring book. The little girl looked up and Jordan asked, "Anyone hungry?"

"Me," Kyra said clapping her hands.

No embarrassment there, Jordan thought as she set the basket down and began unloading the food, setting out a thermos of lemonade, and paper plates. "Good. I've got cold fried chicken and macaroni and cheese." She purposefully made her eyes go big as she leaned down and whispered to Kyra, "And brownies for dessert."

"Yay brownies," Kyra shouted, clapping her hands again.

"But first we eat chicken," Jordan suggested.

Turning to take Hutton out of Lilly's arms, she stared into the woman's big green eyes and saw tears glistening in the corners. "I just can't believe you brought lunch, and came out here to see us."

She placed a hand on Lilly's thin shoulder. "That's what friends do, Lilly. In fact after we eat, there's something I need to talk to you about."

As they spread the feast out on the table, Jordan noted the trailer's small kitchen was spotless and smelled of disinfectant. There wasn't a dirty dish on the counter or in the sink. She wished she could say the same thing about her own kitchen because in her haste to prepare lunch she'd left hers a mess.

By the time the five of them, women and kids alike, hungrily dug into the food, the awkwardness had vanished. The kids created a noisy and boisterous backdrop. After they ate their fill of chicken and potatoes and pasta, they started on the brownies.

"Okay, so the kids will have a nice sugar high that might possibly prevent them from taking a nap any time soon. But what the hey, they're having a grand time."

"They are," Lilly agreed as she took another bite of brownie. "These are delicious. I mean, well, everything was good, but these...you're a fantastic cook."

"My mother spent years as a caterer. She's better than I am at main dishes though. I managed to pick up a few pointers from her over the years and can only hope that will be enough to run a B & B. But my contribution to Mom's business was mainly desserts. I'm good at desserts. I won't lie, though, I'm nervous about opening my home to people with particular taste buds. I know I'm not the world's best cook. Okay, maybe nervous isn't the right word, actually I'm more like scared to death. What if—the guests drive up and don't like the looks of the place? What if—they want their money back? What if—they don't like the rooms, or the food? The food might be the least of my worries."

Lilly smiled. "But what if they like the way the place looks and what if they like the rooms, and there's no what if about it, they'll love the food."

"I want to believe that. I want to think that it's got to work. But, it's just—what if I open on time, but I can't make a go of it? You need security more than I can offer right now, Lilly. That's why I haven't brought you on board yet. You'd have to give up your assistance from the county."

"I thought it might be something like that, but I just wasn't sure. I thought, you know, maybe you didn't trust me or something since my ex is in prison."

"That isn't it—at all. I don't want you to give up your only source of income on a risk."

"You know Jordan I could still come out and help you get the place ready to open, dust, do laundry, you know, as a friend. I'd bring the kids with me and maybe if you just provided us with lunch."

"You can't work for just lunch." But then a thought occurred to her. "What if I paid you with something other than money, like a barter system? I might not be able to afford a salary right now anyway or the promise of a regular job until I'm open for business, but I can feed you and the kids at lunch time, plus you can bring home any other food from all the recipes I've been trying out lately." She looked around the trailer. "What else do you need?" Before Lilly could answer, Jordan spotted several pieces of paper tacked up on the refrigerator door. She got up to take a closer look. "What are these?"

"Those are just some doodles. I like to draw when the kids are down for a nap."

Jordan stared at what looked like to her were a lot more than doodles. They looked like works of art, water-colored oceanscapes, and a few portraits of the kids. "Oh, Lilly. I think you've got more talent than you know. We may have just hit upon the very thing you have to barter. These are good. Do you have anymore?"

"You want my doodling?"

"Honey, these show real talent." The wheels were turning inside Jordan's head. "When I open, we could frame these and put them in prominent places around the house for sale. I bet these will be gone in a heartbeat."

"You're joking, right?"

"Far from it. Organize your portfolio, and the next time we get together, show me what you've got. And Lilly, can you cook?"

"Not as good as you but we get by." "Want to learn?"

Chapter Eleven

Over the next week, Nick stayed so busy installing drywall, bathroom fixtures and laying new flooring he barely had time for anything other than eating and sleeping. Physically exhausted from the work, he no longer woke before two a.m. even managing a good solid six hours of sleep every now and then before the dream kicked in or Scott infringed on his psyche. His sleep routine was far from perfect, but it was a vast improvement over the past year.

Jordan had her own demanding list of chores to get done. She finally finished painting the last bedroom. By the end of the week, they were both so worn out they decided they deserved a breather. As their reward, Jordan packed the three of them a picnic basket filled with lemonade and sandwiches. With spring in the air, they all traipsed down the trail to the cove and the beach. They'd no sooner spread out their blanket on the sand than Nick looked out over the water and said, "Is that what I think it is?"

Jordan got to her knees, put a hand on her forehead shading her eyes and scanned the horizon for any movement on the water. All she saw were vast layers of blue coupled with lusty waves. Just as she was about to tell him she didn't see anything, something huge and gray splashed up out of the water a good hundred yards from shore. "Oh, my God. Is that a whale? That's a whale." She got to her feet, grabbing Hutton. She told Nick, "Get the binoculars." When he just kept standing there staring out to sea, she reached into the picnic hamper herself and dug around until she pulled out the binoculars.

"Who carries field glasses?"

"Standard picnic gear. Can't go to the beach unprepared. Never know what you might miss," she explained as she searched the horizon for any sign of the giant mammal. She had to wait several minutes, but when the whale resurfaced, she sucked in a breath and said, "It's a California gray. I'm sure of it. Want a look?"

"You bet." He took the binoculars from her and watched as the whale came up for air again. "Wow. What a sight. Look, there's another one off to the right. There." He handed the binoculars back to Jordan.

"What are the odds we'd see two migrating gray whales over lunch."

"It was your idea and what an idea it was. I'm starving though." He sat back down on the blanket and dug into the basket. Grabbing the thermos he poured two generous plastic cups full of lemonade, placed them on the blanket. Absently he picked up Hutton's sippy cup already filled with apple juice and handed it off to her just as he'd seen Jordan do. As if he were an old hand at knowing the baby's eating habits, he automatically peeled a cheese stick from its plastic wrapping and placed it gingerly into a little fist. Hutton hungrily began gnawing on the stick.

When Jordan finally put down the binoculars, she turned to see her daughter already enjoying lunch. The significance was not lost on her. Here was a guy not used to kids, yet he had taken to her daughter as naturally as anyone in her immediate family had. She could get used to this, get used to Nick being there for both of them. She wanted to ask him what his plans were after they opened, but she was afraid of his answer, afraid he'd tell her he had no intentions of staying in a dinky town like Pelican Pointe. She decided she didn't want to know any more than that.

She wanted to enjoy the day, enjoy the time she had left to spend with him while he was here.

After finishing their sandwiches they stretched out on the blanket and watched as Hutton ran around on the beach after Quake. But it didn't take long for both dog and baby to run out of gas and begin to wind down about the same time. When Hutton began rubbing her eyes, Jordan picked her up, announcing, "It's time for someone's nap."

"Give her to me," Nick suggested.

"And what are you going to do with a cranky baby?"

"We're going to curl up here and take us a nap. Aren't we, Hutton?"

Yeah right, Jordan thought, see if she goes to sleep like that. But she handed him the baby anyway. Five minutes later, after she'd packed up the basket, she looked over at the pair lying side by side on the blanket. Both had their eyes closed. Amazed, she dropped down beside them, stretched out her legs to relax in the warm sunshine.

Forty-five minutes later Jordan came awake only to see Nick grinning at her as Hutton lay sandwiched between them. Rubbing her eyes, she told him, "She's never done that before. I've never done that before."

"What? Take a nap at the beach?"

"Yeah. I need to put her down so she'll get her nap out and not wake up cranky though."

He got to his knees. "You get the basket and blanket, I'll carry Hutton."

As she folded the blanket before grabbing the basket, Nick stood to the side watching her. She looked radiant. When had he ever used that word to describe a woman, any woman? Never. But he couldn't deny how he felt at this moment. Watching the sunlight glisten off her hair, she all but gave off vibes of pleasure. And when was the last time he'd relaxed enough to fall asleep during the day?

When they got back to the house, just like he'd done before, he laid Hutton down in the crib. He went through all the rituals of tucking the baby in as he'd seen Jordan do. It hit him like a fist to the gut. Contentment. Joy. Love. At the realization, he sucked in a ragged breath and all but staggered out of the room. He quickly made his way outside onto the front porch where his knees buckled just in time to plunk down onto the steps. In love? How the hell had that happened? He didn't believe in love, certainly not marriage. His gut rippled with nerves. What now? he wondered. And what did he intend to do about it?

It was later that afternoon when they were all three once again outside sitting in the backyard in the Adirondack chairs enjoying what promised to be a beautiful evening that Nick got up and disappeared around the corner of the house. Jordan heard water running from the outside faucet. Moments later, he came back, grinning, carrying two huge super soaker water guns in each hand.

Jordan saw the gleam in his eye and knew what was about to happen. "Nick Harris, don't you dare!"

He cocked one brow before sending a steady stream of water her way, hitting her squarely in the chest, soaking her shirt. Rising to the challenge, she got to her feet, grabbing the other gun from where he'd dropped it on the grass. She darted around after him, firing at will. They exchanged shots, running and dodging each other's firepower. Soon Hutton and Quake joined in the chase. Before long, all four of them were soaking wet.

Nick plopped down on the grass, wringing out some of the excess water by squeezing the tail end of his shirt. "Good way to clean up Hutton and Quake every night, don't you think? Take them both out back here and hose them down every night before bed with a couple of super soakers. Less hassle."

"Sure, that'll work. I see mother of the year in there for that." She grabbed a rubber bone lying on the lawn and Quake immediately started playing tug of war.

"When's Lilly start to work?"

"After Easter. That gives us three weeks, plenty of time to put the finishing touches on everything, get the rooms ready before the doors open. That should give us enough time, don't you think?"

When Nick merely nodded, Jordan went on, "You should see the way the woman draws and paints. And the portraits of her kids. They look professionally done. She might be able to make a living as an artist if she could get some sales under her belt and—oh, my God! Why didn't I think of that earlier? What if she could do that during the upcoming street fair?"

"Good idea. Portrait artists are fairly common at street fairs."

"They sure are." Jordan got to her feet and started pacing. "She could earn some extra bucks, too. Do you suppose doing something like that might jeopardize her stipend from the county though?"

"Wait. Think about it for a minute, Jordan. The fair's only days away, I'm pretty sure it's probably too late to get a booth. And even if she could, what makes you think the good people of Pelican Pointe, namely Sissy Carr, would allow Lilly to go anywhere near the street fair to pick up a little extra cash? Murphy mentioned Sissy acts like she's the queen of this thing. And Bran Sullivan, the vet said something about her trying to run the show. She isn't going to like it much if Lilly comes along at this late date and starts raking in money for her portraits. Then there's the booth fee. Who pays for that?" He scratched his chin. "I'll be happy to put up the money but something tells me good old Sissy is going to put up some resistance there."

Her shoulders sagged. "You're right. Well, that's a damn shame. These aren't caricatures Nick, these are honest to goodness beautiful portraits."

"I believe you. You still want to go this Friday?"

"I think it'd be fun. But I was thinking Saturday might work better."

"What and miss the parade?" He asked, grinning.

"I recognize sarcasm when I hear it. Okay, you talked me into it. You haven't lived until you've seen a Pelican Pointe parade."

"I was thinking of taking Murphy up on his offer to go fishing. They're taking Wade's boat out Tuesday planning to spend the night on the water."

"Like I said before, you should go. Wade Hawkins is quite a character."

"How so?"

"He's a retired history professor, a staunch environmentalist, and considers himself something of a local expert in the paranormal."

His eyes widened. He cocked his head. "You mean ghosts?"

Jordan laughed. "That's exactly what I mean. The man's got this wild head of white hair and when he starts talking about spirits and ghosts, his stories just pull you in. It's really more like a hobby, I guess. But last winter he told me he planned to write a book about his experiences. He's serious about pursuing ghosts though. You know, he's been out here a couple of times with some electronic meter and gizmo, claims his sensors went crazy. Says he wouldn't be surprised if we had a ghost or two living right here."

Nick thought of Scott. Hell, he'd been the one to bring his ghost here with him. Cautious, he tried for the right words. "Have you seen any signs of that in the two years you've lived here?" He searched her face for any sign she was thinking about Scott, but Jordan simply laughed. "No. But don't think I haven't thought about using every angle I could to get tourists in here.

If guests want a ghost story, I'm not above making one up."

Nick's breathing leveled off. So she hadn't seen Scott's ghost. Weird. Was he just haunting him, then? "Wild head of hair, huh? I think I might have seen Wade walking around town. Pelican Pointe seems to have its share of quirky residents."

"Yep. You know, I was thinking I might head to church Easter Sunday for services. I gave up going when Scott left, especially when I found the town wasn't that friendly. But I've been thinking, I might give it another try. Want to go with us?"

He shook his head. "I think I'll pass. I'm not much of a churchgoer."

"Well, if you change your mind, I'd welcome the company. The last time Hutton and I went everyone gave us a wide berth."

"Why's that?"

"Beats me. But I'm not going for them, I'm going for me. And besides, me showing up always gets a reaction of sorts."

He took a long look at her face; he saw the teasing look in her eyes. "In that case, count me in." For some reason, he didn't want her walking in there alone.

She smiled. "Good. We'll show up together and give 'em more fodder for the rumor mill."

Over the next couple of days, Jordan worked on her idea, the idea certain to help Lilly out financially during the street fair. To make it happen, she placed a few calls to Carla Vargas and subsequently met with Murphy who promised he'd make it happen. She ended up bringing a cynical Lilly on board less than twenty-four hours before the street fair.

By the time Friday morning rolled around, even Hutton sensed the excitement in the air as the three of them headed into town for the parade.

Parking was a problem, but they finally found a spot two streets over in front of the animal clinic. Once they dragged out the stroller, got Hutton situated, they headed for Main Street carrying their own lawn chairs.

As soon as they rounded the corner, they saw the crowd and smelled hamburgers cooking on a grill somewhere near the food court set up in City Park. The town was a veritable madhouse. With school closed for spring break, parents dealt with anxious children of various ages, who ran around dressed in costume either waiting to be part of the parade or waiting for it to begin. After walking down Main Street for a good ten minutes, Nick and Jordan finally found space enough to set two chairs together in the parking lot at Murphy's Market. They positioned the stroller between them and waited.

At a few minutes after ten, they heard the high school band strike up the sounds of an off-key rendition of *It's a Small World After All* and watched as the band began the march down Main. What they lacked in musical talent they made up for in enthusiasm. As the band got closer, spectators jumped to their feet, applauding. Hutton began clapping her hands too. And Jordan smiled as she watched her daughter get caught up in the music and the movements of the other kids dressed in their snappy, red and white band uniforms as they strode past.

Decorated in red, white and blue streamers, Murphy's vintage 1954 Chevy pickup followed on the heels of the band as it rolled past while the mayor stood in the bed throwing out candy to the kids along the parade route.

After that came one of the county patrol cars with at least six kids hanging out the windows as the car flashed its lights and intermittently hit the siren. That too, got Hutton's attention, but the noise scared her. When she puckered up to cry, Jordan leaned over to console her and bumped heads with Nick who had thought to do the same thing. Jordan looked over at Nick to see him grin widely, and then watched as he reached down, as if he'd been doing it forever, and pluck the baby out of her stroller. In a soothing voice he reassured her, "Don't cry, Blondie. No one's gonna hurt you while I'm around. You can count on that." In response, Hutton buried her head on Nick's shoulder and grabbed a fistful of his shirt just to make sure he wasn't going anywhere.

Watching him gently pat her back and alternately bounce her, Jordan had no doubt he meant every word of it. She didn't know when it had happened, but sometime during the last week, he seemed to have shed his uneasiness around Hutton. And lately, she'd noticed how much more relaxed he was in general, more at ease with everything he did around the house as if he were finally settling in, leaving some of his stress behind.

Soon Hutton lifted her head, smiled into Nick's face and put both of her hands on the sides of his head, shaking it back and forth. Jordan saw him laugh, shake his head to and fro for her pleasure, and watched as he bit playfully at her little fingers. The man had completely calmed her down. When he turned her attention back to the parade, he had her waving back to the other kids without any fear of the loud noise from the siren. In less than two minutes, Nick had completely dissolved Hutton's scary moment.

Jordan's stomach fluttered. Her heart felt like it turned over in her chest. She had no doubt the man would make a good father. Unfortunately, he didn't even know it.

A Dually came into view, pulling a flatbed trailer where Ricky Odem's bluegrass band was perched precariously on the back, performing their song, Rain

Vickie McKeehan

Mountain. The next thing she knew, Nick's bouncing had become dancing and Hutton was clapping her hands to the music as Nick moved back and forth in time to the rhythm of the song.

For the next twenty minutes, much to the delight of the crowd, various decorated cars and pickups filed slowly past while the participants dispensed candy and Mardi Gras-like beads to every adult and child alike who lined the street.

At the tail end of the parade, a ragtag bunch of kids who'd decorated their own bikes and skateboards waved flags and signs at the crowd as they proudly marched to the sounds of one, lone fife player, a sixty-ish man with a mane of wild, white hair. Bringing up the rear, flute to his mouth, Wade Hawkins in a sign of protest to Sissy Carr, led these stragglers down the street to kick off spring to what was perhaps the loudest cheer of the day as people got to their feet, applauding either their children or Wade's efforts, Jordan wasn't sure which. She leaned over to Nick, explaining, "That's Wade for you. He's a rebel at heart."

Looking at the faces in the crowd, Jordan had forgotten how much fun this could be. Why couldn't the townspeople come together like this every day? Willing to forgive and forget how nasty they'd been to her over the past two years, Jordan smiled in relief that maybe there was hope for this town after all.

Nick had never watched anything so amateurish. Or so much fun.

"There's something I have to do," Jordan told him suddenly as she pulled him along through the crowd. He followed, carrying Hutton in his arms while she pushed an empty stroller toward a row of booths set up a long Beach Street.

As they passed the food court, Nick sniffed the air like a hunter on a scent. The smell of meat cooking over a grill was too tempting. "While we're here, let's get a burger. I'm starving."

"In a minute," Jordan said absently as she hurried along at a fast clip. When they reached a white-canopied tent at the very end of the row with the flap open, Jordan pulled the stroller to a stop and stepped inside still pulling Nick along with her. Sitting in a folding chair, with a sketch pad on her lap, Lilly looked up at them and smiled nervously. Kyra sat in the empty chair while Joey played within arm's reach inside the mesh Pack 'N Play Jordan had provided. There was nothing else in the tent except a small pedestal table large enough to hold a glass tip jar.

Nick smiled at Jordan. "Son of a gun, you did it." He'd never been more proud of anyone before in his life. Knowing what kind of a fix Lilly and her kids were in, the fact that Jordan had pulled this off for Lilly said more about Jordan Phillips than anything else could have. His heart swelled with some undefined emotion he'd never felt for another woman. He wanted to reach out and kiss her. But he held back.

"Murphy pulled some strings. And Carla approved it as long as Lilly draws for tips and doesn't actually charge anyone for the portraits. That way, she isn't employed by anyone and she can keep all the money in the tip jar as a donation."

Jordan looked at Lilly. "Did the kids catch the parade?"

"They did, we just slipped back inside."

"Have you been busy?"

She pointed to the tip jar. It had a handful of bills in it. But it was still early, not even eleven o'clock yet. "Murphy and Carla came by, got their portraits done, and then a couple of tourists from San Francisco."

Jordan pushed Nick into a chair. "I want one of Nick and Hutton."

"You don't have to do that, Jordan."

She insisted, "I want one of Nick and Hutton. You're good, Lilly. I know exactly where I intend to hang them." She didn't have a clue. "When you're finished with these two we'll take the kids out for lunch. I bet they're hungry by now."

"You don't have to babysit or feed the kids for me, too." "Nick's hungry, aren't you, Nick?"

He smiled, getting into his role. "Starving. We ate breakfast early. And the smell of burgers is getting to me."

Lilly giggled. She often giggled around Nick. As she picked up her sketch pad to begin drawing Nick's face, she glanced up to see Wally Pierce standing in the open entrance to the tent.

"Hey, Lilly," Wally said nervously.

Jordan exchanged looks with Nick as if she'd just realized why Wally would show up inside Lilly's tent. His service station might have been across the street, but somehow Jordan didn't think Wally Pierce was here because he needed a drawing of himself.

Easy going, Wally Pierce had taken over running his father's service station two years earlier after his dad's heart attack. As the only mechanic within fifty miles Wally could have pretty much gouged everyone who walked through his doors except that he happened to be an honest, hardworking guy who'd grown up a local. Wally knew everyone in town as well as the engines in their cars. Even though his work kept him hopping six days a week, he made a point to go surfing every day after he got done with work. Since he lived in a tiny house, near the waterfront, he walked to work in spite of owning a classic SS Chevelle muscle car. The only vice the guy seemed to have was surfing. Winter or summer, if Wally wasn't at his service station on Beach Street, he spent his time in the water. Tall and gangly, with hair down to his shoulders, he even looked the part of a surfer. Even though he had just celebrated his twenty-ninth birthday, Wally had no steady girlfriend, mostly because he worked and lived in a town with less than three thousand people, where there was a short supply of single women his age, especially pretty ones like Lilly Seybold. Wally knew she had two kids. They'd been right there with her when he'd put a retread on her car. But since that day, he hadn't been able to get her out of his head.

"Murphy says you can draw."

"Some," Lilly replied shyly.

Nick glanced up at Wally and recognized male interest when he saw it. "She's got talent. Show him what you've got, Lilly."

Ten minutes later Lilly tilted her sketch pad in Nick's direction. He looked back at a perfect rendition of himself. Jordan had been right. This was no caricature, but rather a good likeness of his face. "Looks just like me."

Lilly tore off the sheet with Nick's portrait and handed it to Jordan. She immediately began sketching a wriggling Hutton who wouldn't sit still on Nick's lap. Leaning over Nick's shoulder, as if in a supervisory capacity, Jordan whispered in his ear, "Told you she had talent."

Another ten minutes of watching Lilly had Wally growing more and more fascinated. Even a mechanic who knew nothing about art recognized talent when he saw it. When she finished Hutton's portrait, he took it out of her hand. "You are good. I'm next," he said, as he took Nick's place in the chair.

Realizing Wally's interest in Lilly, Jordan decided she'd have to keep an eye on him. But not now, she thought, as she gathered up Joey and took Kyra's hand. "We're off to get lunch."

As soon as she stepped outside the tent, she spied all the people waiting in line. She shot a grin in Lilly's direction. "Girlfriend, you may have a cramp in that hand of yours before nightfall. You have a line out the door." With that, Jordan and Nick headed off with the kids, leaving Lilly to renew her dream as an artist, even if briefly.

The food court consisted of ten booths set up along the grounds of City Park. As they approached the commons area, they spotted booths offering burgers, ribs, BBQ, and tacos from smoke-filled grills manned by busy cooks. Other vendors pushed their funnel cakes, homemade ice cream, and kettle corn. A slew of cardboard tables draped with vinyl checkered tablecloths lined the foot paths where the crowd competed for a place to sit and eat the food they'd bought.

Nick stood in line behind ten other hungry souls at a booth called The Burger Hut which had a banner stretched behind the grill claiming to serve the thickest, juiciest burgers at the fair. While he ordered the food, Jordan took the kids and went in search of an available place to sit. Pushing Joey in the stroller and carrying Hutton while poor little Kyra was forced to follow and keep up as best she could, Jordan was on the second sweep around the commons when she spotted a group of people getting up to discard their trash. She laid claim to the table like a shopper at a shoe sale. Once Kyra got settled in, Jordan waved wildly until she caught sight of Nick carrying a red plastic tray laden with burgers, hotdogs, fries and soft drinks enough for five people.

As soon as he sat down he began doling out the food. "I got hotdogs for the kids but just in case I bought an extra burger. There's fries and lemonade instead of soda."

"Good job. Are you sure you've never been around kids before, Nick?" Jordan teased with a twinkle in her eye.

Nick stopped in mid handout, saw the mischief in her eyes, and then grinned. "I'm fairly certain I'd remember."

Without embarrassing him any further, she turned to the kids. "Kyra do you want a hamburger or a hotdog?"

"Hotdog," the little girl said, clapping her hands in anticipation.

"Hotdog," Joey echoed, clapping his hands like he'd seen his sister.

"Dog," Hutton added, making it unanimous.

After getting the kids fed, they spent the next couple of hours walking up and down the rows of booths looking at displays of handmade jewelry, hand painted ceramics, a needlepoint exhibit, and homemade quilts. A few beach scenes caught their eye done by a few of the local artists that they agreed would look good decorating the guest rooms, but the art was way out of Jordan's price range. Maybe she'd ask Lilly if she could paint something similar. After seeing her talent, Jordan had no doubt the woman could draw just about anything.

Jordan was enjoying the browsing when she suddenly came to an abrupt halt. She turned to face Nick, who was pushing the double stroller with Joey and Kyra asleep inside. "You must be bored out of your mind. This is all such girly stuff. Would you like to go home?"

Home, now that was a new concept, he thought, as he stared at the woman he'd been watching walk. "Actually, I'm having fun. The kids are asleep. It's a nice day. We're getting plenty of fresh air and sun. What could be better?"

At that moment, he saw Jordan's face go white at something or someone behind him. He didn't even have time to turn around before Sissy stomped up to Jordan in a fit of something just short of rage and stood inches from her face. Jordan stepped back. Sissy shook a finger in her face. "I know what you did. You paid for that woman to have a booth here, got Murphy to make an exception even though she missed the deadline. And that is just wrong, wrong, wrong! She missed the deadline! She shouldn't be here."

"What possible harm could it do, Sissy? Lilly's hurting no one."

"She didn't follow the rules and neither did you! You can't just come into town whenever you feel like it and do things your way!" Sissy screeched at the top of her lungs.

"Oh, and you always follow the rules, do you? Sissy, take a look around, this fair is for the townspeople of Pelican Pointe. Lilly is part of that whether you like it or not. So what if she got a late start."

Sissy cut her off. "This isn't about me. There were other people who wanted a booth, others that would have paid more money for the privilege, but we turned them down because they missed the deadline. You and Murphy will pay for this. You bitch!" With that Sissy stomped her foot and stormed off, followed on her heels by Kent Springer in hot pursuit.

"That woman is a piece of work," Nick said as he watched the pair tromp off in a fit.

Jordan shook her head. "I think we should go check on Lilly, make sure Sissy doesn't make trouble for her in front of everyone."

But when they got to the tent, Lilly was fine. Much to Jordan's delight, her tip jar was overflowing. Wally, she noted, was nowhere in sight.

With the kids still napping, Nick and Jordan took another swing by the food court again giving in to the temptation of a funnel cake, covered in a generous portion of powdered sugar and cinnamon. After watching Nick devour two at one sitting, Jordan decided she should try to make one of her own, maybe drizzled with a combo of chocolate and cinnamon icing.

By the time they finished the cake, the kids were stirring. They spent an hour inside the fenced-off area where Bran and Joy had set up a petting zoo. Inside were four new lambs, a couple of calves, a chestnut-brown pony and six starved-for-attention frisky puppies. With the help of Nick, who never left her side the entire time, Hutton touched, petted, or sat on every animal there. As she ran around after a lamb almost as big as she was, Nick commented, "She has the same disposition as her mother."

"What's that supposed to mean?" Jordan asked, trying to balance Joey and Kyra simultaneously on the same pony.

"It means," he said, as he turned to meet Jordan's eyes, "you both have such sweet temperaments, nothing much pisses either of you off."

Jordan's heart lurched. Little by little this man was slowly chipping away at her heart, replacing despair with something very close to love. If it hadn't been for turning her attention back to Joey and Kyra who were squirming way too much for their own good on the pony, she was sure the stupid look on her face was enough to reveal her thoughts. She didn't dare let him know how she felt. Because a man like Nick was a love 'em and leave 'em kind of guy. If he knew how she felt he'd take off back to L.A. before she could finish. Ben Latham had labeled him a major player. Logically, she didn't understand how she could have fallen for him in such a short amount of time. But it didn't have to make sense.

Jordan Phillips had fallen all the way in love with Nick Harris!

Around five o'clock just as the country and western band started tuning up for the evening, Lilly decided to close up shop. She'd been at it since ten that morning. As she counted out her tip money, she felt like doing a happy dance right there in the park. Her kids were happy. She was happy. How long had it been since she could say that? It had been such a good day she felt like bursting. She headed out to find Jordan and Nick.

Lilly found them in the park playing with the kids. "Guess how much money I made today, Jordan? Guess?"

Without waiting for a reply, she bubbled, "Two hundred dollars. I've never had so much fun doing what I would have been doing just sitting in the trailer. Thanks for everything you did for me today. Both of you. You watched the kids. I couldn't have done this without you guys."

Nick waved off her gratitude. "Hey, don't thank me. I didn't do a thing. The booth was all Jordan's idea."

Jordan shook her head. "That isn't true. Without Murphy and Carla it wouldn't have happened."

"But it did and even though I thanked Carla and Murphy this morning, this was your idea Jordan. I just can't thank you enough."

Jordan smiled. "Take the kids home, Lilly. I'm sure you'll have no problem getting them to sleep. Nick and I practically wore them out. Uh, Lilly you might want to give them both a bath. That petting zoo has all of us smelling like sweaty little farmhands."

"Are you sure you still want to watch the kids tomorrow and Sunday? You don't have to, you know. I can..."

"You can't draw and watch two little kids, Lilly. Just drop them by the house in the morning." She pushed at Lilly's shoulders. "Now go. Enjoy your evening."

As Nick watched Lilly pull out of the crowded parking lot, he turned to Jordan and put his free arm around her shoulder. "You're something else, you know that?"

"I'm just trying to be a good neighbor which is more than I can say for some of the other Pelican

Pointe residents. Sissy was just downright rude today. And wrong."

"Sissy isn't anyone's good neighbor." As they zigzagged their way across the crowded parking lot between the cars, he leaned into her and whispered, "What do you say we stop and get some of those ribs before we head home for supper? That way you won't have to cook."

She shook her head and laughed, poking him playfully in his own ribs. "I never knew you were such a chowhound. You've been eating all day."

But when a cranky Hutton began to rub her eyes and fuss, Jordan pulled on Nick's arm, changing direction and headed toward the SUV telling him, "If you want ribs you better get them to-go. She's so tired she's cross. I don't think she'll make it much longer. Give her to me and I'll take her to the car, get her settled in while you get the food." Nick handed over the baby and sauntered off back across the parking lot for the barbeque booth. Over her shoulder, as she climbed into the seat holding Hutton, she yelled to his back, "and could you get some of that potato salad...and maybe some of those sweet potato fries."

He laughed and hollered back, "Sounds like I'm not the only one hungry. I'll try to make it quick. Be back in a jiff."

From the bank parking lot, Kent watched the scene play out. He thought about following Nick and getting in his face. But that really wasn't his style. Not to mention, it would tip his hand. What he'd really like to do is to get that war widow alone for about twenty minutes, maybe teach her a thing or two about what she'd been missing out there all alone before the motorcycle jockey rode into town. Kent licked his lips. Just the thought of getting Jordan alone had him checking out where Nick had gone. What Sissy didn't know wouldn't hurt her, he decided. Just his luck though he saw Harris heading back toward Jordan. Too bad, he thought, he'd have to savor the widow for another day.

On his return Nick spotted Jordan sitting in the rear seat of the car rocking Hutton back and forth to sleep. He opened the door as quietly as he could and offered, "I can have us home in fifteen minutes."

"There's no rush now, she's sound asleep. But I have to put her down in the car seat to make the trip home. She may not like it very much. You might want to cover your ears," she told him, as she gently began to transfer Hutton from her arms into the car seat and awkwardly buckle up the sleeping baby. To Jordan's surprise, Hutton squirmed some, but other than that was pretty much out like a light.

That night their high spirits from the festive day continued long after they pulled into The Cove. Once they got Hutton to bed, they feasted on the ribs, each drinking a beer with their meal. Watching Nick lick his way down the last rib bone, she jokingly said, "I think that's the most I've seen you put away since you came here. You don't eat my cooking like that."

"You're kidding, right? I love your cooking. But ribs and wings have always been my top two weaknesses. That and beer."

"I can tell." When he started to help her clean up, she pushed him toward the hallway. "I believe there's a recliner with your name on it waiting for a Lakers game. Go. I can get this." She gave him another nudge toward the door.

Glancing at his watch, he edged out of the room. "If you're sure, I'll just grab another beer and head out to catch the tip-off."

Since she hadn't cooked, cleanup took less than fifteen minutes. But when she got to the living room, she found Nick stretched out fast asleep in Scott's recliner. Even though the television blared with the noise of a game in progress, she couldn't take her eyes off him. He had such a peaceful look on his face, it was all she could do not to reach over and run her fingers through his coal-black hair. Her pulse quickened. Oh, so tempting, she thought. But she didn't dare. What was happening to her? She forced herself to reel in her emotions and picked up one of her decorating magazines off the coffee table. She got comfortable on the sofa, curling her legs under her and started absently thumbing through the pages, not really seeing anything clearly. She glanced up, her eyes unwillingly drifting back to Nick.

He'd been part of her life for less than a month. She wasn't sure how it had happened or when, but watching him so peaceful in sleep, she realized she didn't want him to leave. Ever. As she gazed at his sleeping form, she wondered how he'd handle that little bit of information. And then knew… He'd run the other way so fast he wouldn't even bother saying adios. She sighed. *Oh, God, what have I done? I've fallen in love with a guy who has a list of conquests from here to L.A., herself included.*

That weekend during the street fair, from ten in the morning to six in the evening, Jordan and Nick looked after Kyra and Joey while Lilly worked the fair. Lilly had protested about the babysitting, but Jordan had insisted, telling her that if she wanted to pay her back, she could work on a couple of beach scenes for the guest rooms if she had any downtime during the course of her day.

When the street fair ended on Sunday night and Lilly came to pick up the kids, she sat down on the couch in the living room with tears in her eyes. Clutching her purse, she said, "I made more than six hundred dollars over three days. Can you imagine that? I have enough to pay you back for the booth fee."

The booth fee had been two hundred dollars. But out of the goodness of his heart Murphy had waived half of that. Something she was certain Sissy didn't know about. No way was Jordan going to take a hundred dollars from Lilly. Instead, Jordan neatly changed the subject. "Were you able to work on those beach scenes?"

Lilly brought out her sketch pad and showed off several landscapes, a few in glorious watercolor. Where she'd found the time to do that, Jordan didn't have a clue. But these were good, every bit as good as the ones she'd seen at the street fair.

Jordan studied them, swallowing her emotion. "These are exactly what I was looking for, Lilly. I think they'll look wonderful on the walls upstairs. How much do I owe you?"

"Oh, Jordan. They're yours. No charge. I've never had so much fun as I did this weekend. If I had canvas I could make you something really nice, but these are just pencil drawings, a few in watercolor. I want to pay for the booth rental."

"Believe me these are more than just pencil drawings. They're lovely. Okay, it's a trade. I'll take these in exchange for the booth rental fee. Will you help me frame them?"

Lilly's eyes met Jordan's. She knew what Jordan was doing. She'd never had a friend as nice. "If you're sure."

"I am."

"Then I'd be happy to."

Chapter Twelve

The next day, Lilly started to work three days a week at the B & B—Mondays, Wednesdays and Fridays from nine to three. When she wasn't helping Jordan with the usual household chores like dusting and polishing and laundry, Jordan sharpened Lilly's culinary skills in the kitchen. They baked bread, all kinds of desserts, and experimented with an array of new ways of preparing Italian puttanesca to a simple tasty, Chinese stir fry.

Lilly's presence allowed Jordan to finish getting the guest rooms squared away as well as the rest of the house. She put the last coat of paint on the upstairs hallway, the landing and the new walls in the bathroom while Nick spent his days spreading much-needed layers of insulation throughout the attic. It was messy, physically hard work for both of them. But it exemplified what Murphy had said about the two of them making a good team. While the big jobs were mostly independent of each other and kept them busy apart, they also spent a good deal of time together doing the everyday, mundane things that were part of life as a cohesive unit.

They settled into a routine starting with breakfast, which they each took turns preparing. After that, they'd work on their own separate projects until one sought the other out for advice or a question or until lunchtime brought them together again for the midday meal. But in the afternoon, usually after Hutton woke from her nap, they'd make the time to do some activity together.

The three of them would likely go down to the beach or take a bike ride up and down the driveway or just sit in the porch swing and watch Hutton play with Quake. After that they'd drift into the kitchen where they'd organize dinner prep together and discuss what chores needed doing either for the next day or the next week. After supper, they would usually clean up the kitchen together or maybe watch one or two programs on television until it was time to get the baby ready for bed. The ritual always included story time for Hutton. Whenever they'd get her off to bed, they'd spend quiet time just the two of them in front of the fire either talking, or reading or spending time on the computer. Without knowing it, without even trying, they had both settled into a pattern anyone with brains would have recognized as a solid family unit.

Two nights in a row they had even necked on the sofa like a couple of randy teenagers, going at each other hot and heavy. But each time just when things started to lean toward the bedroom, Nick made up some excuse to leave, pulling away from her. His behavior was starting to annoy Jordan.

On Wednesday morning after the street fair, just after breakfast, Jordan packed a cooler with sandwiches and beer and watched Nick head off on his motorcycle to meet up with Murphy and Wade at the waterfront.

Jordan had to admit the fishing trip couldn't have come at a better time. Not only did Nick need a breather from all the physical labor, but the sexual tension between the two of them was reaching cataclysmic proportion. And his pulling back every time was making both of them edgy. They'd almost had a testy argument that very morning over the runniness of eggs. Any other time it might have been laughable if the sexual frustration hadn't been getting to both of them.

She wasn't sure what to do about it either, just as she wasn't sure what to do or think about Nick. At times, it was as if he were two different people. He could be helpful, charming, considerate, but the minute she tried to amp up the closeness, he'd pull back, even if he had to leave the house to do it. She was pondering those thoughts, when the doorbell rang a little after nine in the morning. Jordan set Hutton down to go answer the door and was surprised to see Carla Vargas standing on the porch with an anxious look on her face.

"Carla what a nice surprise." But Carla didn't look like it was nice at all, in fact she acted nervous. And she was dressed in a suit, carrying a heavy-looking briefcase. Her stomach fluttered as it flitted through Jordan's mind that this early morning visit looked official. After all their precautions had they put Lilly's stipend in jeopardy?

"Jordan, how are you this morning?"

Jordan opened the screen door and let her inside. "Fine. I've got coffee and some banana walnut muffins still warm from the oven."

"That sounds fine. But...this isn't a social visit...this is... professional." Carla looked around the foyer and into the living room as if she were trying to find someone. It wasn't until her eyes landed on Hutton that Jordan began to worry. At the sight of Hutton, Carla's demeanor became all business.

"Professional? What do you mean?"

"The county—social services received a complaint."

"A complaint? I don't understand." She thought of Mr. Taggert and wondered why he would call social services complaining about noise.

"Someone called the county and said they saw bruises on Hutton."

Jordan's mouth dropped open. "What? That's— impossible, that's—ridiculous."

"I know, but surely you understand we—I have to check it out, Jordan. Pelican Pointe is part of my territory."

"But... When? When did they say they saw bruises on her?"

"At the street fair. I told my supervisor it was ridiculous and that I didn't believe one word of it, but it's my duty to check out reports, for the file. It's my job."

Clearly taken aback, Jordan tried to act normal, tried to maintain her composure as she led Carla into the kitchen. On automatic, she got coffee cups out of the cabinet and plates for the muffins. But her hands were shaking so much the dishes clanged together. "Can you tell me who made the complaint?"

"It was anonymous. The person said they saw Hutton in town at the fair and she had noticeable bruises on her arms and legs. My supervisor said they sounded very convincing." Instinctively, Jordan's hands flew to her mouth. Convincing enough that a social worker came out to inspect her child, she thought, as she began to cry. "I knew the people in town didn't like me, I've known for almost two years they didn't want me here, but this is beyond that, beyond comprehension." She turned to pick up Hutton before dropping into a kitchen chair. She set the baby on her lap and immediately began to undress her. Hutton, as toddlers will do started to squirm in her arms. But she managed to pull down the child's pink overalls and showed Carla the baby's legs. There were no bruises anywhere. On automatic, Jordan began to shed Hutton's white long sleeve top to bare her arms for inspection. "I'm sorry to have to do this."

It took barely fifteen minutes from beginning to end, but Carla did her job. She examined Hutton from head to toe, even removing her diaper. Afterward, she breathed a sigh of relief and said quietly, "That's it, Jordan. You can put her clothes back on. They were obviously mistaken."

"More like mean is what they were, Carla. Why would anyone be that mean?" An image of Sissy during the street fair, mad as a hornet, flitted through her head. "I haven't done anything to these people. They've never liked me. That much I knew. But this—turning me into social services, how could they hate me that much to jeopardize my child to the system."

"Jordan, you have plenty of friends in town."

"Name one."

"Murphy likes you. And there's Lilly."

"Murphy's nice to everyone. But he isn't really a friend, is he? Besides Lilly there isn't another soul in town who has taken the time to come by for a visit or to get to know me. But to do something like this—to be so mean to turn me in for something so serious, something I didn't even do—it's unimaginable."

Carla began to break apart her muffin. "This is good."

"Just like that you can talk about food?"

"Yeah, I can." She reached over and patted Jordan's hand. "It's okay Jordan. I'll file the report that it was totally bogus. Everything will be fine."

"Are you sure?"

"It's over as far as social services is concerned."

Jordan blinked tears from her eyes and blew out a shaky breath. "Thank God."

On board Wade's twenty-foot fishing trawler, Haunted Lady, it took Nick four hours to catch an undersized, scrawny perch. The fish reminded him why he'd never had the patience for the sport, if you could call it that.

As the boat rocked and swayed Nick, Murphy and Wade leaned back in deck chairs with their fishing lines thrown over the railing and dangling in the water, taking in the sunny day. Nick hadn't fished since summer camp when he'd been twelve. Something about the memory was a lot more fun than the actual event. But he didn't dare share this sentiment with Murphy and Wade. Although years older, the two men were a kick. They had spent the day taking turns rehashing old stories about the early smugglers in the area, the ones Jordan had mentioned. And when Wade started entertaining them with local ghost stories about the area, pirates and smugglers alike, it prompted Nick to ask, "You really believe in ghosts, Wade?"

"I do. In fact, I had one some years back that wouldn't leave me the hell alone."

Nick cocked a disbelieving brow at Wade and found himself genuinely fascinated at the prospect that someone else had seen a ghost. "At the time, had you experienced, you know, any type of trauma that might have brought it on?" Nick asked, trying to sound nonchalant.

"Trauma? No, no trauma," Wade answered.

Nick prodded further. "So what did you do? How'd you handle it?"

"Well now, I'll tell you. Most ghosts linger around, bugging the hell out of people because they have unfinished business. Once they finish whatever it is keeping them earth bound, they usually move on. I was a novice when it happened to me, kept keeping me up at night making the lights go on and off, making things move around, you know, real cheesy stuff. Anyway, I put up with it for several months before I contacted a specialist out of Savannah who makes a career out of the paranormal. Why do you ask?"

"Jordan said you brought your electronic gizmos out to The Cove and got a hit."

"I did, but didn't get an apparition, no materialization of any kind, just a lot of energy. So much so it was off the charts. That was after Scott died. I figured it was him, you know, watching over her."

"You didn't mention that to her, did you Wade?" Murphy asked, horrified at the prospect.

"I might have mentioned the fact that my sensors went crazy and she might have a resident ghost or two."

"Jesus, Wade. A woman living alone out there with a child. Are you nuts?"

Nick had to chuckle. "I don't think Wade got to her, Murphy. She's pretty well-grounded." He suddenly found the whole thing ridiculous. It's true he'd seen Scott in material form more than once, but he'd also brought the image back with him from Iraq, back to L.A. along with a shitload of lingering guilt. Scott never bothered much with moving things around or blinking lights, but liked making a nuisance popping up out of the blue. Now that he thought about it, he considered the whole thing laughable. He decided to chalk it up to an overactive imagination and a whole lot of survivor's guilt.

When Wade went into detail with yet another ghost story, Nick realized he missed Jordan, even though for the past couple of days the sexual tension had him working like a fiend to stay busy, to keep his hands off her. He knew with all the necking they'd been doing he had upset her with all the conflicting signals he'd sent out. But he couldn't help it. If he'd given in and taken her to bed, he'd have a helluva mess on his hands. But he couldn't deny what he wanted. He wanted Jordan in bed, under him, moaning as he came inside her. It's all he thought about.

Big mistake. She was Scott's wife. Had been, he corrected. But damn, lately every time he was near the woman, he wanted to get her naked and horizontal. You didn't do that with another man's wife, a man who'd been your buddy. And yet, that's all he could think about doing. What kind of a friend was he anyway? Scott deserved better.

He looked out over the water at the horizon. Fishing wasn't exactly a contact sport. It gave a man plenty of time to think. And all he could think about was Jordan, the way she smelled, the way she moved, the way sunlight brought out the gold in her hair. He'd never missed a woman before, but he missed Jordan like he'd miss his next breath.

And even though Wade and Murphy expected him to sleep on the boat, he'd already decided not to. They'd already said they would motor back to the pier, drop him off if he wanted. He had decided to take them up on the offer. He'd already planted the seed, telling them he still had a lot of work left to do that he couldn't put off. While that was true, it wasn't the truth. He worried about Jordan in that big house alone with just Hutton for company. He knew how silly that was. After all, she'd spent almost two years there alone before he ever showed up. But a blind man could see she was lonely. And he'd be damned if he was going to spend the night out on the goddamned water fishing when he could be spending it with her. Maybe he'd make it back in time to read Hutton a story.

A guy could hope.

As soon as he reached the apple-green and white sign at the bottom of the long driveway leading to the house, Nick cut the engine on the Harley. Even though it was only a little past eight o'clock in the evening, on the off chance Jordan had already put Hutton to bed, he didn't want the loud noise of the motorcycle waking up the baby.

In the darkness, he crawled off the bike and wheeled it silently down the path the rest of the way. When he reached the side of the house, he parked it beside the porch. It wasn't until he reached the bottom step, when he'd removed his helmet that he thought he heard a noise and turned to see Jordan sitting in the porch swing—alone—and crying. He moved so fast, his big feet tripped on the porch steps trying to close the distance. Dropping down on one knee in front of her, he asked, "What's wrong? Something's wrong, Jordan, talk to me."

Jordan sobbed out, "Someone in town turned me in for hitting Hutton, for abusing her. They...they called social services. Carla Vargas was out here today, made an official visit. They said...they told social services Hutton had bruises, purple bruises on her little body. Why would they do that, Nick?"

Seething at the news, he wanted specifics. "Carla was here? Today? What exactly did she say?"

"This morning just after you left. I tried to put it behind me, tried to get some work done, but I...I don't like it here anymore, Nick. I don't want to stay. I...these people are mean. The whole town must hate me to do something like this. I can't live here anymore."

"Whoa, come on, let's get you inside. You're shivering. I'll build a fire, fix you some tea, and we'll talk about this."

He pulled her out of the swing, keeping his hand on her shoulder while his other hand slipped into hers. Once inside, he started to head to the kitchen to make the tea when she said, "There's brandy in the liquor cabinet. I think I'd prefer that instead."

Nick poured a generous amount into two snifters, and brought the glasses over to where she sat on the sofa. He took a seat next to her. Staring into the fire, Nick struggled to calm down. He glanced over at Jordan sitting next to him, watching the fire just as intently. The woman had every right to be upset. Without thinking, he touched her arm, rubbing his hand up and down trying to get her warm. She sniffled and rubbed her nose. Even with eyes rimmed red, her nose runny, the woman looked adorable. "Talk to me."

"I've given this town over two years to come around. It's time to pack up and head back to San

Francisco, back home to my family." She took a gulp of brandy. The alcohol burned her throat all the way down to her belly. But she didn't care, she felt like she needed glasses of the stuff just to get Carla's visit out of her system. She'd have the memory of having to undress her own daughter in front of a social worker stay with her for too long.

Nick listened, but didn't think she really meant it. She'd worked like a dog trying to get this place ready to open. But she was hurt and angry and maybe a little scared at the moment. She had every right to feel that way. It was that combination of things that had her wanting to run without a fight. She wasn't thinking straight. "Your husband had a dream, right? It's almost a reality. Just a few more weeks and you'll open, guests will start showing up for real. Then things will look a whole lot better. Everything will turn around."

"If people in this town are that low, that mean, maybe I don't want it to turn around, maybe I don't want to be around people like that. Did you think of that? Maybe I don't want my child growing up in a town like Pelican Pointe. Maybe this is the wrong place to have a dream, the wrong place to make it happen." She finished off the brandy and let it slide down, warming her insides before getting up and going over to pour herself another glass. She felt so cold even being this close to the fire. How could she ever have thought these people would ever warm to her? Scott. Scott had told her they would that's how, she thought, as she threw back another drink from the glass she'd just poured. Once you got used to the taste, the liquid wasn't nearly as fiery.

He smiled into her warm brown eyes. "There is that."

The brandy loosened up her tongue. "Look, Scott's gone. He isn't coming back. I've given some thought about what you said that night at the cove. Scott had this memory from childhood about this little town that he loved so much, but that little place doesn't exist. The people here simply don't live up to the image Scott painted. He went on and on about these people. Other than Murphy have you met anyone here who's nice? Have you met anyone here who's worth knowing? And Lilly doesn't count. I mean she counts. You know what I mean, she and Scott didn't even know each other. These people treat Lilly just as badly as they do me. Look at Sissy. What possible reason could Sissy have for begrudging Lilly a little extra money?" Jordan paused, staring into the gold liquid in her glass before adding, "I think it was Sissy who made the call." With that bad taste in her mouth, she drained her glass.

He thought about that and remembered the scene at the fair. "Figures. She'd do it just for spite to stir things up, pay you back for getting Lilly the booth."

She poured herself another brandy and drank it down. "Exactly. She's the only one with a real grudge against me." Her words started to slur.

Before she knew what was happening, Nick dragged her down onto the sofa with him and into his chest. Her head began to spin. She let it fall to his shoulder. She felt him stroke her hair. The warmth of the fire and the brandy began to settle her nerves. Or was it Nick, having him here? She relaxed into his body. His shirt felt worn and smooth and smelled a little like the ocean, or maybe fish. She closed her eyes reveling in the intimacy of this moment.

He turned her mouth up to meet his. It tasted hot from the warmth of the brandy. When she licked at his lips, he lost what little control he had and deepened the kiss.

He made her tingle all the way to her toes. She tilted her head back to allow him better access. Her breathy sighs poured into his mouth. He felt her body loosen, relax, knew the exact moment she let go and got caught up in the kiss.

She moaned. "When you touch me I can't think...touch me, Nick."

He turned her in his arms, sighing into her hair. "Shhhh. You've had a rough day. You need to relax, baby." His thumb found her nipple through her shirt and circled it until it pebbled. He slipped his other hand beneath the waistband of her cotton shorts. And found her moist and hot. While his fingers moved back and forth, back and forth, she moved with the rhythm stroke for stroke. His mouth stringed kisses from her temple to her neck and back again leaving a wet trail. "This'll make it better."

"Oh. Nick, don't stop."

"Hang on to me, Jordan, just me." As she clung to him, it took every fiber in him to steady his breathing and concentrate on getting Jordan to climax. With each sigh he felt her body surrender a little more, a tremble here, a tremor there until seconds later she came into his hand with a shudder and a low, sultry moan.

With the tension drained from her body Nick kept his arms wrapped around her holding her tight. "Better?"

She looked up at his face with a dazed, satisfied glow, and ran a hand along his jaw. She all but purred in a drained voice, "Nick, don't leave me tonight."

"I'm not going anywhere."

"Make love to me, Nick."

"You're plowed, honey."

"I am not." She did feel a little drunk. "You wanted me relaxed, I'm relaxed, that's all. I want you. Period."

He took her chin and tilted it up so he could see her eyes. Despite the glazed look, he was tempted. "Listen to me, Jordan. When I take you to bed the first time, I want you completely aware of what you're doing. I don't want you regretting it the next day."

After several minutes of silence, Nick glanced down and saw the alcohol had finally kicked in. She was snoring softly. He held her like that for nearly an hour before carrying her to bed. Dropping down on one knee on the mattress, he gently laid her on top of the comforter before maneuvering her body and legs under it, covering her up.

He sat down on the bed next to her. For the longest time he watched her sleep, inhaling her scent, imagining what it would be like to sleep in here, wake up in this room, this bed alongside this woman every morning. He stroked her hair. Then silently he bent down and kissed her forehead. Then gingerly kissed her nose, her mouth, barely touching his lips to hers. She moaned slightly. He wanted more, so much more. But it wasn't right to want more. Reluctantly, he forced himself to get up, to leave.

Methodically, he went out into the entryway and checked all the doors to make sure they were locked tight before going back into the living room to douse the fire and cut off the lights.

As he made the trip across the yard to his studio apartment, he glanced up at the stars and said softly to no one in particular, "It should be you here, Scott. I'm so goddamn sorry."

Chapter Thirteen

Jordan woke to Hutton babbling over the monitor. Her head ached—no it was more like—it pounded. She took a deep breath and thought she smelled coffee, but she was probably imagining it. When Hutton's baby talk turned to fussing, she knew there was no chance for a quick shower. She swung her legs over to the side and realized she was still wearing the shorts and shirt from the night before.

It hit her then. Yesterday. Carla Vargas had stopped by—but not for a friendly visit. No, after Carla assured her that the complaint would be filed away as having no merit, she'd still spent the day upset. But for Hutton's sake she'd kept it together until last night— when Nick had come back. Nick. The last thing she remembered was his hands—doing things to her. She grew warm remembering his gentleness, the tender way he'd treated her. She'd felt safe in his arms for the first time since...

Damn it. If only she hadn't fallen asleep. Was there some cosmic force at work keeping Nick out of her bed? She was beginning to think so.

Fifteen minutes later, she carried Hutton into the kitchen. Nick stood at the stove, forking bacon onto a paper towel. He cocked his head and gave her a once over. "I heard you get up. There's coffee."

She inhaled the aroma. "Thank God." After she locked the tray in place on Hutton's high chair, she poured coffee and watched as Nick got out the sippy cup, filled it with milk and handed it off to the baby, who eagerly took it. Funny, she thought how quickly he fit into our lives as if he belonged here. She snorted. *Try convincing Nick Harris of that.*

Nick walked to the cabinet, pulled out a bottle of aspirin, dumped two into Jordan's palm. "You look like you could use these."

"Thank you." Jordan eyed him over her cup. She wondered if they were back on an even keel. For some reason it didn't feel awkward after last night. She sucked up her courage and finally said, "You should have stayed last night, Nick."

He laughed. "I wanted to, but you were sauced. Even a player knows the rules." He continued with breakfast, letting the bacon cool as he cracked eggs into a skillet to scramble. Trying for a detached mood, he calmly asked, "How'd you sleep?"

Okay, so he wanted to play it cold, she could do that. "Like a rock."

"Good. You needed it."

She sipped her coffee, wanting desperately to recapture the easy banter they once had between the two of them. "Catch any fish?"

"A couple. I had no idea about Carla's visit, but I wanted to get back here. I missed being here, missed you and Hutton." As he busied himself dumping some of the eggs onto a plate and taking it over to Hutton, he let his words hang for effect. When he looked up at Jordan, their eyes locked. She couldn't keep up with his moods or gauge how she was supposed to respond so she went with the truth. "I'm so glad you came back last night. You must have known I needed you. I'm sorry I feel asleep."

"Hey, you needed a shoulder, I was there." Grabbing bread, he stuffed four pieces into the toaster. Filled up two glasses with orange juice. "And I needed to be here with you, too."

"Last night I was ready to give up, just pack up and go, but…"

"You didn't mean it."

She smiled sheepishly. "I was angry."

"It was a rotten thing for someone to do, call social services like that."

She blew out a breath. "Well, I need to get over it. I don't have time to dwell on petty stuff like that. Carla says it's over and I have to believe her, otherwise—"

"Good because I have something that might make you feel better."

She walked over to where he stood, touched her hand to his face. "Do you ever. And it certainly did make me feel better."

His lips curved. "Get your mind out of the gutter. It's a surprise," he said casually as he sat down at the table and dug into his food. He pushed the platter of eggs toward her. "Here eat your eggs before they get cold."

"You're going to make me wait?" Scooping up eggs onto her plate, she chewed at her lip.

He grinned. "Aww, I didn't know you were so impatient."

"Very funny." But she nibbled at her bacon clearly contemplating what it might be. "Is it a good surprise or a…"

"Definitely good," he said as he took a mouthful of eggs, and then slowly buttered his toast obviously enjoying the idea of making her wait.

"So I'll like it, because I really don't want a bad surprise this early in the morning. Why don't you just—give it to me. Now." She smiled at her own joke.

"It's more fun this way, you saucy wench, a side benefit to watch you so—impatient."

Just then someone knocked on the back door. When Nick looked up, he saw Murphy standing on the back stoop. Nick let him in and noticed the man looked upset. "I thought you were fishing."

"Carla called me last night. Left a message on my cell, which I didn't find until this morning. I was too upset to fish. Wade and I both came back in. Thought I'd stop by and tell Jordan what a rotten thing it was they did. Tell her I'm in her corner."

"Want some coffee?"

"Sure."

Nick motioned for him to take a seat at the table while he went over to the coffee pot. He looked over at Jordan, saw she had tears in her eyes.

"Thanks, Murphy."

He reached to give her a hug. She noted how much he smelled like fish. "Once I got Carla's message I wanted to get out here, tell you not to let this get to you. She said not to worry. She'll take care of the paperwork. It's done now Jordan, put it out of your mind. It's obvious whoever made that call was just trying to make life tougher on you, hoping you'd run." When Nick brought over his coffee, Murphy sat back down at the table. "I didn't mean to stop by so early, didn't mean to interrupt breakfast."

"We were done. You just wanted to make sure Jordan wasn't about to leave. She isn't. Want some eggs?"

Before Murphy could respond, Jordan blurted out, "I'm sure it was Sissy."

"What makes you think it was her?"

"She was angry that we gave Lilly the booth. Plus, she's never liked me."

"Oh, that. Sissy's always upset about something or other, always mad. Just last year she threatened me with a recall. She always makes idle threats. It's her national pastime. Nobody much pays attention. It's just Sissy's way."

"No. I think she made the call, Murphy. Of course, I'll never really know for sure."

"It's over, Jordan. I'm here to tell you to put it behind you. Now that I know you aren't planning on packing up, I feel better. I'm here to tell you to forget it and move on."

She nodded. "I'd just told Nick the same thing."

"Then we're in agreement. You're staying right here in Pelican Pointe. And yeah, I wouldn't mind having some of those eggs and a couple of slices of bacon."

It made no sense for Jordan to dwell on someone as petty as Sissy Carr. She wasn't even certain that it had been Sissy who had placed the call and would probably never know for sure. She decided she needed to spend some time outside tending to her herb garden. She had neglected her plants while trying to get the inside of the house ready. Gathering up Hutton, together they headed out to the garage to get her gardening tools.

For the next hour she busied herself digging in the dirt, pulling weeds, watering, trying to take her mind off the past twenty-four hours. Every so often her mind drifted to the last thing she remembered, falling asleep with Nick's arms wrapped around her. Even though this morning there had been no mention of her mind-shattering climax, replaying it had her stomach fluttering, her pulse kicked up, she grew warm, and not from the sun.

She could kick herself for falling asleep. She obviously was terrible at sending a man signals that it was time to take her to bed. Maybe she'd make a candlelight dinner tonight and seduce him.

Content to dig in the dirt and pull weeds, she lost track of the time and was startled when she heard a car making its way up the long, narrow driveway. She got up, dusted off her jeans, before scooping up Hutton and hurrying around to the end of the house where she ran into Nick, who had obviously heard the car, too. At that moment, Jordan was stunned to see Hutton reach out her arms for Nick. Obliging, Nick dusted off his hands on his jeans before plucking her out of Jordan's arms. As soon as they all three rounded the corner, Jordan spotted a pickup truck, loaded down with furniture in the bed, ambling up the drive. She took off in a run, yelling back at Nick, "It's my sister, Ellen. Looks like they brought the rest of the furniture."

By the time Jordan reached the pickup, it had pulled to a stop and the female passenger, a woman in her mid-thirties with the same dark blonde hair coloring but worn in a short bob, popped open the door and slipped out. Just before the two women started to hug, Ellen pointed to Jordan's clothes and said, "Why are you so filthy?"

"I've been digging in the garden. I'm so glad to see you." Ignoring the dirt, Ellen pulled Jordan into her arms, wrapping her up. Just then, the man who had been driving the truck came around to the other side.

"Don't I get a hug too?"

"Of course, I'm so glad to see you both. I thought you were coming down next weekend. Why didn't you call?"

"Because Sammy's soccer league starts and it was either now while Mom and Dad could watch the kids or not at all. So we decided to bring down the last of Aunt Sophia's antiques. And when Mom and Dad offered to let the boys spend the night, we jumped at the chance to get away. The Cove is always so beautiful this time of year."

"And Ellen wanted to surprise you. Looks like we did." Turning to Nick who was holding Hutton in his arms, he reached out a hand. "I'm Tom Downey, Jordan's brother-in-law." Spotting the dog at the man's feet, Tom asked, "Well, what have we got here? Looks like Hutton's got herself a new puppy."

As the men shook hands, Nick introduced himself. "Nick Harris. And the puppy is Quake."

Behind the men, Ellen whispered to Jordan, "Oh, my God, that's Nick? What a hunk. Not hard on the eyes, is he? I still can't believe you're letting a stranger live with you."

"Don't start. He's living over the garage and you know it. Besides, he's been a perfect gentleman."

As is the language of sisters, Ellen eyed Jordan with doubt. "You sound disappointed."

Jordan nudged her sister in the ribs. "Shut up. He's more like a godsend." Or a saint, she decided. Just how many times could one woman throw herself at a man before he got the message? "And wait until you see the work he's done, the progress we've made. Because of him, we might actually open on time."

It didn't take long for Tom to commandeer Nick to help him unload the furniture out of the truck bed. For the next thirty minutes the men were busy carrying in antique beds, along with matching chests and dressers into the house and up the stairs into the guest rooms.

Later during dinner, Ellen and Tom did their best to pull information out of Nick. At first, the conversation seemed strained and awkward, but when the talk turned to what progress Nick and Jordan had made on the house, they were soon discussing how to put the finishing touches on the place before opening day.

Tom wanted Nick to know, "I can't believe how much work you've gotten done since the last time we were here. You have me until we leave. If you want, I can help you carry in the rest of the furniture from the garage. That way Ellen can help Jordan get the rooms set up. And if there's time I'd be happy to help you finish laying that flooring I saw up in that second bath."

"That'd be great. There's a broken window in there that has to come out though. Just haven't gotten around to it yet."

"I saw that. There was a lot to do to this old house, Nick. Scott didn't have enough time before…" His voice trailed off when he realized what he'd said. He looked over at Jordan, remorse written on his face. "Sorry."

"Don't be silly, Tom," Jordan remarked trying to make Tom feel better.

Tom sucked in a breath. "Well, we can't have the guests using a bathroom with a broken window, now can we? If you order the glass, I'll help you put it in." He gave his wife a quick look as if to say, "Help me out here, dear."

Ellen took the hint. "I notice you're taking one room at a time, finishing it before moving on to the next. That makes sense."

"Nick pointed that out right after he got here. Before, I was all over the place. I never seemed to be able to finish one thing before I'd move on to something else."

"You were stretched too thin."

Tom took a drink of iced tea and said wistfully, "I was hoping to get in some surfing before going back tomorrow. Do you surf, Nick?"

"I do."

"Then maybe Jordan will let us use Scott's boards. What do you say, Jordan?"

"Tom, how can you say such a thing?" Ellen asked in a huff.

Jordan reached over and put her hand on top of Ellen's. "It's okay. Scott's boards aren't a shrine. And it isn't a federal crime to bring up Scott's name." She turned to Tom. "Go ahead and use whatever board you choose. Scott wouldn't want them sitting there gathering dust. Nick's already surfed. And when we have guests they'll be using them as well. Scott bought them and wanted them used."

Ellen turned to stare at her sister. Silently, she wondered if maybe there might be something going on between these two. To Ellen, Jordan didn't look as miserable as she had at Christmas. Could it be she'd already begun to heal? As soon as she heard Nick's next comment, she was sure of one thing, these two definitely had a vibe going.

"Jordan and I picked up one of those baby seats for Hutton. We've been taking bike rides down to the road and back. You should see Hutton get into the ride."

Ellen looked from Nick back to Jordan, and noticed the funny expression on her sister's face. That couldn't be love, she decided. It was too soon for her sister to have that goofy look on her face when it came to a stranger. Not knowing what to make of them, Ellen switched topics. "How are those recipes working out I sent you?"

"Still experimenting. I haven't tried the Cornish game hens yet, but up to now Nick and Hutton have been acting as my guinea pigs. What do you think of the chicken?"

Without stopping to think, Tom revealed, "It's a little dry."

Losing her patience with Tom, Ellen put down her fork, scolding him, "Tom, do you have to say the first thing that pops into your head every single time. For goodness sake, Jordan's doing the best she can. And I for one happen to think the chicken tastes delicious."

Jordan smiled over her wine. "Down girl. Tom's just being honest. I need to know what works and what doesn't before I have a house full of guests and complaints about the food."

In an attempt to make amends, Tom offered, "I do love this bread."

"It's brioche. It's actually fairly simple to make. I found the recipe in one of Mom's old cookbooks," Jordan explained. "Do you remember when we were kids those appetizers Mom used to make with Bisquick for our sleepovers?"

"The ones with pork sausage and cream cheese? Oh, God, I remember. Those might make an interesting breakfast dish for the buffet. And they were super simple to throw together."

"Aunt Sophia's dresser looks good in the room with the bay window, don't you think?"

Ellen couldn't help noticing that Jordan practically beamed. It had to be because the house was starting to take shape.

"Nick and I had this idea to name the rooms, like some of the other B & Bs do. We were thinking maybe an ocean theme, or maybe a shell theme, something like The Dolphin Room. What do you think?"

Ellen looked uncomfortable. She wondered if Jordan realized she kept referring to them as we, like they were a couple. She wondered if this man might be taking advantage of her sister's vulnerable state. She needed to find out. But instead of ruining dinner with questions, Ellen kept silent. She continued to listen as the three of them brainstormed names for the rooms and bantered ideas back and forth until Jordan got up to get dessert. When she brought back individual apple and cinnamon tarts, Jordan set one down in front of Tom and told him gently, "I hope this makes up for the dry chicken."

"Now Jordan that was no reflection on your cooking. You know I'm not really that fond of chicken."

"Don't worry about it. If you'd let me know you were coming I'd have planned on grilling steak. So, it's your own fault."

Everyone dug into the tarts and Nick sighed, "What this woman does with pie should be outlawed."

Again, Ellen watched as Nick looked longingly at Jordan. Every time Jordan moved the man's eyes drifted to her sister—and lingered there a little too long. By the time Jordan poured fresh coffee, Ellen had decided there was something going on between these two. And when Hutton made it clear she wanted out of her high chair, Ellen sat stunned as Nick got up to get a wet washcloth to clean up the baby's face as if he'd done so a hundred times before. There was something telling in the gesture, something familiar, as if the three of them were completely at ease with each other.

But Jordan paid no attention to Ellen as she stood up to take Hutton out of Nick's arms. "This little girl needs a bath. We're off to scrub off some of this food."

"Yell if you need help," Nick volunteered jovially before taking his seat to finish his coffee and dessert.

But as soon as Jordan disappeared into the hallway, out of earshot, Ellen kicked Tom under the table, signaling it was time for the Spanish Inquisition. Ellen picked up her wine glass and got comfortable. With a little too much eagerness in her tone, she stated flatly, "I've tried nice. Now I'll just get to the point. She isn't over Scott."

"I believe you're right," Nick said evenly.

Ellen looked at Tom for support, hoping he'd jump in with his own tough questioning.

But Tom was a disappointment. "I really like your Harley. What year is it?"

Without waiting for Nick's reply, from across the table, Ellen stared down her husband. "Tom, don't you want to ask Nick about his work, if he makes a decent living working as a carpenter?"

Finally, picking up on the hint, but clearly uncomfortable doing so, Tom asked, "Uh, is there plenty of work for a carpenter these days?"

"Actually, I'm an investment banker," Nick revealed smoothly, sipping his coffee.

Ellen came close to spitting out her wine. Quickly recovering, she jumped on that. "Why would an investment banker be working as a handyman?"

From carpenter to handyman was a big drop in a few short minutes, Nick mused, as he picked up his coffee cup again. But he good-naturedly played along with the nosy sister. "I took a leave of absence to recharge and ended up here along the coast." Nick immediately sensed Ellen's distrust. He couldn't in good conscience blame her for it.

But it was Tom who frowned at his wife, ignored the glare she sent his way. "What do you think of the location of this place, Nick? Do you think she's got a chance of making it work? Will she get the traffic she needs to make a go? We're worried about her all alone out here."

Nick sighed. He didn't blame them for that either. "Location isn't the problem. The hostile town is another matter. It isn't that they aren't supportive, because they aren't, but I can just picture someone pulling off the I-5 or the 101 maybe lost, needing to find lodging for the evening. Then them making their way into Pelican Pointe and having someone in town telling them they have to go all the way into Santa Cruz for a room just for spite. She won't get much help out of Pelican Pointe."

Ellen's probing attitude fell away. "We're on the same page there. I can just see that happening. The whole family fears for her down here by herself. We've tried without success to talk her into moving back to the Bay." Ellen shook her head. "She's stuck out here in the boonies trying to keep this stupid dream of Scott's alive no matter how ridiculous it is."

Nick stared at Ellen over his cup. "Some dreams are important enough to keep alive, don't you think?" He turned to Tom. "To answer your question, she'll get the traffic depending on how aggressively she marketed the place in the early stages. And from what Jordan's told me, she's done a good job of getting her name out. She's almost booked up for May. Did she tell you that? She has reservations coming in daily for June. She could use a full summer. And another extension on the loan wouldn't hurt either." He'd been waiting to hear from Charlie on that score, but so far there'd been no word. He shot a look at Ellen and found her staring at him. "She's doing all she can."

Impressed with the man, Ellen relaxed somewhat. "We're getting the word out, telling everyone we meet about the B & B. Some of our friends from church have already booked rooms for May, celebrating an anniversary, or a birthday." She took a slow sip of wine, eyed the man at the end of the table before adding, "I just hope she can run this place by herself."

It was eight-thirty that evening when Nick and Tom settled down in front of the television in the living room with a cold beer to watch the Giants take on the Dodgers at home. "Are you a betting man?" Tom asked, propping up his feet on the coffee table.

He wasn't, but he was a die-hard Dodger fan who, in that other life, had once held season tickets, box seats behind home plate to be exact, for a number of years. "Depends. What's the bet?"

Tom took a drink of his beer. "I've got twenty that says McDonald doesn't go the distance."

Nick considered how many full games McDonald pitched last year and calmly replied, "You're on."

While Nick and Tom watched the ballgame, Jordan and Ellen sat at the kitchen table looking through magazines searching for cute decorating schemes for the guest rooms. As if she couldn't wait a minute longer, Ellen looked up and asked, "You aren't falling for this guy, are you?"

"What makes you think that?"

"Come on, Jordan, the man's a hunk. And every time you open your mouth, it's 'we' did this and 'we' did that."

Jordan looked genuinely baffled. "Oh, for God's sakes Ellen, it's a habit. I was part of a 'we' once, now I'm not."

Ellen felt immediate remorse. "Sorry, I just don't want to see you hurt. But tonight at dinner you had this look on your face."

"A look? I had a look on my face."

"You look happier than I've seen you look in—a long time—and sort of moony."

"You're concerned because I look happy and in your opinion moony? I can't win with you, Ellen."

"He won't stay, Jordan. I don't want you hurt again."

Jordan sighed and put her elbows on the table. "Why would an investment banker want to stay in a rundown B & B working as a carpenter? He doesn't think any better of the town than I do either. They yanked the welcome mat out from under his feet just like they did mine. Of course, I know he won't stay somewhere he doesn't like, or doesn't feel welcome. Hell, no one would. Well, except maybe for Scott."

"I worry about you alone out here. If Scott were alive I'd give him a piece of my mind for dragging you out to this place and then leaving you."

Jordan gave her sister a disbelieving look. "You do realize how ridiculous that sounds, don't you? When Scott went to Iraq he had every intention of coming back. It isn't his fault he didn't."

Ellen looked apologetic. "Okay I deserved that. But you know what I mean."

Jordan smiled. "Unfortunately, I do."

Three and a half hours later, Tom dug a twenty out of his wallet as he and Nick stood in the kitchen. "I never did like the Dodgers," Tom admitted without rancor.

"That's too bad. I never liked the Giants. I do, however, like taking your money," Nick assured just as evenly, as he dumped their empty beer bottles into the recycling bin.

"Giants will rebound tomorrow night, you watch."

"Sure they will," Nick said rolling his eyes. Grinning, he took Tom's twenty and headed out the back door.

Chapter Fourteen

After breakfast the next morning, the women put the men to work moving the remaining furniture from the garage into each of the upstairs guest rooms.

Once they got each piece delivered to the various rooms, at the direction of the women, they helped in the general placement of everything knowing full well the women would more than likely change their minds several times before they were satisfied with the end result.

The labor took most of the morning. But by noon the two men were ready for a nice break. They donned their wetsuits and took off to the cove to surf, gladly leaving the women to their own decorating schemes.

Because it was Friday and Lilly had no way of knowing Jordan had company, she showed up with her kids right on schedule. After initially feeling like a third wheel with the two sisters, Lilly eventually felt more at ease once they all sat down to lunch. Over homemade spinach and artichoke pizza, they chatted about their kids, and then moved on to how best to decorate the guest rooms.

"Lilly here is quite the artist. She's provided some original beach scenes."

"I'm looking forward to seeing my watercolors in the rooms."

"The plan is to put at least one framed watercolor up in each room, not just for decoration but to market Lilly's work. Ellen brought some new frames that should look great."

When they'd swallowed the last bite of pizza, anxious to get started, Ellen asked, "Should we split up or tackle one room together until we finish it?"

"Let's complete one room until we're done, less work for Lilly and me when you head back to the Bay."

With everyone in agreement, while the kids napped, they got to work upstairs, first getting the furniture arranged the way they wanted. From there, they started throwing together the decorating schemes for each room using different kinds of shells, depending on the theme they'd chosen, then hanging a coordinating landscape.

Standing in one of the larger guest rooms, they'd dubbed The Coral Room, Lilly suggested, "Along with the original watercolors, what if we used some of your favorite photographs of the coast, pictures you've taken on trips that have special meaning to you. We could blow those up, mat and frame them. I think pictures like that would look wonderful in here."

Jordan agreed. "Good idea, Lilly. I can dig out some of our old photos of the coast we took on the trip up to San Francisco a couple of years ago, maybe use those frames Aunt Ginny gave me for a wedding gift. Remember those art deco ones I never knew what to do with? They're stored somewhere out there in that black hole of a garage. And, if I haven't said so lately, thanks. The place is really starting to come together. I don't know what I'd have done without everyone's help."

Ellen smiled and put her arms around Jordan. "No problem, honey. What are big sisters for?"

"And friends," Lilly chimed in, feeling more like a part of something than she had in years.

Down on the beach the men walked out of the water carrying their surfboards. Tom pointed to the sea cave back under the trail and said, "There's a dinghy stored in there. If you're up for it we could motor out to Treasure Island, check it out. Scott loved that place. You should get a firsthand look."

Nick stared at Tom. Jordan had suggested he do just that. But he had been hoping he could persuade her to take the trip with him especially on his inaugural trip exploring the island. Suddenly, Hutton popped into his head. It was strange to be considering how a child impacted the activities you planned. There would be no motoring out to the island together unless they could get someone to watch the baby. "Do you think they'd like to go with us?" He shot a thumb over his shoulder toward the house.

"Might. But I don't think Jordan's gonna want to take the baby out in a dinghy. I know Ellen would have a fit if I had suggested taking one of ours out at that age that far in a little boat."

"So do you think Jordan would mind if we took it out?" Nick wasn't fooling Tom.

"You want to see it with Jordan? Don't blame you there. But I think she'd be okay with you getting out there today. Why don't you plan a picnic and take her out there once you get a good look at the place. She'd like that."

A little uncomfortable knowing Tom saw through him so clearly, Nick wondered what it must be like for Jordan every time she thought of Scott. It had to be any number of times during any given day. How long would it take for her to stop hurting every time someone mentioned his name? For that matter, would the hurt ever subside or lessen? Hadn't she seemed so much better lately in that regard, less sad, less depressed? Even he had to admit the image of Scott had stopped popping up so often. His nightmares were less frequent, less severe. He was getting more sleep. Of course, he said none of this to Tom as they approached the entrance to the cave where the dinghy was stored.

"You never know what you'll find in this black hole," Tom muttered as they made their way inside the cave. In spite of the darkness he spotted the dinghy bobbing in the water, moored by a rope looped around the spiky arm of a rock. He pointed to the boat pushed back inside a good ten feet out of the weather. "This thing's almost like new. Scott only took it out three or four times before leaving."

The cave was surprisingly dry and large, a narrow cavern of about ten feet wide that snaked into the dark another fifteen feet back. As they looked around in wonder like two twelve-year-olds in awe of what nature managed to provide, Nick thought of Scott. "Every kid's dream. I would have loved growing up here as a kid." It was a far cry from the way he'd grown up at the military academy. "It must have been something to have this place all to himself as a kid."

"It was. When I first met the guy he told me it was like living the Swiss Family Robinson kind of life. You have to remember his parents died when he was five and his grandparents took him in. This place, this house was a haven for him. I was only down here once with him right after he and Jordan bought the place. Next thing I knew, he was gone."

The dinghy was heavier than it looked. It took both men to drag the boat out of its resting place to the edge of the water. Once there, Tom looked at Nick and said, "Let's do this for Scott, what do you say?"

Nick gave him a nod in agreement as he waded out into the water pushing the boat toward the horizon. With the current, it took twenty minutes of motoring to reach the rocky shore of the little island. As they got closer, Nick cut the engine and immediately saw the place for what it was, a veritable paradise for any young boy, willing to spend his days exploring. Heck, it was pretty cool even for two grown men. Nick was the first to hop out of the boat. Looking around, he exclaimed, "This place is amazing."

"Yeah. We could probably do some serious fishing out here. By any chance you staying put?"

"Thinking about it. But Jordan might have something to say about that."

"You like her I can tell."

He nodded, not sure that he was ready to have this discussion knowing every word he said would be relayed to Jordan's sister in no short order.

As if sensing the other man's thoughts, Tom assured him, "Look, I love my wife, but I won't tell her what you don't want her to know. I can keep things close to the vest."

Nick seriously doubted that. But instead of voicing his concerns he repeated what Tom already knew. "Jordan's been through a lot. She isn't anywhere near ready to move past Scott. I plan on being here until the place is up and going. I won't leave her in the lurch, if that's what you're worried about."

"I was thinking more along the lines of the future."

"I'm staying put until I know she's got a handle on everything."

Tom patted Nick on the shoulder. "You're a good man, Nick Harris. I can leave in a better frame of mind knowing you're here for her. Thanks for that."

With Tom in the lead, sharing what Scott had told him about the island, the two men went off to explore the little slice of land as if they'd just discovered a new continent like a couple of fifteenth-century Spanish explorers.

That afternoon, by the time Nick showered off the sea salt and sweat, it was almost supper time. He'd played away the day surfing, exploring and now it was time to get some work done. But he was surprised to find Jordan and Ellen sitting in the swing on the front porch with Hutton and Tom a few feet away admiring the Harley.

When Tom spotted Nick, he asked, "Would you mind if I took Ellen for a little ride? I've been trying to talk her into one of these things, but she thinks they're dangerous as hell."

Nick looked skeptical. "Can you handle it?"

Tom looked slightly insulted. "I took motorcycle lessons hoping Ellen would see how skilled I was and cave. So far, she hasn't. But I can handle it."

"What about a helmet? I don't have a spare."

"Got it covered." At that, Tom headed off toward the garage. A few minutes later, he came back holding a motorcycle helmet.

Nick raised a brow. "Don't tell me, you found that in that black hole of a garage. Is there anything that isn't stored in there?"

Tom laughed and winked in Jordan's direction. "You didn't tell him? Our Scott was a major pack rat."

Jordan smiled as if remembering. "That he was, Tom. There's no telling what you'll find stored in there either. The man shopped online and seemed to collect anything and everything. And refused to throw anything away."

Holding up the helmet, Tom turned to Ellen and gave it his best shot. "Okay, baby, what do you say we go for a ride on this bad mother? A Harley, Ellen, come on."

Ellen stood up and walked down a few steps. "Promise you won't do anything crazy?"

He put a hurt look on his face. "Me? You're safe with me, Ellen. You know that." He held out his hand and she walked the rest of the way down the steps taking the helmet from him.

"Okay, but I better come back in one piece. I'd hate to explain to the boys how their mother cracked a tailbone on the asphalt falling off a motorcycle."

Tom winked at Nick. "If the worse happens, I died a happy death on a Harley." When Ellen gave him a blank stare, he simply shook his head and crawled on the bike.

Jordan watched as they headed down the driveway toward the road. "I can't believe he talked her into getting on that thing. She's a big old 'fraidy cat, pure and simple, wouldn't even try a skateboard when we were kids."

Nick couldn't resist. "And you would?"

"You bet and I've got the scars on my knees to prove it." He took a slow gaze up and down her legs, lingered long enough on her trim, fit waist, settled on her hips and the shorts she wore and then purposely stared at her knees. "I don't see any scars so I guess when they get back, you'll just have to prove it."

"You're just a real badass on a Harley, aren't you, Nick Harris?"

He grinned at that as the bike roared its way back up the driveway. Ellen swaggered off. "That was fun. And we didn't end up as a splat on the road, either."

Unsnapping his helmet, Tom told Nick, "I told you I could handle it."

Nick turned to Jordan, lifting a brow in challenge. "Come on Jordan, give it a try. Your sister's one up on you."

Clearly interested, but hesitant, she chewed on her bottom lip. "How fast would we go?"

"I promise to keep it under a hundred."

Jordan's mouth gaped open. Nick shook his head and moved to straddle the bike. "You're too easy. Come on. Live a little. I promise to take it nice and slow."

Ellen shed her helmet and handed it off to Jordan. "Go for it. I've got Hutton covered."

Climbing on the back of the bike behind Nick, Jordan tentatively put her arms around his waist. The first contact was nothing more than a light hug, bracing for the bike to accelerate. But when Nick hit the gas, it gave her an excuse to wrap him up. It felt a tad awkward to have her arms around him again but as they cruised down the driveway, she found herself more relaxed, holding on to him felt natural. By the time he got to the road and made a right turn, she forgot to feel self-conscious and locked her arms for real. As soon as he got out on the open two-lane road however, he instinctively kicked it up a notch. The increase in speed had Jordan sucking in a breath and holding Nick firmer, tighter. With another increase in speed, she let herself enjoy the pace, the rhythm of the road and the wind. And slipped her fingers underneath his Tee.

Nick had one thought. Her body felt amazing up against his. Her thighs vibrated into his. When the road curved and he leaned into the turn, she did the same. He felt her nipples through her Tee burning into his back. When a couple strands of her hair whipped out from underneath the helmet, he caught her scent and wanted to pull the bike off the road and bury himself inside her.

Knowing he needed to rein in his thoughts, he sighed into the ocean breeze hitting his face. This was a buddy's wife. A dead buddy. Would that wedge always be there? he wondered. He needed to step back, find a way to... Hell, who was he kidding? That ship had sailed. Many more nights like the other night and taking cold showers wouldn't even be a possibility.

He laughed at that. The only thing that seemed to work was the fact that Scott kept getting in his way. And he wasn't sure how to break free of that.

Eventually, he spotted a clearing ahead and reluctantly pulled off onto the shoulder, turned around, and headed back south.

When the motorcycle pulled to a stop in front of the porch again, Jordan swung her legs off, unbuttoned her helmet and threw her arms around Nick. "I never thought it would be that much fun. With the wind in your face, it feels like you're flying. Thank you for the most exhilarating ride of my life."

He'd liked to show her another kind of ride entirely. He was certain he could make it more exhilarating than the one on the bike. But as he unsnapped his own helmet, he couldn't help but get a kick out of her excitement, so much so, that he completely missed the fact that Tom and Ellen had witnessed her impromptu hug.

That night, after dinner, the four of them were sitting in the living room relaxing with a glass of wine, talking about the grand opening when out of the blue Ellen pointed to the piano and suggested to Jordan, "Come on, play something for us."

After the last time, after seeing Jordan so upset and emotional just remembering her time spent here alone, Nick answered for her, "Jordan bought a new Teddy Thompson CD the other day, how about if we listen to that instead. She doesn't fool me one bit; I think she's a little in love with the guy's voice."

Unbelievably touched, Jordan knew what he was doing. "You know Nick, I feel better about things tonight." She got up and walked to him. Bending down, she gave him a light kiss on the mouth before moving over to the piano. "Tonight, I'm taking requests."

For the next two hours, Jordan played anything and everything from Elton John tunes to Tchaikovsky, keeping everyone in stitches as she periodically stopped long enough to tell silly jokes.

"Why do potatoes make good detectives?" Jordan asked, before waiting a beat to deliver the punch line. "Because they keep their eyes peeled. Okay, old joke." She looked over at Tom and noticed he was nodding off. "Uh-oh, looks like I'm losing twenty-five-percent of my audience."

Tom jumped awake, shaking off the dregs of sleep. "Sorry, but I'm about done in. It was all that furniture moving."

"You mean all that surfing," Ellen corrected.

"Look, when I start falling asleep sitting up it says I've had too much wine." He stood up. "It's been fun kids, but I'm off to bed."

Ellen stood up too, yawned and arched her back. "I'm anxious to try out our room and that bed. I'm packing it in, too."

"Party poopers," Jordan said to their backs, as she started collecting their empty wine glasses to take to the kitchen. Nick picked up his empty beer bottle and followed her.

"Don't you owe me a surprise?" she asked casually as she loaded the dishwasher with their glasses.

He grinned. "Thought you'd forgotten."

"A woman never forgets the promise of a surprise."

He walked toward the laundry room, pausing when he got near the upright freezer in the corner. From the side, he retrieved a large box from its hiding place. She stood mesmerized at the gesture as he dragged the thing over to where she stood near the doorway. It wasn't wrapped. Recognizing the logo, her hand flew to her mouth. She stared in awe at the box containing the Mauviel copper cookware set she'd coveted for over two years. Any other woman might be let down at getting pans as a gift, but not Jordan. She dug into the box as if it were Christmas morning. "Oh, my God, how did you know?"

He watched as genuine pleasure spread across her face. He laughed. "Are you kidding? You practically salivated on the page every time you got to that section of the catalogue. And if that wasn't enough you have a sticky note as a bookmark with your wish list spelled out."

"But they're so expensive, Nick. You shouldn't have."

He rubbed the back of his neck. "I felt kinda funny buying a woman a bunch of sauce pans, but…"

Reverently, she touched the copper through the plastic protective wrapping. "Oh, Nick. I love them. Mine are ancient, hand-me-downs from my mom's catering business she used for almost twenty years. These are…perfect. Thank you. What's the occasion?"

He reached out and tucked a strand of hair behind her ear. "Early grand opening present. You're the best cook I know. You deserve the best."

She reached to take his hand, planted a kiss on the palm. "So do you. When will you ever see that, Nick?" She purposefully rested her other hand on the side of his face.

He cleared his throat and started to pull back. She recognized the gesture. This time, however, she spoke before he did, "At some point, you have to give me a chance. Let go of whatever's troubling you. Talk to me, Nick. Is it a woman? Were you so in love that she hurt you?"

Slowly, he lifted her hand from his face and held it, kissing the palm as she had his. "If I could talk about it, you'd be the one I'd tell. You have to believe that, Jordan."

"Somehow, I know that's true. Just remember, when you're ready. I'll be right here."

He paused when he got to the back door. Just before turning the knob, he looked at her and said, "And just so you know, I've never been in love enough for anyone to hurt me."

Until now.

Chapter Fifteen

The next morning, Jordan had tears in her eyes as she watched Tom's truck head down the long drive as they headed back to San Francisco. She and Ellen waved to each other until the truck made the right turn at the road and disappeared out of sight. As Jordan slowly made her way up the steps, eyes full of tears, she bumped solidly into Nick's chest as he stepped out on to the porch carrying his motorcycle helmet. A shaft of panic hit her, alarm lodged in her throat as she realized Nick too, was leaving.

Nick saw the unease in her eyes and pulled up short. He took her by the shoulders. "I need to pick up the glass for the bathroom window before Ferguson's closes."

Jordan's face lit up. "You're coming back."

"Of course, I'll be back." He shot her a grin. "In fact, why don't I take the two prettiest girls in the county out to dinner when I come back? You can fix those Cornish game hens some other time. Tonight, let someone else cook for you."

"The Hilltop is open until eight."

"I had someplace else in mind, like Santa Cruz. We can be there in thirty minutes, have some dinner, walk the pier, show Hutton the boardwalk lit up at night."

Joy flashed across her face. "We'll be ready when you get back."

As Nick flew along the Coast Highway on his bike his mind whirled in a hundred different directions. He didn't really want to be going into town right now and certainly not making a trip back to Ferguson's. What he really wanted was to get his hands on Jordan, feel her body draped around his, her legs wrapped around him.

Deep in lusty thoughts he was almost to Pelican Pointe when a set of iron gates off to the left caught his eye. His heart dropped out of his chest. He hit the brakes, causing the bike to skid dangerously to a stop in the middle of the road. Jesus. God. Shaking, he shot a U, heading back the way he'd come. He pulled up in front of the gates that led to Eternal Gardens, obviously the town cemetery, knowing instinctively this is where Scott had been laid to rest. How had he missed this place in the time he had spent here? He'd traveled this road dozens of times. Why had he not thought to find Scott's final resting place before now? Why hadn't he asked Murphy where Scott was buried, the one man in town who knew his secret?

Slowly he made his way past the gates and onto the grounds. He got off the bike and walked among the headstones. Eternal Gardens wasn't that big. It took him just a few minutes to locate the right spot. When he spotted the marker, he dropped to his knees to read the headstone.

David Scott Phillips
Beloved Husband and Father
Died In Service to His Country

Nick opened his mouth to speak, but couldn't make the words come out. Tears filled his eyes. He reached out to touch the headstone and for the first time noticed the fresh flowers. Lilies. Crimson stargazers, Jordan had called them. It didn't take much imagination to picture her in this spot, sitting with Hutton. How often did she come here? he wondered, as he sat down on the grass and rested his head against the cool marble.

"It's just my body and bones there, bro. My spirit's right here, alive and kicking."

Nick's head snapped up. He swore. "Jesus. Would you stop doing that?"

"You should be used to me by now."

"Well, I'm not. So, cut it out."

"Okay. But one of these days you're gonna wanna talk. Until then…"

"Wait…"

But it was too late Scott was gone. Nick sighed and laid his head back down on the cool marble.

Back at The Cove, Jordan's bedroom looked like a cyclone had hit it. Clothes were thrown over the bed, on the floor, and her closet looked just as bad. She'd gone through her entire wardrobe to try to find just the right thing to wear. She knew it was silly, but she couldn't help herself. She wanted to look good tonight. After thirty minutes, she finally settled on a floral print sundress. She might have to squeeze to get into it but it'd be worth it. When Hutton crawled out from under a pile of clothes halfway between the bed and the closet, Jordan asked, "Which earrings should I wear, the pearl drops or the gold hoops?"

Hutton answered with a long string of babble. "You're right the sundress looks better with the hoops. Hoops it is.

Okay. Now we pick up this mess and get you fixed up. We want to look good tonight, baby girl."

Even before the SUV reached the highway to Santa Cruz, Jordan noticed how quiet Nick had been since he'd gotten back from town. Her imagination kicked into overdrive as she tried to figure out what had happened there to make him so sullen. Anything was possible. He'd left the house in a good mood and now it didn't take a genius to figure out that the life in his eyes looked drained as if it had never existed. Determined to get to the root of the problem, Jordan asked jovially, "Did you enjoy surfing with Tom?"

"Yeah. It was great. The area has a good breakpoint, not too much undertow. You should have come with us. You need to get out more, Jordan."

"I'm out now thanks to you. I got three more reservations this morning for June."

"That's good. You could use a busy summer."

Softly she pointed out, "I noticed Nick you didn't come back with the glass. Did something happen in town? Did someone say something to upset you?"

Nick shook his head. He knew she was worried about his behavior since getting back from the cemetery, so he lied. "Got there too late. Ferguson's was closed by the time I pulled in." He turned his eyes from the road for a moment and asked, "When's the last time you went anywhere, Jordan?"

"Hutton and I spent Christmas in San Francisco with my parents."

"Christmas? That was months ago." He looked back at her. "Did you take something for the depression?"

She blew out a breath. "Doc Prescott came out once and gave me a prescription, but I never got it filled." When he started to protest, she explained, "Hutton was three months old. I was breastfeeding. I didn't want to take medication. I wasn't sure if I started taking something I'd ever be able to stop."

He sucked in a breath. "Jordan, did you even see a professional, talk to a grief counselor?"

She shook her head again. "I guess Hutton was my sounding board."

Nick reached for her hand, gave it a squeeze. "I'm sorry you've had it so rough." He could kick himself now for his reluctance in making the trip, for taking so long to get here to help. But he couldn't say that. How much longer could he keep his secret? He didn't know the answer to that, but he knew it damned sure wasn't going to be now and it wasn't going to be tonight. No way was he going to ruin this evening out with Jordan. It might be the only one he ever got.

Once they arrived in Santa Cruz, Nick found a parking place near the pier. Like most couples with a baby they had to unload the car, which meant the stroller came out of the back first, then they eased Hutton out of her car seat before grabbing the diaper bag. Even a novice like Nick knew there was a method to the unloading. He'd already discovered that you never went anywhere without the diaper bag, which weighed a ton because it held a lot more than diapers, like a supply of food, the necessary sippy cup, extra clothes, a clean dry washcloth just in case you needed to do an emergency cleanup, and the essential baby wipes for cleaning up after a poop.

After getting Hutton settled in the stroller, they headed toward an upscale restaurant out over the water. But as they got closer, Jordan realized where he was taking her. The same restaurant where two years earlier she and Scott had eaten their final meal together before he'd shipped out. She swallowed, hard. And stopped walking. Could she go back in there?

When Nick realized Jordan was no longer walking beside him, he turned around and saw she'd stopped. Nick had no way of knowing the restaurant held such painful memories for her. Determined to give her a nice night out, he gave her his most charming smile. But before he could say anything she said, "We can't, Nick, this place is way too expensive. What if we just grabbed a hotdog on the Boardwalk, maybe catch the sunset out over the pier?"

He thought she was worried about the money so he draped an arm around one shoulder and prodded, "Jordan, I didn't just spend forty minutes in traffic to eat at a hotdog stand. Besides, you look amazing tonight in that dress. We're not wasting that on a hotdog stand and we can see the sunset from the restaurant." When he realized she wasn't moving, he got more serious. "Jordan, don't argue with me about this. Tonight we're going to eat in a nice restaurant. I want you to enjoy yourself."

She gave in because it felt ridiculous not to. It was just a restaurant after all. She was able to take that first step by telling herself that Hutton had never been there. It was a new experience for her daughter. Well, not really, the last time Jordan had been here, Hutton had been about the size of a pinto bean.

Fortunately, the place wasn't crowded. They were seated almost immediately and the hostess provided a high chair for Hutton. But one look at the menu told Jordan the prices hadn't changed. They were still outrageous. So she did what she'd done with Scott almost two years earlier, and ordered the clam chowder, adding, "I'm not really that hungry."

But Nick would have none of that. He gave her an annoyed look and told the waiter, "We'll take a bottle of your best cabernet and two steaks cooked medium."

When the waiter left, she leaned across the table. "How do you know how I like my steak?"

He lied. He couldn't very well mention that her late husband had told him a good many things, little tidbits of things he hadn't wanted to know then but now circled in his head, like how she liked her steak. "Lucky guess. It's a known fact the majority of people like their steaks cooked medium. I just went with the percentages."

Jordan looked skeptical, but began to relax. It was hard not to. He was trying so hard to see to it she had a good time out. By the time the wine arrived she was determined to enjoy it. "This is a big step up from the Hilltop."

"I should hope so. But I do kind of miss those God-awful, pink waitress uniforms Margie makes everyone wear."

Jordan laughed and began to unwind.

Over dinner, she watched in astonishment as Nick fed Hutton some of his baked potato. When he saw the look on her face, he laughed. "Hey, I've watched you enough times, I know the drill. I'm a quick study. I think I must be doing this right, she's chowing this stuff down..."

"Like she's never had a baked potato." She was, too. Her face was covered with food. When Nick took the initiative and ordered chocolate cake for dessert—a piece for each of them Jordan marveled at the cost, "Nick, that's twelve dollars just for dessert!"

"Would you stop worrying about how much everything costs."

When the waiter dropped off the dessert, Hutton was no dummy. Spying the chocolate, she clapped her hands together and squealed, "cake."

Nick spooned up a bite and stuck it in her mouth. He looked over smugly at her little chocolate mouth and crowed, "Cake. That's the magic word. Hutton's getting into the spirit of the evening. Although, it isn't as good as your mother's, but then she didn't have to slave over a hot stove."

"You make it sound like I'm chained to the kitchen. Because Mom was a caterer I grew up cooking and baking. I enjoy it."

"I know you do. You even make your own blackberry jam. I never knew a woman who didn't ignore the kitchen entirely, let alone actually enjoyed creating something from scratch. You make it look so easy, like it comes natural to you."

"Well, I wouldn't say that. But I love making up new dishes. There's a joy in that."

"It shows in every dish."

Once they left the restaurant, Nick took over pushing the stroller and they headed down the pier to the Boardwalk. They rode the carousel with Hutton six times. They showed Hutton all the lights along the pier. They walked through the arcade where Nick won a huge bear shooting skeet. By the time the fireworks over the water ended, Hutton was out like a light.

On the drive back to Pelican Pointe, Nick glanced in the rearview mirror at the sleeping baby. "We wore her out. Maybe we shouldn't have stayed for the fireworks."

"But the fireworks were the best part. And the carousel. Did you see the look on her face when we sat her up on the horse for the first time? Shoot. I should have remembered to bring the camera."

"I should have used my iPhone. I wasn't thinking. She was a little scared on the carousel at first. That look on her face was priceless."

"It was. That's why I should have had the camera, so I could capture that moment. The look on her little face said it all. What if you only get that look once, Nick? We missed it."

"Nah. We'll bring her back."

We will? She wondered if he meant it, but refused to dwell on that tonight. "That bear you won is bigger than she is." Jordan laughed and realized she'd just spent hours with Nick and hadn't thought of Scott once after leaving the restaurant. She sighed. "It was a wonderful evening, Nick. I haven't had such fun in— gosh, so long I don't remember. Thank you."

He took her hand in his and brought it to his lips. "My pleasure. I'm glad you had a good time.

"Oh, I did. The best."

When they got back they put Hutton to bed as a team. When they got the sleeping baby tucked in, they stood there a moment and watched her sleep. Nick leaned over and placed a chaste kiss on Jordan's forehead. Just the slight brush to her skin had every nerve in his body tingling.

Looking up in his eyes, she whispered, "I'm so glad you're here, Nick."

"Are you?" He put his hands on her waist, drew her into him. With his body he backed her out of the baby's room, out into the dark hallway, bent his head, found her mouth.

Acting on instinct, she sucked in his tongue. Glorious heat, wet and wonderful, spiked between them. She melded into his taut chest. But just when things started heating up for her, once again, Nick ended the kiss, backing away. In the dark hallway, she heard, rather than saw, his sharp intake of breath.

"I've got to go."

He started the move past her, but she grabbed his hand. "Not this time, Nick."

He shook his head. "I can't." He saw Jordan swallow hard, saw the rejection in her eyes. "It isn't you."

Tired of the rebuffs, she retorted, "Oh, really? You could have fooled me. I'm tired of making an ass out of myself with you. I just don't get you, Nick. One minute you're the epitome of seduction, the next you play devil's advocate. Are you purposefully trying to be mean, sending me so many mixed signals? When it gets right down to it, you obviously aren't that attracted to me."

"Are you nuts? You're the most beautiful woman I've ever known." He ran a hand through his hair and realized it wasn't just a line. "I'd love nothing more than to take you to bed, make love with you. Don't you get it? It takes every single cell I have inside me, not to. I'm not ready to be a substitute for—" He'd almost said

Scott. "Your husband." There he'd said it. "You don't think I saw your face tonight when we got to the restaurant. Stand there and tell me you weren't thinking about another time, another place...with him."

"I..." How could she deny it? "Nick..."

He lifted her chin. "You don't have to say a word, baby. Let's face it, you aren't over him. And I'm not quite prepared to be his stand-in. Every time I'm near you, I think I am, I think I can be. But this is too important, maybe more important than anything I've ever done."

With that he turned and walked down the hall, leaving her standing there with her mouth gaped open. Seconds later, she heard the back door open and close.

Like all the other times, Nick had gone. And she was left alone.

Chapter Sixteen

The next morning when Nick didn't show up for breakfast Jordan knew something was wrong. She didn't have the heart to go looking for him either. What would she say? She wasn't certain she could assure him that she had indeed put Scott completely behind her. At the same time, she resented being put in the situation where the decision was all on her. Why should it be? Couldn't she simply have sex with the guy and be done with it?

Who was she kidding? Of course she couldn't. Nick was right about that, the next step was too important to simply jump in the sack. She had Hutton to consider.

But she wanted Nick, she knew that much without a doubt. She just wasn't absolutely certain she was ready to take that next step. No doubt he had read that indecision, her hesitancy, like a book. Had she been that easy to read each time they'd gotten close? Maybe all this time she'd been the one sending the wrong signals.

Okay, so she wasn't a major player in the game. She glanced at her hungry daughter waiting patiently for breakfast. No, she wasn't a player, she was a mother. Instead of dwelling on her lack of a sex life, on automatic, she poured a bowl of cold cereal for Hutton, something she rarely did.

Jordan drank her obligatory first morning cup of coffee, wondering all the while where Nick was. As if she were missing an arm, she went to the kitchen window and longingly looked out across the lawn to the studio apartment. If she had the slightest bit of courage she'd walk up those steps over the garage and see if he'd packed up and left for good.

While Jordan spent an agonizing morning over him, Nick had taken another trip to the cemetery. Sitting at the foot of Scott's grave, he looked around at the peaceful surroundings. What the hell was he doing here anyway? He'd meant to stay and help. Now he'd only complicated Jordan's life and his own. He ran a hand through his hair. "Damn you Scott, this isn't what you wanted. What kind of a mess have I made of everything now? Come on, damn it. You haven't been able to leave me alone for a year." He got to his feet, defiant. "You wanted to talk yesterday, well here I am." He paced up and down the length of the plot. "Now, I get the silent treatment. Come on, you son of a bitch, talk to me. What am I supposed to do now?"

By the time Jordan heard his motorcycle head up the driveway a few minutes before noon, she was a walking set of nerves.

For one thing she'd spent hours painstakingly preparing a French casserole for lunch using one of Ellen's recipes, a recipe that had seemed off with each ingredient. But for something different or more like special, she had even set the table in the dining room where she now stood nervously waiting like a schoolgirl for him to walk through the door. Should she pretend to be busy doing…something? Screw that, she thought, as she heard his footsteps on the porch.

But when he came striding in, her courage took a nosedive. He looked simply heartbroken. She fought the urge to ask where he'd spent his morning, what he'd been doing with his time. Instead, she tried for lighthearted to put him more at ease, maybe take that pained look off his face. "I should've known you'd decide to show up around mealtime. We missed you at breakfast."

Nick took one look at her standing in the dining room, saw that glow on her face that seemed to be constant and immediately his spirits lifted, like he'd come home. He noticed the table set in the dining room with her good dishes and asked, "We having company?"

"No. But I made something special, just wanted to try it out on my two test subjects."

He put his motorcycle helmet down on the hall table along with his keys and eyed Hutton, who had toddled over to him. As he bent down to scoop her up, Hutton held her arms outstretched and said, "Da."

At that one word, his heart slammed in his chest. Had Jordan heard? From twenty feet away he met her eyes, and realized she must have, even though she said nothing. Instead, she disappeared into the kitchen, leaving all her emotions like him, bottled up, unspoken.

"Hey there, Blondie. Let's go wash up and have us some grub. You hungry? I'm starving."

Minutes later, Nick came back, quickly slipped Hutton into her high chair and took a seat at the table. He ran a hand across the front of his T-shirt. "I feel slightly underdressed."

"It isn't that kind of special. I just thought we'd eat in here to be different."

"Whatever the reason, everything looks great."

"Looks gate," mimicked Hutton, clapping her hands together, waiting for the food.

"Looks like your pigs are ready and waiting at the trough," Nick joked.

Smiling, Jordan began passing around the food. "Let's hope it tastes as good as it looks."

But it didn't. After taking her first taste Hutton scrunched up her face and spit it out. Jordan looked at Nick who was a tad more subtle than the baby. He concentrated on his salad, pushing the cheesy main dish around on his plate without meeting her eyes. Jordan caught Hutton's arm in mid windup just as she was about to hurl the stuff over the side of her tray. "Well, judging from the panel of experts, I guess I can take the French casserole off the dinner menu."

Diplomatically Nick offered, "It might have limited appeal."

"Or no appeal. You'd think with all that cheese it would taste better. Maybe I should stick with what I know best and serve simple, basic fare, forget about fancy dishes."

"Fancy's overrated. Nothing wrong with simple."

Getting up from the table Jordan asked, "Who wants a peanut butter sandwich with homemade blackberry jam?"

Nick leaned closer to Hutton's high chair and worked on getting her to do a high-five with her little hand. "Now we're talking. Aren't we, Blondie?"

Later, as she picked up the dishes to carry into the kitchen, Jordan joked, "Nothing like eating peanut butter sandwiches off the good plates in a formal dining room to make the meal more elegant."

"Well, it was organic peanut butter. And you could market that jam of yours."

He followed her into the kitchen carrying the bad-tasting casserole. "Do you think Quake would eat it?"

"I don't want to make him sick. Chunk it down the disposal."

Nick began scraping the vile concoction into the sink. When she saw he intended to help her with the dishes, she shook her head, telling him, "Go on. Keep an eye on Hutton. It won't take me long to clean this mess up and start the dishwasher. I'll put her down for her nap after I get done in here."

"Are you sure?"

"Positive."

As soon as she had the kitchen cleaned up, she headed down the hallway to the living room. Before she rounded the corner, the quiet told her the TV wasn't on. There were no voices, no giggling, and no sounds of playing. She stopped and stared. Nick was sprawled on the rug and Hutton had curled up beside him with her little arms resting on his chest. In a matter of minutes they had both fallen sound asleep. Unbelievably moved, Jordan sat down in the nearest chair. Her eyes blurred with tears. Her heart felt like bursting with the love she had for this man.

That afternoon, they packed up their beach gear and headed down the trail to the cove to spend the rest of the day near the water. It didn't take five minutes before Hutton and Quake were soon running around on the beach. At one point, Hutton tripped and fell, started crying and before Jordan could reach her, Nick had her bundled up in his arms, instinctively brushing the sand off of her face and out of her eyes, telling her, "Hey there, it's okay. Shhhh, don't cry."

Jordan watched carefully as Nick bounced her daughter up and down before gently sitting her back down on the sand, trying to distract her with a plastic shovel as he moved sand back and forth. Forgetting the tumble, Hutton soon started to get the hang of the shovel. With wet sand she began work on piling the stuff into a mound. With his big hands Nick began to shape the mound of sand into something resembling a castle.

She wasn't sure when it happened exactly but slowly Nick had broken that block around her heart, allowing her grief for Scott to find another place to dwell. There was no doubt in her mind he had finally managed to push that pain and anger to a new place. Each day with him here, the sorrow around her heart lessened and now...

Jordan suddenly remembered she hadn't put sunblock on Hutton and dug into the diaper bag for it.

She took the bottle over to where Hutton sat in the sand and started trying to rub the sticky stuff onto her face and arms. Not wanting to be interrupted, Hutton protested by squirming, then fussing until Nick pulled her onto his lap and said, "Come on, Blondie, Mama's got to get this stuff rubbed in so you don't burn like toast."

If anyone had been watching, the three of them looked like any young family, two parents struggling with a resistant toddler, who were trying to get the child to comply without much of a fuss. The way he interacted with Hutton, no one would have believed the man had no experience around a baby. As Jordan turned to put away the sunscreen back in the bag, it hit her then, how her daughter had called him Da when he'd walked in the house.

But then, she also remembered he'd all but ignored it. Didn't the man realize how special it was for a baby Hutton's age to utter the word Da for the first time?

When the wind suddenly kicked up and the clouds rolled in, Nick looked at Jordan and warned, "It's time to pack up and head for the house. Storm's brewing. Looks like we might get rain."

They started packing up their gear, started heading up the trail toward the house. Nick carried a tired and dirty Hutton, while Jordan and Quake followed. Loaded down with the diaper bag, beach towels and blanket, Jordan had trouble climbing the hill. Nick suddenly turned back to her and said, "You okay?"

"Remind me again why we have to bring so much stuff with us."

He chuckled. "I keep asking that myself."

As soon as they got to the back door, Nick kicked off his sandals before stepping inside. Jordan did the same before making her way into the mud room. Nick sat Hutton down on the floor and Jordan immediately hurried to strip off Hutton's dirty clothes. "Time for a bath, dirty girl. Look at you, sweetie, you've got sand in your hair."

"Need help?"

"Nah, I think I can handle this. Where's that super soaker when you need it?" She picked up a dirty Hutton and headed for the bathroom. Nick laughed, as he heard her say, "I think we'll need the garden hose to get you clean tonight, sweetie."

He picked up the dirty clothes from the floor and headed into the laundry room. After dropping their beach clothes into the washer and starting a load, he yelled after her, "If you think you won't need me, I'll head for the shower myself. Hutton isn't the only one grubby."

It was true. The sand stuck like glue between Hutton's toes, under her fingernails, in the creases of baby fat on both arms and on the backsides of her knees. Jordan was just as bad. So once she got to the bathroom, she decided to forego the bath. She'd be better off taking Hutton into the shower with her and scrubbing them both clean at the same time. Stripping out of her clothes, she turned on the water and the two of them stepped inside, making a game out of removing that extra layer of dirt.

Later as they dried off, Jordan thought she heard pots and pans rattling in the kitchen, but she couldn't be sure. Her stomach rumbled from hunger. If she was hungry, Hutton probably was too. She hurriedly dressed them both then headed into the kitchen to fix supper.

At the door, she paused and stared at the man standing at the stove. While Jordan and Hutton had showered, Nick had fixed macaroni and cheese and put a gourmet frozen pizza on to bake. He was in the process of taking the pizza out of the oven when Jordan appeared carrying the baby on her hip.

Her hair was still wet. She wore shorts and a T-shirt and the baby wore some purple romper thing. He stopped long enough to gape. The woman looked absolutely amazing.

The man never ceased to astonish her, she thought, as she took one look at the plate of macaroni and cheese, already dished out and cooling on the table. She settled the baby in her chair, secured the tray in place and gave her a spoon, which Hutton promptly discarded and went to eating with her fingers.

Thunder rumbled in the distance and made Hutton shriek. "Loud!"

"It's okay, sweetie. It's just thunder."

Jordan gazed at the frozen pizza. It wasn't what he'd fixed but rather that he'd taken the initiative to prepare dinner while she'd been busy with Hutton.

"This looks good, Nick. Thanks."

"No problem. I would have called for delivery, but…"

"There isn't any," she finished for him muffling a chuckle. She dug out paper plates from the pantry and began to set out napkins and utensils on the kitchen counter.

"I'm pretty self-sufficient in the kitchen as long as it's out of a box or the freezer. Want a beer?"

Remembering they usually took turns with breakfast duty, she wondered why he was being so modest. His pancakes tasted better than hers. "Sure. I could throw a salad together to go with the pizza."

He reached in the fridge and took out two beers. With a nod of his head, he gestured to the bowls on the counter. "Got it covered."

"You're pretty handy in the kitchen, Mr. Harris. You did all this while we showered."

"Give me a microwave and I'm in my element. And besides, we guys don't take as long in the shower as you women." Nick found a pizza cutter, cut the pie into neat triangles, set it down on the counter between them.

"Watch it," she said jovially, "There were two of us and more dirt per square inch." She took a pull on her beer. "This looks delicious. I think we all worked up quite an appetite this afternoon." She picked up a slice of pizza and took a bite. "Ahh, nothing like pizza for good old comfort food."

Digging in, he smiled. "It isn't as good as yours, but this brand is the best frozen pizza on the market. I'm surprised Murphy stocks it. It'll do in a pinch when you're in a hurry or starving."

At that moment, thunder rumbled again, this time louder. "Storm's getting closer. I hope the roof holds. I did the best I could with the spotty patching job," he assured her, as another wave of thunder roared overhead, this time shaking the house.

Hutton shrieked again and put her hands over her ears, which spread cheesy stuff to her clean hair. "Loud!"

Nick reassured Hutton, "Thunder's just clouds bumping together. It'll be okay. It might just blow over or we might see some rain. The flowers need the rain."

"Rain," Hutton repeated.

As they ate their meal, the rain held off. But by the time they got an exhausted Hutton to bed and stepped out onto the front porch, fat drops of the wet stuff began to fall in earnest. They watched as lightning streaked across the night sky in the distance. "Looks like we're in for a stormy night."

"Looks like." They weren't going to discuss the weather again, were they? Jordan wondered. She'd already made up her mind. "I have spice cake leftover from yesterday. Would you like a slice with some coffee?"

"Sure. If we can have it in front of the fire."

She headed back inside and he followed. While she disappeared into the kitchen, Nick went to the living room to start a fire. The rain picked up as it beat down on the recently patched roof. "I hope like hell the patch job holds."

"Do we need to get out the buckets just in case?" Jordan teased, as she walked in carrying a tray laden with cake and coffee.

"It might not be a bad idea as backup." He sat down next to her on the sofa, picked up a fork, took a generous mouthful of cake. "God, this stuff is addictive. Your desserts are the reason I've gained five pounds over the last few weeks."

Eyeing his trim waist, she laughed. "You could use the weight, Slim. You don't exactly have a lot of excess mass on you," she said, reaching for her own plate. She forked over some of the cake and concluded, "As with everything you do around here I have every confidence in the job you did on the roof."

Their eyes met. "Your belief in me is…remarkable—and new."

"Somehow I doubt that."

"Once upon a time, I was cocky. Lately, not so much." He reached over and ran a finger along her cheek. "Have you any idea how beautiful you are, Jordan?"

She smiled as she picked up his hand, lightly kissing each one of his fingers. "Your pickup lines need a little work."

"You're perceptive. That's just one of the things I like about you." He leaned over and touched his lips to hers. She tasted like spice. The kiss was tender, gentle, lips lightly touching. Then as if control finally snapped, he took the kiss deeper and felt Jordan melt into his chest.

"Damn," he groaned and started to pull away. "I shouldn't have done that."

Refusing to give in to defeat this time, she pulled his head back down to her, teased his mouth open again with her tongue. Hunger gnawed in her belly. "Don't run tonight, Nick. Don't lock yourself away from me again." To lighten the moment, she teased, "My ego can't handle anymore rejection."

But the look in his eyes told her he wasn't getting the joke. "Don't you understand? This is killing me because I want you, but..."

"I've been ready for some time, Nick. I just haven't been able to convince you." When she saw his brow crease, she drawled, "Don't think it to death, Nick. Trust me on this."

That was all Nick needed to hear. "Aww, baby. I've waited to hear you say that for so long." Pulling her into him, he closed his mouth over hers.

Jordan thought the kiss just might liquefy her bones. Knowing he needed to hear the declaration, the words, so there was no mistaking her intent, she whispered in his ear, "Take me to bed, Nick."

He closed his eyes. A sigh of relief escaped. If she knew who would be here with her, who would be kissing her, loving her made all the difference in the world to him. He'd never waited this long to be with anyone before. Ever. Tired of waiting, tired of the torture he felt every time he got near her, every time he touched her, he picked her up and carried her into the bedroom.

As he made his way to the bed the rain picked up outside. He could hear the thick splats hit the bedroom windows, fall harder on the roof, as he simply dropped down on the bed, settled her on his lap.

In the dark, their tongues waged a playful little tug of war before he moved to nuzzle her neck, began to trail kisses down to her breast. He nipped at the bud of a nipple through her cotton shirt increasing her arousal. As he laid her back on the bed, she reached for the bedside light. But he stilled her hand and distracted her by planting another mind-shattering kiss on her mouth. He pulled her shirt up and off, unhooked her bra in one adept motion. Her breasts tumbled out. His breath hitched. "God, you are so beautiful."

He covered her mouth with his again while his long fingers found her breast and toyed with the rose-pink tips.

He trailed kisses along her jaw, down her neck until he found her breast with his tongue, suckling, relishing.

He ran his thumb down her cheek. "Do you know how much I love seeing the sunlight hit your hair just so? Or the sleepy look on your face first thing in the morning when you walk into the kitchen? Or the way your eyes get that certain sheen whenever you watch Hutton play with Quake? Or the concentration on your face every time I catch you standing at the kitchen counter creating one of your dishes from scratch?"

"Nick, you say the sweetest things." She started working on getting him out of his clothes. "But you talk too much." She reached to lift up his T-shirt.

But again, he stilled her hand. Instead, he moved both of her hands down to the bulge in his jeans. "Touch me, Jordan. I've waited so long to have you touch me."

"I will, everywhere. I want you, Nick. I've wanted you for so long." She began working the buttons open.

He kicked out of his jeans, left his shirt on. Although she'd already seen the scars, he didn't want to alter the mood and have to explain how he got them. Determined not to ruin this moment, his mind shoved away the images of the past two years and concentrated on the woman under him.

Beautiful Jordan somehow sensed his self-consciousness and focused on the moment as well. She began to nip and tug at his bottom lip, began to work her body in tune with his. Everywhere his fingers lingered he made her feel like a roaring furnace.

He kissed his way down her body, stopping to suckle at each rose-pink tip, to lick at her belly button, to savor each taste of her skin. Each time he went lower his tongue sought to tingle and touch, nibble and nip.

"Oh, Nick, please," she begged as he sampled and tasted her inner core and sent her over the edge in no time. It hadn't taken Jordan long to pop.

"God, you taste so sweet," he breathed into her.

And then with patience and care, Nick busied her mouth, while his fingers gently stroked every nerve in her body to life again. Trailing kisses to her shoulders and breasts, he coaxed her with his words. "That's it, baby. Give it up again, just like before, just like that. Come on now, do it for me. That's it, sugar."

After another glorious wave engulfed her, he quickly got rid of the shirt. In Jordan's blissful state she never noticed his scars.

Testing with his thumb he found her slick and hot, and shifted into her in one smooth motion. Building thrusts slowly at first, he fought to make it last. But it had been too long for him. The minute she matched the rhythm beneath him, he lost control, and found everything he'd waited for, in her.

Chapter Seventeen

Nick came awake, gasping for the next breath. Sweat dripped down his face. He sat up, looked around the room and blinked.

Jordan. He was in Jordan's bedroom. Scott's bedroom. He checked the time on the clock beside the bed. Four-fifteen. My God what had he done? Just as he started to crawl out of bed an arm snaked out and latched on to his. In a husky voice, Jordan wanted to know, "Where you going, Nick? It's still pouring outside."

Without saying anything he scrubbed a hand over his face. How could he face her?

"You're shaking," she said as she nibbled his ear, noticing he hadn't said a word in response. "I bet there's something I can do to help with that."

If only that were true, thought Nick, if only she knew the truth. If only she accepted him unconditionally. "You don't know me," he whispered hoarsely in a dry throat. He couldn't even bring himself to look into those gorgeous eyes of hers. After making love to her, he couldn't even face her. How would she take the news knowing he couldn't save her husband? What would she say when she found out that he was the reason he hadn't come back? She'd turn him out for sure. And what would he do then? He couldn't take the chance.

He started to crawl out of bed again.

But Jordan surprised him. She snuggled into him, using her body to push him back down into the pillows.

She had him right where she wanted him. Nuzzling his throat, in a sleep-filled raspy voice, she groaned, "No need to be afraid of me, Nick. I don't bite. Much." Even in the dark shadows, he could tell her smile widened. What was left of his heart shattered, filled with so much love for this woman he couldn't contain his need. No matter how wrong it was, he wanted her again. He snaked out an arm bringing her on top of him. "You make me crazy."

"That's the idea. Let go, Nick. Think of me, just me."

Head to toe, body to body, Jordan took control. It was her turn to sample and taste as she worked her way down his chest and belly, leaving sweet kisses on the scars he'd finally revealed but didn't want to talk about. When she took him into her mouth, she knew he'd finally let go when she heard the groan of pleasure over and over again.

And at long last, Nick let her shelter him from all the regret of the past year, as he once again lost himself completely, in Jordan.

The first thing she realized when she opened her eyes was that the storm had passed. Sunshine drifted through the curtains, instantly warming the room. The second thing she noticed was that the space beside her was empty. She sighed. After a night of lovemaking he'd run again like a scared rabbit. She glanced at the clock, six-thirty. Had Hutton slept late? Tilting her head to one side, she listened for any signs of Hutton's movement through the baby monitor. When she didn't hear a sound she decided to take the opportunity of golden silence and jump in the shower.

Fifteen minutes later she walked in to the kitchen. There was Hutton sitting in her highchair stuffing her face with blueberry pancakes. Nick sat at the table working his way through his own short stack. When he looked up, caught her standing there in the doorway, his heart felt like it flipped in his chest. He might have been torn between running and telling her the truth but he knew one thing. He was all the way in love with her. Shooting her a grin, he drawled, "Morning, sleepyhead. Want breakfast?"

He started to get up but she motioned for him to stay seated. After pouring a cup of coffee, she went over to him. After kissing him handily on the mouth, she worked her way between him and the table, straddling his lap. She whispered in his ear, "When do we get to do what we did two hours ago…again?"

Considering what they had done to each other earlier, he nibbled her ear and throat. Need sprang to life inside him. His heart raced. "First chance we get. Hutton's nap is when exactly?"

"The trick is to tire her out. That's my job." She nibbled his ear right back before trailing wet kisses down to his mouth. And whispered, "Sex with you makes me work up an appetite. I could eat a horse." With that, she got up and went over to the counter to fork over her own stack of pancakes.

"I always heard it was the shy, quiet ones you had to worry about. Now I know for sure." A new hunger rumbled in his lower belly just watching her from across the room.

"That's your first mistake."

"What?"

She tilted her head. "Thinking I'm shy and quiet. But I'm willing to work on rectifying that misconception."

From across the room they locked eyes with each other. But when Hutton started dropping sticky chunks of flapjacks from her high chair onto the floor, it was Nick who stood up, started doing wipe-down duty. He sat Hutton down on the floor to play.

True to her word at ten-thirty Jordan put Hutton down for a morning nap, then went in search of Nick. She looked all over the house before finally drifting outside onto the upstairs balcony where she spotted him below standing near the cliffs, with his hands in his pockets, looking thoughtfully out to sea. Instead of shouting out for him to come back inside, she decided to go to him. Then a thought occurred to her. Grabbing one of the blankets out of the box at the foot of the bed, she ran downstairs, stopping just long enough to pick up the baby monitor from its cradle on the kitchen counter. For what she had in mind, they would need to be able to hear Hutton.

With her arms full and her heart bursting with lustful thoughts, she raced past the courtyard and toward the cliffs. Breathless, she snuck up behind Nick, dropping the blanket at his feet. She wrapped her arms around his waist. "Hutton's asleep."

Nick put his arms around her and kissed her on the temple. "I'm in awe of this view."

"It is beautiful here at this spot. You can see the entire cove from here."

"Yeah. But I wasn't talking about that view." He took her face in both of his hands. "Now, this one, I'm not quite used to, it seems I can never get my fill. This is the one I'm particularly fond of staring at, studying, especially these chocolate brown eyes of yours."

"Ahh, well, I brought a blanket. I thought we could..." Her voice trailed off as he took her mouth. The kiss had a slow burn erupting into a blaze.

But when it finally dawned on him what she was hinting at, he said, "A blanket? My kind of woman." And started peeling her out of her clothes as they dropped to the soft grass. Together they managed to spread out the blanket as they rolled in a tangle of arms and legs and body meshing into body.

Nick promised himself this time he'd slow down and enjoy the leisurely perusal over every texture and taste of her skin. But the minute Jordan began to unbutton his jeans, the fire ignited into a furnace. They couldn't get to each other fast enough.

"Hurry, Nick!" Jordan said impatiently as she slicked her tongue along his torso, driving him into madness.

"That's all I want to do when you touch me, Jordan, is hurry. I can't seem to slow down or get enough of you."

On his back, stretched out, he watched as Jordan slid down his body and straddled him, quickly taking him into her. As she began to ride at a fast clip, all he could think about was how he couldn't get deep enough. It would never be deep enough. He tweaked and played with her rosy-tipped nipples as she moved in and out above him. When she let out a low moan of satisfaction, he simply lifted his hips and began to pump faster, draining himself and the sorrows he'd felt earlier into Jordan.

Later, as she zipped up her jeans and stepped into her sandals, she asked, "Tell me again why we waited so long to do this?"

He chuckled at the breathless way she huffed that out and shook his head. "We're making up for lost time."

She giggled like a school girl. "What were you doing out here anyway, Nick? You looked deep in thought."

He lied. Again. "Just thinking about my list of chores. My morning was already planned out until this vixen came along and sidetracked me." He slipped on his tennis shoes and quickly added, "While I don't mind the distraction, it's past time I replaced the broken window in that upstairs bathroom. I picked up the pane of glass yesterday." He failed to mention he'd spent the better part of that morning at Scott's grave before making it into Pelican Pointe where Ferguson had actually opened up on a Sunday for the guy slowly becoming his best customer. It wouldn't do to dwell on that now. He picked up the blanket and gave Jordan a light kiss on the lips before quietly telling her, "The minute Hutton goes down for her afternoon nap, find me. I promise to make it worth your while."

As they started back to the house, she threw him a sultry look, and said simply, "I'm counting on it."

Once upstairs, he got to work. His first order of business was to get the cracked pane out of the frame without getting glass everywhere. It didn't take long to realize there was no way around that. The pane of glass cracked into three not-so-neat pieces. He did his best to tug on each pane until they all popped out of the frame. But not cleanly. Shards of broken glass stuck to his fingers. After painstakingly cleaning up the pieces, he picked up the new pane of glass and eyed the measurements. Damn Ferguson, he thought, and realized the cut was off just a fraction. It would probably be a tight fit. Swearing, he weighed his options. He could take it back to Ferguson's and have him trim it down or, he could try to force it into the frame. If he could get the piece to flex slightly, it might just work. Gingerly, he positioned the pane into the frame, gently applying pressure to the glass. Suddenly the glass popped back, broke off sharply, and sliced a gash across his left wrist straight across the artery.

Blood spurted out of the cut.

At the sound of breaking glass, Jordan ran into the bathroom in time to see blood gush from the wound. Grabbing a towel, she applied force on the gaping cut. "We need to get you to the clinic. Keep the pressure up while I wake up Hutton." When Nick didn't move, when he just kept sitting there, she saw the dazed look on his face and realized he might be going into shock or something. She yelled, "Now, Nick. Move."

Pelican Pointe had one doctor, Jack Prescott. In his mid-fifties, he'd moved to the area after spending twenty years as chief resident of emergency medicine in one of San Francisco's busiest ERs. Burned out, he'd retired on ten acres of coastal ranch land to ride his horses, go fishing when the mood struck, or surf when he got the urge.

That had been six years ago. Much to his frustration, as soon as the town realized they had a bona fide former superstar surgeon in their midst, they hadn't let his retirement stick. Residents started showing up at his house at all hours for medical advice or treatment for everything from common stomach ailments to the flu to broken bones. When his wife grew tired of people coming and going in and out of their house at all hours, she put her foot down and decided it was time he open a clinic in town with regular hours.

Located two blocks off Main, in an old, but renovated Mission-style house, the clinic consisted of six rooms, a waiting area just inside the door, a small kitchen where patients could get a cup of coffee or a soft drink, a bathroom, and three exam rooms filled with donated equipment. If you didn't want to make the trip into Santa Cruz for a medical visit, the clinic was your only option.

Jordan threw open the front door and stepped into the crowded waiting area with Hutton on her hip followed by an ashen-faced Nick holding a blood-soaked towel to his wrist. Looking around the room, there were at least four patients ahead of them. But Jordan wasn't in the mood to wait or offer niceties. She pushed Nick into the nearest empty chair and stormed up to the receptionist's desk. "We need to see the doctor. Now."

Nineteen-year-old Gina Purvis held up a clipboard and a pen and said absently, "You'll need to fill this out and wait your turn."

Not to be dissuaded, Jordan shook her head. "You don't understand. I've got an emergency. This man's sliced open his wrist, the cut is deep and he's bleeding from an artery. We're not waiting." With that, Jordan started down the open hallway looking for either Dr. Prescott or at least someone more qualified than a snotty teenager. Gina jumped up from behind her computer in an attempt to block Jordan's way. But Jordan beat her to the open doorway by a good two steps. By this time she had a good mad-on and had no intentions of letting Gina or anyone else stop her.

When the doctor, a six-foot-two broad-shouldered man, emerged from one of the rooms, he almost collided with her and the baby knocking them back a step.

"What's this?" Dr. Prescott wanted to know. "What's all the commotion?"

"I've got an emergency. He's cut his wrist, maybe the artery. It's bleeding badly."

"Bring him back here and let's take a look."

Jordan went back out to the waiting room, grabbed Nick's uninjured arm and pulled him down the hallway to the exam room. She helped him up on the table. When Dr. Prescott peeled back the towel, fresh blood immediately spurted out. He donned a pair of latex gloves, pushed Nick down on his back before he passed out from blood loss, and began wiping away blood with a sterile cotton pad. He stepped over to the counter, pulled out a suture kit from a drawer, and then filled a syringe. "I'll give you a local anesthetic that way you won't feel a thing." Over his glasses, he asked Jordan, "How'd this happen?"

"He tried to force a new pane of glass into the frame. It snapped in half and the sharp end sliced right through his wrist."

The doctor began to clean the wound. "You're damn lucky. A millimeter the other way and you could have bled to death."

"That's what I was afraid of."

"Now, you sit yourself down there with that baby, Jordan, I'll have him fixed up good as new." Then to Nick, as he forced the needle into his hand, he insisted, "If you're going to work with glass, son, you've got to remember, glass don't flex."

Weakly, Nick managed, "I'll keep that in mind."

An hour later, while Jordan ran into the pharmacy to get his prescription filled, Nick sat in the passenger seat of the SUV. Hutton slept peacefully in her car seat in the back. The nap they'd both eagerly anticipated earlier was now obviously not gonna happen. When Nick looked over, he saw Murphy strolling up to the driver's side of the car.

"Heard about the excitement."

"Jesus, word travels fast in this town. Is there anything not on the gossip track?"

"Let's face it Nick, you being here has given this town more to talk about than we've had in two years. We just don't know what you're gonna do next."

"Glad to be such valuable entertainment."

"Oh, we appreciate it. And Doc wanted me to remind you that, glass don't flex, son."

"Ha. Ha."

While waiting for Nick's prescription, Jordan walked down the aisles carrying a basket, picking up a few items she needed. When she looked up and saw Sissy bearing down on her, she swore under her breath. She wasn't much in the mood to put up with Sissy's mouth today.

"Doing a little shopping, Jordan?"

"What do you care, Sissy?"

Still pissed that the call to social services hadn't sent Jordan packing, Sissy went into plan B just because she could. "You know, Scott told me why he had to marry you."

"What? Scott would never say such a thing and especially to you. Why are you so mean and nasty, Sissy? Is it just your nature or didn't life work out the way you planned?"

Sissy threw back her hair and tossed a box of condoms in Jordan's basket. "You better take these, Jordan. You wouldn't want to trap Nick the same way you did Scott. Face it, the whole town knows Scott had to marry the little tramp from San Francisco. At the time he brought you back here we weren't even sure that baby belonged to him."

"So that's what you've been telling people, isn't it? Well, I wondered what story you'd conjured up for your own spiteful benefit."

Sissy snorted, "Knocked up's what Scott said, that's the only way you would've ever got a man like Scott to the altar."

"Is that so? You wanted Scott in high school, didn't you, Sissy? Well, get over it."

"We went steady. I had his senior ring."

"Until he asked for it back. Scott was never serious about you."

"That's not true."

"Oh, yes, Sissy, it is. Because he found out you were a catty, gossipy, hateful bitch, who'd sleep with a crowd. Scott dumped you, Sissy, and never looked back. Need I remind you about the rock concert, October senior year, when you went to San Francisco, got drunk and slept with the entire band. And let's not forget December of that same year when you slept with the entire basketball team. Oh, yes, Sissy, Scott knew. You didn't fool him for a minute." Jordan picked up the box of condoms and hurled them through the air at Sissy's face. "I think you probably need these much more than I do. Now get out of my way, Sissy. And please, do me a favor. In the future never, ever speak to me again."

Back at the cove, Jordan tucked Nick into the bed they'd crawled out of that morning. Sitting on the edge, she poured out two of the pills in her hand and reached for a glass of water. "Dr. Prescott said to take it easy. He didn't prescribe pain pills to have them sit in the bottle."

"Jordan, it's a simple cut on the hand, not major surgery."

"That took fourteen stitches to close, Nick. Now do I have to treat you like I do Hutton when she doesn't want to do something? Do you want me to hold your nose to get these down your throat?"

Annoyed with her, he took the pills out of her hand, threw them in his mouth and downed the glass of water. "Satisfied?"

"About this, I believe I am. Now get some sleep." She tucked the blanket around him, kissed him lightly on the cheek, and walked out of the room, closing the door behind her.

Fifteen minutes later the Percocet kicked in and he was down for the count.

Later when Jordan went in to check on him, she saw him thrashing about in bed, mumbling in his sleep. Moving to him, she saw how pale he was, how wet with perspiration he felt. She went into the bathroom, wet a washcloth and brought it back to the bed. Sitting down beside him, she started wiping his forehead, then his entire face. She touched his cheek with the back of her hand. He bolted upright almost knocking her off the bed.

"No. No. No. He isn't dead...he isn't..." "Shhhh. You were dreaming, Nick."

"What time is it?"

"Almost five. You needed the sleep, baby." Continuing to mop his brow with the washcloth, she was surprised when he stilled her hand. "Don't. Don't be nice to me, Jordan. I don't deserve it."

"That's ridiculous. You show up and turn this place around. Because of you, we might actually open on time. You're a good man, Nick." Trying for a lighter tone, she kissed his mouth, long and hard. "And just remember, I personally know exactly how very good you are."

He gave her a weak grin, but fell back on the pillows. "I'm not."

"What's troubling you, Nick? Talk to me. Tell me what's wrong."

"It's something…I have to deal with on my own."

"You don't, you know, have to deal with it like that. People often think they do, but talking about it helps."

"I've been to shrinks."

"No shrinks here, Nick. It's just you and me." She picked up his uninjured hand and kissed the palm. "When you're ready to tell me, I'll be right here. I'll bring you some supper."

"No. I'll get up. I need to get up, Jordan."

"Okay. Want me to help you stand up?"

"I can do it. Thanks."

"Big tough guy, aren't you?" She almost thought she saw him smile. But she left him to manage on his own.

A few minutes later he walked into the kitchen, wearing jeans and a button-down shirt he'd left open because he couldn't work the buttons. She had to admit he had more color in his face. He didn't linger too long in the doorway though because he didn't look all that steady on his feet. When he passed by where Hutton stood, he bent down and tweaked her little nose. "Hi there, Blondie. How's my best girl?" Feeling a little nauseated, he dropped into a chair at the table and put his head in his good hand.

Jordan brought him over a plate already filled with roast beef and potatoes. "Can you eat with your left hand or do you need some help?"

He picked up a napkin. "It smells so good I may lap it up like Quake."

Smiling, Jordan offered, "I could spoon feed you like I used to do Hutton before she got to be such a big girl."

Hearing her name Hutton toddled over and tried to crawl into Nick's lap. Because of his wrist, he struggled to get a good hold on her and pick her up one-handed. But Jordan reached down and picked her up, telling her, "Sweetie, Nick has an owie. He hurt his hand. See the bandage? And he's trying to eat his dinner."

"It's okay, just set her down on my leg and I'll hold onto her with one hand." Grinning, he added, "And maybe I'll let you spoon feed me after all."

"What do you say we spoon feed Nick his supper, Hutton? You need to learn how to use a spoon first though, huh?"

Jordan slipped Hutton into her high chair, freeing up both hands. She set a plate of already cut up meat and potatoes in front of her daughter. Out of the corner of her eye, she watched with amusement as Nick tried to cut his meat one-handed. Instantly taking pity on him, she went over and sat down next to him, took the knife out of his hand. "I have special training in this area, Mr. Harris. And you'll find I'm very good at what I do."

His mouth went dry. He forgot about food. Another kind of craving hit him. He'd never seen anyone slice meat with such seductive style. "It's always the quiet ones."

"Mmm," was all Jordan said while she continued with the byplay. She cut up each piece of meat, fed him a little at a time, alternating between the meat and potatoes he loved. "You know, Mr. Harris, if you stay here long enough you'll find The Cove is an all-inclusive B & B. We provide certain services above and beyond what's expected, you might say an array of goodies. Our amenities are known worldwide, sort of like guests with benefits."

He leaned over so only she could hear. "If they're anything like what I've sampled already, I'd say I've hit the lottery. But maybe you should limit a few of those services to only me."

"Oh, I plan on it, Mr. Harris. You're on our very special guest list."

That night, Nick was restless. Even with the pain pills, she noted that he woke up several times in a cold sweat just as he had earlier that afternoon. It seemed to Jordan that whatever was bothering him was so painful it even affected his subconscious. Lightly, she touched his face.

He jerked with a start.

When she saw his eyes pop open, she moaned softly, "That isn't exactly the reaction I was hoping for."

"Jordan." He drew in a breath, let it slowly escape. "I…I was dreaming."

"I know. Let me make it better." She rose up on one elbow, leaned into him and put her mouth on his lips, drew in his bottom lip, tugged. She placed a hand on his stomach and skimmed her way lower. She took him in her hand. He was already hard.

He raised one brow. "You want to fool around…now?"

"I was seriously considering it. But…if you're in too much pain…"

Vickie McKeehan

He rolled over her with the purpose of ending up on top. Instead, he grabbed at his wrist, groaning at the hurt and immediately rolled off of her.

"Be careful, you'll cause your stitches to open up." Patting his chest, she prodded playfully, "Looks like I'll have to do all the work."

His lips curved despite the intense pain in his wrist. "I promise I'll make it up to you."

"I know you will," she reasoned. "But until you're a hundred percent, I'd say it's all on me," she promised, as she skillfully began to work her way down his body.

Chapter Eighteen

Despite the energy-draining sex, Nick couldn't get back to sleep. Jordan, however, snoozed peacefully beside him. After lying awake for the better part of forty-five minutes, he couldn't take it any longer. He decided to get up and take Quake outside to pee. As quietly as he could he slipped out of bed and into his boxers, then managed to get his legs into a pair of sweat pants one-handed. When he got to the foot of the bed, he stopped to scoop up the sleeping Quake from the rug. As he crept out into the hallway he realized a walk outside would do them both good. Even if it was two-thirty in the morning and one of them was still half asleep. The dog looked up at him through bleary eyes as if to say, "What the hell did I ever do to you? I was dreaming about digging up a whole slew of bones."

Carrying the dog, he did his best not to make a sound as he opened the back door and stepped out into the crisp night air. The stars twinkled down at him as he made his way out onto the lawn. He hadn't bothered with shoes and the lawn under his bare feet tickled wet with dew. A chill shivered through him as he sat Quake down to pee and caught a movement out of the corner of his eye.

A shadowy silhouette stood near the end of the house about thirty yards away.

Great, thought Nick. Scott hadn't shown up at the cemetery for two days in a row and he picks now to put in an appearance. Nick didn't figure it was a coincidence that he'd just crawled out of Jordan's bed, either.

But Quake let out a growl. As Nick stepped closer and got a better look at the figure he realized it didn't walk like Scott. And it sure as hell was too big for a damned rabbit. Not a ghost, not a rabbit. Nick knew the minute the shadow of a man spotted him.

Nick thought he heard Scott's voice. "It's not me, you idiot! Go get him!"

Barefoot, Nick tore off after the guy as he rounded the corner of the house in a dead run. Hot in pursuit, he had no idea what he intended to do if, no when, he caught the guy. All he knew was the man couldn't be lurking around the house in the middle of the night out of the goodness of his heart. Even though the guy had a good head start, Nick shot down the driveway after him.

Weeks of physical labor had him in better shape than when he'd arrived. It didn't take long for him to catch up. Before the guy reached the end of the driveway, at a disadvantage with only one good hand, Nick threw his shoulder into the man just as he got to a Cadillac Seville. The tackle sent the man's body flying into the vehicle, head first. With a loud thud, Nick heard the guy's head connect with metal. The impact knocked the guy out cold.

Nick turned him over and recognized an unconscious Kent Springer.

With his hands tied behind his back with his own belt, Kent came to sitting upright in one of Jordan's kitchen chairs. Dizzy, he looked around the room and knew he was in deep shit. Kent watched as two fuzzy women, who when merged together looked a lot like Jordan Phillips wearing a bathrobe, stood at the counter making a pot of coffee. He tried to come out of his fog, but his head hurt as if a couple of jack hammers drilled simultaneously through the rock inside his brain.

As soon as Nick saw Kent come around though, he glanced over at Jordan. Fear had his throat tightening. What he'd discovered beside the house made him sick to his stomach. Nick turned to face Kent. He needed to make this sorry excuse for a human being understand just how much Jordan meant to him. He leaned over where only Kent could hear. "Are you awake enough to hear me, Springer? Because I want to make absolutely certain you understand what I'm about to say. I found the gas cans you dropped right where you left them. You sorry son of a bitch, you planned on setting the place on fire, didn't you? Are you aware just how much trouble you're in?"

Kent stammered, "I...I...have money. I'll pay you...and Jordan of course. This is a misunderstanding."

"Shove your goddamn money. Why did you do this, Springer? Why?"

"I...I've wanted this land since before Phillips bought it. We can strike a deal you and me."

"You piece of shit. I've already called the sheriff." When Jordan wandered over to where he stood over Kent, he immediately stopped talking. Nick automatically reached for her hand, needing the contact. When she leaned in to him, he tucked a strand of blonde hair behind her ear. "Thanks for the coffee, but I want you to head back to bed. I'll wait for the cops to show up."

She understood what he was doing. "I'll leave you two alone...for now. I'll go throw some clothes on. I want to make sure I'm around to watch them arrest this jerk."

Nick nodded. "Then go get dressed. The sheriff should be here any minute."

As soon as she'd disappeared down the hall, Nick turned back to Kent. "Just so you know I've been trained by the military. I bet I know fifteen different ways to maim and cripple a man...permanently. If I ever catch you anywhere near The Cove again, if I so much as see you anywhere near Jordan Phillips or her daughter after tonight, I'll make sure you experience ten of them firsthand. Are we clear?"

Known throughout the county as a straight talker, a no-nonsense kind of guy who ran a clean department, Sheriff Brent Cody stood talking to the newcomer Nick Harris, watching as his two deputies, one of whom was his brother, Ethan, concentrated on taking a few more evidence photos and dusted for fingerprints. They'd found two gas cans and a set of footprints around the side of the house that matched the shoes Kent had on.

Brent turned to Pete Danson, his other deputy and a twenty-year veteran, and instructed, "Get those molds done, will you? We're taking no chances this time around. And take pictures of his shoes."

The minute his brother, Ethan, had arrived on the scene and learned the complaint involved the low-life, scum-sucking Kent Springer, he'd called Brent who had driven in from Santa Cruz to oversee Kent's arrest personally, making sure there were no mistakes and the evidence gathered was by the book. If Brent intended to make the charges stick, his team had to be meticulous. None of them were taking any chances Kent might walk.

"What exactly do you mean this time?" Nick asked.

"I've been trying to get something on this guy for four years, ever since I took office. There have been rumors, complaints about him bribing county officials and the like. But this is the first time I have something concrete." He slapped Nick on the back. "Good job. I hate to think what might have happened if you hadn't caught him in the act. There's enough gas in those cans to light up this place like a bonfire."

Nick shuddered at the thought. "He'll probably make one call to his lawyer and be out on bail by noon." And if that happened, Nick wanted to make sure Kent wouldn't be a threat to Jordan.

"Maybe. But this time I plan to throw the book at Mr. Springer. In this state first-degree attempted arson is a class B violent felony. After I talk to the DA we throw in trespassing, attempted burglary, maybe even stalking. Who knows? Maybe I can get the woman he beat up last Christmas to press charges now. I intend to make this a lot harder for him to talk his way out of than last time."

"Sounds like a real prince of a guy."

"Between you and me and the fence post over there, the guy is a scumbag. Not many people in Pelican Pointe know this, but it's pretty much common knowledge around Santa Cruz. Lady he was having an affair with last fall went missing. Kent was the last known person to see her alive. And Kent had been stalking her, making threats, leaving nasty messages and sending her e-mails. She pressed charges for that, but before he went to trial the woman disappeared."

"Wow, you think he killed her?" Nick's blood pressure spiked. He looked up just in time to see Ethan Cody escort a now handcuffed Kent down the length of the driveway to the squad car. "Do you mind if I have one last word with him?" Nick asked Brent.

"You aren't going to take a swing at him, are you?"

"If I were, I'd have done that long before I ever made the call to you guys."

Relieved, Brent said, "Fair enough. By all means, be my guest."

As Kent passed by, Nick fell in lockstep beside the two men, accompanying them on the walk to the car. Just as the three of them got to the squad car, just as Ethan pushed the handcuffed Kent into the back seat, Nick leaned down to whisper something in Kent's ear.

When he was done, Nick walked back up the drive to where Brent stood.

"What was that all about?"

"I reminded Mr. Springer that if I ever catch him anywhere near The Cove again, I could guarantee he'd never be able to father anymore children and he'd walk with a limp."

Brent busted out laughing, slapped Nick on the back again. "Remind me, Mr. Harris, to never piss you off."

Later that morning as Jordan stood at the stove pouring pancake batter onto the grill, the phone rang. She picked up the cordless. "The Cove Bed and Breakfast, Jordan Phillips speaking. May? I'm so sorry but we're full up for May. But how about the second weekend in June?"

Sitting at the kitchen table drinking his fifth cup of coffee, Nick watched as Jordan flipped through the reservation book she kept on the corner desk. Good, another reservation, he thought, as he remembered he needed to follow up with Charlie in L.A. Knowing firsthand how long it took a loan committee to act, Nick realized they were quickly running out of time. They had less than ten days. A lot was riding on that decision. If the committee refused to give her another extension he might be forced to confess his secret. Confessing his secret meant finally coming clean. Coming clean jeopardized their relationship. She'd know he'd been lying to her from the start.

Just the thought made him edgy. He got up to take over for her at the stove while Hutton amused herself inside the bottom cabinet digging into Jordan's assortment of plasticware. The baby hadn't yet had breakfast but under the circumstances of the morning sensed that she needed to somehow be patient with the adults where food was concerned.

One-handed, he plated scrambled eggs then scooped up Hutton from the floor. After struggling to get her into the high chair with one hand, he poured milk into her sippy cup. Two months ago if anyone had dared to suggest he could make a toddler happy or knew her routine almost as well as her mother, he would have laughed in their face. But somehow this whole domestic picture worked.

When Jordan hung up the phone, Nick went over to where she stood, leaned in and kissed her hard on the mouth. With his one good hand, he tipped her chin up for better access and just for good measure because he could, he kissed her again.

"What was that for?"

"That was for me."

"You need sleep."

"I've gone without sleep before."

Jordan sighed and rested her head on Nick's chest. "I hate to think what might have happened if you hadn't gotten up when you did. You must have heard him, Nick. That's the only thing that makes sense."

He'd spent the morning thinking the same thing. But then he remembered he'd heard Scott's voice just before he'd gone after Springer. Maybe Scott had somehow prodded him to get up and go outside. "I don't want to think about what would have happened if that son of a bitch..." He glanced quickly in Hutton's direction, knowing she was prone to repeating everything that came out of his mouth. Thankfully, she seemed to be engrossed in her food. "Sorry. I need to watch my mouth."

"Nick, why do you suppose Springer did this now? I've been out here alone for almost two years. Why didn't he do something before now?"

Thinking about what Springer had said to him, Nick visibly paled, but he knew she deserved the truth.

"Springer wanted the land, Jordan, since before you guys bought the place. The closer it got to you opening the B & B, making it a reality, the more desperate he got."

"He wanted our land? I'm so glad you were here, Nick."

"Sheriff Cody hopes to put him away for a long while. Try not to worry about it."

"Why would I worry when you're here to protect us, our knight in shining armor?"

"I hate to tell you Jordan but that armor's a little tarnished."

"Not to me it isn't."

He looked into her eyes then, saw his own soul. He touched his lips to hers. The kiss started out slow, but soon built to red-hot longing. Just as stirred, Jordan ran her fingers through his hair, doing everything she could to make sure he knew how she felt. Before the morning was over, she wanted him to know this was what she wanted, he was what she wanted.

Thinking she was worried about getting the place ready to open on time, Nick misread her intent. "It'll be okay Jordan. We still have almost two weeks. I'll work round the clock if I have to."

"No you won't. There's no need for that. You have one good hand. I don't want you opening up those stitches. We're as ready as we're going to get. And if we aren't, it doesn't matter. You've done all you can. I want you to know, I'm glad you came to Pelican Pointe. I want you to know how happy you've made me these past months. In fact, because of you I've been happier these past months, more so than I've ever been in this house. You brought me back to life, Nick. Remember that when you're practicing that stubborn, sulky mood of yours."

"You humble me Jordan. I don't deserve you."

"I'm sorry you feel that way, Nick. Because Hutton and I definitely know we deserve you."

At that moment Lilly appeared in the doorway of the kitchen. She stood there anxiously holding Joey on her hip while Kyra held on to her mother's skirt. Self-conscious at the intrusion, Lilly cleared her throat, hoping to get someone to look her way. "Sorry to interrupt. I stood out there on the front porch and knocked for five minutes but no one answered. Is everything all right out here?"

Jordan tugged out of her infatuation-with-Nick-trance. She had a business to run and no more time to spend stroking Nick's fragile ego. If he didn't know how she felt, she didn't have time to draw him a map.

"We had a little excitement around here this morning," she told Lilly. "Get the kids settled around the table and I'll tell you all about it."

Chapter Nineteen

Easter Sunday arrived with a pastel-blue sky and plenty of official spring sunshine. Jordan left Nick in bed sleeping while she got up with Hutton in time to squeeze fresh orange juice, prepare pecan waffles and cinnamon rolls from scratch. She even fixed a tray with whipped cream and fresh strawberries. When Nick walked in a little before seven, the kitchen smelled like a French bakery. Hutton sat in her high chair already stuffing her face with a mixture of Cheerios and gooey pastry the evidence of which was plastered in her wisps of blonde hair.

Eyeing the spread on the table, he said, "Someone's been busy."

"Take a seat." She handed him a steaming cup of hazelnut coffee. "There's warm maple syrup." She smiled and added, "A feast fit for a king, payment for going to church with us."

Nick dug into the waffles. "What kind of reception do you think we'll get."

"You mean besides mouths dropping and whispering?" She snickered. "Who knows? Who cares?"

"You really don't?"

"Not in the least. As far as I'm concerned, this town doesn't deserve either of us."

After breakfast Jordan cleaned up Hutton and wasted no time getting her dressed in the brand-new lavender dress trimmed with white daisies she'd purchased online two months earlier. Hutton was easy.

It was getting herself outfitted that might be the problem. Hunting through her closet proved to be depressing. Everything seemed familiar and outdated. She struggled to find something sensational to wear. She tried on outfit after outfit until finally settling on a buttery sundress she'd forgotten all about hidden in the back of her closet.

As Hutton entertained herself by trying to put on a pair of mismatched high heels, Jordan fussed with her hair, wondering when she'd last had it cut. "Up or down, Hutton? Which looks better?" Through the baby babble, Jordan nodded, "Right. As shaggy as I am, I should wear it up. I haven't got time to fool with it too much anyway. But a couple of twists here and a pin there, and voila, we have the California version of a French twist. These people don't even like us anyway so why should we try so hard to look good for them." But it wasn't Pelican Point she wanted to impress. She wanted to look good for Nick.

Glancing at the clock, she snatched up Hutton's matching lavender hat and grabbed the baby. They both ran out into the hallway where Nick stood in the foyer dressed in a charcoal-gray suit and a crisp, white dress shirt he'd picked up the previous Friday at Cranston's, the only store in town that sold men's clothing.

Jordan sucked in a breath. The man looked as though he'd stepped off the set of one of those reality bachelor shows. She looked him up and down. "For a former investment banker turned carpenter slash contractor you clean up awfully good."

Nick eyed the yellow sundress. And her long legs. "Right back at you," he squeaked out, trying to downplay his reaction because his knees had wanted to buckle at the sight of Jordan in that dress. The woman looked good enough to eat. As they walked out the front door, he caught a whiff of her scent and whispered to her on the way to the car, "You sure you don't want to change your mind. I think I could come up with a more interesting way to spend the morning."

"Oh, sweetie, that's my plan for when Hutton's taking her afternoon nap."

As he crawled behind the wheel, with his one good hand on his heart, he muttered, "Who knew the quiet ones would turn out to be insatiable?"

Twenty minutes later, they were greeted with plenty of stares from the other freshly scrubbed parishioners as the three of them settled into a wooden pew in the last row near the door.

Holding Hutton on her lap, Jordan wasn't surprised when Ethel Jenkins turned in her seat, leaned over the back, and offered to take the baby into the nursery. "Pastor Whitcomb has a tendency to be long-winded especially on Easter Sunday." Her raspy voice was not the least apologetic as she went on to explain, "Actually the man prattles on most Sundays as a matter of record. Trust me when I say that baby will be better off in the nursery."

Jordan politely declined, telling Ethel, "No thanks. If she gets restless we'll just take her outside. That's why we're sitting in the back by the door."

Ethel looked anything but placated, but said nothing more as the organ music alerted the congregation to the Easter processional.

For Nick, sitting in church was surreal. It seemed since coming to Pelican Pointe, since getting mixed up with a widow and her baby daughter his life had become something he didn't even recognize, nor would anyone else. He hadn't been inside a church since Ben Latham's wedding six years earlier. But his awkwardness at being there vanished as soon as he looked over at Jordan. Her big chocolate-brown eyes met his. His heart beat a little faster as he slid his hand into hers. As they stood up together to join the rest of the congregation in singing a hymn, he assured himself of one thing. This wasn't as bad as he'd thought it would be. He could do this. He looked around at the stares they were getting and widened his grin. Jordan had been right. They had shocked everyone just by showing up.

As it turned out Ethel Jenkins was correct about Pastor Whitcomb's long-winded sermons. Long before the service officially ended, Nick and Jordan had to slip out the backdoor with a restless Hutton, never knowing the stir their presence in church had caused until much later.

Over the course of the next week, Nick and Jordan poured everything they had into getting The Cove ready for opening day. With Lilly showing up every day, there was no shortage of finishing touches to be done.

They framed Lilly's beach drawings, as well as several photographs Scott had taken at Big Sur and along the California coast. They dusted and polished every stick of furniture, sanded and re-stained hardwood floors, and even replaced the glass in the bathroom window without slicing open another wrist.

They fitted beds with soft, cotton sheets and draped them with brand-new, downy comforters, plumped pillows, coordinated rugs and throws, and accessorized the rooms. They stocked the bathrooms with plenty of fluffy white towels, put out baskets of potpourri and little soaps and made sure the place had all the personal touches that made B & Bs homespun and special.

But with one a week to go before their first guests arrived there was still a long to-do list. Even though Nick's hand was on the mend, he still couldn't hang drywall, still couldn't bend his wrist, still had trouble gripping certain tools like a claw hammer and saw.

After an especially grueling Saturday spent setting tile, stopping drippy faucet leaks, and making sure there were no other major plumbing problems, Jordan and Nick were exhausted. Sitting outside on the front porch taking a rare break enjoying a pitcher of lemonade, Jordan lifted her glass to Nick and said, "It's been a good run, Mr. Harris. I'm so proud of us."

When he just sat there without raising his glass in a toast, she put her glass down and asked, "What's wrong, Nick?"

"The loan committee in L.A. wouldn't go for another extension. I'm sorry, Jordan. I've known for a couple of days. I just didn't want to say anything." He couldn't believe they'd turned him down. It had to be because of his extended leave of absence. So much for long-term loyalty, he thought miserably.

"Oh. I guess we'll just have to make this happen on our own then, won't we? Nothing's changed, Nick. It's still pretty much us against them anyway. It's always been like that. Don't worry about it."

"You're amazing, you know that? Here I've been trying to figure out how to tell you. I was afraid you'd drop like a rock. I should have known better."

"Yes Nick, you should have. When will you? Know that is."

He realized they weren't talking about the loan. "You'll do fine here, Jordan."

To Jordan that pretty much said it all. Nick was telling her the only way he could that he didn't plan on being around much longer. She fought off the sadness that grabbed at her heart. Why did it seem like every man she fell in love with couldn't stay with her? There had to be something missing inside her that prevented them from sticking things out. She pushed off the porch and said quietly, "I need to go start supper."

"Jordan."

But she no longer cared to discuss it. If he couldn't see what was standing right in front of him, she certainly wasn't going to point it out...again. She refused to beg. In a huff, she walked past him into the house.

Nick knew he'd upset her. Her demeanor didn't improve over dinner. During the meal when Hutton threw her food on the floor, something he'd seen her do two dozen times before, in an unusual display of irritability, he watched as Jordan lost patience and scolded her. When they finished the meal instead of cleaning up the supper dishes together, Jordan disappeared with Hutton to get her ready for bed alone. As story time approached, when a fussy Hutton wouldn't sit still long enough for Nick to read to her, Jordan simply gathered her up without saying a word, and left the room, tucking her into bed without him. He waited a good thirty minutes before he realized she didn't intend to rejoin him in the living room. He wasn't sure what to do. Should he go into her bedroom, barge in and crawl into bed with her? She'd given him the cold shoulder all evening. He waited around for another twenty minutes before finally giving up.

That night, for the first time in three weeks, Nick slept alone in the studio apartment.

*"**Jordan might be** having some trouble adjusting to small-town life. The last letter I got from her she sounded so depressed. I know she misses me, but I'm hoping while I'm gone the people in town will be good to her."*

"As great as you say this town is, why worry?"

Scott's ever-optimistic nature had him changing the subject. "I can't believe you don't have anyone special back home, waiting for you, Nick?"

Nick laughed. "As a matter of fact I have several waiting, but none that are special. They're only special in the moment, Scott. Try to take a walk down memory lane and remember your single days. You haven't always had Jordan. And I know for a fact before you met her you were exactly like me."

That got a grin out of Scott. "That's why I know what it's like. Before Jordan, I was stuck in that kind of life. Now, it's different. Jordan means everything to me." But he couldn't ignore how her e-mails lately had seemed to be hinting at how unhappy she was.

The sound of artillery fire broke the moment. A rocket exploded.

"Look out incoming."

They heard the sound of another explosion and then watched as the truck directly in front of them exploded. Pieces of shrapnel hit the Humvee. Then all of a sudden the Hummer became airborne. It didn't take a genius to know they'd hit an IED. The smell of burning oil and fiery smoke filled the air. Landing on its side, Nick started to move, to crawl out of the vehicle. He turned to Scott. "Are you all right?"

"I think so, funny though, I can't feel my legs. I think I'm pinned."

From the back of the vehicle, the gunner, Jones from Sacramento, groaned in pain.

"Hold on, Scott, I'll get you out." Nick started working on freeing Scott, but he had difficulty getting a good grip. Blood was everywhere. Despite Nick's best efforts, he couldn't seem to get Scott to budge. Scott was bleeding badly.

"Nick stop. Stop. Help Jones. Get him out first. He's in bad shape. Just look at his head."

Despite the command, Nick continued to pull on Scott's shoulders trying to wedge him out of the vehicle. "No, I've almost got you loose."

"That's an order, Lieutenant Harris, Jones first, then me." Nick crawled to the back, and kicked open the back door.

He easily slid out of the space before reaching back inside, pulling Jones, hefting him to his shoulders and out of the vehicle. Nick carried him away from the Hummer to the other side of the road to safety as quickly as he could. Running back, Nick got to the Humvee and crawled back inside, once again wedging into the small space beside Scott. Nick started working on getting the twisted metal away from Scott's legs. It was slow going. He saw Scott start to lose consciousness. "I'm here, Scott, talk to me."

Grabbing underneath his shoulders, Nick began to pull him up to no avail. He then went to work trying to bend the metal holding Scott in place. Only then, did Nick see how badly Scott was injured, how much blood he'd lost.

"Nick, listen to me. Listen to me. Stop. Promise me, Nick, you'll see to it that Jordan and Hutton are okay? Promise me, Nick. She's unhappy. Jordan's been unhappy for months now."

"Shut up, and help me get you out of here. Turn sideways a little more. Move to the damn right a little more, will you? The damned metal is everywhere. Turn the other way for a second."

"Tell Jordan how much I love her. Nick, I want you to hold Hutton for me, okay? Are you listening to me? Promise me, Nick...you'll hold Hutton. I so wanted to hold her just once. Take care of Jordan, Nick. Take care of them for me. See to them, Nick. Save Jordan, Nick. She's unhappy. Don't let anything happen to them. Promise me, Nick."

"Shut up, will you? You're going to make it out of this tin can if I have to ..."

Just then, the gas pouring out of the tank ignited, causing the Hummer to explode in a fiery ball, throwing Nick out the back. Badly wounded, he tried to get up, but he couldn't get to his feet. He started crawling in the sand toward the burning Hummer. He heard voices getting closer. Two soldiers ran toward him. It was the last thing he remembered before passing out.

Nick woke up inside a tent, a field hospital, with a doctor standing beside his bed, studying a chart. But as he did his best to focus on the room, the doctor looked as if he were far away. Through bleary eyes, Nick mumbled, "Scott, where is Captain Phillips. Scott Phillips where is he? Did he make it out?"

A nurse approached the other side of the bed. He heard her voice. "He's asking about his buddy I take it. It isn't the first time."

The doctor nodded. "I'm sorry Lieutenant, Captain Phil- lips didn't make it."

Nick closed his eyes. Tears ran down his face. "I screwed up. I couldn't get him out. I promised him I'd get him out of that goddamned tin can."

Nick came awake. The trembling was back. Perspiration pooled down his body. He ran shaky hands through his hair.

The clock by the bed read three-forty-five. After going weeks without Scott haunting him, the dream was back. Nick tried to shut out the sounds and smells of that day.

He couldn't shake the image of Scott's face for that last time. He remembered every line, every crease on his face. But it was the look in his eyes that would haunt Nick till the day he died. Scott had known he wasn't going to make it.

Nick looked around the studio apartment. The loneliness hit him like a moving freight train. He yearned for Jordan.

How would Scott feel about that? he wondered. God help him, he couldn't help it, but he couldn't shake Scott's own words. How could any man in his right mind not fall in love with a woman like Jordan? Scott's words. How many times had Nick heard him say that?

Suddenly, it became clear what he had to do.

He dressed quickly, making his way through the dark out to the Harley. As quietly as he could, he pushed the bike down the driveway and then as far along the road away from the house as he could before jumping on and starting the engine. He roared off, heading for the highway.

Twenty minutes later, just as the sun tipped the horizon pink, Nick found himself standing over Scott's grave. Touching the marble headstone, he sucked in a wobbly breath. "I'm here. You wanted me here. I'm here. I'm doing the best I can, Scott. I'm taking care of Jordan and Hutton just like you wanted."

He ran a hand through his hair and started to pace. "Ahh, Hutton, Hutton's amazing. She's this little person who smells all soft and cuddly. She looks just like Jordan but with your eyes. You were right about that Scott, she has your eyes. But God Scott, Jordan is beautiful, inside and out. You were lucky there, bro. She's everything you said she was and more. But here's the thing...damn it. You sent me here to take care of them and...damn it, Scott, I couldn't help it. I've fallen in love with Jordan, with Hutton too. When you sent me here, you didn't think of that, did you? And what am I supposed to do about that now, huh Scott? What the hell am I going to do now?"

His breath hitched. A sigh escaped. "The Cove's just like you said it was, a great place to raise a family. Not the town, though, nor the people. The people suck, Scott. You were just flat out wrong about Pelican Pointe. What were you thinking there, bro? The people here couldn't care less about anyone but themselves. You knew Jordan wasn't happy here. That's why you bugged the hell out of me. You knew. You knew she was miserable. You wanted me to come here to take care of her."

Out of steam, spent, he dropped down on the grass. He sat there tears rolling down his cheeks. "I'm sorry I couldn't get you out of that damned Hummer. So, damn sorry. I wasn't quick enough. If I'd reacted sooner... What is it you want from me? I'm doing all I know to do. What is it you want?"

Scott sat down on the grass beside his friend. "Come on, Nick. You're a good man. One of the best soldiers I've ever seen in combat. You know exactly what to do. You always have."

"Not this time. Didn't you hear what I said? Goddamn it, I'm in love with Jordan."

"I knew you would be. Took you a little longer than I thought it would. Let go, Nick." Scott put a hand on Nick's shoulder. "You need to revisit what happened that day, bro. You're all mixed up inside. Let go of the guilt you've been carrying around. It's eating you up. You're wasting these days with Jordan, spoiling them. Let go of the guilt, Nick, before you ruin everything."

And with that, Scott was gone.

For twenty long minutes, Nick sat there, teary eyed until suddenly he wiped his nose and jumped to his feet. For the second time that morning, he realized what he had to do.

He climbed on his bike and roared off toward town.

As he passed the Pelican Pointe city limits sign Nick drove like a man possessed. Sunday morning half the town must still be asleep. But he looked up and spotted all the cars parked in the church parking lot. Perfect. Just the people he wanted to talk to. He turned the motorcycle into the lot and killed the engine. Getting off the bike, he removed his helmet and stared up at the stained-glass windows, the huge, colorful images of Jesus and the cross.

Although, he wasn't dressed for church, not even close, he stomped toward the double doors, looking for a fight. He hadn't even bothered to shave. Red-eyed from crying, even though services had already started, he stormed inside, almost daring anyone to stop him. When that didn't happen, he made his way down the aisle of the small auditorium to the podium where Reverend Whitcomb stood in mid sermon. The pastor just assumed he was late and walking to a seat in the front pew.

But Nick passed the rows of pews filled with parishioners. He recognized a few of the faces in the relatively small crowd. There was Murphy and Ferguson and Wade Hawkins and old man Taggert. There was Wally Pierce, who sat next to Lilly and her kids. Nick ignored their looks of surprise. When he looked up at the wide-eyed pastor, who had stopped talking and stood there with his mouth gaping open, Nick took advantage of the momentary silence and hopped up the steps to the dais. Several members of the congregation began to protest. But Nick barely heard any of them. He thought he heard Murphy's voice, thought he heard Murphy tell them to sit down and be quiet.

Angry that Jordan might be at risk to lose everything, angry over how the town had treated her, he was in no mood to be conciliatory. "My name is Nick Harris. Some of you know me, most of you don't. But every one of you here knew Scott Phillips." He adjusted the pastor's microphone and repeated, "Scott Phillips, the National Guard soldier whose hometown was Pelican Pointe, California, the soldier who lost his life a year ago in Iraq, serving his country.

"Scott grew up here. You knew his grandparents. You knew him as a boy. You knew him as a man. He had history in this town. You knew him when he moved back here to raise his own family, when he brought his wife back to this town, a wife he had to leave when his Guard unit got called up. He left her behind in your care while he served his country, while he did the right thing. And what did any of you do for Scott in his absence? What did you do for his wife and daughter? Did you lift a finger to help either one of them?

"I can tell you what he thought would happen. He thought you'd take care of Jordan while he was gone. He thought you'd help her get through a difficult time. He might have even thought you'd help get his dream up and going. He trusted you with what he loved the most, his wife and daughter. And how have you treated them in his absence?"

At that moment, Murphy got up from his seat, followed by Carla Vargas. They both walked to where Nick stood as if to lend support.

Nick kept right on going. "Scott loved Pelican Pointe. God knows why. There were days when that's all he talked about. How great his hometown was, how great the people were. How the people in Pelican Pointe would do anything for anybody. Why he believed that, I have no idea only that he did. But you and I know that isn't what happened.

"I served with Scott in Iraq, in the same Guard unit. While we were there, he saved my life on more than one occasion, but when it came time for me to save him, I fell short. I didn't pull him out of that Hummer in time and he…died. I might have failed Scott then, but know this…I won't fail Jordan now. All of you are letting his dream die. His dream's in jeopardy. Every day you turn your back on Jordan, you're letting Scott Phillips down."

Nick looked out at the faces in the crowd. A few hung their heads and refused to look up or meet his eyes.

"Know this though. I won't fail Scott a second time. He deserves to know his death meant something and that he died for something that mattered. He deserves to know that Jordan and Hutton will have a home, that they'll go on strong without him. Scott deserved to see his dream come true. Even if it's from up above. That's all I have to say."

Nick swallowed hard and handed the microphone back to the preacher. He strode down the steps, past the parishioners and outside, leaving the doors clanging together and the stunned congregation, strangely silent.

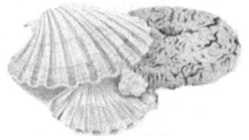

Chapter Twenty

Breakfast had come and gone without Nick. His motorcycle wasn't parked out front. As the morning stretched on, Jordan had a funny feeling, almost a nagging, creepy feeling in the pit of her stomach. By mid-morning she began to wonder if Nick might have taken off. The idea saddened her. But as sad as she felt, it also made her mad.

The only way she'd know for sure if he was gone was to head over to the studio apartment to see if his things were still there. She was just about to scoop up Hutton and do just that when she heard multiple vehicles pulling into the driveway.

Her stomach fluttered. A sick feeling began to spread from somewhere inside. Picking up Hutton, she slowly walked to the front door and stepped out onto the porch. When she saw Murphy getting out of his truck, followed by Ferguson, and a few of the other townspeople, dread washed over her. "What's going on here, Murphy?"

"What all needs doing, Jordan? Point us in the right direction. We're here to help, better late than not at all."

"Where's Nick?"

"Isn't he here? Didn't he come back from town?"

"No." A wild fear flitted in her brain. She stared at Frank Martin and Wally Pierce before turning back to Murphy. "Why is everyone here?"

Before Murphy could answer, Frank Martin, the banker walked up and stood behind Ferguson, followed by Edmund Taggert. Jordan saw the sheepish look on their faces. She mechanically told Taggert, "I'm sorry about the noise we've made this week, I really am, but we have to finish before Friday."

Taggert shifted his feet but shuffled forward. "It ain't that. I just got to say, that man of yours has guts. Not many men would stand up in church and make an ass out of himself like he done. I'm sorry I caused you so much grief the past two years." The old man shifted his feet again and went on, "I taught Scott to fish. Not having kids of my own, that boy used to come around my place to visit the animals. Got used to him being there. I forgot that, forgot what a character he was when he was little. I want to help you get this place ready."

Before Jordan could speak, Wade Hawkins trudged up behind Taggert, and Bran Sullivan followed him. Before long it seemed as if every able-bodied man in Pelican Pointe snaked behind Murphy waiting for further instructions from the mayor on what to do next. But Murphy merely went into a detailed account of what Nick had said at the church.

Jordan listened but couldn't believe what she was hearing. "Why would he do that? Unless... Oh, my God, Murphy, he's gone, he isn't coming back, is he?"

"I didn't get that impression at all, Jordan. But there's something I probably need to tell you."

Without realizing it, she held on tighter to Hutton. Even the warmth of the spring morning couldn't stop a shiver from tingling down her arms. The last time anyone had uttered those words they had knocked on her door to tell her Scott wasn't coming home. The sick feeling swept over her again. She couldn't shake it. Where the hell was Nick? Why was he not here?

"Then where is he, Murphy? Ferguson's is closed on Sunday. In fact, Ferguson is standing right behind you. I knew it. He's gone. He didn't even say goodbye." She finally let out the choked breath she'd been holding.

"Nick made us remember our hearts. He wouldn't just leave like that."

"What are you talking about, Murphy? Made you remember what heart? You aren't making any sense."

"Exactly. We lost ourselves for awhile, the whole town did, but Nick brought us back. He made us remember we're here to help each other. When rough patches hit us, all of us, we save each other from disaster. Nick made us remember how we're supposed to care for each other as a town, how we should see each other through the rough times. Scott was one of us. Nick reminded us that Scott would have wanted us to help. In fact, he expected better from all of us. We just needed Nick to remind us, to shake us up."

"Start talking Murphy. You're starting to scare me." Truth was, she'd actually gone straight past scared to downright fear.

Murphy sucked in a breath. It wasn't his place, but what the hell. "Nick was there—in Iraq with Scott. He was with Scott when he died."

"I know all that. Get to the point."

"What do you mean…you know? Jordan, Nick blames himself for not being able to get Scott out of the truck fast enough."

"Oh, God. I was afraid of that. That isn't what happened at all." Jordan started to pace the length of the porch. "I knew who he was after that first day. I recognized the name from Scott's letters. He always mentioned Nick this, Nick that. I was just waiting for him to talk to me, to open up, tell me about it himself. I was trying to be patient, give him time to do it his own way. I knew he must be suffering from post-traumatic stress or survivor's guilt. I wanted him to talk to me and tell me in his own time, in his own way."

"Do you know he's in love with you?"

That had her stopping in mid-pace and turning back to Murphy. "I was hoping. Are you sure?"

"Oh, yeah."

"I have to talk to him, Murphy. Where…"

"He left the church a good thirty minutes ago." Murphy scratched his head at that, and added, "Maybe he didn't think you'd want to see him. After all, he felt like he'd failed Scott, maybe he felt like he'd failed you too, and took off." But that didn't sound like the guy who had told the congregation he wasn't about to give up.

"He didn't fail Scott. Oh, God, Murphy you have to get him back. We're wasting time just standing around. I have to talk to him, tell him. I have to straighten this mess out."

Murphy pulled out his cell phone, punched in a few numbers on his speed dial. "Brent, this is the mayor of Pelican Pointe. I need a favor."

Nick was thirty miles outside Pelican Pointe when he looked in the side mirror and saw the flashing lights of a police cruiser, a county squad car. Damn. He reluctantly pulled to the shoulder and cut the engine on the bike. Removing his helmet, he waited patiently for the deputy to get out of his car and walk up to the motorcycle.

"You Harris?"

"Yeah. Is something wrong? I wasn't speeding."

"Got a request to detain you."

"Detain me? Why? I haven't done anything wrong."

"That's not what I heard."

Nick crawled off the bike and stood directly in front of the deputy. "What's going on?" They stood there staring at each other through shaded, reflective sunglasses. Finally, the deputy drawled, "That's a nice bike. What is that a 2008?"

"Nine," Nick corrected, beginning to get pissed. Just then, he caught sight of a vintage pickup truck barreling toward them both and watched as it skidded to a stop on the shoulder, spitting gravel everywhere in its wake. Shocked to see Jordan crawl out of the passenger seat, slamming the door, he eyed the deputy. "What's going on?" And then he realized something might be wrong with Hutton. A sick feeling washed over him.

But the deputy's lips curved slightly before he tipped his hat to Nick and walked back to his patrol car.

Breathless, Jordan ran up to where Nick stood, threw her arms around his neck. She stood there until he slowly, almost reluctantly put his arms around her waist. "What are you doing here? Has something happened to Hutton?"

Jordan sniffed, "How could you just take off like this without even saying goodbye? I don't understand you. I thought Hutton and I meant something to you?"

"What?" He ripped off his shades and set her away from him far enough to stare into those brown eyes. "I'm headed into Santa Cruz to see if I can hire some temp workers. I know it might be Sunday but you never know, maybe one of those temporary day labor places might be open. If not, I can always leave a note on one of the doors for them to call me first thing in the morning. With work so scarce these days, I'm hoping they could send us out some temp workers to help with the final four days of preparation, at least get the drywall in."

Relief engulfed her. "So you weren't leaving?"

"Leaving? You mean heading back to L.A? No, not until we've finished, not until we're open for business." But the minute he met her eyes, his breath backed up. Any thought of leaving her now was an absolute waste of time.

She blew out a breath. "This is ridiculous. I'm tired of playing games." She slipped out of Nick's embrace and started to pace up and down on the shoulder of the highway in a huff. Good thing traffic was light.

Jordan pushed her hair out of her face. "I knew who you were, Nick. From the very first night, I recognized the name. And even if I hadn't, I would have eventually recognized your face from the pictures Scott sent home of his unit. The first night you got here, I reread Scott's letters. You were right there, Nick, in every single one."

"That's why you never asked me about my scars. You already knew. Why didn't you say something?"

"Me?" She looked at him in disbelief. "You didn't seem ready or willing to open up to me. I kept asking you, prodding you, giving you every opportunity to tell me what was bothering you, to talk to me." She sighed and ran her fingers through her hair. "Fact is I didn't press you because I suspect I didn't want to talk about it anymore than you did. I don't think I was ready, just as you weren't. I didn't want to hear what you had to say. But don't for a minute think I didn't want you here with us, Nick. I just didn't realize I'd fallen in love with you."

"You love me?"

"Idiot. Of course I love you. How could I not? You're such a good man, Nick. But from what Murphy tells me your memories of that day—in Iraq when Scott—died are just plain—wrong."

He scowled at her. Absently his hand flew to the scars on his chest. "I was there. I ought to know what happened."

"You'd think you should. But you don't."

"Jordan, you don't understand. I couldn't save Scott. I tried, but I couldn't get him out of that goddamned tin can in time. I wasn't quick enough."

"See, that's exactly what I mean, Nick. You were the one wounded."

"Not at first, not until the thing blew. I should have done something before it blew, reacted quicker. I have to live with that."

She sent him a sad-eyed look, wondering why his friend, Ben hadn't forced him to face the truth long before now. But then she realized Nick probably hadn't spoken about that day to a single soul, not even in therapy to counselors, least of all, to his buddies. "I know what happened, Nick. When someone dies over there they send you a detailed account of what happened whether you want to know it or not. Plus, his commander, a Colonel Marks, came to see me in person. Scott died instantly, Nick. And there was nothing you or anyone could do about it."

"No, no, that isn't what happened. I talked to him. He was alive in that Hummer. We had a conversation before..."

Jordan shook her head, denial she thought, as she began to try again to make him see the truth. "I don't doubt you remember conversations with him, Nick. We all remember how Scott loved to talk. But there is no mistake. Scott died instantly from some type of homemade bomb that hit the vehicle." She took out a piece of paper from her pocket. "I brought the letter. The day you showed up I didn't know you were the one who had been wounded beside him. But I called Colonel Marks the next day. He verified it was you in the Hummer next to Scott. You'd lost a huge amount of blood. They had to cut you out before the gas tanks exploded. You were the one wounded, Nick. Scott was already gone. Even after they got you to the hospital they almost lost you."

"He died instantly." It wasn't a question, as if reality might at long last be sinking in.

Her breath caught. She started crying. "I've no doubt guilt brought you here to me. But I hope to God, you stay because you love us as much as we love you." Her voice hitched. "The other day Hutton called you

Da. She called you that this morning when she asked about Da. Where was Da? I didn't know what to say to her. I think Scott wanted you to come here, Nick. In fact, I'm sure of it."

"Jordan, you don't know the half of it. I promised him I'd take care of you. I've made a mess of this whole thing. He knew you were unhappy. He talked about how sad you sounded in your letters. He must have known you needed me." His voice broke, tears streamed down his cheeks. "He's the reason I came here, but he isn't why I fell in love with you. I love you, Jordan. So much that it scares me. I've never loved anyone more. But I couldn't stand to have you thinking about Scott or his death every time you look at me. And that's what you'll do. Eventually I'll be a reminder of how Scott died."

Hearing that just pissed her off. "You don't give me a lot of credit, do you? You think I don't know how different you are from Scott. Believe me, I know. Do you want me to stand here listing all the ways? If I did we'd be here until Hutton starts kindergarten. When I look at you, when you touch me the way you do, believe me Nick, the very last thing I'm thinking about is Scott. Do you think for a minute he'd want you to blame yourself for something you had no control over? Nick, no one's blaming you, except you. If you can't see how much I love you, then I feel sorry for you."

"Marry me. I want us to have more kids, a brother or a sister for Hutton."

Jordan slumped with relief. Finally, she'd gotten through. She smiled and took his hand, walked to the bike. "Then you'll have to come home, Nick, back to The Cove where you belong. Hutton and I need you to come home."

He reached for her then, molding her body to his and kissed her with everything he had.

Epilogue

"**Y**ou're choking me," Nick snapped, as Ben Latham first tightened, and then straightened the black tie around the collar of Nick's starched white dress shirt.

As best man, Ben brushed off the shoulders of the black tuxedo Nick wore and told him, "Buck up. You don't want your tie coming undone during the ceremony."

"As if. It feels like you're tying a noose around my neck."

"Is that a figure of speech, or some code the best man is supposed to recognize for 'I'm getting cold feet, please get me the hell out of here?' Want me to run interference while you make a break for it?" Ben asked in mock tone, as he took Nick by the shoulders and turned him around to face the full-length mirror on the door in the studio apartment where, hours earlier, the groom's party had been relegated to fend for themselves.

"No. I'd just like to have enough air left in my lungs to say 'I do' when the time comes that's all."

"Bitch and moan, bitch and moan. You finally find a beautiful woman who's willing to set aside your sordid past long enough to marry you and all you do is bitch. Who says there are no miracles left in the world?"

"I can always get another best man, wise ass."

"Ah, but I keep you on your toes. Why'd both of you decide to change the name of this place anyway? I saw the new sign out front. Promise Cove Bed & Breakfast. Has a nice ring to it." Just then, Ben took out an envelope from the inside breast pocket of his own tuxedo. "By the way…"

"Aww, you got me a gift certificate. I'm touched." Nick said absently, as he attempted to fluff some style into his still-long hair with his fingers.

"Not exactly. Something Scott gave me a couple of weeks before he died. At least I think that's when he wrote it. All I remember is he gave this to me shortly before he, you know, to give to you should anything happen to him and he didn't make it back. I put it in my gear, forgot all about it. Sheryl came across the envelope the other day going through some of my stuff I brought back from Iraq."

"But that was more than a year ago."

"I know. What with you in the hospital and me coming back home to Sheryl and the kids I just tried to put it all out of my head. Last thing I wanted to do was sort through that gear when I got back stateside. But Sheryl found this buried in my duffle, asked me about it."

Ben handed the envelope off to Nick, but when he saw the scowl on his face, he held up his hands in protest. "Hey, don't shoot the messenger. I guess Scott must have had one of those premonitions, you know, that he wouldn't be coming back."

"You didn't read it?"

Ben looked insulted. "It isn't addressed to me now is it?"

Nick ripped it open and took out the single sheet of paper inside. "Is this some kind of a sick joke?"

"Not at all. What's it say?"

"You know what it says, asshole. Scott didn't write this."

"Honest to God he gave it to me." Ben reached to take the letter back. "You know as well as I do that's his barely legible scrawl. He had the most God-awful handwriting."

Nick's eyes grew wet.

The message read: Take care of my girls, Nick. I know you won't let me down.

Dear Reader:

If you enjoyed *Promise Cove*, please take the time to leave a review. A review shows others how you feel about my work. By recommending it to your friends and family it helps spread the word. If you have the time, please Tweet/Share that you've finished *Promise Cove*.

If you do write a review, by all means let me know via Facebook or my website.
I'd love to hear from you!

For a complete list of the author's other books please visit her at.
www.vickiemckeehan.com

Want to connect with the author to leave a comment?
www.vickiemckeehan.wordpress.com/ blog
www.facebook.com/VickieMcKeehan

Go to the next page for a preview of
Hidden Moon Bay

Vickie McKeehan

Prologue

Four months earlier
Chicago, Illinois

Trouble was about to overtake Emile Reed. The interview had not only been a disaster but had run longer than expected. The parking garage had almost emptied out, leaving behind the dim glare of cheap fluorescent lighting.

Not paying attention, her mind on her ruined career, she failed to hear footsteps come up behind her. An arm jerked her back into a hard, muscled chest. Then a huge, sweaty hand covered her mouth. Despite stiffening her body in response, he yanked her backward then sideways, dragging her toward the stairwell.

She fought. She kicked. She did her best to scream, moving her head wildly back and forth, but the huge hand refused to budge. By sheer force he dragged her in the direction of the stairwell. She resisted the only way she could. She dug her heels into the cement to try to stop his progress. But ultimately he was too powerful and manhandled her into the stairwell, shoving her face up against the concrete wall.

The hand over her mouth was replaced with a cold piece of steel at her throat. He slowly turned her around. The knife he held came into focus. A pair of icy, silver eyes stared back at her through the slits of a ski mask.

The second she felt the point of the knife prick her skin, felt liquid trickle down her neck, it crossed her mind if she didn't find a way to fight she was going to die.

Her assailant tightened his grip.

A raspy voice threatened, "I'm here to make sure you don't testify. Once I give you a Colombian necktie, no one will come forward to squeal."

The man stood so close, Emile smelled his stale, cigarette breath. Tattooed knuckles held the shiny weapon with one hand while the other reached to unbuckle the snap of his jeans.

His mouth curled into a sneer. "But first, what do you say we have ourselves a little fun?"

The blade left her throat long enough to slice at the buttons of the Oxford shirt she wore.

She gaped in terror as the plastic bits dropped in sound-less flight to the cement. The steel made another sweep toward her chest while his free hand squeezed hard the tip of her right breast through her bra.

Emile brought her knee up, connecting to his crotch. The instant she made contact, the second he doubled over in agony, she closed her fist and with an uppercut to his throat, punched him harder than she'd ever hit anything before in her life.

The man staggered backward.

The second she heard the metal of the knife clang to the concrete, she reached out and shoved him with everything she had the rest of the way down.

She grabbed for the handle on the door. The door came back hard, hitting him in the side of his head. He crumpled to the pavement.

Emile didn't wait for him to land. She shot out of the stairwell running in three-and-a-half inch Jimmy Choos until her feet protested and her lungs burned. All she could think about was getting away from the stairwell.

And the man sent to kill her.

Now, as she sat inside her little BMW 323, stopped at the light on Lake Shore Drive and the ramp to the expressway, she did her best to stop shaking and catch her breath, tried to calm down.

Absently, she clutched at her tattered shirt with no buttons. She shuddered. Even though it was mid-May and a warm muggy night, she felt like she'd landed on an iceberg. She turned the car heater up to high.

She'd fought. God help her, she'd gotten away.

But for how long? The man sent to kill her, sent to deliver the message, had gotten through. Big time. How long had he been following her through the parking garage? Why hadn't she noticed him sooner?

Because she'd been too deep in thought about the stupid interview she'd blown not twenty minutes earlier. It was too late now, she realized. No sense beating herself up. But from now on, she planned to be more careful, a lot more careful.

When the light turned green, she breathed out a ragged breath and pressed down on the accelerator, screeching onto the 55 ramp, gaining some serious speed. She spared a nervous glance in the rearview mirror. It didn't look as though anyone had followed her, at least, not yet. Since she couldn't be sure, as soon as she could, she merged into the steady stream of traffic, changing lanes until she'd reached the farthest one. And simply drove and drove and drove.

She wouldn't be going home. At least not any time soon. They'd be waiting for her. She thought of her cozy little condo she'd owned for four years and how she'd painstakingly picked out every stitch of furniture there one piece at a time. She let out a sigh, knowing how much she'd miss it.

But it was too dangerous to go back.

Her mind raced with options. She could head east to New York State where her mother lived. But that was a fairly obvious destination for anyone looking for her. Same with going south to her sister's in St. Louis.

She couldn't go to them; she couldn't risk putting the people she loved in harm's way.

No, she'd already made too many mistakes and bad decisions for that. She could head north to Toronto where an aunt lived. But anyone who knew her might be able to find out about any relatives she'd used on past employment applications for personal references.

Still gripped by panic, she tried to think.

She couldn't stay in Chicago. If she had to, she'd drive clear across the country.

She knew one thing though. No matter what she'd promised the feds, she couldn't go through with it, wouldn't put her family and herself in danger any longer.

If she'd been worried about testifying, appearing in court before today, before that maniac in the parking garage, she was absolutely terrified now.

Because she was certain of one thing: Jeremy Dochenko had no intentions of giving up until she was dead.

Don't miss these other exciting titles by bestselling author

Vickie McKeehan

The Pelican Pointe Series
PROMISE COVE
HIDDEN MOON BAY
DANCING TIDES
LIGHTHOUSE REEF
STARLIGHT DUNES
LAST CHANCE HARBOR
SEA GLASS COTTAGE
LAVENDER BEACH
SANDCASTLES UNDER THE CHRISTMAS MOON
BENEATH WINTER SAND
KEEPING CAPE SUMMER (2018)

The Evil Secrets Trilogy
JUST EVIL Book One
DEEPER EVIL Book Two
ENDING EVIL Book Three
EVIL SECRETS TRILOGY BOXED SET

The Skye Cree Novels
THE BONES OF OTHERS
THE BONES WILL TELL
THE BOX OF BONES
HIS GARDEN OF BONES
TRUTH IN THE BONES
SEA OF BONES (2018)

The Indigo Brothers Trilogy
INDIGO FIRE
INDIGO HEAT
INDIGO JUSTICE
INDIGO BROTHERS TRILOGY BOXED SET

Coyote Wells Mysteries
MYSTIC FALLS
SHADOW CANYON
SPIRIT LAKE (2018)

ABOUT THE AUTHOR

Vickie McKeehan's novels have consistently appeared on Amazon's Top 100 lists in Contemporary Romance, Romantic Suspense and Mystery / Thriller. She writes what she loves to read—heartwarming romance laced with suspense, heart-pounding thrillers, and riveting mysteries. Vickie loves to write about compelling and down-to-earth characters in settings that stay with her readers long after they've finished her books. She makes her home in Southern California.

Find Vickie online at
https://www.facebook.com/VickieMcKeehan
http://www.vickiemckeehan.com/
https://vickiemckeehan.wordpress.com

www.ingramcontent.com/pod-product-compliance
Lightning Source LLC
Chambersburg PA
CBHW020216260626
47156CB00002B/400